# Praise for [illegible] Crow and Dianne Fox's *Tatterdemalion*

"Luscious urban fantasy."

~ *My Reviews and Ramblings*

"A love story set within a deeper, much wider story about society and acceptance."

~ *TwoLips Reviews*

"Highly recommended." A May Recommended Read

~ *Reviews by Jessewave*

"Gritty urban fantasy setting...a simply great story. Get this as soon as it's available."

~ *Three Dollar Bill Reviews*

"Hits the ground running and never slows until the final word has been devoured and savored."

~ *Fallen Angel Reviews, Tatterdemalion is a Fallen Angel Reviews Recommended Read!*

"Those who love shifter stories are sure to love this one."

~ *Literary Nymphs Reviews*

# Tatterdemalion

*Anah Crow and Dianne Fox*

Samhain Publishing, Ltd.
577 Mulberry Street, Suite 1520
Macon, GA 31201
www.samhainpublishing.com

Tatterdemalion

Print ISBN: 978-1-60928-082-6
Digital ISBN: 978-1-60928-037-6

Editing by Anne Scott



First Samhain Publishing, Ltd. electronic publication: May 2010
First Samhain Publishing, Ltd. print publication: April 2011

# Dedication

If this were a book that either of us had written alone, we each would have dedicated our book to the other. With both of our names on the cover, we dedicate this book to the family and friends who have made our work better through their support and kindness. We would particularly like to express our appreciation of the four-footed, furry family members whose determined interference never fails to keep our priorities in proper order: petting now, writing later.

# Chapter One

The steel table at the center of the operating room would hold a body with the arms and legs spread wide. Lindsay knew it was waiting for him and pressed his bare feet to the floor to slow the inevitable. Technicians dragged him into the ring of fluorescent orange shapes painted on the concrete. Runes—they spoke, but not any language Lindsay knew. He only knew to be afraid of them, and of what waited for him inside the circle.

He screamed when the technicians tried to strap him to the table. He fought, fragile elbows and knees thrown like weapons. He screamed when they stripped him naked to apply the electrodes. His decaying teeth snapped on the air, ground against each other and splintered dentin. He knew what was coming. A broad-shouldered man in a crisp vanilla jumper jammed a black rubber gag in his mouth when he opened up to scream again.

"That's better, isn't it?" The man's hand covered his mouth and nose, cutting off his air. "You know they don't get good results when you make all that noise." The man straightened and patted his cheek, letting him breathe again. The air was cold, like steel and concrete, and it stank like rubber, choking him. With no other way to resist, Lindsay lay there and shook so hard with the cold that he couldn't struggle against his restraints anymore.

"Never learns, that one," the other tech noted, shaking his head. He was at the far side of the room, waking up the big computers lurking there, turning on the cameras.

The beetles on the ceiling came to life, flashing bright and turning their single eyes on Lindsay, moving so close that he could look up into one. His terrified and distorted face looked back at him as he stared up into the lens that was taking his picture out to where a hundred eyes and more would see him.

*Father, can you see me?* Of course he could. His father could see him. His mother could see him. Somewhere, beyond the lens and the wires, they were watching, waiting for him to be cured. That was why they'd brought him here. He clung to his certainty that when he was better, they'd come and take him home. The lonely life he'd once longed to leave seemed like a paradise now, and he wanted to go home. Lindsay reached for his magic, but it was hidden behind the drugs, like he'd never been magic at all. He was trapped here, in this body and in this place.

"Lindsay." It was a woman speaking. Her voice was soft and pretty and rich, like his mother's. She sounded gentle, but she could be so cruel. "This won't take long." She always said that. But what was time when he was in agony? "I need you to concentrate." One of the technicians slid a needle into his vein and pushed something into him. It burned cold and made his heart stagger.

*Concentrate.* He was shaking too hard to focus. His heartbeat sounded like thunder in his head. The usual drugs wore thin and the new serum ripped through him, laying him open. The real test hadn't started and he was already in pain.

"Can you hear me, Lindsay? We're going to start now." The computers hummed. The beat of his heart pinged and echoed off the bare concrete walls. Lindsay stared into the blackness beyond the rings of lights like halos all around him, trying to will himself out of his body. A door opened and the woman entered, her heels clicking sharply on the floor.

"You've been doing very well lately," she said. He couldn't see her—the lights around him were too bright. "Let's try this one more time." She put a velvet cloth on his chest. It was so warm and soft. He didn't know when he'd felt that last. The curtains at home, maybe, where he used to hide from the adults stalking the halls like specters. There was something heavy hidden in the cloth and she unwrapped it, spreading the velvet over him. *So warm.*

She fit something icy and heavy around his throat. He tried to gasp, but the gag made it hard to inhale. She closed the stone collar with a click and put the locking pin through with a tiny, silvery noise. There was a collar for his throat, a cuff for each wrist.

"You look like royalty," she said affectionately, when she was done. She took the warm velvet away from him and she put an icy hand on his forehead. "Only very special mages got to wear this, you know." When she leaned in, he could see her eyes, clear and glassy as common marbles. "*Celare*," she whispered. And then she was gone, clicking away from him. "Start the experiment."

Lindsay whimpered as the collar began to do its work, silencing and neutralizing his magic, the magic he had just started to feel once the drugs had been flushed from his system. Every time they brought him here, he was sure he wasn't going to scream, but he screamed anyway. He shook and writhed, trying to escape the artifacts locked around his neck and wrists. The gag didn't stop him from screaming, it only muffled his agony enough that he wouldn't interfere with the carefully calibrated machines that measured his power and his pain.

Time stopped, then disappeared completely. There was no time here, just magic filling him up from within, magic crawling under his skin, magic wailing to be free. The pain was worse than anything he'd known. The drugs and the hours in restraints never came close to this. He screamed through the gag and tried to rip his wrists and ankles free, over and over again, until they were hot and slick with his own blood. Fighting for breath between screams, he looked up into the eye of the camera and saw an alien staring back at him.

White, it was so white, and its eyes were wide and almost black. Like him, it was crying. But the alien wasn't crying tears, it was crying blood, blood that welled up in its eyes and ran down its colorless skin.

"The readings are maxing out, Dr. Moore," someone said in the distance. "Heart rate is over two hundred. The containment field is holding. Prepared for stage two—the guided experiment."

"Lindsay." The woman's voice was all around him, snapping like a whip. "Lindsay, I need you to listen to me. You're going to make an illusion of rain in the room. Do you hear me? Make it rain in the room."

He couldn't hear anything but his blood pounding in his ears, couldn't see anything but a haze of red. His body twisted with agony, and his stomach lurched. His magic, his magic that they had kept from him, his magic was filling him up and searing his bones and drowning his lungs and burning his brain. He slammed his head against the steel table over and over, trying to break his skull open, trying to let some of it out.

"Are you sure about this?"

"He can hear me. He's ready. *Regere.*"

There it was. The crack in the wall. Lindsay didn't understand the word, but his magic saw the gap in the restraints before the echo of the command had faded.

*Rain. Let them have it. Let them have a flood.* The ceiling cracked and water crashed in, sweeping the equipment across the floor. The lights in the halos overhead exploded one by one, going out in blinding showers of light and glass.

"Holy shit! We've got to get him out of here." One of the technicians flung himself against the rushing water to unlock Lindsay's restraints.

"Don't touch him. It's not real," the woman snapped over the intercom, her voice edged with hysteria. "You were told what to expect."

"Help me! He's going to drown." Lindsay's feet were loose and the man fought to undo his wrists and the strap over his waist. Water crashed against them and sent the gurney spinning as it sucked the technician under.

"Open the doors," the other man was screaming, throwing himself against the locked doors at the far end of the room.

There was the sound of the locks clicking open, slowly, too slowly.

Lindsay curled up on his side, clawing at the last restraint on his wrist. The waves crashed around him and he pushed the water out into the halls, pushed it up into the air ducts, washing everything clean.

"Get to him. Sedate him again," the woman was shouting in the background. "*Celare*," she said desperately. "*Celare!*"

The gap was closing, the collar was tightening again. Lindsay's magic seared his nerves as the collar forced it into his body. He spat out the gag, struggling for breath so he could scream, so he could end everything, end the pain.

"*No!*" The word ripped up from his gut, tore free of his spine, and exploded out of his skin. The collar blew apart in a hail of shrapnel. The cuffs followed a moment later, shredding his skin with stone flechettes.

And then, instead of nothing, he could feel everything. He was everything. Tied to nothing, bound by nothing, he was a hundred minds at once—a thousand, even. He breathed a thousand breaths a second, spoke a thousand tongues, laughed, cried, smiled, frowned, opened his eyes, closed his eyes, saw through every eye. Every soul was under his skin.

"Stop!" he screamed, trying to make the torment end. He saw the face of every person who had caused his pain, clenched his will around their hearts and minds, and ended them all. Curling up on his side, clinging to himself, trying to hold himself in his own skin, he vomited blood and bile. "No more," he whispered with his ruined voice, between sobs. But there was nothing to answer him, only silence.

When Lindsay opened his eyes, the techs were lying on the floor, the dry floor. It was as though nothing had happened but that they had gone mad, clawing to escape, soiled themselves, and died. There was silence from the observation room above. The camera lens was black and unmoving. Lindsay's own blood-streaked, tear-stained face stared back at him, and he realized what he'd done.

All dead. He got his wrist loose and slipped off the gurney. There were no alarms ringing, no voices, no footfalls. No one was coming. He fell to his knees. His legs wouldn't hold him up, so he crawled through the open laboratory door and out into the hall. He dragged a white coat from one of the bodies in the hall to cover himself.

At the stairwell, he used the railing to pull himself to his feet. Surely, someone would notice soon. They would search for him, and they would find him. He tried to hide himself with an illusion, but pain made the world go dark. Clinging to the railing, he pulled himself up again with almost nothing but the force of his will.

Up one flight of stairs, then two, he had no idea where his strength came from. He stumbled over a pair of bodies wound together in the dark stairwell, under the red exit light bathing everything in a bloody halo. The door opened when he fell against it, and he tumbled outside.

It was freezing outside and it was night. The snow fell in thick clots, nothing like feathers, and so fast he could hardly see through it. Falling down the stairs hurt, but it was a pain he understood. He clawed at the fender of a car until he got to his feet. One staggering step at a time, he stumbled into the dark. The snow covered up his footprints.

Even the guard at the parking-lot exit was dead, slumped over his open cash register. A man in a black car leaned back in his plush seat, arm extended, coins still in his palm, and snow was slowly shrouding his dead body. Lindsay crept past, clutching the white coat around his thin, cold flesh.

Lindsay staggered a block, maybe two, hidden by the snow, clinging to the shadows beside the buildings that lined the silent street. Distantly, he could hear sirens. They were coming. He tried to run, but only ended up on his hands and knees in the snow. If he couldn't run, he would have to hide. Getting to his feet, he took two steps and fell again. First, he would have to crawl.

He crawled in the snow and the muck, shoulder to the wall of a looming building, until an alley yawned open and he fell into it. The ground was littered with nameless fluids, with glass and twisted metal and rotting wood, refuse thrown out of sight and out of mind. He crept to the only open dumpster—a listing, rusting hulk—and, with the last of his strength, he pulled himself into it.

He slid between wet, folded cardboard boxes, his weight carrying him toward the bottom. As he slid, more trash slipped on top of him and the dumpster shifted, the lid falling shut with a crash. It was dark in here and not as cold as it was out in the wind and snow. Whether he wanted to get out or not, he was here to stay. He curled up in his new bed and tried to keep warm. He was so cold and tired and empty, a burnt-out husk. There, in the dark, he fell asleep and the cold slowly leached away the little bit of life he'd managed to preserve.

Dane had just leapt off the top of the subway at the 207th train yard, on his usual rounds of the city, when he smelled strange ozone. It had a different taste than the oil- and grime-saturated power of the subway line, a different smell than the burnt Bakelite reek from the transformers upwind. This had the touch of magic to it, nothing that came from the shifting of the sky or the machines of men. He crouched in the shadows and cast about for the source of the scent.

There was alcohol on the air, and unwashed flesh, a hint of rot. Dane grimaced as he located the mage who smelled of a little power and a great deal of sorrow. He was a bent thing, dragged down by his filthy overcoat and bags of cans. Dane paced the shadows, following him for a while, his long stride easily keeping up with the other man's shuffle.

They left the train yard and headed for the river, for the haven under the University Heights Bridge. Dane crouched on the cracked concrete wall that shored up the riverbank and watched him go. If he weren't so accustomed to seeing his people reduced to that, he might have spared a thought or two for anger or pity. Instead, he filed the scent and sight away under "harmless" and turned his face into the wind pulling at his long, dark hair.

"I'm listening," he whispered, a bit impatient. There weren't many places he could go that the wind wouldn't find him in time. He wondered what it wanted this time.

"I need you," said the wind, tangling in his wild hair and tickling at his ears. "Come."

Dane was already moving at the word *need*, his four-limbed feral gait carrying him faster than any human could run. He swung up to the rooftops to race across the top of the city, under the heavy clouds, and dropped down to lope through narrow alleys, staying to the shadows. At last, he swung over an iron fence and into the empty yard of an old hostel in a row of brownstones. The French doors of a third-floor room were standing open and the light poured out from within, but Dane could see no one on the balcony.

"Up," the wind urged, pulling at him. Dane went up the trellis, over the balcony, and up farther still to the roof, graceful and silent.

The old man was waiting for him, face turned into the wind, a thin black silhouette against the milky winter sky. The snow parted around him like a curtain pulled back, leaving his silver hair and black robe unmarked.

Now that Dane had arrived, the urgency faded, to be replaced by his usual temper. His voice scraped the silence like a rusty saw. "What is it, Cyrus?"

"Go to Washington." When Dane drew near enough to see him clearly, Cyrus's face was whiter than the New York snow. "The laboratories. You know the ones."

Dane's nose wrinkled, but he nodded slowly. "I know them." He wished he didn't. The one time he'd gone to scout them out, the smell had lingered in the back of his throat for more than a day. Vivian, the third member of their little cabal, had said it was psychosomatic. Dane disagreed. There was something about suffering and the fear it brought that didn't easily wash away.

"Take the car," Cyrus said, as Dane turned away. That was enough to make Dane stop. The wind swirled snow around them both, dragging Dane's long hair about, pulling tendrils to catch in his beard. "You will find a boy there, outside, if he lives." Cyrus's eyes were black stars in his pale face. He swayed from the effort of his magic working, drawing the winds whistling through the streets of Washington to whisper to him on the rooftops of New York City.

"I will," Dane promised, his voice dropping to a gentle rasp. He held out one huge hand to Cyrus, careful of his own claws. "After you come inside."

"The wind..." Cyrus began to protest faintly.

"Is about to knock you on your skinny old ass," Dane said bluntly. The argument was familiar and Cyrus's thin hand was already drifting into Dane's, fluttering like a snowflake. Dane closed his hand over it and guided Cyrus to the door on the roof that led into the house.

In Cyrus's room, which had once been an upstairs dining room complete with huge glass doors and beautiful balcony overlooking the old garden, Dane helped Cyrus out of his damp coat and settled him into a chair by the fireplace. The hearth was dark and full of ash, so Dane stacked wood to light it again, ignoring Cyrus for the moment.

"Time is of the essence." The old man sounded too tired for the words to have much effect.

"No use me getting the kid if I'm bringing him here to meet your frozen corpse," Dane said stolidly, working on lighting the fire. He was grinning behind the thick, wet curtain of his hair. His priorities and Cyrus's clashed more often than not, as Dane didn't feel the same urgency about following arcane visions that the aeromancer did. He enjoyed the conflict more than a little. The fire caught on twisted newspaper and dry twigs, and gnawed the wood.

"Dane." Cyrus's brittle voice cracked on his name.

"Cyrus." Dane rose and crossed the room to shut the balcony doors. The snow had already come in and streaked the wool rug with white. It was as cold as the rooftop in here.

"Stop enjoying yourself."

"Yes, Cyrus," Dane said insincerely.

"This is important." Cyrus thumped his fist on the arm of his chair, a small noise in the large room.

"So are you." Dane brought a wool blanket from the bed and tucked it over Cyrus's lap with careful movements. The scene was more than a little incongruous: the wild-haired, hulking feral caring for the slender, aging prophet. There was no one there to point it out, though. No one had been there for years. No one but Cyrus and Dane and sometimes Vivian, who was as alien as they were and just as inured to it.

The window by the bed was still open a crack. The wind whined and lapped at the crack before slipping in to find its master, rippling Cyrus's hair and tugging at his sleeves.

"Find him." Cyrus put one cold hand on Dane's wrist, gripping like a bird's talons. Tension flowed from him in slow waves, seeping under Dane's skin.

"Have I failed you yet?" Dane gently detached Cyrus's hand from his wrist and turned to go.

"Not yet," Cyrus admitted. When Dane looked back, he was huddled and small in the chair, cast into odd patterns of light and dark as the fire struggled to breathe. A twitch of Cyrus's hand and the air swirled around the flames, coaxing them higher.

"And I won't." Dane closed the door behind him. He was heading down the back stairs when he heard Cyrus's voice once more. It was soft and far behind him, inaudible to anyone but the wind and the fire in Cyrus's room, inaudible to anyone but a beast with ears that could catch the flutter of fear in a heartbeat at a hundred paces.

"Not for some days."

Dane stopped dead on the stairs for a moment, his mind caught on the words. And then the beast in him shook off all concern about tomorrow. All that mattered was now. He dug under his layers of ragged clothing and pulled out a chain with several keys on it, picking the one for the sleek, black Cadillac he would be driving tonight.

It was snowing heavily when Dane got to DC, white clots that spattered on the windshield and clung and melted into a slurry of half-frozen water. The wipers scraped and flung the slush aside, but it was still a miserable drive. The car was stuffy, even with the vents open and the windows cracked. The air was full of exhaust and rust and rubber and oil, a thick smear of civilization over Dane's delicate senses.

The cell phone rang and Dane flipped it open. "What is it, Viv?" No one else called him.

"I'm on my way to the scene," she said. He could hear the breathlessness in her voice, the hum of her car. "I've been speaking to my people. I still can't say what's happened, but they're treating it like a biological terrorist attack, which works for us."

The place would be crawling with Army and Homeland Security. Dane growled as a transport truck passed, sluicing the car in a wave of slush and muck. "Explain."

"They've quarantined all of Walter Reed. They won't know what they've lost for hours. You can find it before then. I think I know what you're looking for." Now, Dane could hear sirens. She must have been getting closer to the Institute of Pathology.

"What is it, then?"

"Moore is a hack, but she can rate power." Vivian's fingernails chittered on a keyboard. She was using a computer or something like it while driving again. Dane and Cyrus had never taken to technology the way Vivian had. "I'll give her that. The only inmate she has who could have that wide a sphere of influence is a kid named Carrington. This is a big deal, Dane."

"Carrington." Dane didn't care much about these things, usually, but he recognized the name. "Isn't he a general or something?"

"Spokesman for the armed forces, among other things," Vivian said. "You remember. That's good. Mother's a socialite from some cereal-empire family. It made the news when they had him committed about two years ago."

"Cereal empire. I hate this country." Dane shook his head and picked up the pace as the rest of the traffic was wisely slowing in the storm.

"Yeah, one of those poor-little-rich-boy stories. I feel bad for the kid. Or, man. He'd be nineteen now. Dane, they cannot afford to lose him. They'll kill him first." Vivian paused, the sound of her car engine died, and there was another voice.

"I'm sorry, ma'am, this is a restricted..."

"I have clearance."

"Go ahead, but stay clear of the red zone. We're still testing for biologicals."

Vivian's engine murmured to life. "Sorry, Dane. I was saying..."

"They'll kill him before they let him go, if they don't simply kill him outright. I hear you. I'll get him." Dane wasn't concerned about the soldiers and agents crawling around the building or the neighborhood. "Cyrus said he got out. I'll find him."

"The girl may be here." Vivian's voice was low and Dane felt his muscles twitch involuntarily. He hated mind mages.

"Did she bring the dog?" he growled.

"I can't imagine she wouldn't. They need to find this kid, Dane. This isn't just humans playing here." Dane could hear the undercurrent of loathing in her voice that echoed the feeling under his skin. "Be careful."

"I will be." The idea that he could get the drop on his old enemy left Dane smiling.

"Pay attention." Vivian's voice stung his ear. "Dane. The boy, and nothing more. You can play with Jonas another day."

"I can focus," Dane rumbled.

"You have about four hours until they finish processing the building." Vivian's tone softened slightly. "Be quick, but be careful. You're not immortal, you know."

"People keep reminding me." Dane snorted with irritation. "I'll be fine. I'll call you when I have him."

“Good luck,” she said, and he could hear her smiling.

“I don’t need luck,” he snapped. “You know that.” She was laughing at him when he hung up the phone. Now he could pay attention to driving hard, to get there soon. The dog and the girl had a head start, but Dane was older and wiser. He was looking forward to this.

He parked, badly, several floors up in a garage next to a mall. He took note of the numbers painted on the wall as he slipped over the railing and dropped into the dark of the loading docks. There was a crackle and splash as he broke through a thin crust of ice and landed up to his ankles in water. Moving too fast to get wet, like a cat, he was gone before the water could wash in over his boots.

Dane glided through the streets and alleys of the capital like a revenant, his long, dark coat swirling around him with the wind. Crouched in the doorway of a shuttered shop to let a police car pass, he murmured, “I’m here.”

Dane had no idea if Cyrus was still awake, but if he was, the wind would take him the message. The air was mad with tension and anxiety. Even if he hadn’t been forewarned, he would have been wary tonight. Closing his eyes, he breathed and let the world speak to him.

The wet, snowy night couldn’t muffle the footfalls and muttered voices, the growl of engines and the crackle of radios, and the scents of hunters and hunted. Dane’s eyes flew open, staring into the distance far beyond the opposite wall, focused on nothing, and he growled low. He flicked his tongue against the cold air, tasting.

He dropped to all fours, moving in his strange, rolling, animal gait, his heavy head swinging as he sought out the strands of scent that beckoned the beast. Instinct kept him hidden, kept him in the shadows while his mind was consumed with the hunt. The urgency was here and now, the same as that which drove Cyrus. Dane entered the moment of it and it drove him, too.

The scent of suffering and fear grew heavier as Dane

hunted. The wind was with him, dipping into some distant alley and bringing him what it found there, drawing him along narrow streets. When he was near, when he could taste iron on the back of his tongue along with the sweat and fear of something dying alone, he scaled the side of a darkened building and cruised the rooftops.

The gap between roofs, where Dane stopped to peer down like a gargoyle, was only a few yards across. Almost no light fell between the buildings, but it was enough for Dane's feral sight to make out the blocky shapes of dumpsters and the snow-tufted trash pushed into haphazard heaps. He tensed, leaning forward to make the leap into the dark, when the wind shifted. Instead of leaping, he moved out of sight, grinning like a demon. The wind had been in his face all this time. He hoped it had kept him hidden.

Dane could hear the heavy, booted footfalls of a man keeping an almost lazy pace down in the alley. The sound stopped and the man inhaled. It was all Dane could do to stay still. *Jonas.* The thrill in his veins was like fire, like lightning, and he licked at his long teeth in anticipation. One more step, and another, and another—every one brought the man deeper into the alley. The real prize was all but forgotten. That moment had changed into another, and Dane was airborne, falling from the sky with the thick snow.

Dane's aim was perfect, even without having seen his goal before he leapt. Jonas was moving already, but not soon enough. He went down under Dane's mass with a thick crackle of bone and tendon parting. Pain seared through Dane's side as four long claws gouged through skin and muscle to catch on his ribs on their way to his heart. Dane's laugh was caught in a snarl of pain, but the rush of adrenaline swept it all away. They rolled through the slush and puddles and Dane got his teeth into Jonas's neck, a snap of fangs that filled his mouth with hot blood. There was a flurry of limbs and claws and fists before they parted, gasping, to face each other in the dark.

"Dane." Jonas had his hand to his neck to staunch the flow of blood while his flesh knit itself together far faster than Dane's own body was healing. The faint light glinted off deadly claws extended from his fingertips. Dane's belly was still holding his insides in and his head was too full of blood rage to care about the wounds so long as he wasn't tripping over his own guts.

"Jonas." There was an affection in Dane's voice that he reserved for his favorite enemies. His body was singing with pain and fury and hunger and joy. At times like this, it was easy to forget that he was mortal. He felt so much stronger than his body.

"The girl didn't mention you'd be here," Jonas said, straightening as his spine put itself back together.

"Maybe she doesn't like you anymore." Dane's hand flicked out, claws piercing a trash can as he grabbed it to toss at Jonas's head. Laughing, Jonas deflected it with a punch. "I don't mind doing her dirty work."

"Maybe she wanted to surprise me." Jonas charged, getting airborne at the last minute in a beautiful leap that aimed one steel-toed boot at Dane's face. Years ago, it might have hit, but Dane hadn't passed the time being lazy. Age had only made him faster and wiser to compensate for the loss of his magic. He shifted and caught Jonas by the ankle, using the man's momentum to swing him headfirst into the side of a building. The brick cracked, and half of Jonas's face peeled away to the bone. His neck snapped back, but before it broke, he caught Dane in the wrist with his other foot, almost shattering the bones.

"Surprise," Dane rumbled, ignoring the agony in his arm. Jonas's breath was ragged, stuttering, but even as he was dying, he was healing, moving again. It would have been terrifying if Dane hadn't seen it before, if his own body wasn't humming with remnants of magic that healed him from the inside out.

Jonas grabbed a rusting pipe, wrenching it loose from whatever held it, and brought it around as survival instinct and rage drove him to his feet. The pipe caught Dane in the left side of the head. His jaw and cheek crumpled as he rolled with the blow. While he was catching his balance and rallying to retaliate, Jonas hit him twice more with the pipe, smashing against his right shoulder and his ribs.

Dane let momentum take him to the ground and out of range, and rolled to his feet. He retreated deeper into the alley, buying time for his broken magic to put him back together enough to be able to see out of both eyes. His bones still remembered his old self, but barely, and they settled into place with a groan.

"Down, boy." Dane spat blood and flesh into the muck between them. He let his shoulder drop, let one leg buckle as he backed up, feigning only a little more weakness than was real in the moment.

"You first." Jonas took the bait and rushed him. Dane danced aside, faster than anything human, faster than Jonas could react, and grabbed Jonas by the shoulder and hip. His claws cut through Kevlar clothing that the dry intellect in the back of his mind recognized as a uniform, and got a purchase deep in dense muscle. Dane hurled Jonas toward the end of the alley as hard as he could, despite the screaming agony in his own shoulder and chest. Jonas hit the wall hard, sending fragments of brick and mortar showering around his body as he slid to the ground.

Not satisfied with that alone, Dane grabbed a dumpster with both hands, claws digging into the rusting steel. He whined with pain as he lifted it, his body shaking in protest, but he got it off the ground and brought it down on Jonas as the other man was struggling to stand.

"Stay." Dane sagged against the dumpster, adding his own weight to it as it crushed Jonas, at least for the moment. He inhaled and gave it another shove, grinding it against the wall until it grated on the brick. He leaned on it, pushing hard and making the metal groan, until he could see bright, hot blood running from under it. The red rivulets wound past his boots and he allowed himself a slight smile. "Good dog," he muttered, pushing himself to standing.

The smell of their blood and adrenaline was a fog around him, but Dane could still sense the fading threads of fear and pain that had drawn him here. It took him a moment of staggering through the alley, pawing through the trash of one dumpster after another, until he found something warm under a pile of sodden cardboard. He lifted the cardboard, throwing it into the alley behind him.

What he found looked as discarded as the rest of the trash, a spindly shell of a human body wrapped in a white lab coat. The long, pale hair was as fine as a woman's, but the body smelled male. Dane leaned in and dragged it out with a grunt. The body smelled poisoned too, as though it should have been dying, but the heart was still fluttering stubbornly against the prominent ribs. Dane carefully tucked the body under his coat, against his bloody shirt.

"Lot of fuss for a little thing," he grumbled without any real displeasure. "Let's not keep Cyrus waiting." Holding the body to him with one arm, he scaled the fire escape and disappeared into the dense white veil of the snowstorm covering the city.

# Chapter Two

It was a long time before Lindsay woke. His sleep was as silent and dark as it had always been, though it lasted far longer. There were no dreams in Lindsay's world. He never tossed and turned. Since he was born, he'd only lay where he'd fallen asleep, still and quiet. For him, sleep was the absence of everything. The slightest sound could wake him without dreams to explain it away.

When he finally did open his eyes, there was no segue between sleeping and waking. He was simply thrust into consciousness and the nothing was replaced by terror and confusion: he wasn't alone.

The room was huge, like something out of a fairytale. He lay in a four-poster bed, swathed in soft sheets and blankets. A fire crackled in the hearth across the room and, beside it, there sat a man.

The man filled the chair he was sitting in. He was tall and broad, wrapped in a long, dark coat. His hair fell loose around his shoulders and his face was hidden by shadows and a heavy beard. His eyes glittered in the dark, watching Lindsay.

More tests? Was this a trick? The Institute? He had hoped this was all over—he'd thought he was dead. Perhaps he was. He never dreamed, and there was nothing in his life like this, not anymore.

He shrank into the covers, moving farther from the man, and was surprised when it worked. There were no restraints, nothing at all to keep him in his bed. He tried to use his magic to get away again, but it snapped like a rubber band, recoiling against him and making him gasp with pain.

"No need to be so frightened," the man said. His voice was strange. "Didn't go to all the trouble of getting you just to do you harm."

"The doctors at the Institute went to plenty of trouble to hurt me," Lindsay muttered, pushing himself into the farthest corner of the big bed, bunching the pillows up behind him. He didn't take his eyes off the man. He was never safe.

"Good thing for you I'm not a doctor." The man stood and Lindsay finally got an idea of how huge he was. "I'm just an errand boy." Firelight glittered in a crystal pitcher of water on the desk, and in the set of glasses by it. The man picked the pitcher up with one hand around the belly of it, his long, black claws stark against the curve, and filled a glass. "Thirsty?"

"No, thank you," Lindsay said automatically. Politeness was bred into him, so that it showed even when all his attention was on the strangeness of the man in front of him. Normal people didn't look like that, and doctors certainly never had claws like cats. "I'm all right."

He wrapped his arms around his knees, hugging himself. When his hands slid over his arms, they didn't touch skin, but some sturdy fabric bound around his wrists. His eyes widened and he clawed the blankets back to see his hands. Stone. He remembered stone on his wrists. Terror had him ripping at the bindings, pulling them away from his wrists. His heart slammed against his chest, and he fought to get free.

"Enough." The man's hands were on his. He'd crossed the room in a heartbeat, silently, to stop Lindsay from tearing off his bandages. The claws were gone and his hands, huge and gentle, swallowed Lindsay's up entirely. "Can't have you bleeding all over the nice linens." Up close, he smelled warm and good, cleaner than he looked. "Breathe, little bunny. No one here wants to tie you up."

Panic made Lindsay's heartbeat and breath come fast. He wasn't sure he believed it, but for now, it was true enough.

Everything was unreal enough that he could relax.

"That's better. Don't get yourself excited. They poisoned you. It's making your heart work too hard already." The man let go of his hands and petted his hair back from his face. "Don't want to have to call the healer back so soon."

Lindsay's hands fluttered to rest on his knees. The touch felt good, and it was a struggle not to lean into it and beg for more. No one touched him like that, so gently. He wasn't sure how to react.

"Good boy." The man kept petting him, soothing him. Even as Lindsay relaxed, the man didn't stop. There wasn't anything to it but gentle touches, the way someone might pet a dog or a cat, but that didn't matter. It felt so good. "Thirsty?"

Lindsay had said no before, but this time he nodded. Nodding gave him an excuse to arch into the touches, to pet himself against the man's hands. "Please."

"Thought so. You smell thirsty." The man straightened and went to get the water. "Healer said to make sure you drank, to clean your blood. Cyrus will have my beard if you don't. Best for us both if you have a drink."

The man shook back his hair as he returned. Lindsay could see him clearly. He wasn't human, and he wasn't really handsome, but he wasn't frightening, either. He had dark gold skin, intelligent eyes under a heavy brow, a hawk's nose and high cheekbones. It was hard to make out anything else because of the beard that blended into the rest of his mane.

"Drink." He reached out to help Lindsay hold the glass.

Lindsay wrapped both hands around it. Lack of use and his injuries made his grip weak, but he drew the glass up to his mouth without help and stopped, staring at the clear water for a moment. "Where am I?" he asked softly, glancing up at the man. "Who are you?"

"You're in New York, with people like you. I'm no one, but you can call me Dane. Drink your water." Dane's brow furrowed.

Lindsay flinched at the stern expression. Obediently, he

took a sip of the water. It tasted clean and pure, and he drank more as he wondered what the man—Dane—meant when he said that Lindsay was with people like himself.

"Good." Dane reached out to pet his hair again, like a reward.

The encouragement and petting kept Lindsay drinking, slow and careful swallows that eased the pain in his throat and the dryness of his mouth.

"You'll feel better soon," Dane promised. Lindsay doubted that. He hadn't felt better than this in a long time.

Dane was different from anyone he'd met before—real and solid and warm, like everything else in the room. There was nothing cold or sterile here—even the water had the chill of a fresh spring and no hint of chemicals in it.

"How did I get here?" Lindsay whispered the words, daring to ask another question even though Dane had seemed unhappy with the last one.

"I brought you." Dane gave him a smile that showed a flash of shiny white fangs. "You can thank Cyrus, though. He sent me."

"To find *me*?" Why would anyone care to take him from the Institute?

"Yes, you." Dane stopped Lindsay from spilling his water when confusion distracted him from holding on tight. One big hand held both of Lindsay's and the glass until Lindsay had control of it again. "Apparently, you're rather special. And I hate that place." Dane's expression darkened and his voice dropped to a rumble in the back of his throat. "I wouldn't put a dog in there, even a dog I didn't like."

"Thank you," Lindsay murmured, mustering up a little more courage. No matter why they'd taken him away from there, he was grateful. He dipped his head to take another sip of water, hiding his face in the fall of his hair. Dane stood beside the bed, patient and still as a tree.

When Lindsay finished drinking, he held the glass out to Dane. "Won't they come looking for me?" His parents wouldn't like that he'd gotten away. The people at the Institute weren't supposed to let him leave.

"They will." Dane gave Lindsay that feral smile again as he accepted the glass. "Doesn't mean they'll find you. Don't plan to let anyone take you away, myself."

Lindsay looked out the window, at the night outside, blinking away the stinging in his eyes. "I don't want them to find me," he whispered.

Dane left his side to refill the glass. "They won't. Haven't found us yet, not for years, and we're far more trouble than you. They don't even know what part of the country we're in right now."

Lindsay nodded slowly. "How long was I there, do you know?" he asked, mostly to distract himself. His time at the Institute had blurred into one long day and night of terror.

"Vivian tells me it was two years." Dane put the glass on the bedside table. There was a curious, animal sadness in his dark eyes.

Lindsay could feel the blood draining from his face. That long? His hands shook as he realized he was an adult. Nineteen. He didn't feel two years older. There had been nothing to mark the time. No holidays, no visits, no birthdays. Not even a letter or a card. Not a perfunctory party for the benefit of his mother's social circle instead of having anything to do with him. He didn't know how he felt about finding himself grown. He didn't know how he felt about anything, but he shook with it all the same.

"Shh." Dane made a soothing sound and stroked his hair again. "Lie back. Cyrus will kill me if you fall out of bed on your head or something. It's over now, understand? The past is the past."

Lindsay obeyed, settling into the soft sheets and blankets again, tucking his cheek against a pillow. "Thank you," he whispered, more comforted than he knew he ought to be. He was so cold, still, even with the fire burning.

"You don't need to thank me." As if he could read Lindsay's

mind, Dane took another blanket from the foot of the bed and tucked it around him. "You need to rest." How long had it been since anyone had tucked him in? Dane frowned and Lindsay realized he'd been staring up at that calm, inhuman face. Quickly, he closed his eyes.

It didn't take long for Lindsay to fall asleep again, feeling safer than he had in years.

From his vantage point on Cyrus's balcony, Dane could smell the cold world he couldn't see through the falling snow, and he itched to be out in it. Soon, perhaps, now that he wasn't the only one here to watch over Cyrus and the boy. He knew, before she came up to see him, that Vivian had come home. The wind had brought him a wisp of her voice and the slam of a cab door, not ten minutes ago.

"Where is he?"

"Up on the roof again." Dane didn't turn to greet her. If she didn't know he was happy to see her by now, he wasn't going to coddle her.

"And the boy?" Vivian's heels clicked on the flagstone as she came to stand beside him. Her scent swirled with the wind and filled his head.

"Sleeping again. The healer's been." Dane looked at the slender Asian woman putting her tiny, smooth hand over his where it curled around the iron railing. "Boy sleeps a lot."

"He's recovering. Mortals do that," she chided him gently, tilting her head so that she could see him clearly.

"What did you bring back with you?" Dane had smelled her coming, smelled someone else with her, heard two sets of footfalls, two light female voices, before Vivian had come to find him. "Something for me?"

"That depends." Vivian's smile was slow and wicked. "Do you deserve anything?"

"I left Jonas crushed to a pulp under a dumpster in the filthiest alley in DC," Dane mused. "Think that's enough?"

Vivian's eyes glittered and she stood on her toes, lifting her chin in that imperious way that said she wanted to give him a kiss. Dane bent to oblige her and she kissed him on the forehead. "Definitely," she murmured. This close, he could smell the warmth of her, the faint hint of perspiration between her breasts, under her arms, at the nape of her delicate neck. "One of these days, someone should actually kill that man."

"I do try," Dane pointed out.

"You'd be bored as hell if you ever succeeded," Vivian said loftily. "I doubt the sincerity of your efforts. Come in, Dane. It's cold and Cyrus will come down when it suits him." She turned away, tugging her dark red cloak closer around her.

"Or when I drag his skinny old ass down here," Dane threatened, following her inside. The doors slammed behind him before he could close them and Vivian laughed.

"He hears as well as you," she reminded him, taking off her cloak and shaking it out. She threw it over the back of a chair and settled, holding her hands out to the fire.

"I know." Dane came over to put more wood on, to warm the room. "So, what did you bring me?"

"Her name is Kristan. I've been using her for a while. You'll want to be careful with her. Her magic...she makes people feel things."

"Empath?" Dane grimaced. Of all the magics, the ones that touched the mind were his least favorite.

"If only." Vivian made a contented noise as the fire grew. "No, she controls people's emotions with her body chemistry. Pheromones. As you'd expect, she's a grifter and a whore, but good at both." Her tone was uncritical, pragmatic. "Just watch yourself."

"She's got to sleep some time," Dane said, shrugging. Vivian laughed at him again, shaking her head.

"So do you," she said. "And I think, when you do, I'm going to cut off your beard."

Dane gave her a dark look and was about to respond when the door to the room opened as Cyrus came in. He staggered and Dane was there, one hand under his arm. Vivian was on her feet as well, coming to help with his coat.

"Was there a reason for the noise?" Cyrus asked irritably, ignoring his obvious infirmity in favor of scolding them. "Or were you simply wasting breath?"

"You should know better than to ask," Vivian said tartly, working him out of his coat. "We were being social. People still do that, you know."

"Yes, yes." Cyrus waved her off as soon as she had his coat in hand. "People will always waste time."

"Did you see anything?" Dane asked, once he had Cyrus settled. The older mage glared at him like a wet, angry crow.

"The wind is unclear," he said sullenly.

"You're tired," Vivian said. The look she shot Dane was accusatory. She was far more adept at chivvying Cyrus into resting when he needed it. Dane simply picked him up when he fell over and put him in bed until he got strong enough to get out on his own. It worked well enough, had for decades, but Vivian was never satisfied with their system.

"I can rest when I'm dead," Cyrus snapped. Still, he let his head fall to rest on the high back of the chair. Dane didn't want to think about that at all and he scowled at Vivian for irritating Cyrus into saying such a thing.

"Or you could rest now." Vivian was unmoved by the temperamental behavior and Dane's scowl alike. She brought over a blanket from the bed and Dane carefully tucked it around Cyrus to warm him.

"Tell me about Washington." Cyrus gestured for her to come closer.

Vivian came to sit in the other chair by the fire and Dane sank down to rest on the rug between them. He crossed his arms and rested his head on them, lying on his back near Cyrus's feet. Like this, he could see them both.

"Chaos," Vivian said quietly. "So far, they think it could have been a terrorist attack. Some kind of biological weapon. The entire block is shut down, the building quarantined, as well as all those who worked in it."

"Survivors?" Dane rumbled.

"A few. Dr. Moore, unfortunately. It's too soon to know more. She must have had an artifact on her." Vivian was still, her gaze on the fire as she spoke. "Word is, William Carrington suffered a massive heart attack that night. And Sophia Carrington, well, she lives. But that might be all."

"She was here in New York." Cyrus opened his eyes and Vivian nodded slowly.

"Yes, she was. So was William. Apparently her maid had to stop her from throwing herself off the penthouse balcony that night." Vivian did not sound particularly regretful. "Rumor has it that she's gone mad."

"His magic reached them across all those miles," Cyrus said softly.

The idea of a mind mage who could drive someone mad across several hundred miles chilled Dane in a place nothing could warm. The idea that the same mage was sleeping one floor below should have left him colder still, if Dane hadn't seen time and again that intent was needed to drive such a thing.

The thin body Dane had carried, cradling it even in the car to keep it warm, hardly seemed like it could harness all that power and all that outrage. As Cyrus had ordered, Dane had spent hours watching over Lindsay, watching him heal, watching him sleep, and watching him wake in terror until he got his bearings—every time he woke. There was never even a flicker of threat in any move Lindsay made or any word he spoke.

Dane had come to understand that Lindsay had no idea that he could ask for what he wanted for breakfast, or tell someone not to touch him when it hurt, much less that he could do terrible things to people on a whim. Lindsay had all the fortitude of a china doll. Dane knew the nature of dangerous things, and Lindsay was not one of them.

Dane had been wrong before, though, and was reminded of it every waking moment. There was a limit to his tolerance. No matter what Cyrus ordered, Dane had his own limits, and

Lindsay would not survive it if he ever proved to be anything but innocent of malice.

"One reaps what one sows," Cyrus said at last, his eyes fixed on something far beyond the fire. Dane had long since ceased to comfort himself with that platitude. If it were true, it would hardly bring him any joy when his own harvest was upon him.

Dane was shrugging into his big black coat, getting ready to escape the confines of the house, when he heard Cyrus's door open. Cyrus wanted to speak to him. Dane could tell from the creak of the hinges. Years of familiarity could sometimes tell him more than his heightened senses. He pulled his coat around him and put on his big boots, moving silently.

The truth was that Dane didn't want to talk to Cyrus. He could smell the cold night creeping in the crack under the front door and he was longing to be out in it. The ceilings of the house felt oppressively low compared to the vaulted roof of the sky. The rooms were tiny and the air in them hot and listless. He was crowded on all sides by the smells of others, by their lust and fear and anger. The night and his city were waiting for him.

Cyrus's feet were sounding one slow step at a time on the stairs when Dane pulled the front door open. The wind frisked up to him like a puppy that had missed him, tugged his hair and his beard playfully, and shoved the door open farther so he could escape. Dane had one foot on the step, sinking into a soft, white carpet, when the wind shifted to push him back.

"Leaving will not change what must be done." The wind spoke with Cyrus's inflection, as always.

Dane stopped and stepped back inside, closing the door behind him. "You don't need me here." Cyrus was standing on the first landing, wrapped in a dark green robe, radiating disapproval.

"Who are you to say that?" Cyrus continued down the stairs and Dane could feel tension creep into him as he made sure the older man's bare, age-speckled feet found each step securely. "Do you know what I know?"

"I know myself." Dane was as trapped in himself as he was trapped in the house, confined to familiar corridors and familiar corners, all of them too cluttered with memory for him to navigate with any grace. Everywhere he turned, he was confronted with the present and the past and a future that was indistinguishable from the other two.

"Precisely why I need you. You know yourself." Cyrus stopped on the bottom step so he was eye-to-eye with Dane. "He." Cyrus pointed upward. "Does not know himself, and what he knows, he loathes. I need you to teach him."

"No." Dane almost never refused Cyrus, not completely, but there was no way he was taking responsibility for the fragile man-child he'd brought home from Washington. "He needs caring for."

"You care for me." Cyrus held out his hand and, without thinking, Dane took it to steady him as he stepped down to the floor.

"Who's going to do it if I'm busy with him?" Dane snorted indelicately. "Cyrus, find someone else. Give him to Vivian, send him to Mona, I don't care. Just not me."

"You're afraid." Cyrus's glittering black eyes narrowed and he glared up at Dane. "*Frightened.*" He let go of Dane's hand and headed for the sitting room, where there was a warm fire and a stack of recent newspapers.

"Of him? He's impressive, Cyrus, but he doesn't scare me." Dane followed slowly, stopping in the doorway. His boots were caked in a dry layer of sewer slurry and he didn't want to leave stinking flakes of it all over the sitting room carpet. "Gun's useless if it doesn't have a trigger, no matter how you load it or where you aim." He was restless and he shoved his hands in his pockets to hide it.

"Not of him, *per se.*" Cyrus took a seat in a chair near the fire. "You know my meaning. Don't play the dumb beast with me tonight. Regardless of your opinions, I've decided that you need to be the one to teach him. You're least likely to be affected by his illusions. You'll be a challenge and you can avoid getting caught up in them."

"No good can come of that." Dane shook his head like a horse refusing the bit. "I won't do it."

"You will." Refusing to indulge him with an argument, Cyrus picked up a newspaper and looked through it. Dane waited. "Another suicide," Cyrus murmured, reading the midsection. "They're not even front-page news. How long are our children going to die of fear and neglect, Dane?"

"Survival of the fittest," Dane said roughly, shrugging it off. He'd seen their kind die in myriad ways over the years. He told himself it didn't affect him anymore.

"Lindsay survived his parents, two years in Moore's hands, and an artifact the likes of which were forbidden even in the time of Sumer. He killed hundreds to secure his own escape." Cyrus peered at Dane over the edge of the paper. "Has he not proven his fitness?"

"He's a child," Dane said stubbornly. He pulled his hands from his pockets to cross his arms over his chest. "I'm no nursemaid."

"He's a man. You're being the child here." Cyrus shook the paper out and folded it up in his lap. He folded his hands on top of the paper in turn and gave Dane a piercing look. "How long do you intend to play the stray dog, Dane? Does being the beast that goes bump in the night amuse you so much that you would do it indefinitely? This is not a fairytale, for all that you may be laboring under a faerie curse. It's high time for you to stop playing the animal and start playing the man underneath the skin."

Dane's body was taut. He felt like he could fly apart at the slightest provocation. "I don't play," he said flatly. "I am what I am. You found it useful enough in the past."

"And now I need you to be useful in another way." Cyrus gestured upward, as though Lindsay were sleeping directly overhead. "He is yours. Yours to care for, yours to teach, yours to heal. You know how this must happen. Keep him alive. They are still looking for him and will kill what they cannot have. When he can take care of himself, he will no longer be your concern and you can slide back into the shadows."

There was silence and Dane had no answer but to grind his teeth until his canines began to powder with it. He was angry, angrier still that the undercurrent in him was fear. "My task is to care for you," he said at last.

"So it is." Cyrus picked up the paper and found where he had left off. "There will be fresh tea in the kitchen. You may bring me some if it suits you." He glanced up at Dane again. "I do not do this lightly," he added. "I would not go without your protection unless I felt it necessary."

That was irritatingly soothing to Dane's ego. He took a slow breath to calm his fury and nodded. There was going to be no arguing and, if he left, the wind could find him anywhere in the world he could run and it would harry him endlessly until he came home. "I'll get your tea."

There was nothing else to say. Dane kicked off his boots and hung up his coat before going to the kitchen. Vivian was sitting at the table in front of the tea service, hands cupping a delicate china cup of Earl Grey. There was such sympathy in her eyes that he willed her to say nothing as he came to get the tea.

"It could be good for you," she said, ignoring his glare.

"Viv..." Dane growled a warning for her to shut up.

"At the least, they'll send Jonas for him," she murmured. Her dark eyes were bright with mischief. "You love playing with Jonas." Dane wasn't going to be mollified with that, but it did take some of the sting from the assignment. "When he wakes up and you're not there, he asks where you are," she added, and Dane knew she wasn't referring to Jonas.

For some reason, that made Dane pause. He picked up the tea tray to take to Cyrus. "Why would he do that?"

"Maybe because he trusts you?" Vivian shrugged gracefully, smiling at him. "It really might be good for you, you know, to have something of your own."

"I don't want it." Dane turned away from her, careful not to slosh the milk in the tiny pitcher on the tray.

"It's not always your choice."

"What am I supposed to do with him?" Dane gave up and put the tray back before he spilled something in frustration. Cyrus could wait for his damn tea.

"Be yourself." Vivian shrugged again. "You've never failed at that. He needs someone. And we need him. You don't have to mean it, Dane." She took a sip of her tea. "You just have to do it. It's not like he'll ever know the difference. How could he?"

But that was just it. Where other creatures, human creatures, could lie and deceive, animals were notoriously poor at anything but the most trivial dishonesty. Dane had been trapped in this half-state longer than other men lived, and he'd grown comfortable in it, in his isolation and his feral honesty. There were good reasons why being separated from his more human self had been a relief.

He wanted to tell Vivian and Cyrus both how much this disgusted him, but he couldn't. He picked up the tray instead. "This had better not take long."

Cyrus looked up when Dane returned with the tea and set it beside him. He didn't comment until Dane had handed over his cup. "You will, of course, observe a modicum of decorum with him."

"I'll what?" Dane straightened and crossed his arms over his chest. He was already worn thin with this idiocy about him taking care of the fragile little mage. "Say what you mean for once, Cyrus."

Cyrus sipped his tea and chuckled. "Don't allow your animal instincts to get the better of you, or his to get the better of him. This is not a dalliance, nor is he available to you as entertainment, should you grow bored."

Dane was sorely tempted to walk out. "I'm not an animal, Cyrus."

"Just a warning." Cyrus took another sip of tea. "The last

thing I need is to lose him because you've broken his heart. You do have a certain charm, you know." He gave Dane a look he knew well, all corvine amusement at Dane's expense.

"I'll do what's best for him." If Dane was stuck with this, he was going to do it right, and damn Cyrus's maundering about decorum.

"See that you do." Cyrus turned his attention to his tea and his papers. "Don't coddle him. His training should begin the moment he's well enough. I want to know what he can do as soon as possible."

"Is that all?" Maybe Cyrus wanted some flowers arranged, or some kittens fostered, or some other equally appropriate use of Dane's time.

"For now." Cyrus didn't look up. "Make sure he dresses warmly when you take him out. I don't want to have to call the healer back again."

Dane took a long breath and let it out slowly. Childcare wasn't in his job description. He didn't even have a job description. Sometimes, he wished for one, so he could point at it when he was trying to refuse new things, for all the good it would do him in the end.

# Chapter Three

Lindsay hadn't left his room yet, not today and not before. He'd showered, soaking up the heat from the water. Dane kept the fire going in the fireplace, but a chill always crept in. Lindsay was cold all the time, these days. Maybe he had been before the Institute. It was hard to remember. Even the calisthenics that had been drilled into him one horrible summer at military camp—useful enough now that he was trying to regain some strength—didn't warm him up.

He'd wrapped himself in a robe he'd found in the closet and curled up in the chair Dane used when watching over him in the night. He was sure it was warmer there than anywhere else in the room. Lindsay looked out the window at the cold blue sky. At least he wasn't the only thing that was cold. The door creaked open and Lindsay startled, but only a little.

"Hello, dear." Vivian was a tiny Asian woman, even smaller than Lindsay. Lindsay couldn't begin to guess her age or her origin. There was something timeless about her, as with Dane, that made it hard to compare her with anyone else Lindsay had known.

Today, she was dressed in a bright red pantsuit and had her dark hair pulled back. Her hands were full of shopping bags in a variety of colors. The difference between her and Dane was night and day. She was elegant and refined, while Dane was huge and seemed perpetually shabby.

"I went shopping for you. Dane said you'd been up and about so I thought you ought to have some clothes."

Lindsay tilted his head, watching her, trying to figure out if there was a catch. "Thank you," he said softly. He meant it. "You were able to guess my size?" He didn't even know his own clothing size.

"I'm clever that way." Vivian stopped at the desk and put down the bags she was carrying. "Someone's got to keep everyone in the house dressed. I bought you slacks and such. You'll be wanting to go out soon. I had to guess, so I bought several pairs of shoes. I'll go get those while you take a look in the bags."

"Thank you," he said again, slipping up out of the chair. He pulled the robe tight around himself and padded over to peer into the bags.

He pulled out a heavy, charcoal-colored wool coat, and the gloves and scarf that had been tucked beneath it. It looked warm. He liked that idea.

Vivian returned with three more bags. "Of course, I had to get you a couple pairs of jeans, because Dane said it was nonsense to bring just slacks, that you'd want jeans."

"Thank you," Lindsay said quietly. He didn't know if he would or not. Maybe Dane was right.

"Do you want to try some of it on while I wait, or should I leave you to it?" Vivian gave him a warm smile. "You'll be going out with Dane as soon as you're able."

Lindsay blinked at her. "Going out?"

"Well, you've got to get used to the city." Vivian took boxes of shoes and boots out of the largest bag. "Cyrus has put Dane to the task of making sure you get on okay, that you learn to fend for yourself, get strong and stay safe. You'll want to be working on your magic too, I'm sure."

His magic. Lindsay looked at the boxes so he wouldn't have to look at Vivian. His magic had only ever gotten him in trouble, and he was still trying not to think about all those bodies... Why would he want to use it now? "Of course."

"From what we can tell, your magic is going to be very good for you. It should hide you from anyone who still wants to hunt you down. Well, except for Dane. If anyone can get through it, Dane can." Vivian found socks at the bottom of the bag and handed them over.

Lindsay took the socks and put them on the chair. Hiding sounded safe. He gathered up briefs, slacks and a shirt. No sense putting on shoes without clothes. "How would he get through it?" Lindsay asked, heading for the bathroom to dress.

"He's got exceptional senses." Vivian raised her voice to be heard through the bathroom door. "I'm sure you've noticed that he's not entirely human."

"I...yes." Lindsay fumbled with the clothes. It had been a while since he'd done this for himself. "Am *I* human?" he asked, when he came out of the bathroom. He looked up from fastening the last button on his shirt, through his hair hanging in his face. "I mean...the magic?"

"You are human. But gifted. Magically gifted." Vivian's expression was fond. "You look quite nice in that. I did a fair job with the sizes."

Lindsay looked at himself and shrugged. "Thank you. It fits well." Magically gifted. It hadn't felt like much of a gift, so far.

"You're a handsome young man." Vivian came over, reaching for his throat. Lindsay backed off, instinctively, but then he realized she was only reaching for the shirt to adjust his collar. Vivian didn't seem to notice, or if she had, she didn't show it. "You don't need to worry about going out. Dane will take care of you."

"I'm going today? Now?" She made it sound so immediate.

"You don't have to go today, dear." Vivian sounded more maternal than Lindsay's mother ever had. "Whenever you're feeling well. You could start by looking around the house. Just stay to this floor and the one below. There's a little library down the hall, though what you'd want with books that were old when Cyrus was a boy is beyond me. You're welcome to them, though." She brushed his hair back off his shoulders. "Are you going to want that cut, or shall I leave you be like the rest of the men in the house?"

Lindsay shook his head, reaching up to tug the ends of his hair. "No. I want..." He touched the closed collar of his shirt with his other hand. "I want to cover the marks."

All across his collarbone and low around the back of his neck, scars like acid burns spilled pink over his pale skin. Dozens of smaller scars starburst out from the burns, from the collar exploding against his skin. There were matching scars on his wrists, and worse, wide stripes of scarring where his wrists met his hands, where he'd torn his skin open trying to pull free.

The shirt covered all the marks, but his long hair served as another barrier, another veil between what had happened to him and what the rest of the world could see.

"All right." Vivian stepped back. "Why don't I leave you to play dress-up? Anything that doesn't fit, put it in the hall. Are you hungry?"

Lindsay tilted his head, thinking about the question. "I... Maybe. I think so." Deciding when to eat was another thing he hadn't done for himself in a long time. There were so many things he would have to relearn.

"I'll send Dane up with a meal. Seems he's still the only man in this house who doesn't forget to eat."

Lindsay could have gotten his own food—he was dressed, after all—but he wanted to see Dane again. Vivian was nice, and he liked her, but there was something about Dane that made Lindsay *need* to trust him. Having Dane bring him lunch one more time wouldn't hurt.

Vivian gestured to the clothes she'd laid out for Lindsay. "If you'd rather other styles, let me know. I was guessing at what you'd like."

"This is..." Lindsay looked around at the clothes. "This is fine. Thank you." He smiled tentatively. "I'll tell you if anything doesn't work."

"You can go shopping for yourself, once you have your magic mastered." Vivian folded up the empty bags and stacked them on a chair. "Then you won't have to worry about my sense of style. Dane will come see you in a few minutes."

Lindsay's smile widened. That, at least, seemed like it might be a perquisite to learning to use his magic. Maybe not enough to make his magic seem like a gift, but being free to come and go on his own… "I'll keep that in mind. Thank you."

"You're welcome, Lindsay. Ask if you need anything else." Vivian left him alone, then, closing the door behind her.

Lindsay watched her leave, and went back into the bathroom to look at himself in the mirror. Pale gray eyes stared back at him, two smudges of faded color in all his pale, pink-white skin and pale, white-gold hair. Other than the scars, the rest of the damage from the Institute was gone. Even his teeth were white and perfect again.

He wasn't sure how Vivian had managed it, but the dark blue shirt made him seem less washed-out. If he was going to be responsible for buying his own clothes, someday, maybe he should ask her about it.

After he learned how to use his magic.

Every day since Vivian had brought him the clothes, Lindsay had gotten up and showered and dressed. It felt good, like a piece of normality. He was still tired all the time, and cold, but he at least had enough energy to get himself clean and dressed in the mornings.

Some days, as Vivian had suggested, he even crept beyond the threshold of his room. The first time he had dared to do it, his knees were weak as he stood in the hall and realized that he could, if he wanted, go *anywhere*. He had found the library, which only got bigger the deeper in he wandered, until he was afraid he would lose the way back out. Reading was difficult even if Lindsay knew the language of the books he chose, because his head still hurt so often. Most days, he ended up in a chair by the window, watching the clouds navigate the sky.

Today, he put on dark wool slacks and a blue dress shirt buttoned all the way up to the collar, and the clouds were shaped like fantastic things: dragons, minotaurs, gryphons. Everything in Cyrus's house had a touch of magic, it seemed, even the windows—everything Lindsay saw through them had a mysterious beauty to it, down to the gray street and dirty snow.

The silence in Cyrus's house wasn't like the silence of Lindsay's childhood home. That silence had been oppressive, like every noise Lindsay made was an imposition. In Cyrus's house, silence had a sense of waiting, like the house was holding its breath. Sometimes, the house would sigh, and the air would tug at Lindsay's hair so he knew that the house knew he was there.

Lindsay felt welcome in the house in a way he had never felt welcome anywhere else in the world. When he left the room, his footfalls were muffled by the carpet runners that lined the halls, and the aging loveseats and chaises in the sitting room Lindsay found next to his room still had enough spring and stuffing to be comfortable. Yet, everything was slightly worn, so Lindsay felt as though he could touch without offending. His fingers brushed a worn place on the arm of the big chair in his room and crept down to the grooves carved by Dane's claws. When Lindsay had first found the wear and realized that those marks had been worn while Dane sat in this chair watching over him, the feeling had been indescribably wonderful.

The door swung open as Dane came in, Lindsay's lunch on the tray in one big hand. He didn't seem to change much from one day to the next, always lost behind the heavy fall of hair and the dense beard, his body obscured by loose clothing. For all that he was huge, he was very quiet, even in his big boots. He rarely spoke, either, seeming to be satisfied with whatever his senses picked up, so it was a surprise when he said, "Eat up. We're going out."

Lindsay sat up, startled. "Out?" Vivian had said so, but days had passed since then, and he had almost forgotten.

Dane set the tray on the desk. "Time to learn to fend for yourself." He straightened and looked Lindsay over. "You're well enough."

To fend for himself. To learn to use his magic, Dane meant. Lindsay didn't know that he wanted to learn to use it. If he left it alone, wouldn't everyone leave him alone in turn?

"What good will it do me to learn to use the magic?" he asked, and ducked his head, afraid he'd make Dane angry with him. "I mean, shouldn't I just leave it alone? With all the trouble it's been..."

"Can't not be what you are. They already know what you are." Dane crossed his arms over his chest and shook his hair back so he could glare at Lindsay properly. "Embarrassment to your father, liability to the government, and experiment that got loose. Can't stop being a mage any more than you can stop being Carrington's son. Eat your lunch. Long day ahead."

Lindsay flinched, stomach churning. The reminder of what he was to his family *hurt*. It hadn't taken being a mage to cause that, though. He'd never felt like he was what they'd wanted in a son. Being a mage had only been the last straw. He shuffled over to the desk and sat to pick at his food.

"Didn't say they were right, any of them," Dane added, as he turned away. "They're not. But that won't stop them from looking for you, no matter what you do. Come find me when you're done."

Come find him. Lindsay could do that. He took a slow, calming breath and tried to get through his meal.

Downstairs, the house was comfortingly domestic. The main stairs led to a spacious foyer that opened up to a dining room to one side and a sitting room to the other, and a hallway ran to the back of the house. Lindsay had ventured down once before, in the night, but the sound of voices on the back stairs had sent him fleeing to his room rather than exercise his rusty social skills. To his relief, there was no one in sight but Dane, sprawled in a big chair in front of the sitting room fire, reading a leather-bound book that seemed small in his hand.

Lindsay hovered in the archway a moment, then stepped inside. "...Dane?" His voice broke, and he tried again. "Dane?" Better.

"Ready to go?" Dane looked ready. On further inspection, when he closed his book and put it aside, he'd finally shaved off the beard and he'd pulled back his hair. Exposed, he looked inhuman, rough-hewn and unfinished. He got to his feet and prodded the logs in the fire with the poker, settling them down.

Lindsay looked at himself. Pants, shirt, shoes. He was carrying his coat. "Yes." No. He wasn't ready to go anywhere.

"No sense wasting time." Dane closed the doors on the fireplace and got up. When he turned, he stopped and frowned until Lindsay was about to start panicking, and then he nodded as though he'd come to some conclusion. "Do you know New York?"

"Yeah." Lindsay looked himself over again, trying to figure out what Dane had been frowning about. What had he done wrong? "My parents have a house in Greenwich. I grew up there. Sort of." He checked Dane's expression cautiously. No frown now. "When I wasn't away at school."

"Then you know how to get us to Washington Square Park." Dane stepped around Lindsay on his way to pull a long, black coat from the hall closet. He tugged it on and gestured toward the front door. "Go on."

"You want me to..." Lindsay stared up at Dane, then glanced at the door. He hadn't been out of the house since Dane had brought him here from the Institute. At the Institute, of course, he hadn't been able to go out at all. Thinking back on his childhood, he'd never been allowed to make his own way before. He swallowed hard. "All right." He could do this—if he could figure out where they were starting from. He headed for the door, pulling on his coat and pulling up the hood.

Outside, the world was shades of gray. They were standing on the front step of a tall, narrow house across the street from a small park. The skyline was visible above the trees. Dane stopped behind Lindsay, pulling the door shut. "Train stops a few blocks south," he said quietly. "To the right."

"Thank you." Lindsay shoved his hands into his pockets, finding his gloves. He pulled them out and tugged them on as he walked, keeping his head ducked down so that, between his long hair and the hood, his face was hidden from view.

Dane followed him like a shadow, silently. He let Lindsay lead the way to the stop. Even when he pulled out the pass cards for them, he made no comment, just tapped Lindsay on the sleeve with his before they took the stairs down.

Lindsay clutched the card in his hand, feeling the edges dig into his skin through the leather gloves. At the bottom of the stairs, he had to push his hood back to see, looking around to get his bearings. A map on the wall told him which train he needed—C train, south, to Brooklyn, off at West 4th.

He headed for the correct bay of turnstiles, swiping his card and pushing through. The crowd crushed in all around him, everyone moving in the same direction. His breath came short, panicked, but he kept moving, walking over to stand behind the broad swath of yellow that marked the edge of the cement aisle where the train would stop. He held himself taut, trying not to shake with fear.

Lindsay almost threw himself aside when an arm slid around his shoulders before he realized it was Dane. Dane said nothing as he pulled Lindsay to his side. When someone bumped him again, Lindsay tensed and tucked himself up against Dane. He could feel Dane rumble, deep and threatening, almost too low to hear. Dane didn't scold or criticize Lindsay, and the threat must have worked, because Lindsay suddenly had some breathing room even as Dane shifted to let him huddle closer. After a moment, a big hand ran over Lindsay's hair, touching gently and soothing.

Lindsay couldn't quite keep himself from leaning into the petting. It felt good, helped him to calm down enough that he could breathe more evenly. Dane's face could have been interpreted as stern or dire, when he took a moment to glance down, but the look in his eyes was nothing of the sort.

Dane tilted his head, listening to something far off. "Train coming," he said simply, as though Lindsay wasn't snuggled close to him and his big hand wasn't petting Lindsay's hair, as though Lindsay hadn't been afraid in the first place.

Lindsay closed his eyes, nodding, and tipped his head forward to rest his forehead against Dane's chest again. He'd have to get on the train, just as crowded and even more closed in. Trapped. He tried to focus on the way Dane's hand felt in his hair, letting the soothing sensations keep him from panicking again.

The train came in with a roar and a blast of air, then the doors opened and Dane let Lindsay get on board. It was crowded, but Lindsay managed to find a pair of empty seats. He took the one near the window, glancing up to make sure Dane was there.

Dane slid into the seat next to him. It was like putting up a wall between Lindsay and the rest of the world. Dane slipped his arm around Lindsay without comment and shifted to get as comfortable as he could with his long legs cramped by the seat in front of them.

It was ridiculous how comforting Dane's presence was, how soothing his touch was. Lindsay leaned into Dane, snuggling close, and sighed softly. Ridiculous, but it worked. He trusted Dane not to let anything happen to him. No one was going to steal him and take him back if Dane was right there, Lindsay was sure of it.

Dane acted as though it wasn't happening at all, as though he wasn't cuddling Lindsay to him, or at least as if it was the most normal thing in the world. There was something wary about him; his attention seemed to be everywhere but on Lindsay. He didn't move, didn't speak, and he let Lindsay hide against him the whole way.

The quick and nearly incomprehensible announcement, "WesFoahStreet. SpringstreetNextStop," came just as the dark of the tunnel receded and the train lost speed coming into the station.

"I think...I think this is our stop," he said quietly, standing up. He hoped he was right.

When Dane got up, people moved out of his way, even the thuggish teens heckling a pair of disapproving-looking older men in suits. It didn't seem to be in his nature to project aggression—Dane actually moved with consideration and grace—but few people did anything but draw away from him. He stepped aside for Lindsay to go ahead.

Lindsay moved as quickly as he could, slipping out through the briefly open doors. He could feel the warmth of Dane's body right behind him as the conductor's voice echoed out of the train, "StandCleaOfTheClosinDaws," and an arm reached out to make the warning a reality.

The doors were barely closed before the train headed out of the station, picking up speed as it went. Lindsay looked around, getting his bearings.

The station was cavernous, large and dirty, with the same sweat-piss smell that was ubiquitous in the city. Lindsay let himself be swept along by the crowd of people heading for the exits. He knew, this time, that Dane was with him, right behind him as he swiped his MetroCard and pushed past the turnstiles.

Once they were above ground, Dane shook himself, a subtle version of a dog throwing off water. The cold, damp winter air was cleaner, but still heavy with car exhaust and the smells of vendors, smokers, and the various perfumes people wore.

Lindsay pulled his hood up, staying close to Dane. "Why Washington Square Park?" he asked, peeking from beneath the shadow of his hood.

"It's a good place to practice." Dane scowled at Lindsay a moment longer before continuing, "When you can take care of yourself, you'll need to look around."

Keeping hidden felt safe. Lindsay didn't want to be noticed. He could be seen and recognized and taken back to where he'd been when Dane had found him. He ducked his head, shoving his gloved hands into his pockets, and headed out into the park. He might have to put the hood back later, but he wasn't doing it now. Scowl or no scowl.

Dane didn't put his arm around Lindsay again, but he always managed to be in reach of Lindsay, no matter where his attention went.

The park wasn't the way Lindsay remembered it. The last time he'd been here, the fountain had been dismantled and construction crews had been everywhere. Today, there was more grass and the fountain had moved. The feel of the place was the same, though. People were still playing chess at tables lined up along the benches in the southwest corner, and Scrabble in the northwest corner.

With NYU so nearby, the game players weren't the only ones hanging around, the park was crowded with people Lindsay's own age. If things had gone differently, perhaps he might have been one of them. But things hadn't gone differently, and he was here with Dane, who made him feel safer than his father ever had.

Lindsay made his way past the crowd that had gathered to watch a street performer juggling a knife, an apple, and something Lindsay couldn't make out, maybe a cell phone. He sat on the rim of the fountain, careful to keep his feet out of the water. He didn't know what Dane wanted him to do, but at least there, he could focus on what Dane was saying enough to learn.

"When was the last time you used your magic without any interference?" Dane sprawled next to Lindsay, his attention on the world around them. His voice was low, but carried right to Lindsay's ears.

Without any interference? Lindsay ducked his head, staring at his shoes, thinking about it. The Institute...they'd drugged him, there. What they'd used had pushed his magic down too far for him to reach. Until the end, when *she* had given it back. He remembered the rush, the feeling of being whole, but it hadn't lasted. "I don't know. I think at the Institute. At the end. But there was something... I don't know what you mean by interference, I guess. Maybe before."

"No drugs. No artifacts." Dane stretched his long legs out and crossed them at the ankles. "Just you. Remember what you did?"

Lindsay thought back, remembering the last time. The first time. "There was a party. My mother's friends. Society stuff, not military. My father was there. I didn't want to go to the party, didn't want to be paraded like a show dog. He insisted. He has this way of phrasing things so I know how much of a failure I am, how much he wishes I wasn't his son."

Lindsay looked at his feet again. He didn't want to talk about this, any of it. "I got mad. I didn't even mean to do it. I didn't know I could. It just happened. He was making that face he always makes when he's about to tell me how much trouble I am, how much trouble they go through to fix me. I told him to go to hell. And then...and then he was on fire. I could see it, sort of, flickering around him like shadows, eating at his skin. His face got the worst of it, I think. I didn't realize, at first, what I'd done. That it was me. He was screaming and screaming and my mother came running to see what was wrong, but she didn't see the fire, and that's when I knew."

"Okay." Dane nodded slowly. "Make me think something...whatever it is."

Lindsay looked back at Dane, biting his lip, but Dane didn't seem afraid in the least. "Really?" He didn't want to screw up and hurt Dane.

"I'm a big boy, and it probably won't do much. Seems it works best on people you hate, and I'm thinking you don't hate me enough."

Lindsay didn't hate Dane at all. He didn't say so, though. He just nodded and thought about what to do. He felt around inside himself for his magic and pushed it out, focusing on Dane, trying to make himself disappear. Everyone else could see him, but to Dane's eyes, he wouldn't be there. If his magic was working.

After a moment, Dane chuckled softly and reached out to stroke Lindsay's hair. "Glad you're still there," he said in a low voice.

"Can you see me?" Lindsay asked, frowning. What had he done wrong this time?

"No. But I know you're there." Dane's fingers slid over Lindsay's cheek. "Barely."

Lindsay's magic faded when he stopped paying attention to

it, focusing instead on the feel of Dane's fingers sliding over his skin. He closed his eyes as he turned toward the touch.

"There you are." Dane's fingers pulled away. "Good work. Ready to do more?"

Lindsay sat up, embarrassed at how he'd reacted. Dane hadn't meant it like that, and he knew Dane could sense his responses. "I guess," he murmured, looking away.

"That guy there." Dane nodded toward a tall young man goofing around with his friends. "He's wearing lace-up boots—make him think they're untied."

Lindsay watched the man for a moment, and then focused on him, just as he'd focused on Dane. He imagined his focus a thread that his magic would follow, affecting only the person on the other end. He pushed his magic out, and with it, the idea of untied boots, laces dangling and tangling under the man's feet.

The young man stumbled, laughing, when his friend shoved him. Then he paused, crouching to tie his laces, miming it perfectly, making all his friends laugh.

When the boots were tied, Lindsay relaxed, letting his magic go. He looked at Dane for approval. He hoped he'd done it right. He wanted to please Dane, even if it meant using his magic.

Dane's usually inscrutable expression showed definite approval. "Nice. You getting a feel for it?"

Lindsay scuffed one foot against the cement, nodding. "I think so." It wasn't so hard. One step at a time, one piece at a time. He wasn't so stupid he couldn't manage that, no matter what his father said.

"You need to look after yourself," Dane said. "Make sure anyone who sees you sees someone else, or no one at all. How is up to you."

Lindsay's eyes widened as he nodded. "I'll try." He stood up and tried to get a sense of how many people there were. But that would change, wouldn't it? He couldn't target everyone individually, because some people would leave the park and some new people would arrive. Eventually, he and Dane would leave the park too.

Could he send it out like a wave? Maybe. Should he change his features? Or try to look like someone specific? No, maybe he should just add a sense that he was forgettable, that he looked like no one in particular. He took a deep breath and pushed his magic out in a circle around himself, wider and wider.

The farther he pushed, the harder it got. His head hurt so much, like someone was squeezing his skull around his brain. Lindsay swallowed hard, trying to hold on. Underneath the pain, there were voices, images crowding his mind, but then they faded away.

It wasn't just the voices that were fading. Lindsay gave a whimper as his vision tunneled, blackness seeping in from the edges.

Everything was perfect right up until Lindsay collapsed with a whimper, slumping as Dane reached for him. It was so hard to tell the difference between Lindsay's usual unrelenting distress and something Dane needed to worry about. Dane caught Lindsay against him and first checked to make sure he was still breathing.

Poor little bunny. Dane could tell that the little mage felt safe with him, trusted him, for some reason Dane couldn't fathom, and Dane had walked him right into this particular disaster. Feeling guilty was damned inconvenient. He sighed and pulled Lindsay into his lap, resting Lindsay's head against his shoulder as though Lindsay had fallen asleep, and snuffled in his hair. Lindsay seemed healthy enough and his pulse under Dane's fingers was strong, but the smells of fear and despair were heavy in his hair and on his skin.

Home. Dane picked Lindsay up easily, gathering the gangly body up in both arms, and made for the nearest street. A cab stopped for him quite promptly and the cabbie hopped out as Dane was trying to open the door with Lindsay in his arms. Under his navy turban, the man's dark face was drawn with concern.

"You need the hospital?" he asked as he opened the door. "He sick?"

"No." Dane stepped in without letting Lindsay go. "But thanks. He's got epilepsy. Seizures. He'll be fine after a rest."

The cabbie frowned as he processed this, then he nodded. "Yes, yes. Right. He's sick in the car, it's fifty dollars extra." He scurried around to the driver's side and hopped in. "No hard feelings. Just hard to clean."

"Not a problem." Dane settled Lindsay's head against his shoulder. "He won't be, though." Lindsay looked like he was sleeping, except for the twist of pain on his face.

The driver swung out into traffic. "Where to, then?"

"West 129th at Amsterdam." Dane looked up briefly. "I'll tell you when to stop." He settled in the seat, wondering how the hell he was going to explain this to Cyrus if Lindsay didn't wake up.

Getting back to the house was easy enough. Dane took the back stairs up and brought Lindsay to bed. He laid Lindsay down and took off his boots and coat. "Come on, little bunny," he said, stroking Lindsay's face.

He really didn't want to have to tell Cyrus about this. He tucked Lindsay in and took a moment longer, stalling and hoping Lindsay would wake. He wet a washcloth in the bathroom and sat on the bed. "Lindsay," he murmured, sponging Lindsay's forehead and cheeks. "Wake up for me. This is enough. Don't make me call the healer." Now, he was worried. He patted Lindsay's cheek firmly this time, even as he resigned himself to needing the healer.

Unlike when he was sleeping, Lindsay woke slowly, dragging himself out of unconsciousness. "No doctors," he rasped.

"There you are." Dane was shocked at how relieved he was. "You sound like you need one." He kept petting Lindsay, trying to soothe him. "Or a drink."

"Head hurts," Lindsay whispered, barely breathing the words out. He closed his eyes again.

"I'll get you something. I may need to get you the healer—not a doctor. I promise." He got up slowly, so as not to rock the bed.

"Why does it hurt?" Lindsay asked, not opening his eyes.

"I don't know why it hurts. Just don't move." Dane knew his fear came through in his voice, but he didn't care. "I'll get you someone. I'll be right back."

Cyrus was going to kill him. Dane took the stairs two at a time up to Cyrus's rooms. He'd never failed like this before. Things that could hurt him never frightened him. Since he was a child, he'd avoided being responsible for anything small and fragile enough to die because he'd made a mistake. He'd never been given another person to care for like this, either. Taking responsibility for Lindsay had been against both his will and his better judgment.

The door was already opening as he reached the hall and Cyrus peered out, his expression dire.

"What has gone wrong?"

Dane slid to a halt. "Something's wrong with his magic. He collapsed and, when he woke up, he was in pain. It was fine at first."

"I'll call Mona." Cyrus scowled at Dane. "What did you do to him? She will want to know."

"Nothing." Dane felt a fraction of his age, and huge and awkward and ridiculous. "I asked him to do small things. It worked the first two times, but he collapsed when I asked him to do something more. He was unconscious for the ride home and now he's awake and in pain."

"Go watch him." Cyrus glared at Dane. "Perhaps you won't have to look after him, after all." The door slammed and Dane was left in the hallway, shut out.

He wanted to punch something. Punching things was what he was good at, beating things, fighting, but not caring for things. He wanted to snarl at Cyrus to put him back where he belonged. He kept his hands clenched at his sides as he stalked downstairs.

He was calm, though, when he came back into Lindsay's room. "You okay?" he murmured, closing the door behind him. The anger had faded to a background crackle behind the worry for his... His. Dane was sorrier than ever for it now, for Lindsay's sake.

Lindsay opened his eyes and relaxed visibly when he saw Dane. "I'm all right," he said, but he was still whispering and his eyes slipped shut.

"I'll get that cloth cold for you again." Dane hardly knew what to do. "Cyrus is calling Mona. She's not a doctor. She's a grumpy old lady who lives over a pizza parlor." He picked up the cloth. "I'm sorry if I did this to you." He petted Lindsay's hair back from his face, as though that would do anything.

Lindsay's brow wrinkled. "You didn't hurt me." The firmness that came through in his faint voice made Dane feel worse, in a way.

"Okay. Stay right there." Dane took the cloth and went to freshen it up.

He filled up the whole bathroom, it seemed, all huge shoulders and clumsy feet. He wasn't made to be indoors. The face in the mirror wasn't even human. His hands, when he didn't pay attention to them, like now, were curled and heavy and tipped with black claws. He forced the claws to shift into something that looked like human nails so he wouldn't tear the cloth up while wringing it out.

Back in the bedroom, Lindsay lay in the bed looking as fragile as he had the first night. Dane came over and laid the cold cloth on his forehead. "Mona will be here when she can be. Sorry it's not sooner."

Lindsay tilted his head, seeking out the touch, shivering. "Cold," he whispered.

He smelled distressed, still. It was the same sick smell that had clung to his skin after the Institute. His skin was icy to Dane's touch, in spite of the blankets piled up on him. The fire was hot in the hearth, so that wasn't the problem. The air in the room was stifling.

Dane gave up and lay on the side of the bed, curling himself around Lindsay. It was all he knew how to do at this point, to keep his frail charge warm. He sighed against Lindsay's hair, wrapping one arm over Lindsay's body. "She'll be here soon," he promised, even though he didn't know it for certain. Cyrus wouldn't let them down.

Lindsay curled closer, pressing up against Dane as he always did. "Thank you."

"Don't talk." Dane stroked Lindsay's cheek, tucking his head down so his own cheek pressed against the top of Lindsay's head. "I shouldn't have pushed you."

Lindsay ignored Dane's instructions, this time. "Did you know?"

There wasn't any suspicion in the little voice, in spite of the question, but Dane couldn't help being a bit offended. "No. Hush." All Dane wanted was for the little mage to stop smelling like he was so ill, to stop shivering.

"Not your fault," Lindsay said, sounding almost imperious. He relaxed by degrees, his shivers slowing.

Dane put his fingers over Lindsay's mouth to hush him up. He needed to be quiet, and to rest. Lindsay sucked in a breath, his eyes opening wide, but there wasn't any pain in the noise. Dane moved his hand enough to cup Lindsay's cheek, but he left his thumb on Lindsay's lips to keep him from talking. Lindsay closed his eyes again, tilting his head into Dane's hand. Dane's guilt wasn't Lindsay's problem. What was Lindsay's problem was that Lindsay was ridiculously stubborn at the worst times. For someone so small, such a thing could do far more harm than good.

"Good," Dane murmured. That was better. Dane sighed and relaxed against Lindsay, waiting for the healer to come. He wanted to do more, but didn't remember how, if he'd ever known.

Finally, Lindsay drifted off to sleep. It wasn't an easy sleep—he was still shivering and his face was pinched with pain—but it was *sleep* and not the unnatural unconsciousness that had dragged him under in the park.

"Here." The door swung open, startling Dane. He'd been too busy listening to Lindsay's breath and heartbeat to push his senses outward. "Same one." The voice was Cyrus and the strange three-legged gait was Mona with her cane. The realization came too late to stop Dane from growling as he lifted his head and pulled Lindsay closer to protect him.

The movement and the growl woke Lindsay. He whimpered, pained and fearful, though not as frightened as he might have been if Dane hadn't been curled over him, protecting Lindsay with his own body. Like on the subway, Dane was a huge, warm wall between Lindsay and the rest of the world, keeping him safe.

"Go on," Cyrus snapped. He waved Dane off and Dane let go slowly, rolling to his feet. Lindsay was rigid with uncertainty, but under it was a spike of anger at the way Cyrus spoke to Dane, like he was speaking to a dog. None of this was Dane's fault. Dane was good to him.

"Let me see what's broken." Mona was an elderly Italian woman dressed in a shapeless black dress and thick boots. Her silvery hair was swept back from her face in a tight bun. "You were fine when I left you." She leaned her cane on the bedside table and bent over Lindsay.

Lindsay felt cold all over again, left alone on the bed. He blinked slowly at Mona, trying to focus through the ache in his head, trying to remember when she had seen him last. He didn't recognize her—at least, he didn't think so.

She put one hand on his forehead and the other hand on his chest, tilting her head like she was listening. "Not much wrong with the body," she said after a while. "Something else is wrong." She frowned. "A great shock to the body, but not from the body." Her hand on Lindsay's face was soft and warm. "Whatever it is, you must avoid it. I cannot heal this well. Sleep, eat, stay warm. The worst is past."

"What does that mean?" Lindsay asked. Why couldn't she

fix it? What was wrong with him?

"It means something I can't tell you." Mona pushed Lindsay's hair back to touch the scars at his neck and then picked up his hands, ignoring the way he flinched at her touches. "It could be this. You had a great magic on you. I felt it when I healed you, drawing mine." She looked over at Cyrus. "I know someone who would know the answer."

Cyrus didn't look too pleased. "So do I. We will see to it. Thank you."

When Mona finally released Lindsay's wrists, he tucked them under himself so she couldn't get to them anymore. He scrunched his shoulders up, hiding the scars on his collarbone, and watched Cyrus and Mona, trying to figure out what was going on.

He didn't like this, any of it. He was sick and hurt and he didn't know why, and they didn't seem to know either, and it all had something to do with his damn magic. He'd known it was nothing but trouble.

"What you did to cause this, don't do it again." Mona shook a finger at Lindsay, and he flinched. He wouldn't be doing it again, Mona didn't have to worry about that. He had no intention of using his magic if it was going to make him sick like this.

Mona took back her cane, leaning heavily on it as she left Lindsay's bedside.

Cyrus shook his head slowly. "We'll discuss this later," he said to Dane. Lindsay wondered if Dane was going to leave too. "I have to speak to Vivian first." He offered Mona his arm and helped her out the door.

Dane stood there, his expression inscrutable as always. Maybe another animal could have gauged his mood. He didn't move until Cyrus was out of the room. He tilted his head thoughtfully as his attention shifted to Lindsay.

"What happens now?" Lindsay asked quietly. If Dane wasn't leaving, maybe he could tell Lindsay what was going on.

"They tell us." Dane came to the bed and ran a hand over

Lindsay's hair. "It's not your fault. Relax."

Lindsay shook his head, his cheek rubbing against the pillow. "She said it was. And he's angry."

"He's always like that when the world doesn't conform to his plans. It's not you." Dane watched Lindsay for a moment and lay back down where he had been. "Go to sleep, little bunny. Cyrus is angry at bigger things than you or me."

Lindsay knew he was being presumptuous, but that didn't stop him from curling himself right up next to Dane, where it was warmest. He closed his eyes. "He's not going to make me leave?"

"No." Dane tugged Lindsay against his chest with a grumble. "Too amusing to watch me try to take care of you."

Lindsay sighed softly. His headache was receding, leaving him tired but in less pain. Dane was warm and big. Safe. Familiar. Lindsay liked being so close to him, liked the warmth and the security and the *contact.* Dane was attractive too, and that certainly didn't hurt matters. Lindsay fell asleep almost happy, in spite of his pain and his failure.

Dane was half-dozing—no sense wasting rest time—when the door to Lindsay's room opened. He could smell Vivian before he saw her, and he caught the scent of Earl Grey tea even stronger than her perfume. He swallowed his growl at the intrusion and resisted the urge to curl himself around the little body pressed up against his.

"How is he?" Vivian tiptoed into the room. Dane could hear cups singing ever so softly against their saucers.

Dane didn't answer, but nuzzled in Lindsay's hair and breathed in. Lindsay was better, but not well, and he was limp and heavy with sleep. Usually, he slept lightly, like he was afraid of never waking up again, startling at every little sound. Dane moved carefully to unwrap himself from Lindsay. He never stirred, and that made Dane feel ill.

Once he was on his feet and across the room, Dane murmured, "Shit, that's how. Breathing, but I don't know what the fuck happened to him. I should have thought more about what I asked him to do."

"Not your fault," Vivian said softly. She knew as well as he did what a light sleeper Lindsay was—Dane was forever growling at her for clicking around in her heels on the floor above while Lindsay was resting. "You know you have to get him ready as soon as possible. Tea?"

"No." Dane crouched to build the fire up again. Lindsay's skin was still clammy.

"I'll have some, then." She poured herself a cup and Dane heard her footfalls moving across the room to the bed.

Vivian was one of the few people in the world who didn't cringe or even change scent in the face of Dane's presence, much less his ill temper. Cyrus was another.

He let his thoughts sink back under the surface of the present that was full of enough sensory information to keep his mind out of trouble. He didn't bother with the tools for building up the fire. He used his bare hands and watched the blisters fade as fast as they swelled when he got too close to the flames.

When he straightened and turned around, Vivian was sitting in the large chair by Lindsay's bed, watching him. "He'll be fine, you know."

"I know." Dane couldn't make things better by sitting and staring, and he couldn't go out, so he passed the bed to stand at the window. Outside, the dark was gathering and snow was dusting the ground. He wanted out, out of the stifling heat and the guilt, to roam his city and forget how bad he was at all of this.

"I understand you got the new girl settled in," Vivian said, offering up the thread of conversation. Dane wasn't going anywhere, so he took it. She had that lilt in her voice that said she knew what he'd been up to already, but they could pretend otherwise. Cyrus was never happy with anyone being too social. Dane was damn hard-pressed to feel guilty about it. Cyrus hadn't said a thing about Dane keeping his hands off Kristan.

"Figured you wouldn't put her through *all* her paces. Just

trying to be thorough. She going to be trouble?" The cold was shimmering off the glass, reaching out to touch Dane's skin.

"She's crude and crass, but pragmatic. And she understands when she's got to be working and when she can screw around. Literally or otherwise." Vivian sounded satisfied. "Watch yourself around her. She's got that pheromone thing going on. She's mean too. Got a cruel streak a mile wide, but it's a good thing. I kind of like her, actually."

"You're a mean woman yourself," Dane pointed out. "You're just glad to have someone around who makes you look sweet." He grinned at the face she made.

"Screw you, Dane," she said without heat.

"Are you volunteering? Because I could use something to kill the time." Dane leered at her over his shoulder. It was their game; it hadn't had much meaning in years. Didn't mean he wouldn't have taken her up on it if she'd ever meant it, nor that she would have refused him if he'd been serious.

Vivian rolled her eyes at him, though affectionately. "Not me. I'm supposed to be watching the boy so you can stretch your legs. Or something. Kristan might take you up on it, the way she was complaining about not getting to go out trawling the bars."

"Cyrus sent you?" Dane turned around, feeling hopeful at the idea that he wasn't being punished for failing to take care of the boy.

"You can't sit in here and sulk all night." That wasn't an answer. "There's beer in the fridge. Steak." Vivian sipped her tea and smiled. "I promise not to tell if you don't cook it."

It was Dane's turn to roll his eyes. "And if I'm not hungry?"

"Then you'll enjoy my company for the evening." She looked awfully sweet and harmless for someone so irritating. "You won't throw me out, because it would wake your little charge." As if to make her point, Lindsay shifted restlessly, his expression twisting into a discontented pout. "I'll take good care of him, Dane."

Dane wanted to go over and pull the blankets up that

Lindsay had disarranged and to smooth back the hair that was clinging to his cheek, just to tidy him up. He hated things being out of order. Doing it would only amuse Vivian more. There had been a time, long ago, when things had been more equal between them. "See that you do," he murmured.

Screw pride. Dane took the few steps to the bed. Pointedly ignoring Vivian, he stroked Lindsay's hair back and straightened the blankets. The unhappy expression faded from Lindsay's face as Dane sorted things out, and Lindsay sighed heavily, relaxing into a deeper sleep. Maybe he shouldn't leave.

"Dane," Vivian said firmly. If he didn't leave, she might have something to say to Cyrus about it, and he might give Lindsay to someone else, Vivian or Kristan, to care for. Dane's task didn't involve attachment—attachment could hinder Lindsay's development and Dane's objectivity. As much as Dane didn't want the task, the idea of giving it up was anathema. He wasn't going to think on that, either.

"Going." He left without looking back, without saying goodbye.

Downstairs, he went to the fridge and pulled out a couple beers. The streets were calling, but he needed to stay here to watch over the house. There were bare footfalls on the stairs and he turned to see a redhead coming down. Kristan. She was dressed in an over-sized T-shirt and nothing else that he could see, and she smelled like pure bliss.

Dane knew he had to be careful around her. Viv was right. The girl had crafty written all over her. Along with *luscious*. They understood each other well enough. Things were looking up.

"Is one of those for me?" She stopped at the bottom of the stairs and leaned there, looking him over. Dane didn't have to breathe to know she was interested. He could see it in the widening of her eyes and the tilt of her hips. She was fearless, unmoved by his appearance, and it was refreshing.

"Sure. Got something for me in return?" Dane grinned, letting his gaze wander over her body.

"See anything you like?" Kristan shifted to pose with one hand on her hip, tossing back her long curls.

"Oh, everything." Dane opened a beer and took a drink. "What can I have?" He already knew the answer to that—he'd had most of it already—but it was fun to ask. She smelled so good that it was hard to stay leaning against the fridge looking at her.

"Oh, everything." She laughed at him. "But you bring the beer." With that, she headed back up the stairs.

Dane followed, purring at the sight of her bare legs and the pale curves of her ass. He could already tell he didn't need to worry about this one—no concerns, no consequences. He loved it when things were simple. He needed simple right now, just for a few hours.

# Chapter Four

When Lindsay woke, he was alone and it was morning. He wanted to be sad because Dane wasn't there, but his head was hurting so little that he could hardly complain. He was warm, covered in heaps of blankets, and the fire was still burning in the hearth. When Lindsay pressed his cheek to his pillow, he could smell Dane there, and a long, glossy black hair scrolled across the white cotton like a signature scrawled on fine paper.

No, Lindsay had nothing to complain about except, perhaps, that he had failed yesterday. He tried to put it out of his head, with some success. Dane had taken such tender care of him last night, it made Lindsay feel as though his failure wasn't the end of the world. Lindsay sat up slowly and his head throbbed. No one took care of him like that.

There was a silver tray by his bed, with a glass of water and a bottle of aspirin on it. Lindsay imagined that, among people who were generally kind and did things like that, throwing someone out for being broken wasn't going to be an option. He hoped. He dressed to go downstairs, ready to do something with his day. Surely he could still do small things. He'd try, at least. If he couldn't be useful, he would try to be social instead.

The living room in Cyrus's house was far more comfortable than the one in Lindsay's parents' home. Like the rest of the house, it was actually used for living in, rather than for display. Someone had lit a fire earlier in the morning, so the room was warm and the chair closest to the fireplace was even warmer. It was Dane's chair, the one he'd been sitting in before they'd gone out together so Lindsay could learn to use his magic. Before Lindsay had failed at learning.

*The New York Times* was on the coffee table. It had been so long since Lindsay had read it. He picked it up and, after a moment's hesitation, climbed into Dane's big chair, feeling like Goldilocks. Dane's chair was definitely too big, but that made it just right. It even smelled like Dane, warm and musky and safe. Lindsay subway-folded the paper, curled up and started to read.

He was halfway through the first section when a woman he'd never seen before came down the stairs and into the room, her heels clattering on the hardwood before the carpet silenced them. She was a beautiful redhead, if one were drawn to voluptuous women, dressed in a lilac robe that was barely done up over her heavy breasts. Her wild red curls were in luxurious disarray, tumbling everywhere, and there were bruises visible on the pale curve of her neck and on the inner swell of one breast.

She stopped when she saw him, one hand on her hip, looking like something out of an old painting, back when women's curves had still been considered art.

"You must be Lindsay." Her voice seemed sweet, but there was something in her that put Lindsay on edge.

"Yes," Lindsay said warily. He thought he'd heard her voice before, drifting through the house on the curious air.

Her expression shifted to something that would have been maternal if she hadn't been standing there nearly naked, dressed to seduce. "I'm Kristan. I heard you had a bad day yesterday. I'm glad to see you feeling better." She headed toward the kitchen, tugging her robe closed over her breasts almost absently. "Did anyone make coffee?"

Lindsay wasn't sure how he felt about other people knowing he'd failed yesterday. He caught her question belatedly and shook his head. "I don't know. I didn't get that far." He returned his attention to the paper so he wouldn't have to deal with the twisting in his chest while she was in the room. He couldn't help glancing over at the top of it to make sure she was really leaving.

Kristan stopped in the doorway and tossed back her hair. The move made her robe slide aside to reveal most of one curvy leg. "You're not waiting for Dane, are you?" Her face was a study in concern. "I'd hate to think he was being rude enough to leave you sitting here on my account. He can be such a beast." Her voice was light, softening her words.

Lindsay stared at her. Dane was sleeping with Kristan? He shifted in the chair, suddenly uncomfortable. "No," he said quietly. "I'm not waiting for him."

After the way Dane had curled up in bed with him, warm and solid and safe, Lindsay's mind had offered up dozens of fantasies. Fantasies that had Dane rolling Lindsay onto his back and stripping him down, opening him up and pushing into him. Fantasies that had Lindsay slipping down the bed to lick and suck at Dane's cock. He knew from the musky way Dane smelled that Dane would taste good—so deliciously, perfectly good—sliding over his tongue.

In the face of Kristan's conquest, Lindsay pushed his fantasies aside, shoved them into the back of his mind. It wasn't as though he'd really expected to act on any of them after all. Right?

"Good." She gave him a warm smile. The way she leaned against the doorframe could have been taken out of an old movie. "I'd feel terrible if I got in the way. It's sweet how he looks after you. He grumbles about it, but you know how he is. Did you want some coffee while I'm getting mine?"

"No, thank you." It was instinct to be polite, even now, when he was feeling crushed and uncertain. "I'm not thirsty."

"All right. I'm sure Dane will be down soon. Men." Kristan rolled her eyes at Lindsay as she pushed away from the doorframe. "You look like a nice boy. I bet you wouldn't keep falling asleep on a girl. Time and again." She made a discontented noise as she disappeared into the kitchen.

Time and again. More than just this morning, maybe.

Lindsay had thought Dane...he...well, obviously he'd been wrong. What did he know? He ducked his head, hair falling around his face as he forced himself to focus on the newspaper. Dane could kick him out of the damn chair if he didn't want Lindsay to be there.

"What the hell are you playing at?" Cyrus turned away from the window as Dane shambled in. His face was a mask of disapproval and his eyes flashed with anger.

"What?" Dane knew he was a mess, having just rolled out of Kristan's bed, but that was rarely an issue for Cyrus. He didn't seem to give much of a damn about anything Dane did, so long as Dane did what needed doing. Dane had long since outgrown the days when he'd wanted Cyrus to care one way or the other. Lately, they only had a real difference of opinion when Dane insisted on trying to take care of him.

The wind sweeping in the window swirled around him, tugging his hair in all directions. "Yes, yes, I know..." Cyrus waved a hand on the way over to the desk. Dane knew full well that wasn't directed at him and, given what glimpses he could catch from the corners of his eyes, he didn't want to know what was speaking. Some magics, he avoided like the plague.

"Jonas has come to the city," Cyrus snapped. "And you're off bedding one of my..."

Jonas was here—the idea sent a thrill of adrenaline spiking along Dane's spine. "Didn't see any harm in it." Dane picked up the computer he usually used on the way over to his chair. He glanced at Cyrus from behind his tangled hair, gauging how angry the old mage was. "She's a big girl. Keeps her from going out after it."

"And you." There was anger and derision in Cyrus's voice.

"You want me here to look after the boy," Dane pointed out reasonably. Cyrus got amusingly snippy when Dane's sex life intersected with his awareness. He settled in his chair, eyes on the computer screen. "There's got to be something in it for me, if I'm going to babysit." He didn't intend to admit to Cyrus, now or ever, that he liked his time with Lindsay.

"You haven't touched him, have you?"

Dane wasn't going to dignify that with an answer. He damn well knew that Lindsay was off-limits, for more reasons than Cyrus's fretfulness. But the way Cyrus said it made his hackles rise. His too-sharp teeth ground against each other and he forced the anger down. He knew when he was being baited.

"If you'd let me out to do my job, I'd have found Jonas already," Dane snapped, instead. "And I'd already have a way to kill him." All the fucking in the world, no matter who it was, wouldn't make up for missing out on that. "Let me go."

"No." Cyrus shook his head so that his hair spilled around his shoulders in fresh disarray. Dane opened his mouth to protest, but Cyrus silenced him with a gesture. "We will be watching him. We must be certain who holds his leash. We may even discover where they are. You and the boy will be going to Ezqel."

"Send Vivian." Dane threw the computer over onto Cyrus's desk where it landed with a crash, and he pushed himself to his feet. "Send Kristan. Go yourself. I don't care. I'm not leaving you alone while Jonas is hunting in my city." He'd had about enough of this. Cyrus was his responsibility, not Lindsay, not anything else. "Even if I did, that's the last place I'd go."

The conversation was over. Dane stalked to the door and tried to wrench it open, but it wouldn't budge. The knob turned, the metal creaked with strain under his hand, but a great force resisted him.

"Let me out, Cyrus." The hair stood up on the nape of Dane's neck and a snarl rose in the back of his throat. He hated this show of power and, in the moment, he hated Cyrus.

"This is too important for your feelings to matter here," Cyrus said simply. "What was between you and Ezqel, what is between you and I, what is to come between you and Jonas, none of it matters." Dane turned slowly to see Cyrus looking at him with rare sympathy. "You know it already. The extent of events makes your opinion on this irrelevant. We must know what they know of us. We must know what they have done to the boy."

Dane rattled the door one more time, jerking hard. The wood screamed in protest, but all he did was make a muscle in his shoulder part under the strain. His flesh tingled as it repaired itself.

"Why Ezqel?" Dane knew there were other people who were knowledgeable in similar magics; he'd gone to them in the past, for his own affairs as well as Cyrus's.

"Ezqel stands a greater chance of healing him. And you." For a moment, Cyrus sounded like he had once when he was younger, when he'd looked at Dane out of a face as pale and unlined as Lindsay's. "*You* can refuse Ezqel until you die. Your death will be needless, but you will at least have your pride. You cannot make that choice for the boy. I wish to think you would not. I need you to go. Don't let me down."

Dane sagged against the inside of the door, letting his head fall back against it. "Have I ever?" he asked quietly.

"Not yet," Cyrus murmured.

"And I won't," Dane said, meeting Cyrus's eyes and refusing to look away from the darkness there. "Not for some days. Isn't that right?"

Cyrus's expression shifted to one of real sorrow, and Dane regretted speaking, because Cyrus had enough pain. "I forget how well you hear. Dane..."

Dane shook his head and pushed away from the door. "Don't say anything." Whatever it was, he didn't want to know. "Did Viv get our tickets?" He picked up his computer and took his seat in his chair again. Why he bothered to fight, after all these years, was beyond him. They were locked in their dance.

"You'll find them in your account." Cyrus was still watching Dane, but Dane turned his attention to making sure the computer wasn't broken.

The door swung open as though nothing had been amiss and Vivian stepped in. "I have his documents," she said brightly. There was an envelope in her hand and she set it on

Cyrus's desk. "I think we're all set." Her smile dimmed when she saw Dane's face, but she turned back to Cyrus without comment.

"Go get the boy, then." Cyrus picked up the envelope and sorted through the contents. "We will see if he likes my plans any better."

Lindsay was still huddled in Dane's chair when Vivian found him. Outwardly, he was reading the paper, but inside, he was trying to get Kristan's words to stop echoing in his head. Instead of pictures in the paper, all he could see were the bruises on her skin where Dane's mouth must have been.

Suddenly, he hated her with a passion that did nothing to keep him from hurting as well. He wanted to hate Dane too, but he didn't have it in him. It wasn't Dane's fault that Lindsay was undesirable. Thin. Pale. Wrong-bodied. Broken. Weak. Dane had been good to him for no reason at all—that made him better than Lindsay had dreamed, and it made Lindsay a fool.

"There you are, Lindsay." Vivian's voice was as bright as the sunshine. She was good to him, like Dane had been. Unlike Kristan, she never made Lindsay uncomfortable. "How are you today?"

Lindsay peered over the shield of the newspaper. "I'm fine. Much better. Thank you." It wasn't really a lie. Nothing was wrong with him other than his broken magic and his foolishness.

"Cyrus would like to talk to you."

Lindsay swallowed hard, fighting tightness in his chest and pricking in his eyes. "Have I done something wrong?" It felt like that kind of day.

"No!" Vivian gave him a sweet smile. "Quite the opposite. Cyrus needs you. Go on up to his office." She gestured toward the stairs. "Don't keep him waiting."

Soothed by Vivian's reassurances, Lindsay put his newspaper on the table beside Dane's chair and stood up. "Thank you," he said softly, heading for the stairs. He didn't want to make Cyrus wait.

Lindsay hadn't expected to find Dane already in Cyrus's room, looking disheveled and sleepy. He was sprawled in a large chair near Cyrus's desk, attention on a computer that seemed small in his hands. The sight of him made Lindsay's heart lift until it collided with reality and tumbled down again, bruised, all in the space of a single beat.

Cyrus looked up as Lindsay came in, dark eyes narrowed. "I have procured a passport for you under the name of Cross," he said without preamble. "It is necessary for you to travel to Germany to meet with a colleague of mine."

It took Lindsay a moment to process what Cyrus was saying. He'd been distracted by the realization that Dane had had sex with Kristan and then rolled out of bed and come in here without showering. Dane was sex-mussed and half-dressed, and it looked so good. That was how Dane would look, if...

Lindsay wrenched his attention back to Cyrus. "When?"

"Your flight will leave this evening." Cyrus handed a large envelope over to Lindsay. "In there, you will find your official documents and all of the information you will need for the trip. Your flight will take you to Zurich. From there, you will travel to the Black Forest. Dane will be accompanying you." He cast a glance over at Dane, who looked back and sighed.

That hurt. With all the time Dane had spent taking care of Lindsay, it was a painful shock to realize that Dane didn't want to go with him on this trip. After Kristan's announcement, Lindsay felt like he had to question everything about his interactions with Dane, like he'd misunderstood everything up until now.

"I'll be ready," he murmured. "Is there anything else I need to know?"

"Ezqel is a very old mage, older than I." Cyrus looked so ancient and crow-like that it was hard to imagine anyone being older. Casting another glare at Dane, Cyrus continued. "You will submit yourself to whatever investigations Ezqel chooses to pursue. In this manner, we hope that he will be able to mend you. And you will address him with the utmost respect." Another sharp glance at Dane, met with a roll of Dane's eyes, and Cyrus turned his attention to Lindsay.

Lindsay felt sick at the idea that this man, Ezqel, was going to...to *investigate* what had been done to him. Even the prospect of being healed didn't lessen the horrible implications. "All right."

"This is important." There was some sympathy in Cyrus's voice. "You are not the first to suffer in this way. You will not be the last."

"I'll do it." What Cyrus was saying made sense, but it didn't make the idea any more appealing. He wasn't sure how he was going to survive it. This morning, he would have told himself that he could lean on Dane. Now, he didn't even have that.

Cyrus fixed Dane with another look. "There is no time to waste. The dog and the girl will be searching for you. You must get to Ezqel at once."

Lindsay didn't know who those people were. He didn't know so many things. Nodding, he clenched the envelope in his hands to keep them from shaking.

"A car will be here for you at five. If you have any questions, you can ask Dane or Vivian." Cyrus flicked a hand toward the door, dismissing him.

# Chapter Five

It was cold and miserable in the forest. The Black Forest, Cyrus had said, but Lindsay thought it looked mostly gray. He trudged along behind Dane, carrying a backpack filled with his bare necessities. The steps that didn't land in mushy puddles nearly landed him on his ass, thanks to the ice hiding beneath the wet snow.

Lindsay was terrified, going to face Ezqel without even the assurance that Dane cared for him. How he could've become so dependant on something he hadn't even known existed, in such a short period of time, was beyond him. That, too, was terrifying.

Dane should have been in a good mood, out in the wild, but he wasn't. Even having known him only a short time, Lindsay could tell. There was a point at which Dane stopped being inscrutable and started being grumpy and that point was long past. The ground slid away under Dane's feet as he headed down a ravine. He rode the slide gracefully, managing to stay standing, until he could stop himself against a tree and watch Lindsay's descent.

Lindsay was smaller, lighter, and had the advantage of seeing Dane go first. He stopped at the top and looked at the tilted trees dotting the descent. Biting his lip, he sent himself toward the first tree at a skittering run-slide. He caught the tree with both hands, took a breath, and aimed for the next. The trees kept him upright. He was already frozen to the core, and landing in the snow would only make it worse.

Dane didn't seem to notice the cold, and he didn't seem to get tired. He was an inexorable animal, with only Lindsay keeping him from eating up the miles. He kept moving and leapt the icy, mucky stream cutting through the bottom of the ravine. There, he waited to help Lindsay cross.

Lindsay was shivering and exhausted by the time he got to the bottom. "How..." He had to wait and swallow down his shivers before he could speak again. "How do I get over?"

"Jump." Dane grabbed a sapling in one hand and extended the other. "To me. I'll catch you."

Lindsay swallowed hard and nodded. He eyed the distance and took a running leap, the snow sucking at his feet with each step. He almost didn't make it, but Dane grabbed his hand and hauled him in. He hit Dane in the chest and Dane let go of the tree to wrap the other arm around him, holding him up.

"Okay?" he rumbled.

Shivering hard, Lindsay nodded against Dane's chest. He was gasping for breath, every exhalation coming out in a haze of fog. "m all r-r-right," he chattered. Dane was so warm. He didn't want to step away.

"There used to be a hunter's cottage around here," Dane said. "We'll stop when we find it." He nodded at the steep hill that lay ahead of them. "Up you go."

Lindsay nodded again and, reluctantly, trudged up the hill. The idea of a reward at the end, though, that there would be a place to stop and warm up—which didn't even feel possible at this point—was a relief.

It was growing dark when Dane pointed out the cottage up another hill. The little building was crumbling under the weight of time and the elements; the wood roof was thick with moss that was disappearing under a fresh layer of snow. "This is it. Not much, but it's here. No fire, no magic in Ezqel's woods. We'll manage without."

A soft whimper slipped out before Lindsay could stop himself. No fire. No warmth. He nodded to let Dane know he understood. He was shivering too much to speak.

Dane reached out, and Lindsay took his hand for the last yards up to the cottage. It was slow going toward the top but, finally, they were at the door. Lindsay went inside and slipped his pack off. He dug through to find dry clothes. If he couldn't be warm, at least he could be dry.

Dane followed him in and dropped the heavy pack he was carrying. The first thing he did was take out a sleeping bag and lay it out in the most sheltered corner.

"Over here."

He hung a tarp by pushing tent spikes between cracks in the stone walls and floor, to give some more shelter and to keep in the warmth of their bodies. It was nearly black in the hut, but he set a light up under the tarp. "You'll sleep here. Settle in, I'll be back." With that, he was gone.

Lindsay eyed the tarp doubtfully, but slid underneath with his clothes. He wriggled out of his wet clothes and pushed them out from under the tarp, then pulled on the clean, dry ones.

When Dane came back a few minutes later, he pulled out a chemical hot pack and cracked it carefully, then shook it. He picked up Lindsay's sleeping bag on the way over to the corner. Crouching, he offered both to Lindsay. "Tuck the hot pack under your coat, but over your shirt. It'll get hot enough to burn, but you need it. Then get yourself in the sleeping bag. I'll bring you dinner."

"Are you going to come in too?" Lindsay asked. It felt strange to be so idle while Dane was busy working.

"Not likely." Dane tugged a foil-sealed meal pack out of his backpack and gave it a twist to start the chemical heating process. His expression, shadowed by his loose hair, was almost angry. "You can eat that in a few minutes. Let it warm. And drink this." He passed over a bottle of water. "You need to rest. I can wait."

The temperature was dropping so fast that Lindsay was shivering in spite of the shelter and the dry clothes. He worried about Dane not resting—Dane hadn't slept during the drive from the airport to the forest's edge either—but he didn't say anything. He didn't have the energy.

"Be right back." Dane left Lindsay alone again, ducking out into the heavy snowfall to prowl the woods as the wind picked up.

Lindsay huddled in the shelter and listened to the wind howling around the little hut as he ate. The warmth felt wonderful after all the cold that had filled everything else today.

Nearly half an hour later, the door creaked open. Lindsay startled, scrambling out from the sleeping bag, but he calmed quickly once he peeked out from under the tarp to see that it was Dane. In Dane's arms was a sapling bole to replace the long-lost bar for the door.

"Do you want me to do anything?" Lindsay was still shivering, but his words came out without chattering.

"You need to rest and stay warm. It's going to keep getting colder." Dane shed his wet clothes, hanging them up to dry on a line as he did, until he was stripped naked. Barefoot, as though the icy stone floor didn't bother him at all, he padded over to his pack to get out dry things to wear.

Lindsay was cold, but he wasn't dead. Dane was beautiful and Lindsay had never seen him naked before. Dane's body was human in form, better than human, the perfect human animal. Lindsay watched Dane until he realized what he was doing. "It gets colder than this?"

"Much." Dane got dressed as far as his jeans and stopped, giving Lindsay a stern look. "Lie down. You should be beat. Are you warm yet?"

Lindsay frowned and shook his head. "A little? The heat packs are helping some." They were radiating heat, and his body was soaking it up, but it didn't feel like he was generating any heat of his own.

Dane stood there for a long moment, head tilted as though he were thinking hard about something. Then, obviously having made up his mind, he shook himself and got moving again. He collected his boots and things he would need if he were getting dressed in a hurry and lined them up neatly outside the little haven where Lindsay was resting. "Move," he muttered, ducking in to join Lindsay.

Lindsay moved. He skittered under the tarp and made room for Dane. A lot of room. Dane was big. And half-naked, not that *that* made Lindsay want to move any farther away than he absolutely had to. He watched as Dane grabbed the sleeping bag Lindsay had been curled up in and twitched it over on top of the other that had been intended for Dane.

Dane coaxed Lindsay into the top sleeping bag first, and slid in after him. He was quiet and quite certain of what he wanted. Lindsay was nervous, apprehension and anticipation muddled together in his belly, when he realized what Dane meant to do. He let himself be moved like a doll, though, and snuggled against Dane's chest. When Dane was done, they were both tucked into the one sleeping bag with Lindsay almost lying completely on Dane's big, warm body with Dane's strong arms around him to keep him warm. The spare sleeping bag under them kept the chill of the stone away from their bodies.

"Now, go to sleep," Dane said firmly. He was warm and smelled so good and was *Dane*—the source of all the good things in Lindsay's life. Suddenly, Lindsay felt all too warm, in all the wrong ways. He blushed fiercely, trying to ignore his arousal.

Dane stroked Lindsay's hair soothingly, ignoring or oblivious to how much Lindsay was turned on by the closeness. Lindsay closed his eyes and focused on the petting, letting it soothe him. He was worn out and that was enough to put him to sleep before he embarrassed himself further.

Lindsay was too exhausted to wake quickly, but his body was awake long before his mind. He was still pressed up against Dane and he was so hard. It wasn't just a morning erection. He was surrounded by Dane's smell and warmth and body, and he couldn't help himself. Lindsay didn't know if he'd ever felt so much need all at once in his life. Still half-asleep, he rocked his hips, pushing his body against Dane, instinctively seeking the friction that would get him off.

Dane murmured sleepily and pulled Lindsay closer. That just made it better. Worse. Something. Lindsay woke up a little more as he writhed, but he didn't stop. He needed...fuck, he needed to come. He kept moving on instinct, his breath coming faster. Dane shifted against him instead of pulling away, making everything feel incredible. Lindsay wasn't awake enough to be ashamed as he rode Dane's thigh, desperate to come.

When Lindsay came, he felt so good, lazy and sated, until the rapidly cooling come in his pants brought him back to reality. Horror jerked him awake, to full awareness of what he'd done. *Oh, God.* He tensed up, ducking his head against Dane's chest to hide his face.

"I'm sorry," he whispered, feeling horrified at himself and, on top of that, afraid that Dane would be angry at him. He was alone in this forest except for Dane. Dane held Lindsay's life in his hands in every way, and Lindsay had gone and done *that.*

"Hm?" Dane had the decency not to laugh or recoil in disgust. "Enh. No bother," he rumbled. "It happens."

Lindsay winced, but he was grateful Dane didn't seem to be angry. He knew Dane didn't want him. He shifted stiffly, trying to roll off Dane with as little contact between his groin and Dane's body as possible.

Dane unzipped the sleeping bag to let Lindsay out. "You put a coat on," he warned. "It'll still be damn cold out there. And get another hot pack from my bag if you need it."

"I'll be all right." Lindsay didn't need a hot pack. He did need his coat, though. He wriggled up to the top of the sleeping bag so he could reach it. Dane stayed very still while Lindsay disentangled himself, much to Lindsay's relief. It was still freezing out when Lindsay got free, but it didn't matter. He needed to flee before he had to see the expression on Dane's face over what he'd done.

Lindsay would have been overwhelmed with shame and loathing, unable to meet Dane's eyes, except that Dane didn't seem to care what he'd done. In fact, Dane was in a remarkably good mood and acted as though nothing at all had happened. It was a gorgeous morning. The sun was shining and the sky was blue, promising a beautiful day of melting snow and hard going. At least Lindsay wouldn't be so cold.

They packed up and Dane offered Lindsay his hand as they made their way downhill. That almost made everything better right then, when Lindsay took Dane's hand and Dane gave him that sharp, jagged smile that showed in his dark eyes. They walked out to a clearing and sat on fallen logs in the sun to eat their breakfast. They caught sight of a wandering doe, a few birds and a skinny, irritable squirrel.

Lindsay picked at the fortified chocolate pudding he was supposed to be eating and nibbled a cookie, watching Dane from under his lashes. Dane's attention was on the far verge of the clearing, where the doe had disappeared. Maybe Dane could still see it. Dane knew so much, saw so much, it was hardly worth trying to hide anything from him. Lindsay took a drink of water and steeled himself to say something, to clear the air.

"Dane, I..." He trailed off as Dane's predatory stare shifted to him. It should have been frightening, but embarrassingly it brought another surge of desire. "About this morning, I..." Maybe he'd just die now and not have to see Ezqel or finish this sentence. Please.

Dane rumbled, shaking his head. The wind used that as an excuse to make his hair swirl in all directions. To Lindsay's relief and shame and confusion, Dane was smiling, almost laughing.

"You're young," he said, and the two words were so full of affection that even Lindsay couldn't miss it. And he could see that, as far as Dane was concerned, that was the end of the matter.

For a moment, Lindsay had a glimpse of himself as Dane must see him: funny, awkward, skinny, young. Dane's little bunny. Lindsay remembered watching wolves on television, the indifferent alpha male dozing while a puppy gnawed and wrestled his tail. Lindsay was young. That was all. Dane's world was full of allowances for the likes of Lindsay.

Lindsay realized that he'd been making himself miserable over nothing. Dane hadn't been treating him any differently. He was the one who'd pulled away from the comfort Dane offered. And now, Dane was offering forgiveness for even that. The easy acceptance, the promise of almost infinite forgiveness, was unfamiliar and comforting at once.

Dane returned to tracking whatever hidden things were moving in the distance. Lindsay turned his attention to his food. Suddenly, he was hungry. He polished everything off with more appetite than he'd had in days.

"We're not too far off." Dane squinted up at the sky and looked about as though the trees made sense to him. "We'll be able to make the next shelter before nightfall without any trouble." He stood and shouldered his pack. He was carrying most of their gear, with Lindsay left to manage the necessities he would need if they were separated.

"Does this one have indoor plumbing?" Lindsay asked, laughing. "Or maybe a working heater?" He was in better spirits now, full-bellied and forgiven. He got up and followed Dane, settling his pack on his back.

Dane snorted at him and held out his hand to help Lindsay across an icy patch as the ground sloped downward. The wind blew in his face, pulling back his hair and making him look almost human except for the fangs that showed when he smiled.

"Come on. We need to make good time. The sooner we get this done, the sooner you can have your plumbing and heating." Ahead of them, the way Dane had chosen to go sloped sharply down into a shadowed gorge thick with trees.

"Bribery will get you everywhere," Lindsay said, still laughing.

Seconds later, Dane's head jerked up and, without warning, he threw Lindsay away from him hard enough that Lindsay tumbled down the hill. Something large and dark hit Dane with a dull crunch, taking him down the slope too. They crashed through brush and trees and muck, and the air was full of snarling.

A tree stopped Lindsay near the bottom and he scrambled to his feet, aching all over, just in time to see Dane go past him, quickly followed by a dark blur Lindsay could only assume was one of the people Cyrus had said would be searching for them. Not the girl. The dog. Jonas.

There was nowhere for Lindsay to run, except toward them, so he did.

Dane hit the base of a tree with a sickening crack and Jonas rolled off of him, his momentum carrying him farther. Landing on his feet, Jonas laughed and bared his bloody teeth at Lindsay. "Wait your turn."

Dane was struggling to get up. The front of his sweater was turning dark with blood from a gaping wound in his neck. "Run," he growled at Lindsay. He shed his pack as Jonas lunged for him and his fist caught Jonas in the jaw with a splintering sound.

Jonas's long claws rammed into Dane's chest, coming out Dane's back as his weight carried them both down. Dane got both arms around Jonas, his own claws tearing through Jonas's clothing over the kidneys. Jonas howled, sinking the claws of his free hand into Dane's left side as though he were digging for Dane's heart. Dane made no effort to get away. He dug in deeper, snarling, "*Run.*" The sound of Jonas's bones shattering was sickening.

*Run? Where?* Lindsay wanted to scream at Dane. He couldn't run. He couldn't leave Dane. At least with Dane, he stood a chance of survival out here. His magic might be broken, but it worked a little. He thrust all his magic in one direction, at Jonas, and he had only one thing on his mind: *Stop.*

Jonas stopped. Lindsay almost lost his grip on his magic, he was so startled. Jonas was keening in agony, head flung back, then Dane's teeth tore Jonas's throat open and the noise stopped. Dane flung Jonas away from him like a doll and Jonas fell to earth, thrashing and clawing at his skull, coloring the snow red with the blood spewing from his neck.

Lindsay's sight was blurring, but he gripped his broken magic tighter, feeling it cut him in return, and used it to pour agony into Jonas's powerful form. Dane wasn't done either. He dropped to all fours and moved so fast, a blur, ready to finish the fight.

Lindsay felt a surge of joy and hate so strong it made him stand straight and tall. The pain he felt was nothing and, suddenly, he understood Dane better than ever. He wanted to kill. Jonas was down, weak and broken, and then Dane was on him.

Jonas unfolded like a switchblade and caught Dane in midair, even as Dane twisted to avoid him, sinking his claws into Dane's torso. Dane made a sick, low noise like all the air had gone out of him as Jonas lifted him overhead and threw him toward Lindsay, trailing black blood and flesh. Dane landed face-down in the snow at Lindsay's feet and Lindsay's magic shuddered in his grasp.

Dane tried to get to his knees, but he wasn't getting up. Lindsay couldn't help him—all his attention was still on killing Jonas. All Lindsay could spare Dane was a glance and a cry: "*Dane!*"

Dane managed to drag himself toward Lindsay before his arms couldn't hold him up any longer. His hands gathered up fistfuls of snow and dirt as though he was going to pull himself up again, but then he sighed and was still at Lindsay's feet.

Jonas should have been incapacitated, should have been dead, even, but he still lurched toward Lindsay, eyes wild, head at a strange angle. Terrified, Lindsay backed away even though Dane was limp at his feet, dying. There was no fear in Jonas's eyes, just a wild light as he lunged at Lindsay. He fell short on the first attempt, going down in the snow. Somehow, Dane's bloody hand was clamped around his ankle, but Jonas's fevered eyes never left Lindsay's face.

Lindsay threw himself out of reach, trying to keep his magic locked on Jonas through the pain of its brokenness, but he caught his heel on a root and lost control. The weight of his pack dragged him backward and, as he fell, his magic snapping back to shatter his consciousness, he thought he saw someone standing beyond Jonas.

The figure was dark and still and ominous like a spire against the pale sky. *Help us.* Lindsay tried to speak, to beg, for Dane if not for himself, but then everything went black.

"Such a little thing for so much fuss."

Lindsay's vision cleared like a veil was pulled away from his eyes, and he was looking up into an ageless fae face framed by a fall of deep red hair. The man took his hand away from Lindsay's forehead and straightened, leaving Lindsay staring at the long expanse of his black robes. A snarling, feral noise brought Lindsay upright before he could think to move carefully so he didn't make his throbbing head hurt worse. He scrambled behind the fae man, almost falling again, shaking.

Jonas was less than twenty feet away, pawing at the ground and tossing his head. He turned, on all fours, snuffling the air wetly and licking as though to taste it. There was no light in his eyes, he looked empty. His gaze passed over Lindsay and the man as though they weren't there at all.

"What...?" Lindsay's voice was a thin waver.

"He can't see you. This is the price for hunting in my forest." Ezqel, it had to be Ezqel, held his hand out to Lindsay without looking. "He will not dwell under any roof or know himself until he is found by one who knows his true name." The words sounded like more than words, like Ezqel was branding the world with his will as he spoke.

Lindsay took Ezqel's dry, strong hand and struggled to standing, looking for Dane. Lindsay expected to see Dane getting to his feet, tossing back his hair. But Dane was still on the ground. The snow under him and behind him where he had dragged himself was full of an impossible amount of blood. He had his cheek to the snow as though it were a pillow and his eyes were still open, fixed on some point in the distance. The wind tugged forlornly at his hair and coat, begging him to wake.

"No." Lindsay clawed out of the pack that was weighing him

down and dropped to his knees beside Dane. "Oh, no. Dane," he whispered brokenly, pushing damp strands of hair out of Dane's face. "God, Dane..." He stroked Dane's cooling cheek, his eyes stinging with tears. He'd never lost anyone before. He had no idea what to feel.

Lindsay had tried, but it wasn't enough, not even when it mattered most—he was too broken. Dane was dead. Lindsay's mind could hardly bear the idea. It was too awful to contemplate that Dane was gone. Lindsay bent to press a light kiss to Dane's white, empty face. "I'm sorry, Dane."

"Why apologize? All things live out their purpose." Lindsay's head jerked up and he stared at Ezqel in horror. Still, there was regret in Ezqel's expression. "I did not think this would happen so soon, that it would end this way. Come." He gestured for Lindsay to move away. "I will carry what remains back. There may be some use left in it."

Lindsay flinched, but he backed off obediently, getting to his feet again. He didn't know what to say, what to do, so he stayed still and silent while he watched Ezqel gather up Dane's body. His head hurt, his heart hurt, he was shaking. But he had to keep moving. For Dane, who had brought him this far. Keeping an eye on Ezqel, he backed away to pick up and put on his pack. After a moment's thought, he found Dane's pack, as well, and took hold of it to drag it along behind himself. It was so heavy, Lindsay couldn't lift it, but he couldn't let it go.

Ezqel tugged Dane's coat closed as he rolled him over, hiding the black and red ruin where his belly had been, and picked Dane's body up as though it weighed nothing. He slung the body over his shoulder and straightened.

"Come," he said again. "It's growing cold." He led the way toward the trees he'd come through, where a path ran into the woods.

# Chapter Six

Lindsay followed blindly, lost in his own thoughts, trying to figure out what he could've done differently to save Dane. The fact that Dane was dead kept slipping away from him, and his mind went back again and again, as though it could correct an error and change the present.

Dane's pack dragged sullenly behind Lindsay, wrenching at his arm and nearly bringing him to his knees every time it caught on this root or that stone. Lindsay couldn't bring himself to let it go. It might've had something important in it, but that wasn't why. Dane's clothes were in there, all of them soaked with Dane's scent, and maybe twined here and there with his long, black hair.

The path went places that were not the same as the landscape Lindsay had walked through with Dane. He lost track of their direction by the first turn and hardly noticed how the path widened from a narrow scar in the forest's flesh to a wide, smooth passage between looming trees.

Dane had spoken as though they were a day's travel away, but before Lindsay's pride gave out and he begged Ezqel to stop, he realized that the journey was almost over. The air grew warmer and, at last, they were walking up a stone path, under an iron archway, and into a sleeping garden. A hedgemaze hid the extent of the garden from Lindsay's view, but he could see the still, white forms of statues where the hedge opened into little alcoves. The statues looked so realistic and unique and human, for all that they were marble, that Lindsay was filled with a dread certainty that they were not statues at all.

"We are home," Ezqel said, without pride or enthusiasm, when they passed below another archway. As if at his beckoning, a house stood there, like something out of a fairytale, and a man and a woman waited for them at the door. The house seemed to exist inside a tiny oasis of warmth within the freezing forest. There was green grass here, and roses climbed the trellises by the doors and windows. Lindsay was shivering still, but by now, it was more shock than chill.

"You will go with Taniel." Ezqel stopped on the path. Dane's corpse hung over his shoulder, hair trailing longer than the limp hands, swinging slowly. "I may see you before you sleep, but I think not, by the look of you. Taniel will have questions for you, and you may bathe and eat in the meantime. Izia." He nodded at the woman. "Come with me. We will see if you can get any use of this thing." With that, he took a branching path that led around the side of the house, carrying Dane away.

Lindsay wanted to stop them, to make them bring Dane back. Dane wasn't a thing to be made use of. He wanted to protest or cry out, but he didn't know how to do anything but be silent. Didn't know how to do anything but do as he was told. And, like that, Dane was gone. The world closed over him and only the heavy pack at Lindsay's feet was left as a reminder that Dane had ever been there at all.

"Let me help you." Taniel was tall and thin, with tawny skin, slanted, dark eyes and raggedly cut, silky black hair. His robe, a soft brown velvet version of what Ezqel had worn, hung on him like he was a coat rack. He picked up Dane's pack in one hand, sliding it out of Lindsay's numb fingers before he could protest, and slipped his other hand into Lindsay's in its place. "Come in," he urged, drawing Lindsay toward the front door.

"Where are they taking him?" Lindsay looked back to the path where Ezqel and the woman, Izia, had disappeared with Dane.

"To one of the outbuildings," Taniel said quietly. He was a little older than Lindsay, by the look of him, but that could have been meaningless. "Every place has its purpose. Come, you need to wash, and you're cold." The door swung open as they approached and Lindsay crossed the threshold into Ezqel's home.

Lindsay, through the numb pain of loss, could tell they were in a kind of place he'd never been before. It was not the architecture or the furniture, though that looked like it had been designed from the illustrations of a children's book. The air itself was different, as though there were another element mingled with it. There was light from above, from hanging lamps, but Lindsay was sure the air itself was glowing. His footsteps, and Taniel's, were silent on the stone floor of the foyer.

The door closed behind them and Taniel guided Lindsay past a staircase that spiraled up to nowhere—there had been no second floor or tower that he recalled from outside—and into a huge, warm sitting room. That place reminded him so much of Cyrus's sitting room, down to the chair that should have been Dane's right by the fire, that Lindsay was afraid his next inhalation would never come.

Another staircase wound slowly up the wall of the circular room until it was lost in the shadows overhead. Taniel drew Lindsay toward one of several small doors under the stairs. "A bath is waiting for you. You could shower, instead, but the water would be cold."

"You've already drawn a bath?" Lindsay looked around the rooms, confused. Ezqel must have known they were coming, though, and prepared for their arrival. His arrival. "Where do I...where should I put my clothes?" They were a mess of mud and snow and smears of blood.

"Of course. We have been waiting." There was a small hall, narrow and dim, and another closed door beyond that. "This is the bathing room. I will take you to your room to sleep later. Leave your clothes here. I do not think you will wish to wear them again." Taniel opened the bathroom door for Lindsay.

Blue-tinted light came in through a stained glass window—a maritime scene with a mermaid on a rocky outcrop among high waves—that was wavy with age. The bathroom was a century behind even the most primitive facilities Lindsay had used, with a minimal toilet and shower and a freestanding tub that had a firebox built into it. There were towels over the firebox so that they would be warm, and a robe on a hook beside them.

Lindsay shrugged out of his backpack and coat, looking around for somewhere to put them. He left them next to where Taniel had set Dane's pack and turned to Taniel as he stripped out of his shirt. "Ezqel said you had some questions for me?"

"I do, but you should bathe first, and rest, should you not?" Taniel gave Lindsay a sympathetic look. "Ezqel does not understand things as others do anymore. Izia and I still do. If you have need of some privacy..."

Lindsay shrugged. He hadn't had the luxury of privacy in years, until he'd come to Cyrus's house. At least in this place and time, he had a choice. "Whatever is convenient for you." Privacy would only give him time to lose himself in grief, and that would come soon enough whether Taniel stayed or left.

"We can speak now, if you prefer." Taniel's expression was sad. "I will need to know about your family history and your personal experiences. You can tell me when you wish to rest." He took a book out of a pocket in his robe and perched on the edge of the toilet lid. "Please tell me when you are ready to begin."

Lindsay ducked his head and finished undressing, then slipped into the bath. It was warm and the blood on his hands swirled away quickly. Like that, Dane was gone. Even in the hot water, Lindsay was cold. Without Dane, it felt like he could never get warm again.

"What did you need to know?" he asked, so that he wouldn't cry remembering Dane washing his face with a cool cloth and worrying over him.

The questions began. They kept him busy, kept him thinking about everything except what had happened to Dane. After he'd cleaned up, Taniel helped him into the robe that should have been warm—it was heavy and soft with fur at the throat and wrists, and hot from hanging by the firebox—but Lindsay was still cold.

"Here. You can't go barefoot." Taniel pulled a pair of slippers—Lindsay thought they were slippers, though they could have been shoes from another era—out from below the firebox and knelt to help Lindsay into them.

Dane had always let him dress himself, and Vivian. It was easy, though, to fall back into passivity. The slippers were fur-lined leather and they fit him perfectly, just like the robe. How was it, Lindsay wondered, that they could know he was coming, know what would fit him, and yet not find him in time to save Dane? He had to bite his lip not to sob at the thought.

"Come." Taniel straightened and took Lindsay's hand as though Lindsay were a child. "We must go to the library." So they went, hand in hand, through the faerie house.

They crossed the warm sitting room, where a black cat curled up in the chair that Dane would have favored, and passed the fireplace that was almost as high as Lindsay, a great arching maw full of pale yellow fire. The cat opened its golden eyes to watch Lindsay, the tip of its tail twitching. It could have been a trick of the firelight, but Lindsay thought he saw something sad in its expression before it dropped its head to groom one paw.

On the other side of the fireplace, a door with runes carved over the lintel stood partway open. Taniel led him in and, defying possibility, the room was round as well. Could you fit more round things in a small space than square? Did magic have no corners? It was filled with books, and went up three stories to a domed roof, beyond which was a cloudy sky shedding soft flakes of snow. What was the illusion, the snow or the garden outside the front door?

Taniel led him to a chair at a table near where the wall swelled out like a belly, covered in a mosaic of flames. It was warmer here and Lindsay realized that this must have been the back of the other fireplace—sparks and books rarely fared well together. For a moment, he thought his vision was wavering from exhaustion or hunger or grief, but then he understood that the mosaic was moving like the flames on the other side.

"I will get the family books," Taniel said. "From what you say of your magic, it will not be easy to track your lineage."

Lindsay sat where he was told, cold in spite of the radiant heat from the wall, and stroked the soft black and brown fur at the cuffs of his robe. *Some use left in it*, Ezqel had said. Would the fae mage take Dane's long, black hair or Dane's sharp, ebony claws? Maybe Dane's golden skin would be of use for something.

"Why not?" he asked, to drag his mind away from the morbid images it was dredging up.

"If you think about it," Taniel said, stopping halfway up a ladder with his robes clutched in one hand, "it's very hard to find an illusionist." He smiled at Lindsay. "Especially one who doesn't want finding."

"Good," Lindsay muttered, before he could stop the word. Maybe they wouldn't be able to find him once Ezqel fixed him, none of them. He didn't want to be part of this anymore, didn't want to think of what Cyrus would say or do when Lindsay told him Dane had died.

Cyrus had given Lindsay to Dane. He wondered to whom Dane had belonged. He couldn't imagine Dane belonging to anyone but Cyrus. The way Dane had curled around him, protecting him, was so at odds with the way Cyrus treated Dane, like Dane was just a dog. Would Cyrus even miss him? Had Cyrus even deserved him? Lindsay hadn't.

Taniel came back with a tome the size of his torso and thunked into the chair across from Lindsay, startling Lindsay away from the tears that were threatening.

"Now. We start here." Taniel flipped the book open. It looked like a giant phone book, but from what Lindsay could see, it was all gibberish. Taniel pulled a lens on a necklace out from under his robes and turned the dials around it, pausing to think before deciding on the final setting. Using the lens, he began to read, and as he read, from time to time, he spoke. It was only to tell Lindsay what he was looking for, in which book, but it was enough to keep Lindsay from falling into the pit of grief that yawned open with every breath.

Taniel had four books of Anglo-Saxon mage lines open in front of him and he was squinting at the pages, trying to work out where Lindsay's family might have branched off, when he straightened and shook his head. "Might I take a little of your blood?" he asked, focusing on Lindsay, who had given up on pretending he was fine and had curled up in the chair, watching the mosaic move. "Just a pinprick is all I need. I will go and get a needle from Izia." Taniel closed the books and got up, smoothing out his robes.

Lindsay swallowed hard. He hated needles. "There isn't another way to get the information you need?"

"I could try another way." Taniel looked at Lindsay thoughtfully, and collected the book in which he'd been taking notes. "I will consult with Ezqel, then I must find the correct tools. If you grow weary, I suggest you rest. There is food in the kitchen if you are hungry. I will be some time, if I am to do it without your blood." He flashed Lindsay a small smile. "You are wise. Most surrender such precious things too easily. I will return." He gave Lindsay a bow and hurried out of the library, closing the doors behind him and leaving Lindsay alone in the dusty silence.

Distractions gone, the silence ate at Lindsay's control. He bowed his head over the table and took slow, deep breaths, trying to delay the inevitable thoughts. He had no luck. He could see it all in his mind, the way Dane had thrown him aside, the way Jonas had borne him down the hill, the sounds Dane had made when Jonas's claws tore into him. Lindsay wished he'd done something sooner, wished he'd done something differently, to save Dane. It was all too late. He gave in to the tears, to the wracking sobs, curling in on himself for whatever small amount of comfort it would bring.

The last thing Dane saw was his own hand clutched around Jonas's ankle. The last thing he heard was Lindsay's desperate cry. His name.

Where he went, he had no name. The rising dark was familiar, he had seen it so many times before and always it had faded in the face of his healing. He could feel his heart stutter. With too much to heal, his throat torn open and every organ shredded, his magic couldn't stay ahead of the darkness.

This time, the darkness never waned.

Out of the darkness, pain. It wasn't any pain he'd ever felt before, it was a pain that encompassed his entire awareness, his whole self. It was all his failure, distilled. In the dark, he was nothing but agony. It went on forever. Hell. He was in hell. He'd never believed in it, but he was in it now, and it had no ending.

*Dane.*

He knew that voice. It carried with it the smell of honeysuckle and hibiscus and magic. Crushed grass under his skin, the salt of the sea in his hair, the sun flowing into his bones. Something in him tried to push it away, a dying reflex, but it persisted. The pain was worse, almost enough to erase him entirely.

*Stop fighting me.* The words snapped through his pain. *Now is not the time for your pride.*

Pride. He had no pride. He had nothing but pain and a fading sense that he had once been more than that.

*That's better.*

It was as though he were being gathered up in someone's hands, cradled and lifted out of the dark. Memory rushed through him. Dirt roads, a split-rail fence, a well, chickens scratching in the dust, a dog barking, hooves on packed soil. He could smell a wood stove and evergreens and a cold wind out of the north. His hands were warm in a pair of woolen mittens. The years went by like snowflakes. Sometimes they caught in the wool of his mittens and he could see them, each different than the last, gleaming and perfect.

There was so much he had forgotten, so much he'd wanted to forget. The smell of latrines and mud and blood and gunpowder. Wet wool on his skin and gangrene stench overwhelming every other scent. Starvation and the weight of an iron collar, the cold bars of a cage. Laughter. His blood splashing into a basin.

Cyrus, his hair as black as a raven's wing and his skin unlined, laughing. The wind sweeping across a field and gathering up a storm of flowers. Vivian with her hair bound up in the *ofuku* style, like a souvenir doll in her kimono. Not Vivian. Omasami. Later, she was Vivian, with lace and a cameo at her throat, her waist pulled small as a daisy stem by her corset. His own hands on the corset laces and her chirping admonishments when he was too careful with her.

He wanted to remember those things, not the scream of mortar fire and the wail of dying, not the weight of a stretcher in his hands, not the alien feel and stink of a gun. Human wars were terrible things, against nature. Mage wars were wars of natural forces.

His wings tore out of his shoulders and spread like twin sails, his claws ripped into the earth and flung him up against the pull of gravity, toward the sky. That, he remembered, in his dreams. The wind spoke in his ears and lifted him high, through the night and into the day, into the midst of battle. When mages warred, high in the mountains above the human realm or in the heart of the desert, they fought with storm and lightning and fire, with tooth and claw, with swords and arrows. Dane had fought on faerie soil, on land that was not earth, had torn the throat out of a dragonet, had dragged angels out of the sky.

He remembered the moment that he was broken, the agony of it that was nothing next to the agony of being betrayed, and none of that was anything like the pain of now. Everything in him still raged against that moment. He dreamed that it had not happened and woke in the prison of his own body.

The dog. The dog had never known his own kind, never known the old laws and ways—all the dog knew was the way of men. The dog lived on the edge of the camps, scrounged what the humans would throw him, let himself be used. Dane had pitied him once, let him live, and had regretted it since. He remembered the girl, her halo of dawn-red hair and her eyes like gems. For a moment, he'd thought she could be saved. But things moved on, and she was gone.

And he remembered his failure. He remembered the stink of his own entrails and the smell of snow, the slurry of blood and earth under his knees. A small voice calling for him. Things undone.

"I have him now," a woman said.

Somewhere, an animal was howling in pain.

"Can you shut him up?"

"Patience, Ezqel. He's barely here."

"He shouldn't be wasting his energy, then."

The pain was receding, taking the shape of a body, flesh wrapped around a soul. It dwindled to a pain Dane could know and understand and enfold, putting it away inside him. When the animal fell silent, he knew the voice had been his.

"You need to be still." A woman's small hands pressed his flesh and he realized that he must have been trying to get up. All his impulses were still trying to drive him to his feet, to stop the dog.

*Jonas.* Hate seared his synapses, branding his mind with the reflex. He tried to speak, but nothing came out.

"He wants the dog. Jonas is gone, Dane. I have judged him as I saw fit."

Dane cast about for the source of the voice, but could see nothing. It was so dark. Clawing at his eyes left his fingers wet.

"Your sight will be the last to return," the woman said, dragging his hands away. "And it will take longer if you put out your eyes. I need you to breathe. Try to breathe for me." She pressed her hands against his chest, once, twice, again, and then her mouth was on his like a kiss, forcing her breath into him. His body stuttered and he gagged. Something under his ribs was struggling. "Relax," she said.

Dane felt panic surge through him as his body came to understand that it wasn't living. The silence in his ears was deafening. No pulse. No heartbeat. No rise and fall of breath. He was full of Ezqel's magic, and the woman's, but no life. The woman breathed for him again and he heard the creak of his ribs swelling outward. Her breath was green, like a tree, and full of life that he drew in greedily.

"Come on," she said softly. "Come back." He felt her hands on his chest, passing into him, through muscle and bone. Her magic filled him up and his body drank it in. He felt her shaking as the black in his vision turned to gray. "You have to want this," she whispered.

"He's been trying to die for years," Ezqel said flatly. "I thought he had some use left, but..."

When the woman breathed into him again, Dane took her breath from her, tore it from her lungs, tore Ezqel's magic from him by every thread his will could gather. Rage drove him to take what he wanted, to pillage both of them without consideration for what it might do to them. The woman fell away from him, but still, Dane was not sated.

"Enough." Ezqel's hand falling sharply across his face cleared his sight and broke his hold on their power. Dane sucked in cool air and his pulse stuttered frantically in his ears. He breathed again and his heart spasmed before falling back into its old rhythm. Above him, the snow fell on the curved glass roof of a conservatory.

"I won't have you striking my patient." The woman's voice was cold. Dane turned his head to look for her. He felt a surge of guilt at taking from her so violently. She was a plain woman, unremarkable, and pale as though she had been bled. "Thank you for your help, though," she said to Ezqel.

"He knows little so well as being angry." Ezqel's eyes were fixed on Dane, his jaw set. His hair glowed like a beacon against the greenery in the conservatory, the greenery that was nowhere near as green as his eyes. "I knew you'd come back, if only to spite me."

Dane's mouth still wouldn't work, and what he'd say, he knew would only make things worse. *You were the one who wanted me back*. His mouth was too dry to spit. Rage made his heart stagger and ache.

"You're welcome," Ezqel said archly, to both of them. "Put him in the guest room when you're done patching his holes, Izia. I believe Taniel is looking for me." He drew his hood up over his hair. The sound of hinges and a snake of cold air marked his departure.

Dane tried to ask where Lindsay was. He didn't trust Ezqel not to have dragged Dane back alone to prove a point, leaving Lindsay to Jonas. The words came out mangled, in various languages scraped up out of his memory.

"If you're asking about your friend, he's well enough. Worry about yourself." Izia pried his mouth open with her strong, cold fingers, and laid something green-tasting and leafy on his tongue. She closed his mouth on it with her palm under his jaw. "Keep that in your mouth. It'll make your heart beat evenly. You're all over the place, and you're still bleeding. I'm going to cover your wounds. It may take another day to heal you."

Once, he would never have died. The curse had followed him beyond that threshold, into the black and the pain. Had he really been dead? When the woman returned, he tried to question her with his eyes.

"I wasn't sure we'd get you back," she said quietly. "You're very determined. I can see why you frustrate him so."

Dane rolled his eyes at that. Ezqel deserved all the frustration Dane could cause, except that going to the trouble would bind him even closer to the mage. Now, he risked being beholden to Ezqel for his life. He could hardly work out the meanings of it all. Everything went dark for a moment while he was turning things over in his head, and he forced his eyes open as fear spiked through him. He could still see. His eyes had just fallen shut.

"The herbs will make you sleepy." Izia leaned over him and patted his cheek. "You need to rest."

Dane didn't want to sleep. The idea of going into the dark

again so soon made tension ripple through him.

"You won't die," Izia assured him. "That part is over. You need some fluids and some time to heal, but you're back with the living. Rest will heal you faster than anything else. Let me stop you from leaking all over the place and I'll set you up with fresh fluids."

Dane caught sight of a pole with several limp bags hanging from it. Saline. Maybe some herbal concoctions to replace his blood. It was so strange. He'd never been hurt or sick like this before. He thought he should be afraid, but the animal in him shrugged it off and curled up to sleep. Things went dark again. When the beast slept, so did the man. Everywhere they went, they went together, even to death and back.

It was dark when Taniel put a hand on Lindsay's shoulder and shook him gently. Lindsay found that he was still at the table where he'd sobbed himself to sleep, head in his arms, and there was a blanket tucked around him.

"It's very late," Taniel said. "You slept a long time. I will be going to bed soon and I cannot leave you here. Come and eat, and I will show you to the guest room. I got a great deal done while you slept." A lamp burned on the desk and the light bounced off of several arcane instruments that had not been there before.

Lindsay blinked up at Taniel, confused for a moment, but then it all came rushing back to him. What had happened, where he was, everything. He gathered up the blanket and stood, rubbing at his sleep- and tear-crusted eyes. "I'm sorry. I didn't mean to fall asleep."

"You were tired. Creatures sleep when they need to rest or heal." Taniel offered Lindsay a hand to steady himself. "You should eat if you can."

Dane had often offered to hold Lindsay's hand when he needed support. Lindsay couldn't bring himself to accept Taniel's hand, not just now.

"I'll try," he said, nodding. He hadn't eaten in...a long time.

When they'd stopped for breakfast, sitting on the heavy logs and listening to the birds.

Taniel took Lindsay to a kitchen that looked like an illustration from a child's book, with the fat, old black stove and hanging herbs and the beautiful embroidered curtains. This room, too, had no corners. Beyond the windows, it was night, soft and velvety and dense; Lindsay could almost feel it curled around the faerie house like a great, black cat.

"There's some fresh custard," Taniel offered, coaxing Lindsay as though Lindsay were half his age. "And some biscuits. I could make you tea. Izia's better at it than I, but I haven't seen her all day."

"That sounds fine." Lindsay wasn't sure he'd be able to finish even that. He stood in the center of the room, feeling lost and alone.

"Come, sit." Taniel pulled out the chair nearest the wood stove for Lindsay. It was red with little blue and white flowers painted on the back and arms, like a nursery chair grown large. Lindsay sat, obediently, at the end of the worn wooden table. Someone had cut roses, the blowsy, rude, wild ones, and arranged them haphazardly in a yellow pitcher. Taniel hurried about the kitchen, sandaled feet hushed on the stone floor, robes swishing about his legs, as he served Lindsay up a bowl of sweet, creamy custard with a few biscotti, and set to making him tea.

Lindsay ate, and drank the tea when it was ready, but he wasn't really awake for any of it. He stared off at the old stone walls, feeling sick and sad. Finally, he pushed away the last dregs of tea and murmured, "I think I haven't slept quite enough. You said something about a bed?"

"Yes. Izia is usually in charge of the guest room, but..." Taniel held his hands out to Lindsay. "If there is no fire there yet, I can build you one. I don't know where she is. I'm sorry, it's rude of us. Ezqel must have put her to another task."

"Thank you." Lindsay wasn't concerned about the rudeness. He only wanted to be alone, so he could cry himself to sleep again. He knew what task Izia had been put to and he didn't want to think about it. He slipped his hands into Taniel's and let himself be led.

Taniel took him out into the sitting room, to the staircase that wrapped around it. At the head of the staircase, lamps filled a loft with golden light. Izia came to meet them as they were going up. She looked ragged and exhausted.

"There you are," she said, giving Lindsay a smile. "I was coming to find you." She waited at the top step for them to reach her. "The room is ready for you."

The loft was decorated with two plush chairs and a delicate table between them, and there was a single door that Izia opened as she went ahead. "We only have the one guest room, so I'm afraid you'll have to share the bed," she said in low tones.

Lindsay tensed and tried to stop, but Taniel drew him on in spite of his balking. Who would he be sharing the bed with? Another visitor? Dane's corpse? He felt sick at the idea of anyone near him and it felt like any strangeness was possible in this magical house.

The room wasn't spacious, but it was big enough for a large, four-post bed, a chair by the fire, and a writing desk and chair. It was just like one would find in a bed-and-breakfast, except that the furniture was probably centuries old. A fire burning in the large fireplace was the only light.

Izia smiled at Lindsay again, beckoning him to come farther in, and looked over her shoulder at Taniel. "There was some use left in him after all," she said, sounding pleased with herself. "I have seen nothing like it. I've done nothing like it."

The shadowed half of the bed was taken up by a large body with black hair spilling over the pillows. Dane was sleeping, looking surprisingly young and peaceful. Someone had washed him and shaved him and trimmed his hair, in addition to bandaging him and tucking him in bed with the blankets pulled halfway up his chest and his big hands folded over them.

"He said you should be near the fire," Izia said to Lindsay. "So you wouldn't get cold."

Lindsay just stared. He couldn't believe what Izia was saying, what he was seeing with his own eyes. He'd have thought it was a hallucination, if he could have had those. It couldn't be a dream. He didn't dream. "Dane?"

"Sometimes, there is more to life than a heartbeat." Izia put her arm around his shoulders and carefully led him into the room. "Especially in anyone old and powerful—even more so in one of Dane's kind. Still, he was almost gone. We put the body together so he could stay in it a little longer. He must have things to do, not the least of which seems to be picking fights with Ezqel."

Taniel was on Lindsay's other side, one hand under Lindsay's elbow. "I have only read of things like this." He smiled at Izia. "This is marvelous. I must know all of what you did so I can record it."

As soon as he could move, Lindsay shook off Taniel's grip and rushed over to the bed, kneeling beside it so he could watch Dane's chest move with each breath. Was it real? Dane was breathing. Lindsay bowed his head, resting his cheek against Dane's warm shoulder for a moment while he tried to keep from crying all over again.

"Thank you," Lindsay whispered brokenly, curling one hand around Dane's wrist to feel his pulse. Dane was breathing, his heart was beating. He was warm and solid and very much alive, if pale and thinner than that morning. Lindsay could see the sharp shadows along his jaw and collarbones.

"Ezqel does not take kindly to a death by violence in his woods, nor to the loss of an old student," Izia explained. "And you must know Dane's magic. I am not surprised they sent Death with its tail between its legs, if only in fear of their tempers. This one spent his few waking moments telling me how to take care of you, as soon as Ezqel wasn't there to argue with. There's water on the desk and food in the kitchen, but don't be surprised if he's not interested yet. His insides are still putting themselves back together."

Izia and Taniel stood just inside the door. Izia was leaning on Taniel, looking even more worn than she had before. "Thank you," Lindsay said again. "I'll take care of him." He wouldn't make the same mistakes again, not any of them.

"Sleep well, Lindsay. I will see you in the morning." Taniel patted Izia's hand on his arm. "Now, I will take care of you, before you fall down."

"Only because, if I do, no one will dictate today's events to you?" Izia teased. "Call for me if you need anything," she said as Taniel led her out the door. "I'll hear you if it's me you're asking for."

Lindsay nodded, watching them leave. When they were gone, he carefully crawled onto the bed with Dane, curling up beside him and wrapping the robe more tightly around himself. He watched Dane's chest rise and fall with each breath, daring to reach out and touch Dane's warm, golden skin to reassure himself that this was all real.

*What does it matter if it's not?* If he was dreaming, he didn't want to wake. If he was awake, he didn't want to fall asleep. The only place he wanted to be was right here, watching Dane breathe. When his eyes stung with tears, Lindsay blinked them away as fast as he could so that he didn't lose sight of Dane even for a moment. In spite of himself, after some hours, he dozed off.

In the night, Dane roused enough to move, turning over and wrapping an arm around Lindsay. He nuzzled into Lindsay's hair, breathing in and grumbling contentedly. Lindsay slept in fits and spurts, waking now and then to check if it had all been a lie. Each time, though, Dane was still there, still breathing, his heart still beating against Lindsay's cheek.

It wasn't yet dawn when Dane woke enough to grumble over something in the here and now. "Under the covers," he grumped in Lindsay's ear. "You're going to freeze." The fire had gone to ash and a sharp chill had crept into the room.

Lindsay woke quickly at the sound of Dane's voice. "'m all right," he protested sleepily, but he wriggled around until he'd managed to get himself under the covers anyway. He hadn't wanted to disturb Dane.

Dane sighed, low and contented, cuddling Lindsay to his chest. He was bare except for the bandages around his belly, shoulder and neck. Izia obviously hadn't felt the need to dress him.

Lindsay wasn't dressed either, with just the robe between him and Dane's bare body. He bit his lip and snuggled closer, the robe slipping with his movements. His bare skin slid against Dane's, making him shiver, but he didn't pull away. He wanted to be close, to be able to feel and hear Dane's breath and his heart.

Dane slid a leg over both of Lindsay's, curling around him and wrapping him up in sleek, naked warmth. He seemed purely content like this, oblivious to any impropriety.

Lindsay remembered, suddenly, the way Dane had pulled him closer, had cupped his ass and ground up against him, in the sleeping bag yesterday morning. He'd been so focused on his own pleasure, and then so utterly horrified at himself for not staying in control, he hadn't been able to think. Now, though, he recognized Dane's actions for what they'd been—if not outright approval, then at least acceptance.

Lindsay gave in. If Dane didn't want him so close, Dane could be the one to push him away. Dane had never pushed him away yet. He always drew Lindsay in closer. Lindsay breathed in the clean, warm smell of him and got a rumble of pleasure in return as Dane seemed to relax even more.

Lindsay drifted off again, after a while. When he woke, the first hints of light were streaking through the curtains and his face was pressed into the curve of Dane's neck and shoulder. He tucked himself in closer, seeking comfort in the warmth of Dane's body.

Eventually, reality caught up with Lindsay enough to make him whisper, unsteadily, "You were dead." Saying it aloud, even very softly, made everything more real. Losing Dane had been a harsh blow, one Lindsay might not have recovered from.

"Yes." Dane exhaled slowly. Lindsay hadn't meant to wake

him, hadn't known he was awake, or for how long. "I was. I don't recommend it. I'm sorry I left you alone." He pressed his cheek to Lindsay's hair.

Lindsay shook his head. Dane hadn't let him down, just the opposite. "I'm sorry I didn't stop him in time."

"Not your job, not your problem." Dane's tone was firm, even if his voice was thinner than usual. "My place is to take care of you."

"I don't *care,*" Lindsay answered fiercely. Tears were already welling up in his eyes, and he tried to blink them back. He shouldn't have said anything. Damn it. He was supposed to be done crying. "I don't *care* whose job is what. I don't want you to *die.*"

Dane's expression was inscrutable again for a moment, then it softened. "Okay. Fair enough." He cupped Lindsay's cheek in his hand, rubbing gently with his thumb. Lindsay tilted his face into the caress, soothed to a rather embarrassing extent just by being touched. "I'll do my best not to do it again," Dane promised solemnly. He kept petting gently while he coaxed Lindsay to lie down in the curve of his arm, on his uninjured shoulder. There was blood spotting his bandages, but he didn't seem to be in much pain.

"Thank you." Lindsay settled, nuzzling at Dane's hand and shoulder. He didn't want to lose Dane. The idea that he should let it happen because it "wasn't his job" was terrible. Dane tolerated him so well, even if Lindsay was talking back first thing in the morning.

Finding his hands in his tangled robe, Lindsay slid them over Dane's skin, careful of the bandages. He wanted to feel the warmth, the life in Dane's body. Dane was alive—the fresh surge of realization made Lindsay wriggle with joy. He pressed his lips to Dane's shoulder and collarbone again and again until his tongue was darting out with each kiss to steal a taste of Dane's skin. He was gentle, delicate, careful not to ask for anything more than the contact and intimacy Dane was already allowing him.

Dane's big arm around him flexed as Dane drew him closer, his hand splayed over Lindsay's hip where Lindsay's robe had slid away to leave it bare. Dane's breathing changed and he reached over with his other hand to stroke Lindsay's hair. Approval, not just acceptance.

"Dane," Lindsay whispered, rubbing his cheek against Dane's chest.

"Mm?" Dane made a slight noise of discomfort as he shifted to be able to see Lindsay's face.

Lindsay cupped Dane's face in both hands and stretched up, brushing his lips lightly over Dane's. It was a risk, but one he was willing to take. He'd almost lost Dane—he *had* lost Dane—and he never would've known how Dane felt about him. At least this way he'd know.

Dane kissed him back, less tentatively, and made a soft noise that Lindsay already knew meant he was pleased with something but not about to say so out loud. His hand on Lindsay's hip pulled Lindsay close enough to feel everything. Dane was already hard, hot, and his cock was perfectly in proportion to the rest of his massive body.

*Oh.* Lindsay could hardly breathe. He'd had no idea that it would feel like this to be wanted, and he was sure that Dane did want him, at least a little. His gasp of surprise broke the kiss and he kissed Dane again, quickly, so that Dane wouldn't think that he was done.

Dane pulled away from him, though, laughing quietly as he nuzzled Lindsay's nose with his own. "Missed me that much, did you?"

*Yes, yes, God, yes.* Lindsay's throat tightened up and he couldn't say it out loud. He swallowed hard. "But that's not why," he began hastily. Not why he was kissing Dane. He'd wanted to before, he really had, so much, and then... "You were *gone.*"

That was all that would come out and Lindsay was despairing of ever making any sense when Dane kissed him again, so sweetly, and wrapped Lindsay up in his arms. "I know," Dane murmured. "I knew, little bunny."

Of course Dane knew. Dane knew and hadn't pushed him away, had held him and slept with him and kept him close, always.

Lindsay slid his arms around Dane's neck and pressed against Dane to feel bare skin and bandages against his chest and belly, and to feel more of the proof that Dane did really want him. All the fantasies that had withered and died before were blooming again in his head and that was all that he could think of, how much he wanted Dane. Lindsay pressed his lips to Dane's with a moan, trying to speak with his body and offer himself up.

"It's all right," Dane said soothingly, petting Lindsay's hair. "Gently now."

Lindsay had only a moment to worry that he'd done something wrong when a knock at the door frightened him.

"It's just Izia." Dane petted him again to settle him. "What do you want?" When Dane raised his voice, his tone shifted to something impatient, maybe even angry.

The door creaked open. "Ezqel wants to see Lindsay before the sun is in the next house." Izia didn't look much less tired than last night, though she was standing on her own. "And I want to make sure you don't end up undoing all my hard work."

As soon as Lindsay realized what she was talking about, his cheeks felt like they were on fire. He wanted to hide against Dane's chest, but he took a breath and steeled himself, turning to face her.

"I'll be down to see Ezqel soon."

"There's food in the kitchen. You have time to eat, Lindsay, but not much else." Izia gave Lindsay a smile, but she was stern again when she turned her attention back to Dane. "I'll wait outside a minute, then I need to check your wounds."

The door creaked shut and latched, but Lindsay could feel her waiting outside. Wounds. Dane was terribly hurt and Lindsay was thinking about sex.

"Enough of that," Dane said brusquely, ruffling his hair. He was drawn and pale. The sun had risen enough that there was light to better see him by now. “Go on and eat, before Ezqel decides to undo all his handiwork because I’ve made you late.”

“He’d better not,” Lindsay said, surprising himself with his own fierceness.

Dane laughed and relaxed back into the pillows. “Wait until after he heals you to go defending me.”

“As long as you’re okay, I will.” Lindsay wanted to try to steal another kiss, but he’d had more than he’d ever thought he’d get. Now wasn’t the time to push his luck. Izia said he’d only have time to eat and he didn’t have any clothes up here. He slithered out of bed and straightened himself out, fastening the robe properly and finding the slippers where they’d fallen off the bed.

“You’ll be fine as you are.” Dane sounded so tired that Lindsay looked at him in alarm. “And I’ll be fine as I am, as long as I know you’ll get some breakfast.”

“I’ll eat,” Lindsay promised. “I’ll see you…” He trailed off. He had no idea when he’d see Dane. Today, tonight, how long would it take?

“Soon enough,” Dane assured him. His eyelids seemed too heavy for him and they fluttered shut before he stopped them, but he opened his eyes again and mustered up a reassuring smile for Lindsay.

The door creaked open. “Lindsay,” Izia said sternly. “Find Taniel as soon as you’ve eaten, if he doesn’t find you first.”

“Going.” Lindsay didn’t want to leave, but Izia was here and he was sure that Dane would rather Lindsay not see him like this. With one last longing look over his shoulder, he slipped out the door.

# Chapter Seven

In the storybook kitchen, Lindsay found more of the custard from the night before, and some dried fruit. He ate in silence, thinking about Dane. He was alive. Not only was he alive, but he had *kissed* Lindsay. Lindsay never would've guessed anything like that would happen. He was still feeling giddy from the whole experience. He hoped those good feelings would carry him through Ezqel's tests. When he was finished eating, he went looking for Taniel.

Taniel was busy in the library, bent over a huge book. When Lindsay came in, he looked up and smiled. "Did you sleep well?" He put his pen down and got to his feet. "Ezqel is ready to see you now."

"Yes, thank you." Even if he hadn't, Lindsay's answer would have been the same. He bit his lip. "These tests… Do you know…?"

"There are many ways to do things." Taniel gave Lindsay a sympathetic glance. "I cannot tell you what will happen—even I can't know. Ezqel himself may not know. I will take you to him." He gestured toward a door set back in the shadows of the library.

Lindsay followed Taniel, lagging behind. He was nervous, and Taniel hadn't helped that at all.

Taniel led Lindsay to a narrow stone staircase that wound up and up past locked doors. They emerged through a heavy door at the top of the tower, into a round room that looked like a classic wizard's haven.

Ezqel was seated at a massive desk at the far end, in an alcove lit from above by a globe of light suspended on a chain. He raised a finger when Taniel brought Lindsay in. “My thanks, Taniel. You may go.”

Taniel stopped just inside the door, giving Lindsay a reassuring smile. Lindsay nodded, slipping farther into the room. Not too far, though. He didn’t want to get close to Ezqel. The idea of these tests, whatever they were going to be, was enough to make the meal he’d eaten sit badly in his stomach.

As Taniel closed the door, leaving them alone, Ezqel rose from his seat. “We must know what was done to you.” He stepped around the desk and picked up a stone sphere. “Taniel has traced some of your lineage, giving us some understanding of your potential. Have you seen one of these?” The sphere was larger than a softball, plain but polished.

Lindsay shook his head. It was a rock. He didn’t say that out loud, though. “No. What is it?”

“We call it a *kuni.* Come. Place your hand on it.” Ezqel waited for Lindsay to come to him.

“Is it…?” Lindsay walked closer, but slowly. “Will it hurt?” He’d had enough pain for a lifetime.

Ezqel held it out at arm’s length. “This will not hurt.” His expression was dispassionate.

*This won’t. But something else might.* Lindsay swallowed hard and reached out, carefully pressing his hand to the stone sphere, the kuni.

Ezqel murmured foreign words under his breath and the stone glowed. He tilted his head as though listening. “That’s enough,” he said after a few moments.

Lindsay pulled his hand back immediately. “What did it do?”

“It told me that you’re a mage.” Ezqel chuckled softly. “And it told me more. But most people use it simply for that. Kuni come in many sizes and shapes. Keystones, gateposts, pendants, even a stone in a ring.” He put the kuni back on the stand on his desk. “You need to relax, Lindsay. It’s not as though you're not going to go through with this."

Lindsay focused on his feet. Ezqel was right, he wasn't going to say no. He and Dane had gone through so much to get here. He nodded. "I'm sorry."

"Fear is to be expected. I understand that you've been abused," Ezqel said simply. "I'm afraid you will need to revisit some of that today." He crossed the room to something large draped in black fabric. When he pulled the fabric away, it revealed a mirror. "This will let me see what was done to you. I will know what they know, and I will know how you were damaged."

Lindsay wrapped his arms around himself, shaking as he resisted the urge to step back. "What do you need me to do?"

Ezqel gestured for Lindsay to come closer. The frame of the mirror was ornate, gilding over wood. "You must look in the mirror."

Lindsay could see himself in the mirror, could see the fear on his own face. It was ridiculous, being afraid of a mirror. Wasn't it?

Ezqel ran his fingers over a portion of the wood on one side where the gilding was worn away. The other side had a similar worn spot. "Put your hands here," Ezqel said and, as Lindsay moved close enough to obey, he stepped back to stand behind Lindsay.

The fear was still there as Lindsay stared at himself. He could see his too-pale face and his wide eyes. And right then, it changed. He could see himself, younger, standing in front of his father. It wasn't until the flames started that Lindsay realized what he was watching.

His manifestation.

In an instant, he wasn't watching anymore. He was there, listening to his father's screams and smelling the sickly-sweetness of his father's burnt flesh. "I'm sorry," he tried to say, but nothing came out. His lips didn't even move.

By the time his mother burst through the door, his confusion was gone. He was immersed, living the scene all over again, stammering his frightened explanations like the first time.

There was a flash of light, and Lindsay's parents were gone, his bedroom was gone, and Lindsay was back in Ezqel's tower. He wasn't seventeen anymore, and the man in the room with him was Ezqel, not his father. His heart was racing like it had been in the past, and his knees were weak.

Lindsay had to hang onto the mirror to keep from falling and that let the mirror suck him right back in. This time, he knew what was happening as he fell into the past. He was running, terrified, trying to get away. There was nowhere to go, nowhere to hide. No one to save him. Lindsay screamed as a big hand wrapped around his shoulder, stopping him and jerking him around.

All he got was a glimpse of his father's face before the white light dropped him back into Ezqel's tower. Then it was the sterile green and white of the Institute, his father's big hand on his shoulder again.

"Fix him," Lindsay's father said. "Get rid of it. All of it."

A doctor in a white lab coat nodded, writing something on the clipboard in her other hand. "We'll take care of it. Thank you, Mr. Carrington."

There was a flash again, too fast for Lindsay to escape. The sharp sting of the intravenous line going in, and the drugs were pumping into him. Lindsay screamed, couldn't stop screaming. It felt like pure fire flowing through his veins and eating up everything in its wake.

"Calm down," someone said. A technician in a white jumper. "Give the meds time to work. It'll all feel better soon."

Lindsay's magic bubbled up inside him as he fought the drugs, fought to stay in control of himself, but as they ate their way through his system, his control faltered. He couldn't hold on. His magic seemed so far away, so dull and useless. Even when he managed to find it within himself, he couldn't make it work.

Another flash left Lindsay in the observation room of the

Institute, strapped to the gurney, stripped of his clothes and his magic. “Make it rain,” the doctor said. “Do you hear me, Lindsay? Make it rain in the room.”

Hope sparked in Lindsay’s chest. Would his magic work? Could he use it to get away? He reached for it, finding the silky trail of it deep inside himself, but when he grasped it and tried to pull it to the surface, tried to use it, his magic slipped away.

“Do you see, on the monitors?” The doctor wasn’t talking to him anymore. Her voice was quieter, as though it was an accident that the microphone was still picking her up. She was talking to someone else. Lindsay’s parents, maybe. They were the ones who had brought him here. They were watching, he was sure of it. Watching him being tortured, all in the name of “fixing” him. “The drugs are working. The magic is there. You can see it spark, but he can’t use it. Watch.” Her voice got louder again. “Lindsay. Focus. I want you to make it rain.”

*Flash.* He was back again. The stone collar was heavy around his throat, on his collarbone. He couldn’t breathe. His skin tore as he yanked and pulled at his hands, trying to get out of the cuffs, out of the straps, tried to get *away*, but this time, his magic was within his reach. “Make it rain, Lindsay.”

Lindsay screamed.

He didn’t stop screaming. When the flash brought him to the corpse-littered corridors of the Institute, the screams simply turned inward. He’d done that. He’d killed them all.

The white light enveloped him, dragging him back to Ezqel’s tower. He let go of the mirror, still screaming, and fell to the floor. His hands and knees had barely touched the concrete before he was throwing up, heaving every bit of the small breakfast he’d eaten onto the floor. Between heaves, he was still screaming. He couldn’t stop. He didn’t know how long he’d been falling in and out of the mirror, how long he’d been screaming, but the noises he made were nothing but terrified rasps, and his whole body was shaking with his sobs.

“Are you sure you can’t eat?” Taniel held Lindsay up with

an arm around his waist. The young librarian's face was drawn with concern as he helped Lindsay descend from the tower. When Lindsay had come back to himself, Ezqel was gone and Taniel was there, trying to comfort him without success. "At least a little tea?"

Lindsay's stomach gurgled at the very thought and he shook his head. "No food," he rasped. He wasn't sure he ever wanted to eat again. Taniel had brought him water and he'd rinsed out his mouth, but he hadn't been able to swallow.

"Do you need Izia?" There was another set of stairs up to the guest room that they had to conquer. Taniel was patient, helping Lindsay across the sitting room and up to the safe haven.

"I'll be all right," Lindsay said, shaking his head again. Izia had been with Dane, the last he'd seen either of them this morning, and he was sure she was still tired from whatever work she'd done to heal Dane the night before. "Just...time." He'd thought time would help with the memories, but they were all fresh, all over again.

They were partway up the stairs to the room when Dane found them. Taniel saw him coming and squeaked inadvertently. Dane's hair was in disarray and he was absolutely stormy, wearing pants and bandages and nothing more. Lindsay flinched. After everything else, he didn't want Dane to be mad at him as well.

"Go away." Dane's fury was all directed at Taniel. He reached out for Lindsay. The minute Dane had his hands on Lindsay, Taniel backed away, almost tumbling down a few steps and beating a hasty retreat. Dane gathered Lindsay up to his chest, holding him close.

Lindsay tucked his face against Dane's shoulder and took a slow, shuddering breath. "Taniel didn't hurt me," he whispered. None of it was the librarian's fault.

"That's why he gets to walk away." Dane carried Lindsay to the guest room and kicked the door closed behind him. He brought Lindsay to the bed and laid him in the warm hollow where he must have been resting or sleeping before.

The sheets were so warm, and Lindsay felt so cold. He made a soft noise, rubbing his cheek against Dane's pillow. "Are you all right?" His misery didn't matter if Dane was still hurt.

"Getting better." Dane brought him a glass of water and waited while Lindsay sat up to take a sip. Lindsay's hands shook, and Dane had to help him hold the glass to keep the water from sloshing out as he brought it up to his lips. When Lindsay was finished, Dane put the glass aside and lay beside him, curling around him and pulling him close. "Don't worry about me." He got Lindsay in his arms and frowned with concern.

"Long day," Lindsay admitted, trying to stop shivering.

"You look like shit," Dane said solemnly. Lindsay felt like shit too, so that worked out. "I swear he enjoys making people miserable," Dane muttered. "He's done. We can go soon." He bent his head and nuzzled his cheek against Lindsay's, rubbing like a cat marking his territory.

It felt good, a sweet contrast to how Lindsay felt otherwise. "Why are you so good to me?" he murmured, curiosity rolling over his better sense. He hadn't meant to ask, not ever. He didn't want to jinx this. But the question had slipped out.

Dane shrugged, a ripple of muscles against Lindsay's body. "It works." He snorted softly against Lindsay's neck. "Kinda nice change from the usual, anyway." He purred against Lindsay's throat before pulling back and giving Lindsay a crooked grin. "It does work, right?"

"Mmm." Lindsay nodded. "It's nice, knowing I can screw up and you won't hate me for it." It gave him room to make mistakes. Like being upset about what Kristan had said. He'd been so wrong about all of that. Kristan might have been Dane's lover, but Lindsay was Dane's to care for. He belonged to Dane, and that was something even Kristan couldn't lay claim to. Lindsay burrowed close against Dane's chest, sighing with contentment.

"No reason for me to hate you for anything you did yet."

Dane pulled the blankets up around Lindsay and snuggled Lindsay up to keep him warm. "Hate's something I save for a special few, anyway. Don't think you rate." He chuckled softly, petting Lindsay's hair away from his face.

"Feels good," Lindsay admitted, not talking about the petting alone.

"I go easy on people I like anyway," Dane said, still petting. "You, I like." He shrugged again, his expression sliding back to being as neutral as always.

Lindsay wriggled up enough to angle his mouth against Dane's, pressing a soft kiss there. "I like you too," he whispered, ducking his head into the curve of Dane's neck. He liked Dane a lot.

Dane purred and relaxed into the bed, laying his head in the pillows. "I noticed," he rumbled. He could smell it, probably, or he'd read it in Lindsay's actions long before Lindsay had ever admitted to himself how important Dane was to him.

Lindsay relaxed against Dane again, closing his eyes and trying not to let the memories surface. He could feel tension creeping over him again and his throat got tight with disappointment. Couldn't he be safe here, at least?

One of Dane's fingers, very carefully, found a spot to tickle on Lindsay's ribs. Lindsay squirmed, surprising himself with a giggle, and ended up flopping on his belly to protect his sensitive skin.

Laughing, Dane stopped tickling and patted Lindsay's ass instead. He draped his arm and one leg over Lindsay, pinning him to the bed with warm weight, and pushed his nose into the hair behind Lindsay's ear. Whatever he smelled there elicited a low growl and a soft bite on Lindsay's neck.

It made Lindsay shiver all over. He tilted his head forward, baring his neck. The chill from having been torn open and thrown back together was slowly wearing off. Dane's presence, his protectiveness and his warmth and his laughter, were enough to penetrate Lindsay's misery and wash it back to memories where it belonged.

Dane licked where he'd bitten, tongue rasping slightly behind Lindsay's ear. He growled again, an angry noise, but he kissed Lindsay as though to reassure that Lindsay wasn't the target. Shifting, he pulled Lindsay closer to him, sheltering him under the solid warmth of his body. Lindsay whispered Dane's name, feeling soothed and aroused at once.

Dane tugged the blankets up over both of them and gave a contented sigh. "Sleep now, eat later."

Lindsay made a sound of agreement, tucking himself up in Dane's arms and closing his eyes. That sounded like a perfect plan. Maybe more things later than food. Maybe. He pressed a kiss to Dane's bare chest. It was new to have something so sweet to hope for.

# Chapter Eight

Dane woke before Lindsay, finding his little bunny curled up in a tight knot of anxiety against his chest. He stroked Lindsay's hair and cuddled him until the fearfulness subsided and all Dane could smell was contentment. Outside, the sky was paling with dawn. No one needed to tell him Ezqel wanted to speak to him. He could feel it. The house knew.

"I'll be right back," he promised, kissing the snowy curve of Lindsay's shoulder.

"Dane?" In spite of Dane's caution, Lindsay startled awake, and Dane pulled him close, cursing silently.

"I'm here."

Lindsay twisted and flailed and wouldn't be content until he'd worked himself around to press half-sleeping kisses to Dane's mouth. He was so young, so small, the little bunny. Dane sorted the blankets out once Lindsay was done disarranging them, and petted him until he relaxed.

"I'm going to talk to Ezqel," Dane told him, trying again. It was easy to forget how thin the line between sleeping and waking was for Lindsay, given how still he was when he slept. "Someone will bring you breakfast. You make sure to eat."

Lindsay made an unhappy noise and shoved his face against Dane's throat, his slender arms wrapping around Dane's neck like white vines. It should have irritated Dane, yet it didn't—it was unnatural how it didn't. He felt like laughing, but he didn't want to wake Lindsay further.

"If you don't eat," he whispered in Lindsay's ear, "you won't have any energy to get on with living, little bunny."

With another grump, Lindsay pulled his arms away and sighed forlornly. He peeped at Dane from under his white-gold lashes, his gray eyes hazy with sleep. "I'll eat," he mumbled discontentedly.

"Thank you." Dane kissed him on the head and slid away, tucking the blankets in behind him to keep in the warmth. Lindsay rolled into the hollow Dane's weight had made in the mattress and wrapped his arms around the pillow Dane had used. Dane hoped he stayed sleeping.

Of course, none of their clothes were up here. Who needed Outside things in Ezqel's house? Dane tugged on the jeans and the long-sleeved shirt Izia had brought him yesterday—no, Dane didn't want a robe, thank you, he looked ridiculous in them, like a walking sofa—and went to eat before attending to his old teacher. Ezqel could wait.

"I could wait, but why should I?" Ezqel caught Dane halfway through a rabbit he'd found in the fridge, dressed and quartered and waiting to be cooked. Dane hadn't bothered with that last part. He was starving for flesh.

"Because I'm hungry." Dane bit through a leg bone with a satisfying crunch.

"Your little bunny better watch that you keep your stomach full." Ezqel closed the back door behind him and brought in the pail of milk he'd been out getting, as he did many mornings.

"This is *rabbit*," Dane clarified, taking another bite. It would have been better fresh and hot.

"Why are you so contrary?" Ezqel put the pail on the back of the counter to settle. "Have you learned nothing?"

"I've learned not to waste my time." Dane shoved the last of the rabbit leg into his mouth and got a tin cup from the same hook it had been hung on for longer than Dane had known Ezqel. The enamel was worn away where the handle met the hook, and the handle and the hook were growing thin. He ignored Ezqel's glare and pulled the linen off the pail so he could dip the cup into the warm milk, careful not to get his fingers in it.

"I never disagreed with that. Simply with your definition of waste." Ezqel took the kettle from the bar over the stove and put it on the heat.

Dane washed the rabbit down with warm milk. "Do you like having this conversation?"

"I like it when my students learn something. I keep trying until they do." Ezqel busied himself with finding the right jar of tea, shaking his dark red hair back in a way that made Dane briefly, disconcertingly, nostalgic.

"What if you're wrong?" Dane picked up a front quarter of rabbit. His teeth sheared through ribs and muscle alike as he took a bite. Hunting was forbidden in Ezqel's forest, but the dues the forest owed its keeper were another matter altogether. He met Ezqel's arch expression with one of his own.

"That rarely happens." Ezqel found the jar he wanted, full of dark, shriveled blossoms. He reached in with a beautiful, spidery hand and drew out a dead bouquet for the pot.

"And surviving is the litmus test?" Dane snorted and took another bite. "Funny," he said, when Ezqel didn't answer, ostensibly because the kettle was boiling. "Anyone would think that was my argument."

"You don't seem to have much taste for survival."

"It's harder than it used to be." Dane shrugged. There was no need to point out why. "Don't mind it if it comes, don't mind it if it doesn't."

"You seemed eager enough to live two days past. You know that what I do for him, I could do for you." Ezqel crossed his arms over his chest, scowling outright.

"I had things still undone," Dane said through a mouthful of rabbit. "I'll do them as I am. I've lived with it this long. Besides." He flashed Ezqel a sharp smile full of the twist in his chest. "What's a punishment without a little inconvenience?"

"I shouldn't have bothered." Ezqel pushed away from the counter as Taniel wandered in, too lost in a book to be wary of the tension in the air. "I could have sent the dog to Cyrus to do your job instead of sending him wandering out in the world. Bring the tea when you come up." He left so quickly that he almost knocked the little librarian into the table. Dane stifled the growl that rose at the idea of anyone taking his place, much less Jonas. Ezqel didn't deserve the satisfaction.

Taniel stumbled and clutched his book to his chest, casting about wide-eyed. "I...me?" His question fell on Ezqel's absence and he turned to Dane instead.

"Me." Dane took another bite of rabbit.

"Oh." Taniel seemed relieved, but he wrinkled his nose. "Are you sure you didn't want that cooked?"

"I didn't even want it skinned." Dane crunched the backbone loudly, enjoying Taniel's flinch as much as the taste. "But we can't always have what we want, can we?" He didn't bother to raise his voice, knowing the house would carry it to Ezqel's ears.

"You shouldn't..." Taniel started to say in a small voice, then fell quiet under Dane's glare.

"Shouldn't what?" Izia came clumping in, her purple clogs loud on the stone floor. She took one look at Dane's face and answered her own question. "Ah. At it again. At least you're entertained."

"He started it," Dane pointed out.

"I know." Izia stepped around Taniel and arranged the tea tray with quick, irritated gestures. "Do you ever wonder why?"

"I know." Dane finished off the last bite of rabbit, drained the cup of milk, and went to wash his hands at the old granite sink. "That doesn't change anything."

"Will anything?" Izia held out the tray.

"No." Dane took the tray from her, meeting her sad expression without sympathy. Any pain he felt was so much a part of him, like his brokenness, he felt no desire to let Ezqel take it from him, nor to relinquish it without taking a piece of flesh in trade.

"Not even time?" She let go of the tray and stepped back.

"It's been long enough." Long enough and it was all still the same.

"True." Dane left the room, but he could hear her as well as Ezqel could hear him. "None of us is immortal. Time will change something, some day."

Dane didn't think about things like that. He let the animal fixation on the present wash away the twinge in his chest. The smell of the world crept in through the cracks in the house, the smell of Lindsay sleeping slipped downstairs to soothe him further. All he had to do was get the bunny well again, help Lindsay outgrow him, and the world would settle back into its round.

His mind tried to return to the bed where Lindsay lay sleeping, but his feet carried him on to Ezqel's study in the tower. It was as he had left it last except for the lingering taste of Lindsay's distress on the air that raised his hackles. Lindsay hadn't even been born when Dane had last crossed the threshold into this room.

"Do you know what they did to him?" Time to get down to business. The taste of Lindsay's pain reminded Dane to keep his mind on the present, kept him from going back to dig up old bones.

"The Shackles of Tehut, or a replica thereof," Ezqel said, not looking up from his work. Dane put the tray on the desk and stepped back. "Not going to sit?"

Dane snorted. There was no chair in the room other than the one on which Ezqel sat, making his usual refusal to settle irrelevant. "Old River magic. I thought it was long gone."

"My guess is that they were a replica of the broken set found at Bam several floods ago. You remember the ones. The pharaohs used them to control their mages, like bridling a horse." Now Ezqel did look up, watching Dane pace over to the mirror; Dane could see him in the reflection. "It would have been possible to reproduce that set—the magic was still heavy on it."

"You have that set," Dane pointed out, trying not to snap and let Ezqel have the satisfaction of it. "I don't need a lecture on it. It's supposed to be the last set."

"I've only had it for a few hundred years. Someone had it before me." Ezqel poured himself a cup of tea, meeting Dane's eyes in the mirror. "If I could decipher the bindings back when I was young and foolish, who's to say someone older and wiser did not do that and more?"

"There could be more?" Dane ran a hand over the worn place on one side of the mirror frame. He could smell Lindsay's misery strongly here, soaked into the wood, his vomit soaked into the stone in spite of a good scrubbing. Adrenaline raked Dane's nerves and he felt his claws lengthen, his spine curving before he could stop it.

Ezqel said nothing about it, drinking his tea instead. Dane could smell the flowers, remembered their fragrance over his head and the crushed grass under his back one hot day. "All things are possible, but I could not find them. I searched, as did Cyrus. Their pattern is gone."

"They could be sleeping in lead." Dane forced himself to change to as human as he could go, even as his skin prickled with growing hairs and his teeth nicked twin marks in his lower lip.

"I can see beyond it," Ezqel said simply. "Cyrus has been listening, as well. We know Moore does not have another."

"That doesn't mean she doesn't know how it works." Dane pulled his hand away from the mirror before he clenched the wood and broke it in frustration.

"That's not my concern. I only needed to know what happened to him. The shackles use magic against itself to keep it from the mage. The more powerful the magic, the more power is given over to the binding runes, and so it goes. He overloaded the binding and something in him broke from the force of his magic returning to him. Like the body, the mind can be too strong for its own materials." Ezqel tapped an uneven rhythm on his cup with his ivory fingernails. "I cannot heal the paths of his magic while his magic runs in them."

"You'll kill him if you take it out of him," Dane warned. It would be like Ezqel to forget that killing Lindsay made the entire exercise a moot point. "If that magic didn't work on him, why will yours?"

"His magic found a failing in the artifacts. The world has changed since they were made. Nothing escapes the passage of time. Old knowledge is dangerous for that very reason. Clinging to the past will only wound the future." Ezqel waited until Dane looked at him before taking a drink of tea. "I will bypass his magic. Have you forgotten your lessons?"

"If you put him in a soul jar, I will eat your liver." That thought cheered Dane up immensely. The opportunity only needed to arise.

"Actually, I was thinking more along the lines of a *heksiphage*." Ezqel leaned back in his chair, still tapping his fingers. Dane had threatened to break them once, to get some quiet. "They're becoming more and more common in urban centers." He put his cup down and pointed at a map of the world hanging on the far wall. "Go get that. Mind, you'll have to kill the thing and bring me its heart."

Dane was halfway across the room before he could think to be irritated at being ordered around. He didn't care enough anymore. He wanted this over with. "I'm fine with killing things."

"The most likely form we'll find on short notice is a *guul*. They're bigger than you are."

"Never stopped me before." Dane lifted the map off of its brackets to bring it to the center of the room. It was heavy with precious metals and gems, and it was different than the last time he'd seen it. Then again, the world had changed over that many years.

"This isn't the time for debating your testicular fortitude." Ezqel met Dane in the center of the room, inside the ring of white marble set in the floor. "Put it down." Dane set the map on air and it hovered at waist height. "Go to the artifact room and bring out one of the *jarthalfyr* boxes, the black and silver one. And get the ring case while you're in there."

"I don't need your help," Dane said, trudging to the wall behind Ezqel's desk. He found a place that felt right and shoved at it, putting his will behind the push, and a door that hadn't been there before opened up.

Beyond the door that wasn't, there was a museum of sorts. Dane knew that finding the jarthalfyr artifacts wouldn't be difficult. They were used for guuls and trolls and minor demons—they stank. The ring case was probably shoved somewhere random and he'd have to hunt it down. He tried not to scratch at his scalp and skin. The magic in here pricked his senses and caught on the broken places in him, making him burn and itch.

The black and silver jarthalfyr box was on a shelf with several others of different colors. This one had a rune-chased silver dagger set in the lid. Dane liked it immediately for the way it sang like a tooth thirsty for blood. For convenience, Dane found the null bags—shielded against magic and mundane drips and spills like blood—and took a likely looking black velvet one.

The ring case was, surprisingly, at the back with the other jewelry cases. Dane slipped between a pair of tall, thin alabaster urns with jackal heads, swallowing hard against the way their aura made his instincts scream at him to flee, and pulled the ring case from its place. The power surging from the wall of adornments was so intense it made his head swim. By the time he stepped back out, his shirt was damp with sweat under his hair and his pace was hurried in spite of his pride.

Ezqel didn't move as the door disappeared behind Dane. He was bent over the map, squinting at the detailed jade continent of North America. Dane forced himself to breathe slowly as he put the things he'd brought out on Ezqel's desk and came over to see what was so damn interesting. He could smell blood.

Tiny ruby spheres—Ezqel's blood—were rolling about the world, every one rambling on about its business without leaving a stain behind. Dane watched from the other side of the map as each of them found its way to a different spot in the world and settled. Ezqel murmured and gestured with his right hand and they began to glow.

"That one, I think." Ezqel pointed at a droplet shining brightly in what Dane figured must be Mexico. Ezqel brought his finger to it and it clung to his skin a moment before being absorbed. "There is a guul in Cholula, young and strong and foolish, like the mages it hunts." He passed his hand over the rest of the map and his blood came flying toward him like iron filings to a magnet, to be drawn into his skin. "It should be hungry by the time you get there—I can feel it. Take the boy and find it. It will likely think him as toothsome as you do."

Dane growled at that, low and warning, and Ezqel laughed.

"What?" Ezqel pointed at the map. "Put that back. It's not as if it isn't so. I'd think he had some spell over you if he weren't so crippled."

In a way, it was a relief to hear that, and Dane was ashamed. He picked up the map and returned it to its place. He was a suspicious old beast, wary of the world because he knew his own evil. "And when we kill the thing?" Killing was something he could do well enough, better than keeping something like Lindsay alive.

"Bring back its heart, nothing more. You know how to butcher an animal." Ezqel was inspecting the jarthalfyr box, making it bright with his magic as he tested for flaws. "I can use the heart to hold his magic while I heal the broken parts of him."

"Fair enough." Dane put the world where it belonged and collected the box and bag.

"Take this." Ezqel opened the ring box and pulled out the one he wanted, almost without looking. Dane didn't need to see it to know what it was, either. *Yzumrud.* A heavy, gold thing with a green stone in it, green with hints of blood, like it lived. It fit his finger.

"I don't want it. These will do." Dane folded up the bag and tucked it in the box. He knew how much demonic things stank and didn't want the smell clinging to him more than necessary. "I'll get the thing and bring it back."

"You're not immortal." Ezqel turned on him with the ring held out in a clenched fist. "Did you not illustrate that only a day past?"

"I'll make sure to get the heart before I die, so as not to inconvenience anyone." Dane crossed his arms over his chest, the box in one hand. "Have I let Cyrus down yet?"

"The same illustration applies," Ezqel ground out. Color came to his pale face, staining his lips red and his cheeks rosy. "Let no one accuse you of being wasteful."

"I owe you for keeping my service intact." Dane wanted to hit Ezqel—not that it was a rare feeling, nor would it have been satisfying—and held himself back from doing it so as not to fail Cyrus further. "He said I would fail him, I did, and I won't do it again." He turned on his heel and walked away. Ezqel's fury was like a small sun at his back.

"Not for some days." Ezqel's voice struck off the arches and the high ceiling and bounced around the room, echoing over and over again. "*Not for some days*, Dane. Are you still counting them as men do? Those days are not past. Do you think a little thing like your moment of death would catch his attention?"

Dane stopped at the door, trying to breathe. "No." No, he didn't. He wasn't that arrogant. Dane dying in some stupid scuffle with Jonas was hardly a failure. Ezqel had been there to stop Lindsay from being harmed. Dane had made it that far.

"Let me do this for you."

Dane knew Ezqel wasn't talking about the ring alone, but about what came after. "Why, when you would not, before?" He turned slowly.

"That's my affair." Ezqel held out the ring again. His heavy hair was out of place, his robes slipped off one shoulder farther than the other, his jaw was tight. "Take it." Every little crack in his facade felt like a war trophy.

"It's my *life*." Dane came back to snatch the ring from Ezqel's hand. "My life is not your affair. Not anymore." He held the ring up. "Not because you asked. Not for Cyrus. For my own reasons." He shoved the ring in his pocket. "I am still allowed one or two of those, no matter what I am, no matter what you think of me."

"Dane..."

Dane turned his back on the mage. No worse could be done to him than had been done already, not without damaging Ezqel's own machinations. Dane wasn't fool enough to think anything else mattered, not after all these years. "I'll see you when I've finished what needs doing."

Leaving Ezqel's house was far easier for Lindsay than coming to it had been. Taniel led them out through the gardens in the back and under an archway overgrown with ivy, through a gate. "This path will take you to the nearest town. You must stay on it, though. If you step away from it, you may not find your way again, and I cannot say where you will find yourself." He looked up at Dane. "*You* might find your way, but I don't recommend it. You know his sense of humor."

Dane snorted and hitched up his pack. "I do. We won't stray. I'm not in the habit of chasing white stags."

Taniel stifled a laugh. "No, that's wise. Good luck." He turned to Lindsay and gave him a warm smile. "And good luck to you, also. We will see you again."

Lindsay nodded back at Taniel, giving him an uncertain smile before following Dane away, along the path. "What's..." Lindsay tromped along beside Dane for a moment, gathering his thoughts. "What does Ezqel *do*?" He'd been too terrified to even think about what it was that Ezqel was good at. He'd been too busy being trampled by his own memories.

"You mean the basic magic he was born with? A strange kind of sight, like what they call 'second sight'. He doesn't see things like other people—matter, time, magic. His sight makes him a master of the art of magic. Spells and artifacts and the like." Lindsay didn't know. He hadn't grown up with magic around him, ubiquitous the way it seemed to be now. "It's hard to find him because so many people would simply kill him if they could—he's that dangerous."

Lindsay tried to turn the information over in his mind, tried to process. "Did he save you? Is that how you survived?"

"Partly. The body can live on magic for a little while if it must, and it needs magic to live. That's one reason we have long lives. They gave me enough magic to force what was left of me to keep working. My body and Izia's healing took over." Dane rubbed at the back of his neck and his shoulders drew up defensively.

Lindsay glanced away. Dane was so rarely discomfited about things that watching it made Lindsay feel like he was trespassing. Dane grumbled deep in his chest and Lindsay felt a bit better, because that was the Dane he knew. He kept hoping he'd work out how to take care of Dane the way Dane took care of him. It felt like their relationship had changed since they'd first set foot in the Black Forest. Dane's death had changed everything for Lindsay, but it wasn't that alone.

The kisses. Dane had kissed Lindsay, had kissed him like he *meant* it. Lindsay could hardly stop thinking about it, no matter how he tried to put it aside. Some part of him that he hadn't known existed was still flying high, replaying each kiss whenever his mind wandered.

Maybe they were only kisses, like treats for when Lindsay was good or brave. But it seemed like it should mean something that Dane had kissed Lindsay, was attracted to him, but hadn't simply sated himself and fallen asleep like he had with Kristan, even if Lindsay would have given Dane anything. Maybe that meant something good.

Dane let him have so much, let him take so many liberties. Lindsay didn't understand how his own magic worked, much less anyone else's. He was certain that it would have been rude to ask someone else, but the way it was between them, it felt like he could ask. "Your magic? What...what is that, exactly? I mean, I know about your claws, but...how does that help you heal?"

"Awful curious about magic for someone who just spent all this time saying he didn't want his," Dane teased. He reached out and petted Lindsay's hair, though.

Lindsay leaned into the touch, his eyes slipping half-shut with the pleasure of it. Maybe Dane was only indulging him, but it still felt good. "I don't...I don't know. I want to understand."

"Was a time I would have made short work of Jonas," Dane said quietly. "I used to be a shapeshifter, of a kind. Now, I have a little of it left. Not much."

"What happened?" Lindsay asked, before he could think better of it.

"I hurt someone." Dane's voice was neutral. "They hurt me back."

"Oh." Lindsay was silent for a long time, as they trudged along the path. The walk was far easier, leaving.

How Dane had lost his magic nagged at Lindsay along the way, though. Lindsay tried not to remember the pain and torment that he'd suffered when he'd lost his magic, and before that. Maybe Dane had suffered like that, too. The idea made Lindsay ache inside. It made sense, the way Dane seemed used to pain, how he'd never made anything but that small sound when Jonas had gutted him.

"And Jonas? Was he a shapeshifter too? He's the one Cyrus was talking about when he said the dog would be looking for us. I figured that out. Is that why he kept coming, why he didn't die?"

"He always looks the same. He heals. And he hunts. He's nearly impossible to kill." Dane shook his head and glanced over at Lindsay, his expression dark. "Nearly. We call him the dog because that's what he is. He hangs around on the outskirts of being human, but he'll never be one. He eats what scraps they throw him. Takes their work."

Lindsay was quiet, remembering. "I think I almost killed him. I think...if I wasn't broken, if Ezqel hadn't come..."

"Next time." Dane slung his arm around Lindsay's shoulders. "He'll never see it coming."

Lindsay leaned into it, basking in being included, somehow, in Dane's future, and in the way Dane had faith in him. "Will Ezqel really be able to fix me?"

"If he says he can, he will." Dane turned to Lindsay. "Do you want to be fixed, now?"

Lindsay met Dane's eyes. "I don't want to be standing there, wishing I could push a little more, *wishing* I could do something. I want to be able to *do* it. I don't want to be broken."

He understood it, now, what they'd been saying before. That his magic could be the difference between life and death. That he would need it. That being broken wouldn't save him, it would make him an easy target. There was never going to be another time when Lindsay went through watching someone die because of him, unable to stop it, not if there was anything on earth Lindsay could do to keep that from happening. Not even if it meant putting himself in Ezqel's hands again.

Dane stopped walking and pulled Lindsay into him with the arm around Lindsay's shoulders. His other hand slid into Lindsay's hair, tilting Lindsay's head back to the perfect angle for a fierce kiss. The kiss felt like pride and praise and want all in one hot moment of lips and teeth and tongue, and it warmed Lindsay through to feel it.

"Now you get it," Dane said, when he pulled away from the kiss. His expression was intensely predatory. It sent another rush of heat through Lindsay, all the way to his belly. "You understand. It's good."

Lindsay nodded, trying to catch his breath. "I didn't, before. I didn't know why you kept telling me I'd want something that's been nothing but pain and trouble." He kept his eyes on Dane's. "I do now."

"Good." Dane let go of Lindsay's hair and smoothed it back into place. "It needs to be this way. Come on. Guess where we're going next." He turned them to keep walking.

"Out of the woods, I hope," Lindsay said, obediently following Dane's lead.

"Mexico." Dane grinned at him. "We're going demon hunting." He was like a kid anticipating a birthday party—a very large, scary kid.

"As long as it's warm." Lindsay backtracked through the

conversation a moment and asked, "*Demon* hunting?"

Dane laughed at his expression. "Ezqel needs its heart. It'll be good for you to get out and do something. Can't wait, myself."

Dane had nearly gotten killed, and there he was, reveling in the anticipation of hunting a demon. Lindsay hadn't even known demons existed. He wasn't sure whether he was frustrated with Dane or impressed by his indifference to his recent trauma. "How do we find it?"

"It eats magic," Dane said cheerfully. "And, by association, mages. Should be a snap."

It ate mages. Perfect. Out of the frying pan, and into the fire.

The hotel in Cholula was spectacular, a shimmering white tower with two gleaming turquoise pools and lush gardens inside and out. Dane and Lindsay had a room halfway up, two beds and a lounge, a wide balcony, and a bathroom the size of Lindsay's bedroom back in New York. Vivian, who had made their reservations, had great taste. The tiled floors were cool underfoot, the carpets were soft and plush, the artwork was relaxing, and a mellow breeze blew through, stirring the streaming white curtains. It was too bad they weren't going to spend much time here.

"We should get ready to go." Dane nodded toward the windows that had a view of the setting sun, as soon as the bellhop left them their bags. "Need to get hunting before it's too long past dark. It'll be after food soon, by Ezqel's reckoning. Don't want it to get someone, get sated, and leave us sitting for a week."

"All right. What do you need me to do?" The thing hunted mages, Dane had said, but Lindsay didn't know what that meant for him.

"Be pretty." Dane flashed Lindsay a wolfish grin. "Should be easy enough. It likes to hunt on the seedy side of things, outside the illegal nightclubs and gambling houses. We'll be going there. Lone, drunk victims are easy prey for a thing like that. We'll find it where they are."

Lindsay blinked at Dane. Bait. He was going to be bait. He wasn't used to thinking of himself as desirable, but Dane seemed certain of it. "I can do that. I think." At least he could do *something.* He dug through his bag, searching for anything to wear to a nightclub. Most of what he had was chosen for the cold German winter, not the warmth of Mexico. And certainly not for looking pretty, or easy.

"There's a shop downstairs," Dane added, pulling off his own shirt. "If you want to get some lighter clothes. Whatever you think works best. Pretty's not my forte." He snorted softly at the notion.

"The gift shop might be best. You can tell me if I succeed." He took the cash Dane handed over and gave Dane a grin that he couldn't have stifled if he'd wanted to. Dane liked him. *Dane liked him.* "I'll be right back," he promised.

It didn't take long to find what he needed. The hotel was part of a resort, and the shops downstairs stocked all manner of clothes and things for forgetful tourists. He slipped back into the hotel room and ducked into the bathroom before Dane could ask any questions.

It had been a long time since he'd tried to dress in such a way that he'd attract attention, and these were the first clothes he'd bought for himself since... He stopped that train of thought and turned his attention to his clothes, shedding the ones he wore and digging through his bag of purchases.

The pants he'd bought were black and velvety-soft, and he'd found likely the only long-sleeved shirt in the entire resort. He'd impulsively bought an eyeliner pencil, but standing in front of the mirror, he was afraid it would make him look like a clown. He gave it a shot anyway, tracing delicate lines under his eyes. When he stepped back to inspect himself, he was surprised to see that the kohl brought out the gray in his pale eyes, making them seem more intense.

After he'd cleaned up the pile of clothes and tags he'd left on the floor, Lindsay was out of ways to delay showing himself to Dane. He swallowed hard and stepped out of the bathroom, shrugging uncomfortably. He wasn't sure if he'd managed anything more than making himself nervous.

Dane's rumble was definitely approving. Lindsay was learning to tell Dane's noises and his expressions better all the time. "Someone's going to steal you, not just the guul. I best be careful." He kept his hands to himself, though. He was wearing heavy boots, clean jeans, a wide belt, and a well-worn leather vest. As far as Lindsay was concerned, Dane looked pretty damn irresistible himself.

Lindsay watched Dane tuck a black bag into a pocket of his vest and sheath a long silver knife in his boot. He trusted Dane to find the demon, but maybe he could help. "What should I be watching for?"

"It appears human," Dane said. "The hardest thing for it to hide is its feet, because they touch the earth and the magic seeps away. They look like birds' feet, at least if you have the sight to see through its disguises."

"Can you see through them, the way you see through my illusions?"

"We both can. Anyone with enough magic in their blood can see through a guul's disguise. That's why you won't find it in bright places or with many people—it doesn't want to get too close to the mages it hunts, not too soon. It'll be a man alone, in the shadows, waiting for someone else who's alone."

"Oh." Bird feet. Lindsay would have to remember that.

Dane checked Lindsay over one more time, slowly, and flashed him a toothy grin. "Let's go hunt demons."

Lindsay's cheeks felt warm, and he smiled, looking forward to this almost as much as Dane was. "Let's go."

They took a cab from the hotel to the wrong side of town, and Dane waved off the driver's warnings, given in halting English. "We'll be fine."

It was obvious why the driver had been trying to discourage them from getting out here. Everything seemed dim and shadowed, even the places lit by neon signs. There were alleys everywhere, darker still, and that seemed to be where people were headed. Into those alleys, to the illicit places Dane had mentioned before.

"We pick one, we go in, we grab a drink, we mingle, then out the back. Wander the alleys a while, and back into another. I won't lose you if you don't want me to, so don't worry. Have fun. You have to seem natural." As Dane spoke, he led Lindsay toward a narrow pink door set into a grungy, pale green building.

Lindsay nodded. He could do this. He had to go in and have a good time. Inside, the club was hot, packed with people from one end of the room to the other. Lindsay tucked himself closer to Dane and tried not to seem nervous.

"It's like throwing an illusion." Dane's voice was warm and reassuring in his ear. "Without the magic behind it. Make people believe that you're a happy party boy. Put yourself out there. None of these people know who you are or were, and you'll never see them again. So go on."

Lindsay took a deep breath and nodded again before plunging into the crowd. There was a dance floor, or something like it, where people were grinding against each other. He made his way over and found himself dancing with one man, and another, and another. None of them spoke English, and Lindsay didn't speak any Spanish, but that didn't matter. No one was here for the conversation. Eventually, though, Lindsay looked around for Dane. The big man should have been hard to miss, even in such a crowd.

As if summoned by Lindsay's thoughts, Dane was suddenly behind him, murmuring in his ear. "Time to keep hunting."

Lindsay let Dane lead him out the back of the club. They wandered through the dark alleys until Dane pointed toward an open door where light and music were pouring out into the alley. "Let's go through there."

"All right." Lindsay slipped in ahead, weaving through the crowd. Dane moved past him like they didn't even know each other, and Lindsay saw him disappear into a shadowed corner. He would probably lurk there like he was lying in wait until he caught a scent or decided it was time for them to leave.

Lindsay's pale hair and skin and slender body brought him a great deal of attention, even from women and from men who had been dancing with women. He danced, like he had in the last place, twirling from one person to the next. It was flattering, being so sought-after, but sometimes it was hard to keep his smile plastered to his face.

Hands skimmed his chest and hips, his ass and groin. Some did more than just skim. One of the men he danced with insisted on holding his ass with both hands, tight, kneading as he ground against Lindsay's body. The last man wasn't much different. He put Lindsay's back to his chest and ground against his ass, instead. He dragged his tongue from Lindsay's shoulder to his ear, leaving a trail of warm saliva behind.

When that one let Lindsay go, Lindsay shook off the other offers and headed for Dane. He'd had enough. Too much.

Lindsay found Dane in a booth in the darkest corner of the bar. Dane's back was to the wall. He was holed up there, staring out into the open bar like an animal in its den. Lindsay didn't hesitate to go to him, crawling along the bench to curl up at Dane's side.

Dane wrapped an arm around him, laughing quietly. "Maybe you're too pretty for this town." No one bothered pursuing Lindsay once he was safely tucked up against Dane. "Ready to move on?"

Lindsay shook his head. "No more," he murmured, pressing his face against Dane's chest and taking a deep breath to calm himself. Dancing had been fun, but he didn't like being a piece of meat to be passed around, groped and fondled at will.

"Okay." Dane stroked Lindsay's hair with one hand and picked up his drink with the other. "You want some?" He offered the glass to Lindsay.

It smelled strong, like scotch or rye. Lindsay held the glass in both hands and sipped. It burned going down and he coughed, but took another sip anyway.

"It'll settle you some," he said, loud enough for Lindsay to hear. Obediently, Lindsay had some more. The petting felt so good, soothing. He leaned into it, and into the solid warmth of Dane's body. Dane got him to drink most of what seemed like an unusually full glass of liquor. "Better?"

Lindsay curled up against Dane's chest, nodding. "Better. Thank you." He was buzzed and his anxiety had eased, as Dane had promised.

Dane ran his hands over Lindsay's back and over his hips. "That's good. Need to teach you how to throw those wicked little elbows. Keep the men off you."

"I thought you wanted them on me," Lindsay murmured, rubbing his cheek against Dane's shirt.

"Wanted you to have fun. Careless young mages having fun are what this thing wants." Dane nudged Lindsay's temple with his nose. "Thought you liked men, anyway."

"I do." Lindsay tipped his head back. "I don't like being grabbed like that. It was...I don't know. Too much."

"Now you know. Done partying for the night for sure?"

"I'll go back out there if you want me to." For a moment, he was afraid Dane would make him go.

"Tell me what you want."

Lindsay butted his head against Dane's chin. "I don't want them touching me anymore." He wanted to stay here, with Dane, where he felt safe.

"Fair enough. Anything else?" Dane's hands were warm on his back and hips and over his thighs.

"I want *you* to touch me," Lindsay muttered, shifting under Dane's hands. He liked it when Dane touched him. He wanted Dane.

But a thin line of cold cut through all Lindsay's warmth and pleasure. Dane's gentle smile suddenly felt condescending and so did his question. Dane could tell that Lindsay wanted him, so why was he asking? Why would Dane ask unless he couldn't be bothered to want anything for himself?

Suddenly Lindsay was afraid that he'd been wrong, that Dane didn't want him but was keeping him happy so he'd be good for Cyrus. Lindsay couldn't say what had changed except now he could see how he could be used because of everything he felt. It was so easy to see that his emotions and his pleasure were strings being pulled, and Dane was asking him to participate in his own manipulation.

Betrayal. Even his own body was being used against him, all over again. It was horrible, and it made so much sense, that Dane would be the one to keep him in line. It wasn't like Dane seemed to give a damn who he fucked.

"Actually, you don't have to do anything," Lindsay muttered. He wasn't going to play this game. "You don't have to fucking *indulge* me. I'm not going to fall apart." He pushed away and out of Dane's lap, out of the booth.

Lindsay had to get away so he could think. Being near Dane made him stupid with emotions and hormones that were clouding his judgment. He tugged his fingers through his hair, like he could wipe away Dane's touches, and headed out the back of the bar. He didn't know where he was going, maybe back to where the cab had left them. Maybe he'd be able to get to the hotel from there. He didn't need Dane, not for *that.* He didn't need anyone who didn't want him as much as he wanted them.

The streets were empty and humid, the last of the day's warmth making the standing water from the sewers hang in the air. A thin layer of murky mist mingled with the sweat and makeup on Lindsay's skin, making him feel as dirty and disposable outside as he felt inside. There wasn't a person or a cab in sight. Maybe it would be easier to find a cab on a busier street.

Lindsay knew he was sulking, but damn it, Dane didn't have to be such a dick about everything. It wasn't like Lindsay was going to fall apart if Dane didn't fuck him. Dane didn't need to whore himself out to keep Lindsay in line. Lindsay had nowhere else to go.

Didn't Dane want anything for himself? No one else felt a

burning need to know what Lindsay wanted. And if anyone could tell what Lindsay wanted or needed, wouldn't it be Dane, with his senses that made him seem like a mind reader? Too many fucking questions that Lindsay couldn't answer. He was done with it.

Lindsay wiped under his eyes to make sure his eyeliner wasn't streaking his face. There was a man behind him, walking at an even pace. It was too shadowed to make anything out about him. Otherwise, the street was still empty. A moment later, the man was closer than his pace would have allowed.

Lindsay sped up, wishing he hadn't left the bar so impulsively. He looked around, hoping for the light from another club or some other crowded place.

"You're pretty tonight." The voice was right in Lindsay's ear.

Lindsay's head whipped around and he caught a glimpse of a tall, thin man. Those footsteps hadn't been that close, but there the man was. It wasn't Dane, so Lindsay didn't wait. He ran for the empty intersection he could see in the distance. Whoever it was, he didn't want to stick around for a better introduction. He ran straight into someone, someone who smelled sweet like honey.

"Don't run." Hands closed on Lindsay's shoulders.

Lindsay twisted away and ran again, taking off down an alley. He wanted to get *away*. His breath came fast more from the fear than the running, and his heart was pounding so hard it felt like the man would be able to track him from the noise. Where was Dane? Lindsay was going to die and Dane was going to laugh at him for being stupid.

The man followed him into the alley. His steps scraped on the stones like huge nails on a chalkboard. Every slow step he took was like five of Lindsay's steps, the way that chilling sound got closer and closer. A hand clamped around Lindsay's wrist and yanked him off his feet. "Pretty."

Claws. Like bird talons. That was why it made those noises. The demon had bird feet. Lindsay gulped for the air that was knocked out of him when he hit the ground. He struggled, trying to kick and get away.

When that didn't work, he shoved his magic out instead. He was broken and the magic would knock him out, but he was fucked anyway. Nothing else had worked, and passing out would be worth it, if he could get away. It had worked on Jonas, maybe it would work here too. *Stop*, he thought, pushing his magic at the demon. *Die.*

The guul laughed. It felt like the thing was lapping up Lindsay's magic through its skin. "Oh, so pretty," it praised. It dragged Lindsay deeper into the alley, pulling him by the one arm. Lindsay slid through a slurry of waste and water, kicking frantically, spitting obscenities in fear and outrage. He was nothing but a piece of meat. Nothing he did mattered, all over again.

# Chapter Nine

When Lindsay stormed out, Dane didn't let Lindsay out of his sight, following at a distance. He hadn't done anything wrong, but he was dealing with the aftermath of nineteen years of people doing everything wrong.

He would let Lindsay stomp around for a while, keeping an eye on him to keep him safe. With luck, Lindsay would find his way to a cab and make his way back to the hotel successfully. It wasn't going to do Lindsay any good if Dane had to rescue him, lost and exhausted, and kick the last of his pride into the gutter.

Dane saw a slender shadow far ahead of him on the street, shoulders hunched, head down. He was going to have to work on that. A half-blind, one-legged mugger could jump Lindsay if he kept going around with his head down. The urge to catch up and lecture Lindsay was there, but he put it aside in favor of ducking into an alley. He lost sight of Lindsay for a moment, but he wanted to get up on top of things. His claws sank easily into old mortar as he scrambled up the side.

The buildings in the area were all only two or three storeys, almost all with uniformly flat roofs that served as patio or garden space, and the passages between them were narrow enough to leap. Dane liked old neighborhoods. He caught Lindsay's scent again as he loped along, then a glimpse of the slouching boy-shape as Lindsay turned a corner. Lindsay was young, and Dane never let himself forget it, no matter how old Lindsay's losses made him seem.

Something else caught Dane's attention on a cross-breeze that pulled at his hair—the scent of honey. He paused and straightened to smell the air, raising his face to the wind. Demons often smelled of sweet things. The air swirled, making it hard to tell what direction the scent was coming from. Dane growled and set off toward Lindsay.

Several buildings over, where the homes gave way to warehouses, he caught sight of Lindsay and another man. The smell of honey hit him in the face and turned his stomach. For a moment, it seemed he could get to Lindsay before the guul, but, in a blink, the creature was ahead of Lindsay, reaching for him. Translocation. If it could take Lindsay along, Dane would never find them again.

Lindsay twisted loose of the guul and darted out of sight, then the guul disappeared as well. Dane moved silently along the rooftops to intercept Lindsay's path, swearing internally in a constant stream of profanities that crossed languages, races and eras. He could hear Lindsay's voice, and it gave him hope, despite the fear in it. As he moved, he slipped Yzumrud onto his finger. He had his pride, but that didn't matter when it came to Lindsay's safety.

Dane came to the edge of a building over a narrow alley and crouched there, feeling a wash of déjà vu. It seemed he was going to make a habit of scrapping in alleys over the boy. He gauged the distance and launched himself into the air. Landing awkwardly, he hit the guul, bearing it to the ground.

As they rolled in the muck, he could hear Lindsay scrambling to escape. *Good boy.* The guul threw Dane off like he was nothing at all and Dane's thoughts were lost as he crashed into the side of a building, nearly half a storey off the ground. Falling, he hit the dirt at a bad angle. Things snapped in his left leg as it buckled.

"Ah, it has a guardian." The guul reached out as he struggled to get up. The more his body tried to recover, the weaker he felt. "Better and better."

"Dane!"

*Damn it.* Maybe Lindsay hadn't learned a thing.

Dane threw himself at the guul and took it into a brick wall with so much force that they left a dent where the bricks were shoved in. The guul's human disguise was shredding and its honeyed smell was rotting on the air. It backhanded him across the alley, sending him crashing into the opposite wall with a sick crunch. Air went out of him and things shattered in his back, but some of his strength crept back into his blood.

"Helpful little thing," the guul said sardonically. It must have been drawing off of Lindsay, but Dane couldn't get breath to tell the damn boy to stop and run. At least Lindsay was buying him some time to heal. When the guul straightened, it shed the last of its disguise. At full height, it was taller than Dane, a black, skeletal body covered in taut, glossy skin. It cast about with its heavy head, turning to grin at Lindsay with teeth like knives. "I will have you in a moment."

Lindsay stumbled backward and sank to the ground. The guul was draining him dry and Dane would be next. Dane didn't have much choice here if he wanted them both to live. He needed Yzumrud.

Laughing, the guul turned back to Dane. "Now. The main course." It reached for Dane with talons longer than daggers. Once, Dane would have had a set to match. Now, he couldn't put his bones back together fast enough to get to his feet.

"Eat this." Dane raised his hand and muttered the words to finish a spell in the old faerie tongue. He hadn't used magic like this in years, but the words rolled out perfectly. Fire burst from his palm, a hot white knot of flame that took the guul full in the face. Dane turned his head aside to avoid getting bone and carapace splinters in his eyes as the guul's skull exploded.

It always felt like cheating.

Dane forced himself up, leaning on the wall for support. Any thrill from the kill was lost in the bitterness of knowing Ezqel had been right, Dane had needed Yzumrud. He brought his hand up to stare at the damn thing.

"Bastard," he grumbled, at the ring as much as at Ezqel.

Yzumrud caught the faded moonlight and glittered like laughter.

The dim glint of light on the ring sparked an equally dim memory in Dane, from so long ago he might have been Lindsay's age. Breathing hard, he stared at his hand and the ring as though they belonged to someone else.

The memory of truths twisted by demon magic and the smell of honey over death bubbled to the surface of his mind. Guuls had more power than magic-eating and their illusion played tricks on more than the eyes. Dane had known that once, and Ezqel had known he knew it; they had learned it the same way, each in their own time.

Before Dane knew what he was doing, he'd clenched his fist and twisted, driving Yzumrud and his hand through the wall behind him. A snarl of rage was locked behind his clenched teeth. Ezqel had known he would forget. There was so much he'd forgotten. When he pulled his hand back, the ring glittered still, untouched.

If Dane had remembered, he never would have let Lindsay storm off. If he'd remembered, his need to protect Lindsay would have kept Lindsay too close for the boy to be bait for the guul. They might never have gotten the heart they needed, not like this, and Dane wouldn't have apologized for it, either. They would have found another way.

"I'm sorry." Lindsay's voice was small and shaky, barely loud enough to be heard over the roaring in Dane's ears. It didn't need to be loud to bring Dane up short. Of course Lindsay would think it was his fault.

"Not angry at you," Dane ground out. Another surge of anger, this time at himself, rose as soon as the first was ebbing. "Just..." His vision was tinted red, everything was wrapped in a bloody halo. There was no discussing it now. He turned and pointed an ichor-stained finger at Lindsay. "Not you. Understand?"

Lindsay's body tensed in a reflexive cringe, but he nodded and tried to sit up.

Dane turned back to the smoldering, headless corpse. "Good thing we didn't need that part," he muttered. "You okay?" He flexed the hand he'd used for the spell. Sparks of heat and power were still running up and down his arm, catching on his broken magic and making his skin sting.

"'m good." Lindsay hadn't managed to stand yet and he sounded unsteady, but he was awake and aware. That was enough for Dane.

"Good. Stay that way." Dane spat out the taste of guul that lingered on the air and shook his head. "I hate using party tricks." He hated owing Ezqel. He hated failing.

From his boot, he pulled the long silver dagger. In the dim alleyway, it glowed with an eerie light that pulsed in the runes along the blade. He kicked the twitching corpse onto its back and, straddling it, split it from neck to notch. The resulting stench was unbearable. "Why don't they ever make one that smells *good* inside?"

"I could do without ever smelling honey again."

"Come closer, it'll clear your head." Dane plunged one hand into the open cavity to find the heart. He got his fingers around it, careful not to nick it with his claws. He wrenched it out as Ezqel had instructed, but stringy tissue still bound the thing to its body. A slash of the magical blade freed it completely. Dane held it up for Lindsay to see. It was more than twice the size of a human heart, longer and thinner, and blacker than the night sky. "That wasn't so hard, was it?"

"Except for the part where I made an ass out of myself." Lindsay pushed himself to his feet and made his way over to Dane. He was unsteady but calm, and Dane was proud of him. He didn't even make a face at the demon stench. "Are you all right?"

"Thing eats magic, and don't tell anyone, but I'm not exactly at my best." Dane wiped the knife clean on his thigh and sheathed it again. His back hurt every time he breathed and his leg felt like it was going to buckle if he put too much weight on it. He could feel every bone fracture and blood clot.

"But I'll live."

That was all he was going to confess to, even to Lindsay. He pulled the black velvet null bag from his pocket and slid the heart into it, and tucked it into the inside pocket of his vest. "Are you well enough to walk?" He checked Lindsay over, frowning.

Lindsay nodded, and Dane could tell he was lying from the way he wobbled from that little motion. "I'm sorry," he said.

"That's fine. Get out of the alley. I have to get rid of this thing."

Dane was still blindingly angry, and it surprised him all over again. He so rarely got angry at things other than Ezqel and Cyrus these days, and the worst of it never lasted, always subsiding back to the embers of resentment and old losses. But he was furious that Lindsay had nearly gotten killed again, mostly with himself for failing to do his job. He should have known, even if Ezqel hadn't reminded him about the guul tricks, not to let Lindsay out of his reach, much less out of his sight. Rage was making his head throb.

Lindsay headed back out of the alley the way he'd come. He waited near the corner, staring at his feet, hair hanging in his face. Dane wanted to yell at him to keep his head up, but refrained. This wasn't exactly a teachable moment.

Dane took a few paces back and raised the same hand he'd raised against the demon before. Yzumrud glinted at him again in what little light there was, laughing at him for needing it once more. He spoke under his breath and the corpse imploded in a shower of green sparks and a cloud of yellow gases.

The fire was green and white, flaring so hot that the smell of melting asphalt undercut the vile smoke. When the corpse finally fell in on itself in a fresh fountain of sparks, Dane turned away. It hurt to move, but he was good at keeping his expression neutral.

"Let's go. Are you sure you're okay?"

Lindsay nodded. "I can walk." Dane could smell his blood and fear and pain, but he wasn't about to argue. He'd wait until

Lindsay wobbled enough to warrant an intervention.

"Fine." He stopped and gestured for Lindsay to go in front of him. "Go on. Least if something else steals you, I'll see it." Dane watched him struggle, too proud to ask for help. Lindsay didn't know how to ask for help, and Dane knew it.

Dane caught up in two strides, sweeping Lindsay up in his arms and ignoring how it hurt. It was better than watching. Sometimes, Lindsay could be ridiculous and it was irritating how much like Dane the boy was being at those times.

"I'm not *indulging* you," Dane muttered. That was still pissing him off. No matter what the guul had made Lindsay think, the fact remained that it was damned difficult for one of them to make someone think something they didn't believe in, at least a little.

"It feels like you do," Lindsay admitted softly. "I didn't want to be an obligation, like you had to do anything like that to keep me happy. I...want to be *wanted.* That's all." He closed his eyes, tucking his cheek against Dane's chest.

Dane pressed a kiss to his hair and tried not to get angry again. "It wasn't your fault for thinking it. Well, it wasn't your fault for being stupid about it," he said quietly. "Not completely."

"It's not?" Lindsay's face was full of such desperate hope that Dane wondered, again, what Cyrus thought he was doing giving someone so fragile to him.

"Not completely, no," Dane grumbled, any residual anger temporarily diverted by Lindsay's need to be forgiven. "Demons play with your mind. The sweet smell, it's not sweet. It's the same smell as the other one. You think it's sweet, because you know the smell of honey. Same as the way you felt that made you walk off."

Lindsay sighed, defeated, and sank into Dane's arms. "Still my fault for thinking it. It wouldn't have happened if I didn't believe it, right?" Sometimes, he was too smart for his own good.

"I should have remembered." Dane wasn't about to let

himself, or Ezqel, off the hook. "It was my fault."

"But..." Lindsay started, but fell silent when Dane glared at him. He pressed his cheek to Dane's chest and gave Dane those wide eyes.

"My fault," Dane said flatly. He didn't need this ridiculousness. Right now, he needed to work out where they were so he could get them back to the hotel.

"You killed it, at least." Lindsay's stubborn little voice drifted up from under Dane's chin. He was impossible, and it made him all the more irresistible.

"Who said I don't want you?" Dane shifted so that Lindsay could be more comfortable even though his voice got more angry as he spoke. He was frustrated with both of them. "Cyrus is going to kill me for touching you at all—if I'm lucky, he'll only kill me—and you're going on about how I don't want you? Where the fuck did that idea come from?"

"You didn't seem all that...I don't know. Interested. I guess." Lindsay raised his head to peek at Dane's face. "Cyrus is going to be angry?"

"Not interested..." Dane stopped on a street corner that was barely lit by a single flickering bulb. "Cyrus is probably chewing his own hair. And I *am* interested in you."

Dane could hardly help himself. Lindsay had grace and intellect and beauty and delicacy and strength that hit all of Dane's buttons right. He was everything Dane wasn't, and so perfectly made. What the hell did Lindsay want, poetry? Getting out of that kind of thing should have been an advantage to being with a man, and Lindsay was definitely a man, even if he was still green and new to it.

Dane set Lindsay on his feet and held his shoulders so that Lindsay had to look at him. "Asking what you want doesn't mean I'm not interested. Where'd you get that idea?"

"It just..." Lindsay closed his eyes. "I don't know. I didn't want you to be...tolerating me, or something. And when you asked... I thought if you were really interested in me, it would sound different."

Dane wanted to bang his head on the lamppost, except that his head already hurt. “Maybe I am indulging you,” he admitted. His hands were filthy, so he used the back of the cleanest one to push Lindsay’s lank hair back from his smudged face. “It’s nothing I don’t want. What’s wrong with being indulged? What’s wrong with someone giving you what you need? Sometimes it can fix things nothing else can.”

Lindsay bowed his head. “I didn’t want it to be like…” Dane could guess the rest of that sentence. *…like his parents, being civil to him out of duty instead of love.*

“This is now. That’s what I’m trying to tell you, with everything. This is not then.” Dane dropped his head to nuzzle Lindsay’s nose with his own. “This is a different life.”

Lindsay tipped his head up, eyes closed. He was so young, far too young to be starting over, but here they were. Even if Lindsay had lived all his years free, he would have been inexperienced, next to Dane. In spite of all the terrible things that had been done to him, Lindsay was so innocent, ignorant of so much good as well as so much of the evil in the world. All Dane wanted was to make sure that Lindsay learned the best of things first.

“It’s over,” Dane reminded him, instead of saying what he wanted to say, for fear of sounding patronizing. “Your mother wouldn’t even know your face. She’ll depend on the kindness of strangers until she dies. You nearly killed your father from hundreds of miles away. You could do it again.” Dane nudged Lindsay under the chin with a knuckle, making Lindsay open his eyes. “Your life now. Say what you need.”

Lindsay hesitated for a long moment. “You.”

Dane was a tired, hurt animal, but the answer made him smile, made him warm in places he hadn’t remembered he could be warm. He should have told Lindsay to pick something better, something more useful, something more beautiful, something less broken. He couldn’t. What he wanted wasn’t worth considering here, but he wanted this. “Then you’ll have me.” He pulled Lindsay to him and kissed Lindsay’s soft mouth.

Resting his hands against Dane's chest, Lindsay opened up to the kiss, yielding so easily. "I'm sorry," he whispered when he could speak, his lips warm against Dane's.

"I can't always be there to make sure you survive your mistakes. Or mine." Dane scooped Lindsay up again and started walking. "If you're sorry, make smaller mistakes. So will I. Okay?"

Lindsay nodded, snuggling up against Dane's chest. "I'll try," he promised.

"You're a fast learner." Dane laughed quietly. He could smell Lindsay's sweetness under the muck and smoke and the musk of other men. "But I might have to put you over my knee if you don't hurry up."

"No, thank you," Lindsay muttered, stretching up to butt his nose against Dane's chin. "I won't run away from you again."

"Good." Dane turned up a street that was better lit and they passed people who gave them odd looks. "We'll get a cab soon," he promised. "Get you back to the hotel and you'll feel better."

Lindsay tucked his head against Dane's shoulder, closing his eyes again. Nothing hurt anymore. Dane's blood bubbled with the satisfaction, however muted, of a kill, and the pure pleasure of being claimed. He could have walked the whole way back without a second thought except that he didn't want to make Lindsay wait to get clean. It wasn't only concern for the grubby little bunny, though. Dane wanted to get the smell of other men off of what was his.

Eventually, Dane managed to hail a cab, though it took a handful of money waved at the driver to get him to stop. Even in the cab, he didn't let Lindsay go. It eased Dane's pain to have Lindsay in his arms, warm and alive and safe.

When the cab stopped, Lindsay opened his eyes and raised his head. "We're back at the hotel," Dane murmured, and Lindsay closed his eyes again.

In the room, Dane finally put Lindsay down, tucking him

into a plush chair so he could put away the demon heart. Lindsay yawned hugely and rested his cheek against the back of the chair. There was color under the dirt on his face. The little sleep had done him a world of good. "How's your back?"

"Stings," Lindsay murmured, pulling his feet into the chair and curling up. "Are you all right?"

Dane would feel better when he wasn't carrying around body parts from an animal he didn't plan to eat. From his suitcase, he got the black and silver box that Ezqel had given him for the heart. The black bag that held the heart was still hot, but it hadn't leaked any blood into Dane's pocket. Dane tucked it carefully into the padded box, taking the time to knot the strings of the bag seven times.

"I'm fine. Wouldn't have been a problem except for the dying thing."

Dane took the knife from the sheath under his vest and laid it into the lid of the box where it fit perfectly into an indentation there and glowed blue as the box locked. Once the light faded, he put the box in his suitcase. He started to take off the damned ring and pushed it back onto his finger with a sigh. They might need it again.

"I'm sorry you got hurt. And that I couldn't help. Again." Lindsay frowned. The little scowl was rather endearing, really.

"Getting hurt is what I do." Dane peeled off his vest; when he let Lindsay see him, the last of the scars were still visible. "I get over it. Nice that you care. Thanks." His tone was dry, but he meant the words. He was unaccustomed to the sentiment and it made him feel awkward, as though Lindsay's concern was a coat several sizes too small for him to wear.

"Can you do it a little less?" Lindsay tilted his head. "You're a fast learner..."

Dane stopped getting undressed and glared at Lindsay a long moment before he laughed. "Smartass." Lindsay looked unrepentant as he laughed as well, wretched little brat that he was. It was good to hear him laugh. The animal in Dane couldn't think beyond the moment and the man didn't want to.

Nothing could be wrong in his world when Lindsay laughed like that.

"Come on." Dane kicked off his boots. "We both stink."

Dane's pants were the next to go, and Lindsay was sure Dane could smell the lust that surged in him. He'd seen Dane naked a few times, but the wonder hadn't faded. Dane was gorgeous. As he stood up, though, his lust was dampened by the pain from his back that made him wince and hiss in a breath. "Let me just..." He started unbuttoning his shirt, his fingers awkward and slow.

"Let me." Dane was right there, though Lindsay hadn't heard him cross the room. He ran one hand over Lindsay's hair, so gently. With the other hand, he hooked a claw in the opening of Lindsay's shirt and drew it to the hem. The fabric parted with a whisper and the shirt fell open.

Lindsay stared at his torn, stained shirt. It took a moment for it to sink in that Dane had sliced it open and his razor-sharp claw hadn't touched Lindsay's skin at all. "Oh," he breathed. "Thank you."

"Don't think you'll be wearing it again." Dane pushed the shirt back from Lindsay's shoulders, his warm palms skimming Lindsay's skin, and let it fall. "It's not really you anyway." His long hair brushed Lindsay's cheek and he pressed a gentle kiss to Lindsay's temple. "Let me help with the rest?"

Lindsay nodded. He hurt too much to be able to get his clothes off nearly as quickly as Dane could and, if he was totally honest with himself, the show of control was intensely arousing. "Please. I think I like it when you help." He had little hope of being less than honest with Dane.

"I noticed." Dane sniffed playfully in the hair over Lindsay's ear before he sank to his knees and unlaced Lindsay's boots.

It was such an unfamiliar pose to see Dane in, but Lindsay was beginning to understand that those kinds of things didn't matter to Dane. He was beginning to understand a lot of things about Dane that he hadn't grasped before. Dane had almost died for him—*again*—and Lindsay knew now that these weren't isolated incidents. Dane would do anything he could to keep Lindsay safe. Lindsay hoped that someday he'd deserve that kind of devotion.

Lindsay let Dane help him strip, swallowing hard as he felt the brush of Dane's claws against his skin. His clothes fell to the floor. God, that was really hot. After everything that had happened tonight, he should've been curled up in the corner, shaking and terrified. Instead, Dane's care and touches soothed him and let him move past the fear. Dane couldn't fix everything, Lindsay knew, but he could fix a lot by being who he was and caring about Lindsay.

Dane stood, running his hands up Lindsay's thighs and hips as he did, and all the way up Lindsay's body to cup his face. The touches left a trail of heat in their wake. Lindsay felt like he was burning up, and Dane hadn't even kissed him yet.

Just like the walk back to the hotel, Dane scooped Lindsay up and carried him to the bathroom, only this time, Lindsay was awake and aware enough to enjoy it. He gave Dane sweet kisses and soaked up the warmth and the feeling of being cared for. Wanted. Dane *wanted* him.

Dane settled on the edge of the big, deep tub and turned on the water, still holding Lindsay to him with one arm. His expression was definitely troubled and, though they were both filthy from the fight with the guul, when Dane picked up a washcloth and wet it, it was Lindsay's face he washed first.

Lindsay closed his eyes and didn't move while Dane washed his face. When the cloth moved away, Lindsay opened his eyes again. "What's wrong?"

"Nothing now." Dane kissed his forehead. "Wanted that stuff off your face." The unhappiness was fading from his expression as he studied Lindsay's clean face. "To see you."

"Oh." Lindsay couldn't help but smile. He felt warm through at the idea that Dane liked looking at him—at *him*. Leaning in, he nudged his nose against Dane's chin and kissed him lightly on the mouth. "It's me now."

Dane rumbled, a happy noise, and nuzzled against Lindsay's cheek and neck. He huffed softly there, like a sigh, and then patted Lindsay's hip. "Into the tub." The hot water was getting deeper, swirling around the curves of the tub and sucking at Lindsay's feet as he stepped in. "Izia packed some salves," Dane said, letting go once Lindsay was steady. "I'll see to your back."

"Why didn't I pass out this time? I mean, I used my magic—or tried to, at least. It felt like he was...eating it up, like it wasn't *doing* anything. But why didn't I...?"

"You never got to use it." Dane came padding back in with a couple small jars in one hand. He stopped to get more washcloths and some hand towels from above the sink. "The guul took your magic before you could use it and hurt yourself with it. The magic is in you all the time, like your blood, but quiet. When you drew on it, you made it easier for the guul to take. Whatever was left, you couldn't use enough to do any damage." He stepped into the tub and nudged Lindsay forward, sitting down behind him.

"So I shouldn't have tried to use my magic at all." Even when Lindsay wanted to help, he failed. "It didn't do me any good at all, did it?"

"Not you." Dane caught Lindsay around the waist with a big hand and pulled him back. Lindsay found himself leaning on Dane, his cheek against Dane's chest, while Dane rinsed the muck and gravel from his wounded shoulder. "While it was feeding on you, I had some time to heal."

Lindsay nodded, cheek sliding against the soft, thick fur on Dane's chest. "I don't want to be so helpless anymore."

"You need to keep your head up, to start." It burned when Dane was washing, but he stopped and, after trying to identify the next sensations, Lindsay realized that Dane was plucking debris from the scrapes. "You could get mugged by a lamppost, the way you go around." A kiss on the nape of Lindsay's neck took some of the sting out of the words.

"I'll do better."

"That's all I want." Dane kissed his hair. The longer Dane worked, the better Lindsay felt, especially when Dane put Izia's salves on his throbbing arm and torn back. By the time Dane set the jars aside, the wounds of the evening were fading into nothing but a dull ache and the itch of healing skin.

Lindsay rested and snuggled Dane as best he could while Dane washed his hair. When Dane shifted him aside and moved on to washing his own hair, Lindsay picked up the cloth Dane had used on his face and washed the rest of his body. When he was finished washing himself, he wriggled around in the tub, sloshing water up the sides, to wash Dane, too. It was his fault Dane was all grimy and dirty, after all. And Lindsay wasn't going to pass up the opportunity to touch.

The grooming made Dane purr and he sank to rest his head on the edge of the tub, twisting his long hair up and out of the way of the cloth. Other than that, he was passive and relaxed—all Lindsay's.

Lindsay washed Dane's face last, and once it was clean, he leaned in to rub his cheek against Dane's. Feeling Dane's skin sliding against his own was as intimate as a kiss.

The gesture got him a warm purr and a nuzzle in return, and Dane's big hands sliding across his back as Dane pulled him in close. "Thank you," Dane murmured in his ear.

"It was my pleasure." Settling his body against Dane's in the warm water, Lindsay drew back enough to kiss him on the mouth.

"I know." Dane's voice had that teasing growl, and Lindsay could feel him smile before he kissed Lindsay again. This time, the kiss was less gentle, more open, and Dane left one hand on Lindsay's hip while he got the other in Lindsay's hair to keep him near.

Lindsay pressed himself up to Dane, skin on skin, and flicked his tongue along Dane's lips. This close, he could feel everything, and the warm water surrounding them made their bodies slide against each other like silk.

Dane's hand in his hair tightened as Dane kissed him hard

enough that Lindsay felt the edge of his fangs, how sharp and long they were. Dane's claws brushed against the nape of his neck too, all the little hints that he was in the hands of someone who was barely human at the best of times. And yet Dane was so careful with him. There was a ripple of tension in Dane's body and a low rumble in Dane's chest, yet he was still safe.

Lindsay moaned and rocked his body against Dane's, feeling the proof that Dane wanted him as much as he wanted Dane. That got Lindsay a low growl and Dane's fingers slipping between his ass cheeks. Dane nipped his lower lip and kissed him harder. Arching into the touches, Lindsay moaned again. "*Dane.*"

"Bed." Dane followed the word with another kiss before he pulled back. "I want you in bed," he said roughly, nudging Lindsay's cheek with his nose.

It took a moment for the words to register. "Yes." Lindsay slid back off Dane's lap, out of Dane's arms, and stood up. Once he was out of the tub, he held his hand out to Dane. "Come to bed with me."

Dane let Lindsay draw him out of the bathroom. The lights were out, but the moonlight trickling in through the open balcony doors washed everything in a thin coat of white. They were still sleek and wet, but it was a hot night. Even the breeze making the gauze drapes dance like ghosts was warm. When they got to the bed, Dane bent to kiss Lindsay again, one hand in the small of Lindsay's back to pull him close.

Lindsay slipped away after one kiss and fell onto the bed. He sprawled out, damp skin sticking to the soft sheets, and smiled up at Dane. The way Dane was looking at him was like one of his fantasies come to life, and it sent a thrill of pure pleasure through Lindsay's body. Dane wanted him.

Dane's growl was definitely predatory, a low thrum that sent a shiver up Lindsay's spine. Dane crawled onto the bed and over Lindsay, inspecting him carefully in the low light. Lindsay could make out his expression clearly, couldn't miss the way Dane's tongue flickered over his fangs before he growled again. Dane nudged the hollow of Lindsay's hip with his nose, breathing in Lindsay's scent, and his hot tongue washed across Lindsay's balls.

Lindsay's breath caught in his throat and he arched, legs falling open. Dane's feral behavior only turned Lindsay on more, reminded him how much Dane wanted him.

Dane's tongue was slightly rough and it felt incredible as he tongue-bathed Lindsay's balls and licked up the shaft of his cock. Dane's hands were all over him too, stroking his thighs and spreading him open. Dane purred as he licked at the head of Lindsay's cock, pleased with whatever he tasted there.

"Dane..." Lindsay couldn't keep from writhing. He wanted more, everything, anything Dane would give him.

Dane kept moving up Lindsay's body. His inspection was thorough, but not slow. Soon, he was nipping and licking Lindsay's nipples, then kissing up to Lindsay's mouth. All the way up Lindsay's body, his hands left hot trails of pleasure everywhere he touched. Dane's rough breathing and all his little noises sounded so aroused and possessive. When he finally kissed Lindsay on the mouth again, he laid his body over Lindsay's, covering him.

"Please." Lindsay licked at Dane's mouth, desperate, pleading licks, trying to tempt Dane into more.

"Yes." Lindsay felt the word as much as heard it, hissed against his mouth. Dane kissed him recklessly, sharp teeth and all, before pulling away with a harsh exhalation as though it hurt him to do it. "Stay." He pressed another kiss to Lindsay's mouth. "Like that." Dane wasn't gone long, rolling out of bed to pad over to his bag. He returned with something he'd dug out of it and slid into bed beside Lindsay, pulling him close with a rumble. "Tell me what you want." He didn't make it easy to think, the way he kissed Lindsay's neck.

"Fuck me," Lindsay managed. He couldn't think of anything he wanted more than to feel Dane inside him like that.

Dane's response was to bite him on the neck with a growl, sliding his body over Lindsay's so that his cock rode against

Lindsay's thigh. He stopped biting before his teeth did any damage, and whispered, "Good."

*Good.* Yes, so, so good. Lindsay shuddered and swallowed back another plea for more. "Yes."

Dane pushed Lindsay's legs apart with one of his and Lindsay heard the familiar sound of a lid coming off a jar of some kind of salve. He was mustering up enough thought to wonder what it was when Dane bit him gently again, under his jaw where it was soft and vulnerable, and then Dane's slick fingers were stroking behind his balls.

Lindsay's hands found Dane's shoulders and the back of his neck. "God, Dane," he managed, when Dane's fingers slid over his hole. "I want..."

"Soon." Dane slowly pressed a finger into Lindsay as he trailed kisses over Lindsay's chest and rolled to kneel between Lindsay's thighs.

Lindsay breathed through the strangeness of it. Dane touched that place inside him that made him want to writhe. "Dane," he gasped. "Oh God, *Dane.*" There wasn't any room for worry, here, only pleasure and need and the heat building up in Lindsay's belly, already threatening to spill out.

Dane purred and didn't stop, pushing Lindsay further and further into a place where there was no room for thought. His fingers filled Lindsay up more, stroking inside him exactly where he needed to feel it.

"Please. Dane, fuck me. I want."

Dane was there, kissing Lindsay gently on the mouth and stroking his hair, soothing him. When Dane pulled his fingers out, there was an almost unbearable moment of *nothing* and then the heat of Dane's slick cock sliding into him.

"Patience," Dane said, his voice thick with need. He was moving so slowly, letting Lindsay take him in.

Oh. "Oh, fuck," Lindsay breathed. Dane's fingers had been nothing compared to this. Lindsay could feel his body opening up for Dane, and it felt amazing. He wanted more, faster, now, but Dane's kisses kept him from begging with anything more than soft whimpers.

"Good," Dane murmured, as Lindsay gave in to being patient. Finally, he was deep inside Lindsay, his heavy body pressing Lindsay into the soft bed and protecting him from the world at once. "Better now?"

"Yes." But Lindsay wanted more, so much more. "No. I want. *Move.*" He showed Dane what he wanted, tilting his hips and tightening his body around Dane's cock. The sensations surprised him—how much more full and tight it made him feel—and he gasped out a soft moan.

Dane made a noise that was halfway between a laugh and a purr. "Yes," he said, nudging his nose against Lindsay's. He pulled back slowly and slid in again, letting Lindsay feel all of him this time. He set a lazy pace that was almost too slow except for the way he pushed in so deep at the end of each thrust, making Lindsay moan every time.

Dane seemed indifferent to his own pleasure. When Lindsay managed to focus, Dane was watching him, fixated, and smiling. It was such a rare expression for him, and so gentle. "Better now?" he teased, softening it with a kiss.

"I want..." Lindsay swallowed another moan when Dane moved again. "Want it to be good for you."

"It is." Dane kissed him again, hot and slow this time, pressing their bodies close. "Perfect." His voice was so raw and human right now. "I forgot how good it could be like this."

Dane wanting this—wanting him—was more important than anything else. "So good," Lindsay agreed, losing himself in the pleasure again as Dane moved with more urgency, fucking him harder instead of simply moving to let him feel the sensations of it all. Lindsay shuddered and arched into Dane's thrusts, crying out as heat flashed through him and come spattered Dane's hand and his own belly.

"I like that," Dane purred. "It's so good. I could eat you up." He groaned as he fucked Lindsay hard, shudders running through him with each thrust.

It was everything and nothing like Lindsay had thought it

would be. The way Dane felt, pushing into him fast and hard, the way he sounded, the way he looked—Lindsay's imagination couldn't have come up with something so perfectly beautiful and fascinating. Something so addictive. Lindsay wanted to feel like this—wanted to be the one to make Dane feel like this—again and again.

Dane kissed Lindsay like he really was trying to eat him up, hard and hungry. His rhythm faltered at last and he came with one rush after another.

As Dane relaxed, Lindsay threaded his fingers into Dane's hair and pulled him in for more kisses. Dane rubbed his cheek against Lindsay's and hummed softly, relaxed and contented. Lying down, he drew Lindsay into his arms and curled around him. He settled Lindsay's head on his shoulder and kissed Lindsay's temple and cheek and mouth, purring.

Lindsay snuggled up in the warmth of Dane's body and closed his eyes. The world hadn't seemed this right and full of hope since he'd walked into that room at Ezqel's house and found Dane sleeping in the bed, alive. Lindsay hadn't felt this good and right *ever*.

"Sleep now," Dane rumbled. "Tomorrow, rest." He kissed Lindsay's hair and huffed softly. "You need more than all this mess."

He tugged the covers up and tucked them both in, warm and safe. It was better than any dream, so good that Lindsay clung to being awake as long as he possibly could. As he drifted off, he could feel that Dane was still awake, watching him fall asleep.

# Chapter Ten

The next day, after Lindsay had finally woken, Dane insisted they were still on vacation. Lindsay was pretty sure that Cyrus didn't think anything of the sort and that Dane was going to get in even more trouble, but Dane didn't seem in the mood to hear it. He led Lindsay out to the pool and covered him from head to toe in sunscreen, muttering direly about how pale Lindsay was and how likely he was to burn, and then sprawled out on a two-person lounge chair and promptly fell asleep in the sun.

Lindsay felt a ridiculous surge of affection for him right then. Dane had probably hardly slept all night, watching over him. In the light of day, Dane could get some sleep, knowing Lindsay was well.

Eventually, Lindsay made his way into the pool. The water felt warm to his cool skin, though not as warm as the bath the night before. Some of the pool's other occupants were splashing around in one corner, laughing and having fun. Others were swimming in lanes on the far side, showing off their bodies and athleticism. Lindsay watched both for a while, then rolled onto his back and floated, basking in the warmth.

He was relaxed, for once. Content. There were marks on his skin from Dane's hands and mouth, and the swimming trunks he'd bought from the hotel gift shop did little to hide any of them. At least Izia's salve had made the wounds from the guul fade. Lindsay hadn't used it on the marks from Dane. Up in their room, Lindsay had stood in front of the mirror, behind the closed bathroom door, and just stared at himself for a long time. In the pool, he floated with his arms outstretched, careless of what anyone thought of his body or his scars or the marks of his sex with Dane.

He liked the way he looked, like this, and he knew Dane liked it too. He remembered what Kristan had said, that Dane had rolled over and gone to sleep after having sex with her. That wasn't what Dane had done last night. It was that, even more than the sex itself, that Lindsay would keep replaying in his mind.

Rolling himself upright, he climbed out of the pool and padded over to Dane's lounge chair. He toweled off, crawled up beside Dane and, after a moment's hesitation, snuggled up close. Dane wouldn't mind.

"Where'd you swim, the ice bucket?" Dane grumped, shifting to get his arm around Lindsay. He wasn't at all shy about their relationship, whatever it was, even now. Maybe being huge and terrifying made it easier.

"Fuck you," Lindsay muttered, but a thread of pleasure wound through his tone. "I'm always cold."

"Brat." Dane groped Lindsay's ass in what had to be an affectionate gesture, especially given where his fingers were slipping. "Thought you liked it the other way around."

"Keep that up," Lindsay murmured, "and we'll both find out how much I like it in public." He was already getting hard.

Dane laughed, but shifted his hand to cup the curve of Lindsay's ass and moved his whole body so he could duck his head and nuzzle Lindsay's nose with his own. "Would I do that to you?" The wind picked up and pulled Dane's hair around, tickling Lindsay's cheek with it.

Lindsay arched one eyebrow, a smile tugging at his lips. "Maybe."

"Only if you wanted it," Dane pointed out, his voice uncharacteristically tender. The wind grabbed at Dane's hair again, even though the canvas sides of the cabanas around the pool hung still. Dane tensed and raised his head, listening.

Lindsay couldn't see anything different than when he'd walked up to Dane's chair a few moments before. "What is it?" he asked softly.

"Just listen." Dane lay back again, but the tension didn't leave his body. "Cyrus..." The wind curled around them and a voice came with it.

"Moore is awake," the wind said. "She has sent her people to find you where the dog was last seen. It was the girl who held the dog's leash for Moore while she slept. The girl sent the dog into the forest. The girl has not been seen. No one knows what has become of her." The voice was definitely Cyrus, but hollow and thin with distance, spilling into their ears alone. "This dalliance can wait until Ezqel has what he sent you for and the boy is healed. No more wasting time."

Dane made a discontented noise.

"Go quickly. Vivian and I can do nothing if Moore's people catch up to you there." The wind sighed against Dane's cheek, in his hair, and there were no words left in it, just a caress. Then the air was still again.

Lindsay had thought Moore was dead. He'd killed them all. He remembered that, from the mirror. So many bodies. Maybe she had been. Lindsay couldn't count on death to be the end of anyone, anymore. "Who is the girl? Cyrus mentioned her before."

"They call her 'the girl' because she was so young when she started. Younger than you. Her name is Lourdes. I knew her once. She's a mind mage, and a good one. Too bad for everyone that she ended up where she did." Dane sat up, bringing Lindsay up with him. "The sooner we get this sorted, the sooner Cyrus and Vivian are out of danger."

"I'll go pack," Lindsay murmured, picking up his towel. He played with it between his hands, feeling sick with fear. Would Jonas be back? Was Lourdes going to find him?

"It won't take long to get there." Dane's hands were warm on Lindsay's shoulders and arms. "Breathe. We're leaving. This is all we can do right now."

The flight from Mexico to Zurich was tense. Whenever he could, Lindsay found himself pushing up the armrest between their seats and sliding over to tuck himself against Dane.

Of course, the fear only got worse once they landed. The airport was crowded. Was Lourdes one of the nameless strangers surrounding them? He made himself stop clinging to Dane's hand, but he stayed close, fingers clenched tight around the shoulder straps of his backpack.

He'd never imagined wanting to rush back to Ezqel's cottage. What he'd gone through last time should have been enough to keep him away now, but the promise of being fixed and the threat of people like Jonas and Lourdes coming after him were enough to drown out any fear of repeating Ezqel's tests.

This time, they approached the forest from the village that had been at the end of the path they'd taken on their way out before. As they left the village behind in the falling dusk and trudged through the muck and a thin sheet of snow, a slim shadow broke away from the trees and came hurrying toward them. When the wind tugged the figure's hood back, it was easy to see that it was Taniel, robe clenched in his hands to keep it out of the muck.

"There you are. I feared you would not get this far. Izia is watching the other path for you. Quickly, come." He looked wild-eyed, like a frightened rabbit.

Dane grabbed Lindsay's hand and drew him along faster. "Have they come this far?"

"There are many hunters in the forest." Taniel beckoned them to follow. "Hunters coming into Ezqel's forest, but hunting nothing living there."

"I'm sorry," Dane said flatly. His expression was closed, but his eyes were hot with anger.

"Are they hunting Jonas?" Lindsay asked quietly. "Or are they hunting me?"

"Does it matter?" Taniel gave Lindsay an apologetic smile.

"Either outcome is to your disadvantage, and the events alone anger Ezqel. Trespassers in his forest are like ants on his skin, night and day." Turning back to watch his step, Taniel murmured a spell that could be felt on the air.

Lindsay frowned. He hadn't realized the forest was so closely connected to Ezqel, though he saw now that he should have. The paths, the rules, everything pointed to the forest being more to Ezqel than a simple patch of trees. "I'm sorry," he said, echoing Dane.

"You are not responsible for the evil of others," Taniel said simply. "It is good to see you again, regardless."

"And you," Lindsay said, surprised to realize he meant it. "Thank you."

Ezqel's house was warm and dim when Taniel ushered them in the side garden door. The smell of something cooking—a rich stew, perhaps, and maybe bread—was on the air. "He will want to see you first," Taniel said. "And the item you have brought him. Later, I would like to hear of how you obtained it." His eyes were bright at the prospect of adding to his prodigious store of knowledge.

Lindsay frowned. "May as well share the tale of my stupidity," he muttered. He was terribly nervous about seeing Ezqel again, and about how the hunters might have affected Ezqel's mood. The old mage hadn't been particularly personable before, and Lindsay wasn't looking forward to finding out what he was like in a bad mood.

Dane slid his pack from his shoulder and opened it up. He had to crouch and dig through, but he found the box and offered it to Lindsay. "Here. You should take it to him. It is your healing, after all."

Lindsay swallowed. "I don't suppose he could do it from a distance?" he asked hopefully, taking the box and holding it carefully. He traced the lines of the ornate knife set into the lid with his thumb.

Dane reached out and put a hand on Lindsay's leg. "It

won't be the same if I come with you. Some things, you have to do alone."

"I know." Lindsay tore his gaze away from the box and looked at Dane instead. "Thank you."

"You already survived the worst." Dane gave him a smile. "You're here. Go on. I won't be far, but you won't need me."

Lindsay mustered up a smile for Dane. He glanced at Taniel one more time, then turned and headed for the room where he'd seen Ezqel last.

Ezqel was at his desk, and looked up as Lindsay came in. "You have it. This is good." He held out his hand. "Bring it here."

Lindsay came closer, but slowly. He stretched out to put the box in Ezqel's hand, not wanting to get any closer than he had to. He knew that Ezqel's tests had been necessary, but that didn't make him feel any more comfortable with the old man.

"You'll have to get over that," Ezqel said, not looking at Lindsay. "This thing I am doing for you, it requires you to trust me. Do you even know what will be happening to you? Aren't you even curious?"

"No," Lindsay whispered. "I don't know what you're going to do to me." It wasn't as though he'd had any chance to ask Ezqel about it; Ezqel had been too busy making him relive the most hellish moments of his life. "Will knowing make me trust you more?"

"Maybe. Maybe not. What do you think? Do you care what I'm going to do?" Ezqel tilted his head curiously, waiting.

"I'm not sure," Lindsay admitted. "As long as it works. I don't want to be broken anymore." He took a deep breath. "Will it be like last time?"

"No." Ezqel put the box down and folded his hands over it. "This was a young demon. About the same age as you, at least in its own years. You were fortunate to be in the same time and place as this one. Its magic will help heal you. The heart will draw your magic out, as it did when the guul was hunting you. For a moment, it will be like the heart of your magic. We are putting you on bypass so I can undo the damage without hurting you. And then we will see..."

"See what?" Lindsay stared at Ezqel.

"We will see how well you heal. We will see if you recover completely. It will be an interesting thing to watch." Ezqel smiled. "Watching things grow always interests me."

"It won't get worse than it is now, will it?"

"It will only get better." Ezqel shook his head slowly. "You can only get better if the past is put in the past."

Lindsay nodded. "All right. I guess I'm ready whenever you are." He wasn't, but he might never be ready. He wanted to be fixed, and Cyrus and Dane wouldn't have sent him here if they didn't think it would work.

"You could do something for me, though." Ezqel took up his pen. "A personal favor."

Lindsay pulled his hands up into his sleeves. "What is it?"

"Get Dane to stop being a fool. Tell him to let me help him." Ezqel looked at Lindsay askance. "I thought he'd be done by now, but apparently not." He tapped the box. "This will work on both of you—magic is simply magic, like water is water—but he won't tell you that. He knows it, and I know it, and now you know it. So, I leave it in your capable hands. He has to be conscious, or I'd simply have Taniel club him senseless with a fire iron."

"I can try." Lindsay turned toward the door, half-expecting Dane to be standing there, watching him.

"Isn't there some saying—do not try, only do?" Ezqel gave Lindsay an arch look. "If you succeed where Cyrus and Vivian and others have failed, then perhaps it will be to your benefit. Consider that."

"I don't know that I have any more influence over Dane than they do," Lindsay murmured. "I doubt that I do." He shrugged. "But I will try. We talked about his magic, once." And not since.

"You could be stronger than you allow yourself to be." Ezqel went back to writing. "Consider that, as well."

Lindsay frowned. "What do you mean?"

"I mean exactly what I said." Ezqel didn't look up. "To do otherwise would be to waste my words."

Ezqel and Cyrus were peas in a pod. No wonder they were friends.

Lindsay found Dane in a huge armchair in the sitting room below the guest loft, reading a large book by lamplight. The cat, displaced, dozed on the high mantel, its tail dangling above the yellow flames. The natural light softened Dane's features and brought out the red tones in his hair. Lindsay's chest was tight with seeing him there.

He glanced up a moment after Lindsay came in. "You seem to have survived," he rumbled.

"He hasn't touched me yet," Lindsay returned dryly. He came over to curl up on the floor near Dane's feet, rubbing his cheek against Dane's knee. It felt good and he was quiet a while to enjoy it before ruining everything. Waiting only made him more nervous, though, so he spoke before Dane could ask what was wrong just from smelling his anxiety. "You didn't tell me the heart would fix you too."

There was a thump as Dane closed the book. "Wasn't relevant. He didn't have any damn business..."

"Any business doing what? I know you don't like being stuck. I could hear it in your voice when you were telling me about it before. Why wouldn't you want him to help you?"

"Any business getting you involved in my business." Dane shook his head and put the book aside. "It's not your trouble." He crossed his arms over his chest and stared into the fire flickering in the hearth. "I manage as I am."

"What happened to all the pep talks you gave me about how important it was to have full use of my magic?" Lindsay didn't know if Dane was being stubborn now, or if Dane had been simply manipulating him before. He was hoping for the former, but he didn't understand it.

"That was for you." Dane relented some and reached out to stroke Lindsay's hair. "Your magic is important. Ezqel just wants to win an argument we started before you were born."

It was ridiculous how much being petted helped soothe Lindsay's worries. He crawled up into Dane's lap and frowned at Dane. "How do you know yours isn't? Is winning the argument really so important that you would rather have that than all of your magic?"

"Yes." Dane shrugged, looking utterly unapologetic. "And I know what I am. There are advantages to being freed from being human anyway." He stroked Lindsay's cheek. "Don't worry about the affairs of old men."

Lindsay's eyes slipped shut. "I know what you are too," he murmured, turning into the touch, brushing kisses across Dane's palm. "And I know that your magic is more important than whatever Ezqel did to piss you off." He opened his eyes again, meeting Dane's. "I know that I need you." Not that he expected *that* to make a difference, but he had to say it anyway.

Dane's expression didn't shift for a long moment, but then he drew Lindsay to him for a tender kiss. "I begged him once, and he refused me," he said against Lindsay's lips. "Long, long before you were born."

Lindsay couldn't imagine making Dane beg for anything. It hurt, the thought that Dane would have begged Ezqel for help and been refused. That only intensified his dislike of the fae mage.

"Hasn't he begged you to let him help, now?" Lindsay asked, snuggling closer. Nothing mattered but Dane being well. "Isn't that what this is? Doesn't it mean anything that he wants to help enough that he asked me to help you?"

"This is part of a game. He offered to help me when we were here before, and I said no. He hates to be refused, for all that he refused me." Dane stroked Lindsay's hair back. "He thinks he'll win if you get me to say yes." He kissed Lindsay, and Lindsay leaned into it, trying to get close and begging with his mouth.

*Please. I need you.* Lindsay slid his hands into Dane's hair and pressed kisses up under Dane's chin. He licked at the roughness of Dane's beard over his golden skin, doing everything he could remember animals doing to show submission. "He can't win if you're not playing the game," he murmured, dragging his mouth along the line of Dane's jaw.

"It's not a game to me anymore." Dane pulled back and looked at him for a long time, his big hands framing Lindsay's face, so long that Lindsay began to blush in spite of himself. "If it's what you need, it's done." At last, Dane drew him in and kissed him again, as though there was no one else in the world, much less in the house.

The intensity made Lindsay moan and arch against Dane. He slid his hands over Dane's chest, but Dane's shirt kept him from touching skin. Frustrated, he tugged until the shirt buttons gave way and let him slide his hands underneath. The touches got him soft growls and Dane's tongue slicking through his mouth like he couldn't get enough of Lindsay's taste.

Taniel's cheerful voice preceded him into the room. "Dinner is ready. The two of you must be...hungry."

Lindsay froze, then pulled back from the kisses to see Dane's face.

Dane was smiling, slow and wolfish. "I'm hungry," he admitted, but his eyes were on Lindsay and the light in them had nothing to do with food. Lindsay knew his cheeks were on fire, but Dane's expression was worth any embarrassment. "Thanks. We'll be right there." Dane leaned forward and caught Lindsay's mouth with his own, kissing him without shame or hesitation.

"I'll set your places, then." Taniel didn't miss a beat. His robe swished and the sound of his sandals on the stone floor faded into the kitchen noises.

Lindsay all but melted against Dane, reassured by his response. Dane had kissed him in public before, but Lindsay hadn't been sure how to act in front of people who knew Dane, important people. Then Dane went and acted as though Lindsay was the only person in the world who really mattered. For a moment, Lindsay felt that important. He licked back into Dane's mouth to suck lightly at his tongue, a tease and a reward at once.

Dane slid his arms around Lindsay and held him close, like he was indulging himself as much as Lindsay in the hot, slow kiss. He didn't seem to be in any hurry to end it, but he finally pulled away. "You need to eat," he said, his voice soft and heavy with affection. "It's been a long day. And you need your strength."

Lindsay didn't want to leave this perfect moment. That he hadn't eaten anything but an energy bar since they'd left the airport hardly registered, but he knew Dane was right, so he pressed a quick kiss to Dane's lips and slid back off his lap. He could behave responsibly.

Once Lindsay was up, Dane put an arm around his shoulders and led him into the kitchen. Taniel and Izia were already there, and the food was all on the table.

"Thank you for sharing your meal," Dane said, and it sounded almost formal. He pulled Lindsay's chair out for him and waited for Lindsay to sit.

"Thank you," Lindsay echoed, slipping into the chair. He fought a blush when he realized that Taniel kept glancing at him when he thought Lindsay wasn't looking. He couldn't help but wonder what Taniel was thinking.

Dinner was delicious, but very quiet. Dane ate like he was starving, putting food away with mechanical efficiency. Taniel ate surprisingly little, and Izia had her nose in a medical journal when she wasn't buttering her bread or reaching for more stew. Lindsay ate slowly, but he ate.

After dinner, Taniel collected his dishes. "Ezqel will be working all night, I expect. He said to tell you to make yourself at home indoors and in the gardens, but not beyond, until he is ready to see you again." He gave Lindsay a smile as he turned away.

"Thank you." Lindsay remembered seeing the gardens as he'd walked out of the forest, the last time they'd been here, but he hadn't explored them at all. Maybe he would do that later. "Is there anything else I should do to prepare for...whatever he's going to do to me?"

"Rest," Izia said, glancing up from her reading. "And don't use your magic. You'll need all your energy for the ritual." She gave Dane a pointed look that slid to where Lindsay had undone his shirt.

Dane looked unapologetic as he reached for more bread. He picked up a butter knife and shrugged at Izia.

"I can hardly use my magic anyway." Lindsay ignored the implication of the way Izia had looked at Dane. He didn't need to touch his magic, but touching Dane was another story entirely. "Not if I want to stay conscious."

"That works out then." Izia went back to her reading.

Dane gave Lindsay a smile and took a bite of the bread he'd just finished buttering. Lindsay bit his lip to hide an answering grin and ducked his head to eat his dinner.

After dinner, Lindsay headed upstairs to the room he'd be sharing with Dane. Again. He felt nervous and giddy, all at once. He'd managed to convince Dane to allow his magic to be fixed, but at the same time, he didn't know what that would entail, for either of them. Up in the guest room, he stripped for sleep, still thinking everything over. He hoped whatever happened, Dane would be happy with the return of his full magic.

Dane followed him in a moment later and closed the door quietly. He stood there and watched Lindsay undressing, hands in his pockets.

Lindsay hesitated a moment, glancing over his shoulder at Dane, then kept going. Boots, sweater, pants...everything got stacked by their bags, so he wouldn't have to hunt for it in the morning. Being watched made him self-conscious, made him move slower and more carefully.

"You're filling out." Dane's voice was soft. "Not quite such a little bunny anymore." He peeled his shirt off over his head and shook out his hair.

"I'd hardly moved on my own in two years, when you found

me," Lindsay pointed out just as softly. He was never going to be tall or broad like Dane, but at least he wasn't quite so sickly-thin as he'd been when Dane brought him back to Cyrus's house.

"I could tell." Dane gave Lindsay a smile. "Funny little thing, you were." He skinned out of his pants and padded over to sweep Lindsay up in his arms. "You were a fighter, though. I liked that." He settled Lindsay against his chest, tucked up safe and warm.

Lindsay wrapped his arms around Dane's neck and nudged his nose against Dane's chin. "I didn't know how to stop," he murmured. "Still don't, I guess." At the Institute, all his fighting had seemed hopeless and stupid. Now, it actually felt like the smart thing to do.

"Guess we have that in common." They didn't seem to have much else in common, with Dane so dark and huge and Lindsay so pale and small in his arms. Dane carried him to bed, tucking him into the turned-down blankets and leaning over him to kiss him, slowly and sweetly, as though he were tucking Lindsay into bed. "I'm going to build the fire up so you don't get cold in the night."

Dane left Lindsay snuggled in soft sheets and heaps of blankets while he crouched to put more wood on the fire and adjust the flue so it would burn slowly. Lindsay sighed and settled into the blankets. Izia had said he should rest, and the look she'd given Dane... Well, Lindsay knew she'd meant he shouldn't be getting up to anything with Dane, either.

When he was satisfied with the fire, Dane wandered around the room, turning down the lamps and checking the windows. Lindsay took full advantage of the opportunity to watch Dane move. He was bare, and entirely comfortable with it. His powerful muscles shifted under his furred skin as he moved, and Lindsay wondered if any of Dane's appearance would change tomorrow. It wouldn't matter, though. Lindsay had grown far more attached to who Dane was than to how he looked.

Dane pulled something out of his bag before he came back

to bed, sliding in next to Lindsay. His warm body pressed up against Lindsay's side as he leaned in to kiss Lindsay on the mouth. "Sleepy?"

Lindsay snuggled closer, shaking his head. "Not yet," he murmured. It was hard to truly be sleepy when he was so nervous about what was going to happen to him tomorrow.

"You need to sleep." Dane's hand slid down Lindsay's body to cup between his thighs. He kissed Lindsay again, hungry and shameless about what he wanted, in spite of his words.

Lindsay moaned and arched up into the touch. He spread his legs and wound his fingers in Dane's hair. "Definitely not interested in going to sleep right now," he muttered breathlessly. "Especially not if you're touching me like that." He arched and licked at Dane's lips. "Please don't stop touching me like that."

"Don't want to," Dane confessed. His hand kept moving, stroking slowly, while he kissed Lindsay. "I want you."

"You can have me," Lindsay promised, whispering between kisses. "Tell me what you want me to do. Anything." As long as Dane didn't stop touching him, Lindsay would give him whatever he wanted.

Dane didn't ask for anything. He just slid his body over Lindsay's, slipping between his thighs and leaning over him to keep kissing him. He'd been careful before, but now he was even more tender, going so slowly, as though he was trying to enjoy every moment.

Dane kissed behind Lindsay's ear. "Soon, you're not going to need me anymore," he murmured. He didn't sound sorry about it, he sounded proud.

The pride in Dane's tone warmed Lindsay, but he knew Dane was wrong. "Some kinds of need don't go away just because what's broken gets fixed."

That made Dane purr and bite at Lindsay's neck. He wrapped his arms around Lindsay and shifted to slide the head of his cock between Lindsay's ass cheeks. He didn't say anything else, just let their bodies move together.

Lindsay moaned softly, moving to keep Dane's cock sliding against him. His moans got sharper as the friction built up, making his dick leak precome onto his belly, and he turned his head to catch Dane's mouth again, kissing him wantonly.

Dane shifted and, a moment later, he pushed a hand between them to slide a slick finger into Lindsay. His kisses were as needy as Lindsay's; his usual reserve seemed to have disappeared.

"Please," Lindsay whispered, writhing under Dane. Taking his cue from the way Dane kissed him, he nipped at Dane's lower lip and licked into his mouth, making pleading sounds.

Dane didn't make him wait too long. He got Lindsay slick, then himself, before sliding his cock into place. His hair was falling around him in rough waves, his expression was intense, but then a smile tugged at the corners of his mouth. Lindsay smiled back, tentatively, and leaned up to press a quick kiss to Dane's lips.

"Good." Dane kissed Lindsay back into the pillows and moved faster. He pushed himself up, arms straight, looking at Lindsay hungrily while they fucked. Being stared at like that was like being washed in pure heat.

Lindsay tried to muffle his moans, biting his lip and turning his face into the curve of his arm. Everything felt too amazingly good, and his moans kept coming louder and louder. His cheeks were on fire with embarrassment, but he still couldn't stop.

"They can't hear you," Dane whispered. Maybe he was telling the truth. Lindsay didn't think about it. He accepted Dane's reassurance and stopped trying to hold back or muffle himself. "Their loss. You sound so good." Dane inhaled slowly, breathing in Lindsay's pleasure.

Lindsay's next moan came clearer, louder than the others.

"Like that. Feel it." Dane's voice was rough. He moved harder and faster, rolling his hips to let Lindsay feel all of him.

Lindsay shivered harder, overwhelmed with pleasure. His moans turned into cries that all sounded like Dane's name.

Dane whispered praises and compliments, how beautiful Lindsay was, how much he wanted Lindsay, how good it was to be with him—things he'd never said before. Lindsay soaked it all up, the words filling him up with pleasure just as the physical sensations did. He could never have imagined that someone would have so many words for him, for how wonderful he was, but Dane kept talking, all for him. The rush of emotion added more depth and need to his cries as he writhed under Dane, trying to pull him deeper, trying to feel everything.

Dane didn't stop speaking, not even when he came. His voice got raw, but his words were still sweet and soothing. It seemed like he would never run out of tender things to say, like he had saved them all up for now.

Finally Dane stopped moving and gently disentangled their limbs. He didn't pull out, though. He kept their bodies close and snuggled Lindsay against him, burrowing in Lindsay's hair with a soft sigh of contentment. Dane kissed his forehead and stroked his hair. "Think you can sleep now?" His expression was as affectionate as his features could manage.

"If I say no, does that mean you're going to fuck me again?" Lindsay asked, letting a hint of a grin tug the corners of his lips.

"If I say yes, does that mean you're going to make yourself stay awake?"

Lindsay laughed and wriggled under Dane. "Maybe. Would you blame me?"

"I don't know, I've never been in bed with me." Dane tumbled them over in bed so that Lindsay was on top of him. "You need your rest, though. Tomorrow, things change."

Lindsay braced himself on his hands so he could see Dane, his smile fading. "I know." He didn't know what to think about what Ezqel would do to him. He wanted his magic, wanted to stop being so damn helpless, but his last encounter with Ezqel's magic hadn't left him wanting another taste of it.

"Don't be afraid." Dane reached up to cup Lindsay's cheek with one hand. "I'd go first, but I have to see you better before I let the old man waste his magic on me."

Nodding, Lindsay rubbed his cheek against Dane's palm. The contact was soothing, as Dane's touches so often were.

"Sleep," Dane said. "We'll both still be here tomorrow night."

Lindsay gave in and curled himself against Dane's chest, closing his eyes. He listened to Dane's heart beating like a metronome and let the regularity soothe him into sleep.

# Chapter Eleven

It felt as though they'd hardly slept at all when a knock at the door woke them both with a start. "What?" Dane snapped.

"Ezqel is ready for you," Izia said as she opened the door and peeked in. "You shouldn't eat before you come. He's expecting you both." Slowly, she stepped into the room. In her arms, she carried a pair of black robes. "Wear these and nothing else. He expects you to wash before you come."

Lindsay looked at the robes, then at Izia. "Nothing else?"

"Nothing else." Izia laid the robes over the chair by the fire. "You weren't dressed when you were born, were you?" She gave Lindsay a smile.

"All right." Lindsay wasn't happy about it, but he'd do whatever Ezqel needed so he could have his magic back.

"Don't leave him waiting. He's been looking forward to this since Cyrus contacted him." As she let herself out, Izia gave them both a *look* that said, louder than words, not to fool around.

Lindsay flinched. "Looking forward to it?" He didn't like the idea of anyone looking forward to fucking around with his magic. He'd had enough of that already.

"He doesn't see things like we do." Dane nuzzled Lindsay's temple, but didn't kiss him. "It'll be fine. He's also looking forward to finally getting me to give in to him. We should just go get it done, so we can get back to living."

Dane offered to shower first so Lindsay could stay in the

warm bed a little longer, but Lindsay didn't want to wait. "But I wouldn't get to watch you shower."

"I'm just eye-candy to you, aren't I?" Dane pulled a robe on and held another out for Lindsay. "Come on, you can appreciate my male beauty a little longer before Ezqel has his way with me."

Lindsay slid his arms into the robe. "As long as you're *you*, I don't care what you look like."

"I hope I'm still me, then. I haven't been that other person in a long time."

Lindsay didn't know what that meant, so he kept quiet as they walked to the bathroom to shower.

When they finished cleaning up, Taniel was waiting for them in the sitting room. "Ezqel will see you outside. This is not a magic to be done indoors. I will take you to him."

Naked and outdoors. In winter. Lindsay sighed quietly and pulled the robe tighter around himself. "Does the magic cure frostbite too?"

"It will be warm enough." Taniel led them out through the back of the house, but this time he took another path, one that led toward a tall, gray mountain.

It was, shockingly, warm enough, and the path under their feet was dry. Tiny green spikes of new flowers poked out from under black, rotting leaves. The air smelled like snow with a hint of spring when the wind blew.

"This is a safer place to break magics," Taniel explained, growing breathless. "The stone is very stable, it goes deep, and it draws in power. The water that runs through is clean and carries away excess power, the fragments of spells."

"I'm starting to feel like I grew up with blinders on," Lindsay murmured. "I never would've guessed there was so much magic in the world, or so much...infrastructure for it."

"The human race drifts on the surface of great depths, in every way," Dane said, as though he were quoting something. "You'll learn." He offered Lindsay a hand as the path grew steep. He seemed to know the way as well as Taniel, his feet finding the path without hesitation.

Dane was right, Lindsay thought. When the spring-laden breeze pulled at his damp hair, he remembered all the times he'd felt the wind before and had never known it could have a voice. He'd never known that people like Dane and Vivian and Kristan existed. Lindsay had assumed that Taniel was a human student and now he wondered at Taniel's magic. What was it?

And how did Izia's magic work? She'd saved Dane from death, with help, but she looked like some graduate student playing monk at a party. The kuni that had tested his magic, it had seemed like a normal stone, but someone had made it and polished it. The box that held the guul heart, had Ezqel made it? And what about the ring that Dane had worn to kill the guul? It had shimmered with a red light that reminded Lindsay of the glow in an animal's eyes.

Lindsay was used to living on the surface. At home, he had lived on the surface of all his mother's secrets and wealth and all his father's power. He'd always known, even though it was never talked about, that his father had seen combat and had ordered the deaths of soldiers and had even killed men himself. There were medals to prove it. Lindsay had floated above those depths, but this was different.

Now the depths below him meant safety.

There was awareness in Dane's expression and Lindsay realized that Dane could see into the depths, not just into the mundane dark. Dane had come up from those depths for Lindsay. It was time for Lindsay to leave the surface behind and dive, to swim deep and to learn. He didn't want to be ignorant anymore.

After a while, the trail leveled out to wind along the side of the mountain where it jutted out of the earth, a ragged, weathered face rising to Lindsay's left. Dane moved to walk on the raw outer edge, his bare feet sure over even the sharpest stones. The forest rolled away below them and Lindsay thought he could see, in the distance, the other rise where they'd been when they'd eaten breakfast before Jonas had come. Maybe he was just making it up. Who was he to know where they were in

Ezqel's forest?

The wind pulled at them again and Lindsay clung tighter to Dane's hand. Dane's eyes said what Lindsay needed to know. *It's okay. I won't let you fall.*

"It's just here," Taniel said, carefully negotiating a turn around an outcropping. Lindsay could hear water falling. As they came around the corner after Taniel, Lindsay saw that the path was cut by a silver ribbon of water that plunged down several storeys before breaking into foam and rainbows on the rocks below. "This way." Taniel led them back the way the water came, through a rift in the mountainside so small that Dane had to duck to get through.

Lindsay followed, quiet again. Nervous again. He had no idea what Ezqel was going to do to him, except that it involved the demon heart they'd brought back from Mexico, and that they had to be outdoors because the magic wasn't safe indoors. If it wasn't safe inside a building, how could it be safe inside his body? The passage widened until Dane could walk on the edge of the stream and hold Lindsay's hand, keeping him steady on the worn, damp stone path.

Lindsay would have been embarrassed except that Dane wasn't. Dane never made him feel like being looked after was wrong or weak. Dane made him feel like it was a gift, a gift he deserved. Lindsay wasn't used to deserving anything, or he hadn't been. He was now. It hit him then how much he could lose if this didn't work right on Dane.

Dane's eyes were wide like a cat's in the dim light, and he squeezed Lindsay's hand. "It's okay," he murmured. "It'll be over soon."

Lindsay didn't want it to be over. Not this part. What if, once Lindsay had his magic back, Dane didn't want him anymore? It wouldn't happen, he soothed himself. Dane had seemed so happy at the idea that Lindsay would need him afterward. What if Dane thought, secretly, that Lindsay wouldn't want him anymore? Lindsay leaned his head on Dane's shoulder, watching as Taniel's shadowed form grew darker as the light ahead of them grew stronger.

"And then we can go home," Dane added, kissing Lindsay's hair. Everything would be okay. Lindsay closed his eyes for a moment and wished as hard as he could. He'd never wished for anything, really, because wishes never came true. *Let everything be well.* This was his new life. Wishes came true here.

Taniel led them into a cavern flooded by water from higher up the mountain that pooled here before pouring out the way they'd come and plunging down the mountain. Humidity gathered on the ceiling and dripped from long stalactites. Something growing in patches on the walls and ceiling gave off just enough light to see by. Lindsay had never seen anything like it before.

"Lichen." Taniel answered Lindsay's half-formed, unspoken question. "It feeds on more than just air and stone and water. It knows much. The earth and the things on it, they remember more than man has ever known. But we can't dally." He took hold of his robes in both hands, lifting them above his ankles, and hurried toward the shadowed end of the cave.

*It knows much.* Lindsay let himself be led along, looking up at the lichen a little longer. But what did it know? He was beginning to understand Taniel's obsession with knowing everything.

They went through another narrow passage, this time with the water all the way to their ankles, washing their feet and numbing their toes. They emerged into the light. The vaulted ceiling went up high to a crack in the roof where the sun came in and caught on the crystal edges of the stone, lighting up the whole room.

All around them was the sound of water running. Lindsay realized that most of it came from the spring that welled out of the rock at the far end of the room, but there were little tributaries falling from the ceiling, seeping from the floor, rippling down the walls. The floor was worn with wandering silver streams, tiny veins leading to the pool that rushed out to feed the side of the mountain and the forest.

Unnatural things were here, as well, if magic things were

unnatural. Runes were inscribed all over the floor and walls. At first, Lindsay thought they were gilded, but there was only stone when he stopped to look at one. The shimmer he was seeing was magic, not gold.

It was real. Magic was real. Like stone, like water, like light, it was real and Lindsay could feel it all around him. He could feel his own broken magic yearning for it and falling short.

Ezqel's equipment was in the cave also. Lindsay had seen movies like *Frankenstein* and thought them laughable, but here was the real thing: brass and glass instruments, blue flames and coiling tubes and burbling liquids, shimmering crystals and clockwork gears. A magical laboratory hidden in the side of a mountain, in the heart of a thinking, knowing forest. And in that laboratory, a faerie scientist was working, just like in a fairytale.

"Are you ready?" Izia stepped away from the table that she had been helping prepare, wiping her hands on a rag. Her cheeks were flushed and her eyes bright, as though she'd been working hard since she'd sent them to shower. Ezqel had his back to them, bent over a workbench so that Lindsay couldn't see what held his attention. "I was about to come find you."

"More than," Dane grumbled, before Lindsay could apologize for being slow going up the mountain. The way Dane sounded, it was Ezqel and Izia who'd been slow.

"I need to take some notes." Taniel bobbed at them, a funny little cross between a bow and a curtsey, and scampered off. Lindsay liked him more all the time. He wondered if he would have been like Taniel if his parents hadn't wanted him to be something he wasn't.

"You first." Izia gave Lindsay a smile, rolling down her sleeves and smoothing out her robe.

"Me...?" Lindsay wasn't sure what he'd expected, but it wasn't this. What had he been expecting? The doctor's office? More and more, he felt the huge gap between his knowledge and his new reality. Awareness was only a small step toward knowing. He had so far to go.

"Unless you want to see your friend go first," Ezqel said, not turning around. "But I don't think he'd like that."

Izia held out her hands. "I'll take your robe. You won't need it until after."

*Oh.* It wasn't like Lindsay had any shame, not about that. He just felt so exposed already. "I..." He started to speak, but Ezqel turned to look at him and Lindsay really was ashamed. *Coward.* "Here." He slid the robe from his shoulders, surrendering it to her.

The tiny purr of approval that Lindsay heard from Dane made him flush and stand straighter at once. Dane liked the look of him. Even that small thing made Lindsay's vanity—silent so long he'd thought it dead—rise up and give him more strength.

"On the table." Ezqel's voice filled the room effortlessly. The fae mage stood and came over to the table. Taniel was a step behind with a tray of instruments, including an inkwell and quill, in his hands. "I'll deal with you later," Ezqel said to Dane. There was a dismissive chill in his voice that gave Lindsay pause.

Izia was trying to help him up onto the table, using a small wooden step stool, but Lindsay froze. The fact that he was broken and naked didn't matter a damn. He wasn't doing anything as long as Ezqel was speaking to Dane that way.

"I want him to stay," Lindsay blurted out. Something in him whispered that, though Ezqel was doing him a favor, he'd done one for Ezqel too, something no one else could do.

Everyone turned to look at Lindsay and he sat on the cold stone table quickly, hands in his lap, trying not to shiver, trying to stay brave. "Please," he added quietly. *Please don't send him away.*

The silence was unbearable, finally broken by the shifting of velvet as Ezqel shrugged. "It's not my healing," he said flatly, as though it really were.

Lindsay couldn't look at Dane, in case Dane was disappointed in him or, worse, embarrassed. Instead, he turned his attention to the stone table that was freezing his backside. It was dark silver granite inset with metal and stones, white and red and black. The metal had been shaped into runes that he thought he remembered from somewhere. Maybe from the floor.

"Are you sure?" Izia's voice was soft. She put a gentle hand on Lindsay's arm. "Taniel and I will be here with you. If he stays, he will *see* you."

The way Izia said that word, *see*, made Lindsay realize that she was talking about something other than seeing him naked. Dane would see something about him that even lovers wouldn't normally share. The moment his eyes met Dane's dark stare, he knew. "I'm sure."

Dane stepped into his range of vision, keeping himself the focus for Lindsay's attention. His arms were crossed over his chest and his expression was calm. "You're going to be fine," he said, his voice low. Lindsay met Dane's gaze again and nodded. He would be.

"I was able to identify the particular artifact used on you." Ezqel turned to Taniel, who was standing by a small cart with all kinds of equipment arranged on it, a tall black glass cylinder in the center. From the tray Taniel held, Ezqel took a small gold pot of ink and a black crow's quill. "That will make it easy to reverse the spells."

Ezqel brought the ink and quill over to Lindsay. "I'll make the proper inscriptions to lay the groundwork for the second half of the process, then we'll attach the heart artifact. I only bother explaining this to you so that, possibly, you will stop being quite so anxious. It interferes with my concentration."

"I'll try to stop," Lindsay promised, glancing at Ezqel apologetically. He didn't mean to make anything more difficult.

"I could distract him." Dane smiled at Lindsay. Izia and Taniel both gave Dane discouraging looks and Ezqel exhaled sharply.

Blushing fiercely, Lindsay shot Dane a glare that was softened by the grin tugging at his lips, and ducked his head to hide behind his hair. Dane chuckled.

"Hold out your hands." There was an edge to Ezqel's voice that Lindsay remembered well enough from his childhood—the sound of him trying someone's patience with his wretched needs. Lindsay flushed and obeyed, trying to keep his hands steady. "Don't move."

The ink on the quill that Ezqel lifted from the well was blacker than anything Lindsay had ever seen except for the blood of the guul. When the quill came down on his skin, Lindsay had to bite his lip to keep from crying out. It felt like he was being opened up with every stroke, and the ink was seeping into him. He felt sick, like vomiting or fainting, at the sensation of Ezqel's careful writing passing over the half-numb skin of his scars, over and over again.

The fear Lindsay felt was so much like what he'd felt at Moore's hands back at the Institute, and Ezqel was just as cold and cruel and powerful. Every bit of fear he tried to suppress compounded instead and he could feel himself spiraling out of control. He had to stop. He sucked in a breath, dizzy and terrified and hating himself.

"I told you to hold still."

Ezqel's voice snapped Lindsay back into reality. Only then did he realize what had been rising up in him. Terror. Horror. The smell of antiseptic and steel and electricity. The memory of the cuffs on his wrists that bound him to his bed.

"I'm sorry," he said, and it came out weak and broken. "I'm trying." His hands were fluttering like thin white flags, surrendering.

"That was then." Dane's voice was warm and golden, like the sun streaming down. "This is now, remember?"

Lindsay looked up to see Dane standing right there in front of him, looking at him like there was no one else in the room. *Dane.* The first safe thing Lindsay had known in the world was right there when he needed it—that was why he'd wanted Dane to stay.

"Make him still." Ezqel's frustration was palpable. "I can't work under these conditions."

Dane's hands closed on Lindsay's, huge and gentle. His tender expression washed away all Lindsay's shame. "Try harder," he said, and he sounded angry, but Lindsay knew it had nothing to do with him. Dane had been speaking to Ezqel. There was a long, uneasy silence, and then the quill dug into Lindsay's skin again.

Dane's hands were warm around Lindsay's, and so strong. He leaned in to kiss Lindsay's forehead. "It's nothing," he murmured. "This is now, remember."

Lindsay nodded and met Dane's eyes. "I remember," he whispered, but it wasn't easy to push all that fear aside.

With his hands anchored in Dane's, though, Lindsay could stay still. He didn't move while Ezqel scrawled up his arms, down his spine, on the soles of his feet. Izia handled him like a doll, but he didn't care. But when she lifted his hair away so that Ezqel could get at his neck, Lindsay clenched Dane's hands reflexively as the past rose up again.

Moore's hands, her voice, the weight of the collar being clasped around his throat as she told him he looked like royalty. The smell of the drugs filled Lindsay's head, and he could taste the rubber gag they'd shoved in his mouth. The first line of the quill on his neck made his stomach lurch. He'd thought he was being still, but as the quill drew back, he found that he was shaking.

"I'm sorry." Lindsay was too afraid to move. If he moved, Ezqel would stop, and he'd be broken forever. He tried, clenching his muscles tight, but he couldn't stop shaking. "I won't move, I'm sorry, I just, I'm trying, I…"

Dane's mouth on Lindsay's halted his babbling. It was a long, slow kiss, tender without being chaste, and Dane's tongue washed the memory of drugs and gags out of his mouth. He could feel Dane's familiar jagged teeth against his own tongue, and he pressed into the kiss with a whine he couldn't stifle. By the time Dane pulled away enough to let him breathe, Ezqel was writing again, and Lindsay was calm. He leaned his forehead against Dane's, breathed Dane's breath, and let himself pretend that there was no one else here but them.

Ezqel kept working without comment, the quill pressing hard against Lindsay's skin. The sensation of the sharp point dragging over the twisted, half-numb scar tissue was nauseating, but Lindsay could bear it now. Finally, Ezqel turned away. "If you two are quite finished..."

Dane pulled back. "Only if you are." He gave Lindsay's hands another squeeze and stepped away.

"Lie down." Izia came over to help. Taniel had long since pulled out a book and was carefully making notes about the whole procedure.

Once Lindsay was flat on the cold stone table, he looked around for Ezqel so he could watch whatever the fae mage was doing to prepare for the next step.

Izia came back to stand by his head. "I'm going to make sure you're safe while this happens, that your body keeps working normally. You can focus on me. You're going to be fine." Lindsay met Izia's eyes. She was some kind of healer, he reminded himself. She'd saved Dane, brought him back after he'd died.

Ezqel opened up the dark glass cylinder and pulled out something that looked like a copper and silver octopus with a black body. Before Lindsay had time to wonder what it was, Ezqel came over and put the black thing on Lindsay's chest. The guul's heart. Lindsay had expected it to be ground up, powdered, or made into some kind of elixir. He hadn't expected to see it again, lying on his breastbone, heavy and wet and warmer than his own flesh.

The smell of it hit him with all the memories of that night in Cholula, his stupidity and his terror and the crumpling of Dane's bones and the flash of the knife as Dane butchered the dead guul. It could have been his own shivering making the thing move, but it seemed fresh, still twitching with life.

"This will hurt."

That was all the warning Lindsay had. The first needle piercing his skin sent a fresh terror through him. But there was no burn of drugs that followed and Lindsay realized that all the long, spindly "limbs" of the device had needles at the end. Bypass, Ezqel had said. Only magical, not medical.

Lindsay tried focusing on Izia, but he didn't know her well enough for her to be able to make him feel safe just by virtue of her presence. He turned his head, seeking out Dane instead. Lindsay focused on him, memorizing his features, letting the familiarity soothe him as the needles slid in.

Things grew vague after that. Cold spread out from the points in Lindsay's skin, as though his life were being drained from him. It felt like it had when the guul was taking his magic, only he could feel the icy points where it was seeping away from him.

Izia took his face in her hands and said, "I need you to look at me." Her hands were incredibly warm.

The cold that was even colder than his skin and the sensation of being drained all over again made Lindsay feel sick. He stared up at her with wide eyes.

"You're going to be fine." Her hands were so warm, warmth that pushed into him and fought the cold that filled him. "You're not alone. My life is with yours. Trust me."

"Step away from him." Ezqel's voice was distant and hollow.

There was something beating on Lindsay's chest, faster and stronger than his heart, and there was a strange blue light in the air. Lindsay felt lost, with even Izia moving away from him. He tried to turn his head toward Ezqel's voice, but he couldn't move. Besides, moving his head might have meant seeing whatever it was that was so heavy and alive on his chest. Lindsay knew what it was, and he didn't want to think about it, about what it was doing there.

Instead of his magic being repressed, or kept from him, now it was being drawn out of him entirely. Ezqel moved around him, touching him here and there, speaking words that made no sense. The weaker Lindsay got, the faster the heart beat and the brighter the blue light grew, until it was painful to his eyes. He was so afraid and he couldn't speak. It was so familiar.

Finally, there was nothing left. Lindsay was weak and empty and human, his breath rasping in his throat, his body struggling to survive without an essential element it had known all his life. He had no idea how he was alive. He felt dead, like a drowned man borne up by the untamable water.

Ezqel came to stand at Lindsay's head, placing both hands on Lindsay's temples. He spoke in a strange language, holding Lindsay's head in place like his hands were a vise. There was a hiss and crackle and new light, red and gold mingled with the blue of the guul's heart glowing. Lindsay was burning. The words he didn't know were on fire, burning through his skin. He couldn't move to stop it, couldn't wipe the fire and ink from his skin, because his body was nothing but a husk. All that was left was his mind, trapped in the prison of his flesh.

Ezqel's dark eyes were full of power and nothing else; he was filled to overflowing with it. Pure magic pushed through Lindsay and wetness welled at his throat and wrists. Lindsay's husk was full of Ezqel's power; it seeped into his bones to the marrow.

The broken places in him cried out to be healed and there was the sickening twist of something being set right. Ezqel let go and stepped back with a final word. All the magic that had been taken from Lindsay rushed back in, racing joyously through his body.

Lindsay rolled onto his side, curling up, gasping for breath. His cheeks were wet with tears, but he wasn't afraid anymore. It was like he'd been filled up with pleasure. His magic was dancing under his skin, waiting to be let out. He wanted to roll around and bask in it. His magic ran the course of his body and found it whole again. He felt so peaceful.

"Be still." Ezqel was gently moving him to detach the heart. The needles slid away without pain and the ugly thing fell harmlessly into Ezqel's hand. "Izia."

"I'm right here." Izia draped Lindsay's robe over him and gathered him into her arms, helping him sit up. Lindsay could feel and smell the ink and ichor and sweat thick on his skin.

"Take him to get cleaned." That was Dane's voice, so rough and familiar, like stone under Lindsay's feet. Dane was right there, like the sun. His expression was tender, but there was pain in his eyes.

Lindsay wanted to tell him not to hurt, life was too wonderful to hurt, but his mouth wouldn't make words yet. The things he knew and felt were too big for something as small as speech. He let Izia help him up, and he pulled the robe around himself. As Izia led him away, he looked over his shoulder again to make sure Dane would be all right.

"I'm fine." Dane knew what Lindsay was thinking, just like always. "Go get clean, little bunny."

Of course Dane would be fine. Lindsay put his head on Izia's shoulder and let her lead him back the way they'd come in. Nothing in the world could ever really be wrong again.

The pool in the first room swirled as though it were waiting for Lindsay. The water had been tugging at his ankles all the way down the passage. Izia pulled his robe away from him.

"Go on," she said gently. "It's quite deep, but it's safe."

Lindsay let the water pull him in and the surface closed over him. It was cold, but it was the cold of life. The currents washed him clean and tumbled him over, moving around him like great snakes. For the longest time, he didn't need to breathe. There was so much life in him, he wasn't even cold, and the water wanted him to stay. When Lindsay broke the surface at last, Taniel was waiting for him.

"Izia wants me to check your pulse." Taniel knelt at the edge of the pool. In the lichen glow, he looked like he was made of amber. Lindsay swam to him and Taniel felt for the beating in his throat. Serious-faced, Taniel counted silently, his lips moving with it. "Very good." He pulled his hand away and smiled at Lindsay. "How do you feel?"

"Perfect." It was the first word Lindsay could find that came close. "Where did Izia go?" How long had he been in the water? When he looked over his shoulder at the passage to Ezqel's laboratory, he could see blue light rising. "Are they...did they start already?"

*Dane.* Lindsay scrambled out of the water, searching for his robe. Dane had been there for him when he was afraid, and he should have been there for Dane. "My robe," he demanded, feeling tears well up already.

"Here." Taniel wrapped it around him. It smelled and felt clean, like it had just been washed. Lindsay didn't bother to wonder about it, but shoved his arms in the sleeves. Taniel didn't let go when he tried to pull away. "Lindsay. You need to stay." Taniel's voice was soft but stern. "I'm needed, if you're okay to be left alone."

"I..." Lindsay's eyes stung. "I'm fine." Why hadn't they waited for him?

"It will be well." Taniel helped do up the robe and kissed Lindsay's cheek. "It will be well. I know it." With that, he was splashing back up the passage and into the bright light.

Did Dane have something to hide? Lindsay was heartbroken and ashamed at once. He didn't have any right to Dane. Dane wasn't his. He was lucky that Dane shared so much with him. He fiddled with the ties on his robe, feeling mortal and small and dirty again.

The room was interesting enough. Maybe it was like a waiting room. Maybe not so different. Lindsay trailed his fingers over the lichen. What did it know? And what did it say about Lindsay that *lichen* knew things he didn't?

Lindsay was about to laugh at himself when a noise from the laboratory startled him. It wasn't just a noise. It was a cry, and it came again. There was so much pain in it, so much loss, that he was moving before he could think better of it. *Dane.*

At the opening into the laboratory, Lindsay made himself stop, one hand raised to shield his eyes. The heart looked like a sapphire now, on fire from the inside, incredibly lovely and painfully bright. It beat on Dane's bare chest where he lay on the stone table the way Lindsay had. Ezqel was a stark shadow cutting into the light as he moved around the table, speaking a stream of arcane words in a low voice.

For once, Dane seemed small, what could be seen of him from here, even fragile. His skin was white and marked with wide, dark runes that looked painted on at first glance, but went deeper than the surface, deeper than Dane's bones, even, down into Dane's soul. When Lindsay looked too long, he felt as though he could fall into the darkness of them. Now, he understood the cry of pain and loss.

Blackness welled out of the rifts, spilling over the table, dripping onto the floor like blood. Dane's fragile body arched, fighting. He was so strong. Lindsay remembered how empty his own body had been when the guul heart held his magic, and yet Dane had fight left in him. When Dane cried out again, Lindsay shook with the effort of not running to Dane's side. It was only the faint shadows that seemed to be Taniel and Izia that let Lindsay talk himself into hanging back.

The knowledge that he was seeing what he shouldn't beat at Lindsay's conscience. His heart ached with the need to go and soothe Dane, to protect him. *Stop hurting him.* Ezqel's voice rose, every word like a hammer on an anvil, shaping what lay there. The light swelled again and Lindsay turned away even as he saw something thrashing in the light that cast shadows like wings.

Half-blind, his head ringing with Ezqel's magic and Dane's screaming, Lindsay slunk back down the hall toward the pool. He was shaking when he got there and he sank slowly onto a worn stone in the shadows. The wall of the cave was rough and wet against his cheek, like everything was crying. He wiped his face with the sleeve of his robe, then took a deep breath.

Dane would be fine, Lindsay told himself. It was time to stop falling apart. Taking another breath, he pushed himself to his feet. He knelt at the edge of the pool and washed his face with fresh, clean water until he was sure he wasn't crying anymore. When he raised his head, the light at the end of the hall was gone.

No one was coming for him, but... Lindsay got up and tugged the robe around him. It was his business too. Dane was his business. Everyone knew that, even Ezqel. Dane wouldn't have been healed, Lindsay told himself, if Lindsay hadn't talked him into it. He hoped it had been the right thing.

"There you are," Taniel said brightly as Lindsay, steeling himself for admonishment, stepped into the laboratory. Taniel was coming toward him at his usual hurried scurry. Ezqel and Izia were talking, normal tones instead of the strange rhythm of incantation. There was another voice with theirs, smoother than Dane's, warm and low.

"Is that Dane?" Lindsay asked softly. "Are they finished? Can I come back in?"

Dane was sitting up on the table, arguing with Ezqel while Izia draped his robe over his shoulders—and it must have been Dane because no one else seemed to argue with the fae. It wasn't quite Dane, though, even if Lindsay couldn't see his face from this angle. The set of his shoulders was different, his hair wasn't quite the same, and his voice, when it lifted to tell Ezqel in no uncertain terms to get the hell out of his way, was definitely not the same. Ezqel backed off so he could stand. He was still so very tall.

"You can, yes." Taniel stepped out of the way. "I was just coming to get you."

Lindsay padded in, more hesitant now that he'd been given permission. He wanted to see Dane, to make sure he was all right, but he didn't want to interrupt, either. Dane looked so different. It made Lindsay realize how much his magic being broken must have hurt him. That idea made Lindsay's feet move faster, to get him closer to Dane, close enough to comfort.

"That was a very tightly woven spell. I suspect that I could not have removed it for you before," Ezqel was saying. "Not while leaving you alive." He seemed pleased with himself. The demon heart in his hands glittered like it was made of stone. The metal extensions from it were blackened and corroded. It certainly hadn't looked like that after Lindsay, what little Lindsay remembered of it.

"You say that now." Dane didn't sound like he believed a word of it. He pulled the robe on with a few angry moves and shook his hair back. “Where’s...”

Lindsay came closer. So many of Dane’s individual features were the same: the strong nose and high cheekbones, the soft lips, the same dark eyes and long hair. His skin was still golden, but lighter, and Lindsay could see that Dane’s chest was no longer furred like it had been. So many of the same features, but they seemed put together differently. He was gorgeous, with a beauty that rivaled Ezqel’s. Surpassed it, Lindsay thought. Dane was made of so many good things; his appearance was only a small part of it all.

“Not running around, trying out your new toys yet?” Dane teased. There were no more fangs when he smiled, only beautiful teeth. Slightly pointed, beautiful teeth.

“Not yet.” Lindsay ducked his head, smiling, reassured by Dane’s teasing. “Thought I might wait for you, first.”

“You’re fine, and I’m...” Dane pulled up a sleeve to show that his skin was covered in sticky black markings, “...dirty. Go on.”

“Then go get clean. The water feels good. I can wait.” Lindsay shook his head to show that his own hair was still wet. He didn’t want to “go on”, not unless he had to. He’d stay back here, but he still wanted to see, to get used to the way Dane looked now. Besides, he’d always liked watching Dane.

“I will when I’m ready. You need to eat. I’ll come find you at the house.” Dane didn’t look like he was going to change his mind. “I’m sure Taniel will take you back.”

As if on cue, Taniel was at Lindsay’s side. “You can practice your magic,” Taniel said brightly. “Come on.” He put a hand on Lindsay’s arm and Lindsay gave in, letting himself be led.

Maybe Dane *was* different. Dane had said that he couldn’t remember who that man was, the man he’d been when he was whole. Maybe he didn’t remember the man he’d been when he was broken, or what had mattered to him moments before. It wasn’t as though Lindsay hadn’t been warned. Funny how that never stopped anything from hurting.

# Chapter Twelve

Dane watched Lindsay go, saw the uncertainty written in his slim shoulders. If he didn't have confidence yet, Dane running after him wasn't going to fix it. Dane sure as hell wasn't going to do anything while the past was stinking on his skin.

When Lindsay's smell and the sound of his breathing were long gone from Dane's senses, Dane followed the path to the pool, without a word to the others. He didn't owe them anything. Leaving his robe behind on the rocks, he plunged into the icy water. Magic ran through here, pure magic from the earth, and Dane could feel it washing him clean beneath his skin. He swam as deep as he could, reveling in his new body...his old body. As he broke the surface, he could sense that Ezqel was waiting for him, alone.

"If you're waiting for me to thank you, it'll be a long time." Dane pulled himself out of the pool next to where Ezqel was standing. They were of a height now, more similar than ever. Dane shook off the familiarity even as he looked Ezqel in the eye.

"No. But there's work to be done." Ezqel held out the robe Dane had discarded. It smelled freshly washed, so Dane pulled it on. "My forest is full of vermin."

"Blame Cyrus." Dane pulled the robe closed and belted it as he turned away. He should go talk Lindsay into trying his magic out. He could let Lindsay use it on him again, maybe that would help. Couldn't trust little Taniel to talk anyone into anything.

"I never knew you to turn down the hunt," Ezqel said softly, speaking to Dane's animal ears. "Maybe I got something wrong with those spells."

Hunting. Hunting in Ezqel's forest, even by Ezqel's permission, was never done. Ezqel never gave permission. Once, though, on a green plain long-since swallowed up by a shifting, hungry desert, they'd hunted together. The sun had been a white coin on a bleached-bone sky when they'd set out, the moon a silver sickle harvesting stars when they'd been sated.

"Here?"

"Are we anywhere else?"

Dane wrung his hair out, water spattering on the stones at his feet, while he pretended to think about the offer. In his bones, he had already accepted. Now he had to consider the consequences. "Is Jonas with them?"

"Not this time. They have other dogs, though. Unnatural ones." Ezqel came to stand by the threshold with him, a flicker of red and white at the corner of Dane's eye. Behind them, his magical workshop murmured quietly to itself, just loud enough that Dane could hear it.

"I'll do it, but only so Cyrus doesn't owe you," Dane said at last. A pang of fear spiked in him, fear that he'd try to change and not know how, that his body wouldn't answer, that he'd look like a fool in front of Ezqel for being broken enough that all the magic in the world couldn't fix.

"I don't care why you do it." Ezqel passed him and stepped out into the sunlight. "Your reasons are your own," he said, his voice small in the outside air. "Didn't you say you wanted it that way?"

"True enough." Dane followed, trying to consider how he felt about that. Suddenly, he was blinking in the sunlight. His human eyes were too slow to react. Letting the beast seep in was like grasping air at first.

"North, first. Then the rest of the compass." Ezqel stepped up onto a rocky outcropping. The wind pulled his hair and robes in all directions, buffeting him, and it lifted him as he shimmered into feathers and beak and claws and bright eyes. A gyrfalcon, larger than anything the world had seen in these late days, took the wind under its great wings and became small in the sky.

Dane watched Ezqel soar, relieved to have the moment to himself. Instinct led his feet to the clearest path winding north and he loped along it, bare feet cold on the earth. It was strange to have his body so straight and vulnerable. The wind, growing colder the farther he got from Ezqel's haven, pulled his robe open and bit at his bare skin.

*It has to happen sometime.* The voice was his own, not Ezqel's, not Cyrus's. The wind was empty of Cyrus's presence and his magic—once in a while, the wind let him be alone. *I don't remember. I don't...* It had been so long.

Dane ran until he could hardly see for the wind in his eyes, though his hair caught on branches and his feet cut on stones, until the pressure in his chest was a fire that made him feel human. He knew the mountain, knew this upward slope and the place where it broke. Sometimes, there was only one way to make things happen.

He knew from the slip of the scree under his feet exactly where he was, and that the gap ahead would leave him no choice but to change or find out how deep it went. The forest fell away so that, suddenly, he could see distance and a horizon and the sky arched overhead. The black cross of the bird swung up toward the sun, waiting for him. He remembered miles disappearing under his paws, the bunch of his muscles, the way his claws cut into the earth's skin...

Four paws to the ground, long body like a coiled spring, ears back flat against his skull, he doubled his speed over the last yards to the rift in the mountainside. The gap yawned under him, but he was already stretching out to the ground on the other side. His momentum and weight rippled up into his body as his forepaws hit the ground, translating to his hind paws as they gained purchase and threw him forward again.

The world was different, yet familiar, like coming home after years away. The bird was a speck so high in the sky that he lost it, but he could feel the eyes on him. He didn't need the bird to tell him what was ahead.

Three men. No, two men, and one dog. Dane's muzzle wrinkled and the sneer drew his lips back so that their taste swirled around his fangs. He bit the air as he circled to pick up their trail, coming up behind them.

"That's no bird." The rifle bolt had a sound that never failed to make his blood rise.

The dog smelled him coming and was turning to face him. It stood on two legs, but it was leashed and enslaved no less, straining against invisible chains. Dane cleared it and came down on the man with the gun, dipping his head to tear the man's spine out with a snap of his teeth and shake of his head.

The other one was trying to radio for help—Dane could hear the crackle as the headset came on—but a shadow passed over and, when it lifted, the man's head was gone. The bird laughed and dropped the head as it made for the zenith again. The body crumpled with the jerky hesitation of a thing unsure it was dead.

The dog was afraid, the smell of its sweat and adrenaline stronger than the blood in Dane's mouth. With no master to direct it, it backed away and turned to run. Dane swiped through the tendons at the back of its legs and flipped it over on its back. He pinned it down with a bloody paw and stared, trying to fathom it.

It beat at him with clenched fists and tried to summon magic that never came. It was mad, mad in the eyes, mad in the stink of it, yelping like a dog with a human mouth. Dane killed it with a bite and a shake of his head, and dropped it, spitting out its poisoned blood. The cry of the bird reminded him to leave curiosity to the minds of men. Shaking his head again to clear it, he turned to follow the bird.

Ezqel's forest was vast, but his paths through it followed the laws of magic, not matter. Every step of Dane's paws, every beat of Ezqel's wings, covered miles. The forest was infested with men. Taniel hadn't been exaggerating. Methodically, with the help of the whispering wind, the lion and the falcon hunted every last one and brought them to earth.

The sun set on them at the edge of the human world, next to a burning truck and a crumpled helicopter. The corpses that Ezqel had summoned up out of the forest—once they were dead, he had more dominion over them and they were easier to command—lay in neat stacks, matched with their various body parts, awaiting disposal. The forest still felt uneasy, but at least it was clean.

Dane stretched out next to the flames of the smoldering truck and watched Ezqel peck out the eyes of a man who had, until today, likely considered himself to be firmly in control of many things. The screaming faded to sobs as the bird stepped off the man's chest and, with a flick of its feathers, was Ezqel in his fae form again. What there had been to learn from the man had been disappointingly minimal. Always, they were only following orders.

"Should I let it live?" Ezqel crossed his arms over his chest and looked at the squirming man trying to crawl away on fingerless hands and crippled legs.

Dane rumbled and got up, stretching until his back cracked and his twitching tail nearly caught fire on the burning truck. Sneezing at the offense of smoldering synthetics, he paced over to circle the last of their prey. If they killed it, it was likely that Moore and her kind would be stupid enough to send more, and that would be irritating. He yawned mightily, shaking his mane for emphasis.

"You're right." Ezqel bent to pick up the man's cell phone and, muttering an unlocking spell, pressed a few buttons gingerly. Dane didn't recognize the voice on the other end. "This is over," Ezqel said to it, holding it out in front of him as though he wasn't quite sure what to do with it and didn't want it too near his face. When Ezqel threw the phone at the ruined man and it landed in front of him, the man scrabbled for it and began babbling into it hysterically.

*What happened? Who's there? What do you mean, they're all dead?* The phone echoed the distress back across the miles.

Dane sat and sighed, bending his head to lick some gore from his chest. People didn't learn. Worse, they forgot. If they bothered to remember, no one would have been foolish enough to come into the forest.

"Let's go home." Ezqel stepped back into the forest that opened up for him with a sigh.

Dane didn't bother to argue the semantics of "home" with him, but followed at his heels. After a mile, the path widened so that Dane could pace along beside him. Soon, the path curved around the side of the mountain and they were walking the same trail that Dane had led Lindsay up that morning. Dane drew a breath and remembered what it was like to walk on two legs.

"Done playing the beast?" Ezqel didn't look over at him.

"Who said I was ever playing?" Dane felt small and bare in this body. His skin itched, and his short teeth were on edge. He tugged his robe tighter around him. It was as clean as it had been when he'd shifted; where things went when he was on four legs was a mystery he'd never questioned. They were here, just not *here*. He'd never lost anything. Not yet, at least.

"I know you well enough." Ezqel's irritation was a little bit comforting.

"Do you?" Dane wasn't sure Ezqel did, nor Cyrus, for that matter. They knew what it suited them to know, and they didn't care about the rest.

"Well enough to remember you were more than just a mangy circus animal once." Ezqel did look over now as he led the way around to the back of the faerie cottage. The dusk softened his features, made him seem more human, almost caring. "Best to find out if you still have it in you before you need it."

Dane shrugged. "No sense showing off," he said dryly. A small door hidden at the side of the house swung open for them as they came up the path.

"You're still a bad liar." Ezqel headed up the stairs to his study and was almost around the first turn when he stopped and turned back. Dane stood at the bottom of the stairs, impressed that Ezqel had noticed he wasn't following before getting all the way to the top. "Have something you need to do?"

"Yes." Dane wasn't going to admit that he was anxious to get back and check on Lindsay.

There was perhaps a flicker of concern mixed into the irritation in Ezqel's expression. It was hard to tell with him sometimes. His expressions were not always human and his scents were unique. "Thank you for your assistance today," he said, the words heavy and stiff.

"It was nothing." The flat response wasn't rudeness, it was necessary so that no hint of obligation remained between them. The words of old men held too much weight to be allowed to wander outside the bounds of formality.

Ezqel tilted his head, listening for something, then frowned. "You returned Yzumrud."

"I did. It was useful." Dane put emphasis on the past tense. He'd taken more from Ezqel than he'd ever intended, even if it all had been for his own purposes. The ring sat in the drawer of the desk in the room Dane shared with Lindsay, waiting to be put back in its place. He wasn't taking it with him again.

An exhalation was the only sound of Ezqel's surrender, but it was loud in Dane's ears. "Very well. Have a good evening. I doubt I will see you before you leave."

"I'll give your regards to Vivian and Cyrus." Dane didn't have much else to say, not after all this time.

"If you speak to them before I do." No favors. Not even the small courtesies. Ezqel turned his back on Dane and his next steps took him out of sight.

In the kitchen, Dane washed his mouth out with cold tea and looked himself over. Blood didn't carry through the changes—not on his skin, anyway. He rummaged around and found some mutton and cheese to have with the tea. The utensils he needed to cut and eat were awkward in his human hands, briefly, until he remembered how it felt to use them. By the time he was fed, standing at the counter and watching dark fall over the herb gardens, he thought he had the hang of being human again.

Physically. Washing the dishes, watching his long fingers flicker in and out of the soapy water, he remembered being human-bodied. His human mind, his human heart, those would be stranger to revisit. And, if he recalled them correctly, they would be more trouble than his human flesh.

Lindsay put off practicing his magic. Taniel prodded, but Lindsay reasoned that he'd let his magic settle into his body before he played with it. He didn't really want to find out the hard way that it wasn't quite ready for him yet.

He spent the rest of the day with Taniel, eating, resting, and talking. Taniel was full of stories, a book of endless fairytales that Lindsay now knew were true. By nightfall, Lindsay still hadn't seen Dane again. Dane must've been busy with Ezqel or Izia or getting used to his magic again. Lindsay went up to the room and got ready for bed. He tried to be adult about what he was feeling, but under it, he was just scared.

As he was getting changed, the door swung open. Lindsay turned around, smiling as soon as he saw Dane stepping into the room. Dane was still wearing the robe he'd had on that morning, but it looked somewhat the worse for wear—most of him did, actually. His hair was in disarray and his feet were dirty. He didn't look quite the same as when Lindsay had left him by the waterfall, but he didn't look like he used to either. Somewhere in between—human, with only a hint of the feral.

"Taniel put you through your paces?" Dane asked, as though he hadn't been gone all day.

"Not exactly," Lindsay admitted, shrugging.

"You have to try it sometime." Dane took his robe off and threw it over a chair. "Ezqel doesn't screw up. Usually." His skin was flawless, paler, and he had less body hair, but there was still some in the center of his chest fading into a thin line that led to the soft curls at his groin.

"I will," Lindsay said, though he wasn't sure he wanted to

try it and find out that it didn't work. "Are you all right?"

"Fine. Not dead yet or anything." Dane sprawled on the bed and tucked one arm behind his head.

"Well, I'm glad to hear that." Lindsay crawled up beside him and sat cross-legged.

"What're you looking at?" Dane sighed heavily. "Lie down and go to sleep, Lindsay."

Maybe Dane didn't want to be seen like this. Lindsay didn't want to make it worse, whatever the problem was, so he curled up on his side and closed his eyes. Grown-up relationship. Extenuating circumstances. He'd already had more than he'd ever dreamed, he reminded himself.

"Under the covers." Dane grumbled and tugged the covers out from under Lindsay to tuck him in, getting in beside him. "Unless you got super-heating powers from Ezqel this morning."

"No. You think he'd let me trade up?" Lindsay wriggled under the covers.

"Not likely. He's no fun." Dane tucked Lindsay in and frowned at him. "You'll need to use it sometime, you know."

Lindsay sighed. "I know. I just... I don't want to try, and find out that even after all that, I'm still broken." He shrugged. "I don't know what to do with it, anyway."

"Me either." Dane shrugged, mirroring him.

Lindsay was oddly reassured by Dane's admission. "I think I could figure out what to do with you, though," he murmured, smiling wickedly. "If you're not all worn out from playing in the dirt all day..." He wriggled closer, rolling up so he could nudge his nose against Dane's chin submissively and brush a kiss over Dane's lips. Maybe it would still work.

"I don't get tired." Dane's voice dropped to a familiar purr and his hand found Lindsay's bare hip under the blankets.

Lindsay grinned, nudging Dane until he fell over onto his back. "Prove it," Lindsay challenged, crawling up over Dane and leaning in for another kiss.

"Prove it?" Dane laughed at him, a real smile and a real laugh. It did work. Lindsay felt a surge of triumph and joy.

"How did you want me to do that?"

Lindsay rubbed his cheek against Dane's and sat up again. "I've been waiting all day for you to come back, so I could convince you to fuck me."

"Convince?" Dane grinned and ran a hand over Lindsay's hair, petting him like always. "You looked in a mirror lately?" He slid his fingers into Lindsay's hair, tugging gently. It didn't hurt, at least not in the way that would make Lindsay want to ask Dane to stop. "So, how were you planning to do this convincing?"

"You seem to like it when I tell you what I want."

"You think I'm that easy?" Now Dane was teasing. His voice was smoother than before, but the tones hadn't changed.

"I think you are when you want to be," Lindsay said honestly. He leaned forward, against the pull of Dane's hand, and flicked his tongue over Dane's lips. "But maybe I could kiss you some, if telling you what I want doesn't work, because that works sometimes too."

Dane leaned up for a kiss, his mouth soft on Lindsay's. "You learn fast," he murmured after. His other hand slid up Lindsay's back, fingers tracing the curve of Lindsay's spine.

Lindsay arched into the petting, humming with how good it felt. "You teach well."

Dane kissed him again, more demanding this time, his tongue pushing into Lindsay's mouth. He pulled Lindsay against him and Lindsay moaned softly. He licked at Dane's tongue, sucked at it. He'd used his words, had told Dane that he wanted him, but now it was time to show him.

The sounds Dane made, low groans of pure want, were almost as affecting as his touches. Dane's hand was huge on Lindsay's back, splayed wide to hold him close. He cupped Lindsay's ass with the other hand, stroking between his thighs. Lindsay arched, spreading his legs as far as he could manage, and slid his own hands over Dane's chest, exploring the new territory. The fur was gone, but Dane was still broad and strong. Lindsay could feel the muscles shifting beneath Dane's skin.

A moment later, Dane was tapping Lindsay on the shoulder with the plain salve that had been tucked under the pillows. "Trust me," he murmured. "I'm not tired. Haven't been this not-tired in years."

Lindsay sat up a bit, flushed and wide-eyed, and whispered, "Show me." He took the salve from Dane and opened it up. "I want you to fuck me. Please."

"I will." Dane's hands found Lindsay's ass as he leaned up to bite the side of Lindsay's throat—his teeth were suddenly sharp. "I could do it all night," he growled, sounding terribly feral.

Lindsay shivered hard and pressed into it, all of it. "Please," he whispered again. He wanted exactly what Dane was offering.

"Use that, and you can have anything you want," Dane promised. He licked where he had bitten, purring contentedly.

Lindsay made himself sit up, pulling away from those oh-so-intense licks and bites so he could dip his fingers into the little pot. He braced his other hand against Dane's chest for balance and support as he pushed Dane's fingers away and slid his own slick finger into himself. One, and then another, he fucked himself with them, and he couldn't keep from moaning.

Dane's eyes were dark and hot on him. "That's so good." He curled a hand around Lindsay's cock, stroking enough for some friction. "Pretty," he murmured, as if to himself as much as Lindsay.

"Please," Lindsay answered, gasping with the sensations. For all that Dane looked different, it was definitely him—no one else called Lindsay pretty.

"Whenever you want it," Dane promised. "You look so good, I could eat you." He said it like he meant it, like he'd barely been resisting all this time, and for a moment Lindsay could believe it would be good.

Lindsay pulled his fingers out. "Now."

"C'mere, then." Dane cupped Lindsay's hip in one hand and guided him down. "Let me feel you."

Lindsay went slowly, letting his body adjust. The palm of Dane's hand was warm and smooth against Lindsay's cock. The pleasure of those touches sated Lindsay enough that he could be a bit patient until his body took Dane in all the way. The calm didn't last long, though, when Lindsay moved. Shivers rolled through his body and he gasped, writhing and moving faster. He was suddenly so close, he could feel the pleasure boiling up inside him.

"Yeah, like that," Dane purred. "Let it go. I'm not going to stop."

Lindsay moved faster, fucking himself on Dane's cock without restraint. Dane hissed his approval, hips moving under Lindsay to fuck him harder as Lindsay came, slicking the hand stroking his cock and spilling over the back of it onto Dane's belly.

"Like that," Dane murmured. He seemed to love it when there wasn't any pretense or clinging to self-control.

Lindsay kept moving, wanting it to last. Every thrust made him shiver all over again, and he moaned. He wanted to make Dane feel it too, wanted it so much. This wasn't worth anything if he couldn't make Dane feel as good as he did. "Please," he whispered, as something opened up inside him.

Dane rocked under Lindsay for a long while, then wrapped his arms around Lindsay, tumbling them over, sliding his belly against Lindsay's and making both of them sticky. He kissed Lindsay recklessly, moaning, still moving hard. When he pulled back, he was totally human again, beautiful in a way that didn't seem to exist anymore except in paintings. His eyes were black with pleasure, his full lips swollen from kissing Lindsay, his cheeks like roses under the gold.

Lindsay tangled his fingers in Dane's hair and pulled him in for another wet, messy, hungry kiss. All Dane's reserve was gone. He gasped against Lindsay's mouth, whined his name, kissed him hard and hot, fucking him relentlessly. Without warning, he pulled out and slid down, pushing his fingers in instead. Shivering and moaning, he licked and bit his way down Lindsay's chest until he was lapping up the streaks of Lindsay's come.

"Oh, God," Lindsay gasped, trying and failing to catch his breath. "Dane..." He writhed, moving as much as he could to keep fucking himself on Dane's fingers. Dane's mouth felt so good, so intense, and it felt so good to *know*, to be able to *feel* how much Dane wanted him.

Lifting his head a moment, Dane grabbed the salve and got his fingers slick again before pushing three back into Lindsay. They were long and thick, filling Lindsay up. His mouth came down on Lindsay's cock, sucking it in, tongue sliding out to lick at Lindsay's balls as well. Dane moaned around Lindsay's cock, sucking hungrily, shivering.

Lindsay cried out, his hips bucking to push his cock deeper into Dane's mouth. He tried to settle down almost immediately, petting apologetically even as he kept writhing, but Dane just moaned and sucked Lindsay in again. Every move Lindsay made got more noises from him.

"Dane, Dane, oh, fuck..." Lindsay gasped, his hands clenching in Dane's hair before he could stop himself. He rocked between Dane's fingers and his mouth, his back arching like he'd been shot through with pleasure. "Please."

Dane kept at him for a long time, hungry like he couldn't get enough. Finally, he pulled his mouth off, pulled his fingers out, and pushed his cock back in all at once. His weight came down on Lindsay, barely caught on his elbows, and he kissed Lindsay hard.

"Yes," he whispered against Lindsay's mouth. "Yes, anything." He fucked Lindsay with long, deep strokes, rolling his hips as he thrust. His kisses would have been dangerous if he'd still had fangs, and he gasped Lindsay's name between them, sounding overwhelmed with pleasure. Dane had never been quite like this before. It had always been intense, but this was so much more open than Dane usually was.

*More open.* The knowledge of what he'd done hit Lindsay hard enough to make him gag into the kisses. He struggled to pull away, and to drag his magic back into himself. Oh, God, what had he done? He hadn't understood what he was feeling when he'd done it, but now he knew. He knew and, God, he hoped Dane would forgive him.

"I'm sorry," Lindsay choked out past the tears of shame and fear. He grabbed at Dane's shoulders, trying to shake Dane awake. "Oh, God, I'm sorry. I didn't know..."

As the magic rolled back, Dane pulled away with a convulsive shudder, his face and body shifting through several variations on his usual appearance. He shook his head like a dog shedding water, and clenched his head in his hands like it was about to fly apart.

"Dane... I'm so sorry." Lindsay had ruined everything. He curled up against the head of the bed, wrapped up in a knot of blankets and sheets. "Are you all right? God, I'm sorry, I didn't think it worked like that. I swear I didn't mean to. I wouldn't. Are you all right? Please be all right..."

Dane got up from the bed and went to stand in front of the fireplace, hands on the mantel. He breathed slowly and pushed away, still not looking at Lindsay. "I'm fine," he said, his voice tight.

Lindsay didn't have to see his face to know that he wasn't. Dane's body was taut with something—outrage or distress, either was equally horrible—and every muscle was clearly outlined under his beautiful skin. Lindsay didn't know how to fix it, any of it. He ached to pet Dane's wild hair and to soothe the tension out of his broad back.

"I'm sorry," Lindsay whispered again. He really had ruined everything and now Dane might hate him, might send him away like his father had. And he *deserved* it.

"That's why you practice." Hands on his hips, Dane stood there, looking into the fire. He was still breathing harder than normal, though whether it was from all the pleasure or the upset was impossible to tell.

Lindsay ducked his head, pressing his cheek against his pulled-up knees, and closed his stinging eyes. Dane was right. He hadn't practiced when Taniel had tried to convince him to, and now he'd done something awful. He couldn't imagine how Dane must feel.

After an agonizingly long time, long enough for Lindsay to feel like he was frozen into a knot of despair, the bed shifted as Dane sat beside him and then his big arm slid around Lindsay's shoulders. "No harm done," Dane said quietly, pulling Lindsay against him. "You didn't mean it."

"I swear I didn't," Lindsay promised desperately. "I just wanted you to feel good. And it... It just happened."

"Well," Dane said, murmuring against Lindsay's hair, "you know it works now?" He wrapped his other arm around Lindsay and held him close.

Lindsay pulled the blankets tighter and tentatively rested his cheek against Dane's chest. "I didn't think it would work like that. I'm sorry."

"You didn't mean it." Dane sighed heavily, then laughed a bit. "Good thing you weren't angry." He pressed a kiss to Lindsay's hair.

"I won't do it again," Lindsay promised. He tilted his head back to see Dane's face. He needed to see, to make sure Dane didn't hate him.

Dane's expression was gentle even though his face looked more feral again. "How about you ask first from now on?" he suggested, stroking Lindsay's hair back. Slowly, he leaned in.

Lindsay searched Dane's face for any sign that Dane didn't mean that, but there was none that he could see. He nodded. "I promise," he said softly, waiting for Dane's kiss.

The kiss was slow and sweet, and it felt like forgiveness. Dane gathered Lindsay up, blankets and all, and pulled Lindsay into his lap, wrapping him up safely. "Tomorrow," he murmured, "you practice."

Lindsay nodded, ducking his head against Dane's chest again. He should've known his magic would slip out that way. That was how his parents had found out about him. It felt like nothing less than a miracle that Dane was holding Lindsay close instead of sending him away. It felt so strange to be forgiven, something he'd never experienced before he'd met Dane. Before Dane had found him.

After a while, Lindsay wriggled out of the blankets enough that he could wrap his arms around Dane's neck. He'd hurt Dane, not the other way around, but he was the one being comforted. He wanted to give that back. He knew which of them deserved the petting and apologies.

Dane kissed the curve of Lindsay's neck and let Lindsay comfort him in return. He sighed as some of his tension went out of him, and rubbed his cheek on Lindsay's like a cat. Oh, that felt so good. Lindsay returned the gesture and snuggled up close.

Dane kissed his temple and tumbled him over onto his back, kissing his mouth and pushing at the blankets to get to his skin. He got between Lindsay's thighs once they were out of the blankets, his kisses turning hot and needy.

"Dane?"

"Not done with you yet." Dane kissed him again, hard. He pulled back, his expression serious even though his cheeks were flushed. "I still want you. Just me. Just you."

"Just me and you," Lindsay agreed breathlessly.

Dane let Lindsay open up for him, moving slowly and carefully. His breath was rough again already and he brushed kisses over Lindsay's mouth. "You don't need any magic to make me feel good." The difference was night and day. Dane had been overwhelming and intense before, and that was still true, but he was careful now, in control where he hadn't been before. "You okay?"

Lindsay nuzzled Dane's cheek. "I'm all right."

"Good. Last thing I need is to hurt you." Dane bit the curve of Lindsay's neck, carefully this time.

"You didn't." Lindsay would be sore, and there would be marks on his chest and belly from Dane's bites, but Lindsay didn't care. "You wouldn't."

"Never on purpose." Dane pulled back to watch Lindsay's face. His breath was coming rougher, and his hair fell around them, making everything dim. "You're so pretty like that." Dane's voice was a low purr. He ducked his head and licked up the tender line of Lindsay's throat, growling possessively. He bit the softness under Lindsay's jaw, growling again, pushing in hard.

Lindsay cried out, shivering, his hands clenching on Dane's shoulders. "Please," he whispered. There was something so shockingly good about the possessiveness in Dane's voice, in the way he growled and bit and fucked Lindsay like that.

Dane's breath was hot against Lindsay's ear as he gasped Lindsay's name and came hard. Lindsay whispered Dane's name in answer, nuzzling Dane's neck and cheek, licking and kissing the warm skin there, basking in the heat of having been wanted so very much, but Dane wasn't done with him yet.

He kissed Lindsay on the mouth, fiercely, as he pulled out. Then he did as he had done before, sliding down Lindsay's body to suck Lindsay's cock into his mouth, pushing his fingers into Lindsay as he went. There were no fangs in the way this time, either. His mouth was hot and hungry, his tongue exploring Lindsay's cock again.

"Dane?" Lindsay gasped. He scrambled to pull his magic back in, but there was none. There wasn't any illusion to strip away Dane's self-control this time.

Dane pinned him to the bed with one big hand in the middle of Lindsay's chest. It was like he couldn't get enough, sucking Lindsay off and fucking him with three fingers. Lindsay cried out, rocking between Dane's mouth and his fingers, his noises coming faster and more desperate with every passing moment. He couldn't hold on. Finally, his cries sharpened as he came, and Dane still didn't stop. Dane took everything Lindsay had to give, swallowing him down and purring around his cock.

When Lindsay could think again, he wound his fingers in Dane's hair and tugged lightly as he whispered Dane's name. *Please let it be real, let it not be an accident with my magic again.*

Dane lifted his head and let Lindsay's cock slip out of his mouth. He pressed a kiss to Lindsay's belly, then met his gaze.

Dane looked normal, but Lindsay wouldn't have realized last time either, if he hadn't noticed that Dane wasn't *acting* normally. He bit his lip. "Are you... I didn't... It's you, right? I didn't mess up again?"

Dane slid his fingers out and crawled up over Lindsay's body to kiss him on the mouth. "Me," he murmured, between tender, reassuring little kisses. "All me. Wanted to finish what I started earlier, because I could."

Lindsay relaxed, wrapping himself around Dane as best he could and kissing him back sweetly. "Good," he whispered. "God, Dane, I don't ever want to... I want it to be you."

"I know." Dane curled up with him and held him close, giving him the kisses he needed. "It was a mistake, and I'm not hurt. You'll learn."

"I learn fast," Lindsay promised. He was so glad Dane wasn't angry at him. Dane had every right to be, Lindsay knew, and he planned to do his best to deserve the forgiveness he'd received.

"I like that about you, remember?" Dane pushed Lindsay's hair away from his face and gave him a sharp, feral smile.

Lindsay smiled back, relieved and happy. Pleasing Dane—with anything—was such a good feeling.

"You ready to go to sleep yet?" Dane grabbed some of the blankets and shook them out to cover Lindsay up.

"As long as you're staying," Lindsay murmured, rolling to curl up beside Dane.

"I'm not leaving you yet," Dane said quietly, tucking Lindsay in against him. He kissed Lindsay's hair and cradled Lindsay in his arms.

*Not yet.* Lindsay hated the way Dane said that, but he knew it was true. Once they were back at Cyrus's house, he'd have to get used to sleeping alone again. Being alone again. For now, though, he had this, and he wanted to enjoy it for as long as it lasted.

Dane watched Lindsay sleep. The light of the moon was

more than enough for him to see by; it limned Lindsay's delicate features with a thin line of silver. Lindsay would hardly recognize himself the way Dane saw him now. The moon's pen traced the lines of Lindsay's face that were growing stronger by the day, bringing out the picture of the grown man he would be when his body recovered from years of neglect and abuse.

The moon crept higher and Dane still wasn't tired. Lindsay was a bit restless and Dane didn't blame him. It had been that kind of day. At least Lindsay smiled when he wriggled closer, no more frowning and scowling. Dane kissed his temple and huffed softly in his hair. So sweet. The wind rattled around the window and Lindsay murmured.

"It's nothing," Dane said to him in a low voice. Lindsay didn't wake. Even sleeping, he believed Dane and settled again.

Dane wanted it to be nothing. He closed his eyes and forced the world away. Lindsay's breath skimmed his chest like a little hand petting him to sleep.

The wind whined in the chimney and Dane heard delicate feathers of ash scattering across the hearthstones. *Damn it.* He kissed Lindsay and then worked away slowly, tucking his pillow where he'd been and letting Lindsay snuggle it instead.

Sleeping, Lindsay pouted. Sad little bunny. "I won't go far," Dane promised. The wind rattled the flue. "I will be right there," he hissed through his teeth. He finished tucking Lindsay in securely and finally made his reluctant escape. The cold wasn't going to bother him, but Cyrus would have something to say if he were to hang around naked, so he pulled on his robe.

The windows were surprisingly well sealed, for all that the wind had been tugging at them. At the north-facing window, Dane flicked the brass catches back and felt the weights in the frame dropping as the pane rose slowly. When it was open enough for him to slither through, he slipped out to perch on the wide ledge and pulled the pane back down until his fingers were nearly caught against the sill.

"I'm here," he said grumpily, as though Cyrus didn't know. He set his back to one side of the deep well in which the window was set and his feet against the other, leaning against the glass while the wind pulled at his hair and robe. It was snowing, but the flakes fell against something that was nothing Dane could see, and none reached him.

"You weren't sleeping," said Cyrus. "So don't be such a bear."

Dane sneezed as his own hair tickled his nose. Cyrus was feeling playful. "Am I to have no privacy, still?"

"As much as you need." The wind feathered through his hair. "You never needed much."

"Things change," Dane said.

"Not so much. I speak. You ignore most of it."

"Only the parts that don't matter." Dane looked out past the place where the snow stopped. From here, a layer of snow blanketed the garden that had been, when Dane had been on the ground, green and new. There was no knowing anything for certain in Ezqel's house, nor about Ezqel.

"I think you keeping your hands off the boy matters." Even from thousands of miles away, Cyrus could sound snippy.

"It mattered more to him that I touch him," Dane pointed out. "And to me."

"And you see no danger in that?" The wind snapped at Dane's cheek with an icy finger. "In either of those things?"

"It wouldn't stop me if I did." Dane shook his head. "I never cared much for the rules, Cyrus, and you'll have to live with me having my own opinion again. It's not going to kill you."

There was a long pause that made Dane's chest hollow with dread as he wondered what truth he'd hit upon. Then again, maybe Cyrus was sulking, or talking to someone else. He was just starting to feel ill and cold when Cyrus sighed.

"You are well, then?" Cyrus sounded subdued, or maybe resigned.

"I think so. Better, at the least." He'd been a little better before Ezqel healed him, he knew that much. He'd already felt more whole. Lindsay had as much magic in his little frowns and rare smiles as most enchantments, all but the strongest of them.

"It is good to know."

"You weren't listening to find out if I did it or not?" Dane asked dryly.

"I heard it happen to you," Cyrus said softly. "But I wasn't listening." The wind touched his cheek, gently this time.

"I think it's over," Dane allowed. He hadn't been fully his other self yet, but he'd been human enough, even if not totally of his own accord that last time.

"And the boy?"

"He's not a boy." Dane couldn't help his growl. Lindsay was young and new and tender, but not a boy. "He's grown."

The wind sighed in Dane's ear, but Dane wasn't budging on the matter. "Figure of speech," Cyrus said, at last. "If he's not a boy, what am I?"

"A withered old stick with no sense of humor?" Dane offered, and got his hair pulled for it. He startled himself when he had to stifle laughter. The human in him was more easily amused than the beast.

"What are you, then?" Cyrus snapped.

"A moth-eaten old fur coat." Dane let his head fall back against the stone. "A tattered thing with a little use left in it. To keep him warm enough until he can find something warmer and newer that suits him."

"You're so sure of that?"

"No matter what you think of me, I'm not *that* much of a fool." Dane didn't expect Cyrus to think better of him than that, but he wished it from time to time. Cyrus had little enough reason to change his thinking, and Dane knew it. The way he'd nearly gotten Lindsay killed in Cholula was reason enough and that was only one of many foolish things Dane had done. Lindsay would grow up and move on, if Dane didn't get him killed first.

"You've let him into your bed," Cyrus said, and Dane could hear him rolling his eyes. "And you want me to think you're not a fool?" The wind laughed in Dane's ear.

"Not so much of a fool that I think he'll keep me," Dane rumbled. "Don't worry, Cyrus. You'll have me all to yourself again before you know it."

"I won't have you at all if you don't come back in one piece," Cyrus said, changing the subject as the wind changed quarters.

"That's why I went through all this," Dane said irritably. Now that he'd thought about Lindsay outgrowing him, he was in an ill-temper, and doubly so because he was upset about it at all. "So I wouldn't die so easily. Or did you forget that part?"

That guardians were outgrown was life, Dane reminded himself, forcing down his irritation. It wasn't as though Lindsay would suffer anything terrible and be gone. He would grow and change until he had outgrown Dane and their relationship was altered forever. If Dane had any say about it, it would be one day at a time, so slowly that Lindsay would hardly notice until it occurred to him to be at most a little melancholy over it and no more than that. It was what Dane wanted more than anything, when the human in him could be counseled by the unselfish, steadfast beast.

"I haven't forgotten," Cyrus said, breaking into Dane's argument with himself. "But I have taken steps to see you back here safely nonetheless. Vivian has drawn Moore's attention away from us."

"Is the girl there?" Dane's mind snapped into the present as his hackles rose and his teeth pricked his lip. There, now he was more himself.

"Vivian has seen nothing of her. Moore has made no move and had no communication that suggests the girl has been in contact with her. We think the girl must be after the dog, who has not been seen either, or in disgrace."

Dane tamped down his irrational surge of disappointment at that. "We'll be safe to come in by LaGuardia?" Getting Lindsay home in one piece was far more important than killing Jonas.

"Moore uncovered your actions in Cholula, but our

contacts on the West Coast—at Vivian's urging—convinced her people that the two of you had gone up that way, especially since the trail ran cold in Ezqel's forest. Right now, they are tracking Brenna's people instead."

Brenna. Dane remembered her, and not fondly. The temperamental electromancer made his skin itch, and not just from her ozone and static aura. She was a trollish bitch, and thought as ill of him as he did of her. But he could forgive her a great deal if she kept Moore busy.

"So, they think we haven't made it back here?" Dane hadn't thought to worry about that on the hunt, that some message about his presence would get through to Moore. He'd been too busy killing, too busy in the present. It was his own fault for stopping partway to being fully himself. He'd forgotten how little his animal-self could understand when he was between his true forms.

"No one believes you'd do any business with Ezqel you did not have to do," Cyrus pointed out. His laughter tickled the hairs in Dane's ears, making Dane shake his head. "The word is that you and Jonas are equally unwelcome there, once Ezqel paid his debt by telling you where to find the guul."

Moore was chasing Brenna up the West Coast, the girl was still off somewhere after the dog, and the world was still certain that Dane was fool enough to refuse the aid that would heal him. It suited Dane just fine. He would get Lindsay back to New York, back to the safety of Vivian and Cyrus, and then deal with Jonas.

*Kristan.* Dane chuckled softly. There was bait that no dog could refuse. Sweet meat. She'd forgive him for taking Lindsay as a lover instead of her, he was sure, especially if he could offer her a way to please everyone.

"You're amused by the efforts of others to save your moth-eaten hide?" Cyrus was most certainly not amused.

"Just thinking ahead," Dane said, feeling contented. "I can do that, you know."

"I'll believe it when I see it," Cyrus said. "Come home and

show me." The wind tugged at Dane, drawing him in as though Cyrus planned to pick him up and bring him home on the back of the North Wind.

Dane was ready to go right then, too. Suddenly, he was swept through with a need to return so intense that he wanted to spread his wings and throw himself into the wind. But the new ways had their benefits. "I'll be there soon," he promised. "Both of us will be."

"I'm waiting for you." The wind wrapped around him, tangled in his hair, and he breathed it in. Then, in the next moment, it was gone. Dane was ready to go home.

# Chapter Thirteen

Kloten was crowded and chaotic, like most airports. Staggered announcements came over the loudspeaker in German, echoed in English and other languages Lindsay couldn't keep track of. On the flight in, the rough, guttural instructions had only served to make Lindsay more nervous, more miserable, but not this time. He was ready. Healthy, finally, and steady, even with his backpack heavy on his shoulders. New York, Cyrus's house, was home for Dane. Lindsay hoped that, after everything he'd done to learn and to fix himself, it could become home for him too.

Dane, for once, drew only admiring glances. He was human looking, tall and graceful and stern. As always, no matter where they were, Dane seemed to understand the language well enough. Lindsay let him take the lead. He wasn't as noticeable as Dane, and people tended to not realize he was there, even when no magic was involved. They made it through the line to get their boarding passes, checking their bags, and then to the terminal.

"Do you want anything to eat?" Lindsay asked quietly, remembering that the food on the plane from New York had been horrible, even though they'd been in first class. He didn't expect it to be much better on the way back. He told himself that he was just thinking of Dane's sensitive senses and trying to spare Dane another lousy experience, and that he wasn't trying to squeeze another tiny moment or two of intimacy out of the time they had left.

"We should both eat." Dane squeezed Lindsay's small hand in his big one. "You can't live on air. Pick where you want to eat, and we'll have a meal."

"I couldn't talk Ezqel into letting me trade up for that, either," Lindsay murmured, flashing Dane a smile. He looked around at the fast food kiosks and more traditional restaurants along the hall to the terminal. "There, maybe?" He pointed to a restaurant with neon in the windows and dim lights inside. The illusion of privacy was appealing.

"Whatever you want." Dane steered them that way and held the door for Lindsay. "As long as you eat."

"Anything to keep me from having to eat the stuff they served on the plane last time." Lindsay held up two fingers to the maitre d' and the man led them to a table, where Dane finally let go of Lindsay's hand so he could pull out a chair for Lindsay.

Lindsay soaked up the closeness as he skimmed the laminated menu. Thank goodness for the ubiquity of English in international airports. He found something that seemed edible and spent the rest of his time watching Dane.

Dane put the menu aside. "What're you looking at?"

Lindsay rolled his eyes. "Same thing everyone else in the airport is looking at."

Dane frowned more, but didn't say anything. He just tapped Lindsay's menu. "Know what you're eating?"

"Chicken Oscar. Would you prefer it if I pretended that I haven't noticed the change? You look different, but I still like it. I'm just...getting used to it."

"You don't have to pretend anything." Dane seemed disgruntled, regardless. He wasn't comfortable and it showed, which wasn't normal for him.

"Is it... What's wrong?" Lindsay frowned. He hadn't meant to upset Dane.

"Nothing's wrong. I look normal. It is what it is." Dane leaned back and gestured for the waiter to return.

Lindsay kept frowning. There were four chairs at the table,

but he and Dane were seated opposite each other. It was too far away, Lindsay decided, so he got up and shifted over to sit in one of the chairs closer to Dane. "You are so full of shit," he muttered, as the waiter walked up to their table.

Dane blinked at Lindsay before giving the waiter his attention. He ordered for them both and turned back to Lindsay. "What?"

"You've gotten grumpy every time I've looked at you since Ezqel did his thing," Lindsay said quietly. He'd noticed, every time. How could he not? "So you can't really expect me to believe you when you say nothing's wrong. I'll get used to the change, but…if you don't like it, why don't you shift back to the way you were before?"

"I will when I don't have to be around other people," Dane said flatly. "It's better to look human than not. Drawing attention isn't good for you, anyway."

"You got by before." Lindsay reached out, finding Dane's big hand and rubbing his cold little fingers over it.

"Until you came along, I 'got by' by way of not being in the company of people." Dane turned his hand palm up for Lindsay's touch. "For a long time. Still not fond of it."

"We're almost back to New York, and then you can go back to not being in the company of people." That, Lindsay imagined, was probably the answer to his question of whether Dane would still want him around when they got home.

"Enough of that." Dane put his arm around Lindsay and pulled him close, snorting irritably like a disgruntled bear.

*Oh.* Lindsay relaxed, rubbing his cheek against Dane's.

Dane butted his nose against Lindsay's temple and his ear, purring softly. His cheek against Lindsay's was uncharacteristically smooth, but as warm as ever. Lindsay could hear Dane's purrs—he could *feel* them—and they made him smile.

"You need to eat," Dane murmured. "You're too small, little bunny." He ran a finger over Lindsay's ribs.

Lindsay turned his head to see the waiter heading their

way with a basket of baguettes. "I'll eat," he murmured, wriggling to sit down in the chair again without tumbling over.

Dane reached over to pet him. He always managed to make it feel perfectly normal. "Good. Cyrus might forgive me if you come back with a few pounds on you."

"Is he really going to be angry with you?" Lindsay asked, once the waiter walked away again. He reached out to tear off a small piece of the bread and picked at it.

"Yes." Dane took a drink of his water. "He already is. It's nothing new. When you get old like us, things build up." He didn't look terribly upset, but he wasn't happy either.

"I'm sorry. I didn't mean to cause trouble."

"Eat your bread." Dane picked a piece up and held it out for Lindsay to eat. "*You* are not the trouble here. What's between Cyrus and me isn't your problem."

Lindsay ate the bite of bread and sighed. "I just don't want..."

"Don't want what?" Dane offered up another piece, but he was obviously waiting for Lindsay's reply.

"I don't want you to stop letting me be near you." Lindsay didn't want to cause trouble, he didn't want Cyrus to be angry, and he didn't want to lose the little piece of comfort and happiness he'd found with Dane.

"That won't happen," Dane said simply. "Cyrus and I have been angry at each other about things since long before the last time I looked this way." Dane put his fingers under Lindsay's chin, making Lindsay look at him. "Cyrus gave you to me. He can't take you back. There are rules about these things, older than any of us. What's between you and me is something else. What I did to keep Jonas from having you, I didn't do for Cyrus."

Dane had *died* to keep Jonas from having him. Lindsay met Dane's eyes, stunned by the admission. "Oh," he whispered, hope creeping in. Cyrus couldn't take him away from Dane. There were rules. "Good."

"Eat now," Dane said gently. He picked up the bread he'd

dropped on Lindsay's plate and offered it up again. "Everything's going to be all right."

Lindsay nodded, taking the bite from Dane's fingers and picking up one for himself. He'd shredded the piece of bread without realizing, but at least now it was in bite-sized pieces.

After a moment, Dane leaned over and pressed a kiss to Lindsay's temple. It was a small gesture, but surprisingly intimate. Lindsay couldn't help smiling. Dane didn't say anything else, but he petted Lindsay's thigh under the table, a smile touching the corners of his mouth.

When their meals arrived, Lindsay ate carefully and slowly, and he sank back to curl up in his chair, watching the restaurant staff bustle about.

"Am I going to have to carry you onto the plane?" Dane teased. He'd cleaned his plate and, without asking, tugged Lindsay's over to finish the last of what was there. It took a lot to fuel his body.

"Airports are exhausting," Lindsay murmured. "But I can wait until I'm on the plane to sleep."

"Taniel put you through your paces this morning," Dane reminded him, gesturing for the waiter to bring their check. "That'll wear you out, too." Dane paid in cash, then stood and offered Lindsay his hand. "Come on. Ten hours in a tin can awaits."

Lindsay slipped his hand into Dane's and uncurled himself from the way he'd been sitting in his chair, sorting out his limbs and standing up. "You make it sound so appealing."

"It's ten hours in a tin can with me." Dane gave Lindsay a genuinely charming smile. He was very beautiful when he was human.

"You're right, that is appealing."

Dane drew the usual uncertain glances when they got on the plane. His darker skin and unusual features and his size, no matter how pretty he was, made people nervous at times. Still, on this flight, the flight attendants seemed determined to flirt with him from the start. He ignored all of it and only wrinkled his nose with displeasure at the attention. Lindsay found himself tempted to growl on Dane's behalf.

Lindsay let Dane sit near the window, and flipped up the arms of their seats so Dane could sit partly sideways and straighten his legs without them being in the aisle. After the first offering of drinks and snacks, he leaned over to curl up against Dane's side. The flight attendants may have assumed that Lindsay was too young to be anything but Dane's teenaged son or charge, but Lindsay didn't care. *He* knew better, and that was what mattered.

Dane slid his arm around Lindsay's shoulders and pulled Lindsay close, so that Lindsay was snuggled up against his chest. Maybe it comforted him as much as Lindsay. He sighed heavily, relaxing, and something in his rib cage popped into place with a dull noise that translated clearly enough to Lindsay's ear. "You should sleep."

Dane was right, but Lindsay wasn't ready to sleep yet. He wriggled until he could sit up and kiss Dane on the mouth.

"Going to make all the flight attendants jealous of me?" Dane teased, nipping at Lindsay's lips.

"Of *me*, maybe." Lindsay snorted, butting his nose against Dane's chin. "I think you're overestimating my attractiveness to the general public."

"I'm not overestimating your capacity to make them think you're the most beautiful thing they've ever seen." Dane slid his hand down to grope Lindsay's ass.

"That doesn't seem like a good way to *not* get noticed," Lindsay pointed out.

"Yes, but who would care?" Dane nuzzled Lindsay's nose with his own, smiling. "You might have to ward off worshipers, but people do manage."

Lindsay liked it when Dane teased like this. It made Dane smile, and Lindsay liked being involved with anything that made Dane smile. "Sounds like a lot of trouble," he said, grinning.

"You're young and resilient. I think you'd cope." Dane laughed and kissed him. "You're pretty brave."

Brave. "Maybe." Lindsay could be brave, even if the idea of using his magic still made something in his gut twist and churn.

He wanted more than just these little kisses, and he knew what he had to do to get what he wanted. Pulling back from Dane's mouth, he closed his eyes and imagined them as they had been a moment ago, with Lindsay tucked against Dane's side, ready to fall asleep. He sent his magic out in one careful wave, filling the airplane with his illusion, and then opened his eyes to look at Dane again.

Dane's eyes were searching, his expression serious. "Think it worked?"

A flight attendant pushing a cart passed them by without a second glance. "Kiss me again, and we'll find out."

Dane pulled Lindsay in for a real kiss, hot and shameless and possessive. Dane kissed Lindsay like he wanted to make up for not being able to do anything more. Everything more. Like he wanted to make Lindsay come from that alone. After a long while, he kissed away to Lindsay's ear.

"How did you end up not sleeping?"

Lindsay laughed softly, but this time, he was more than willing to sleep. He was sated, worn out and feeling blissful. He tucked his cheek against Dane's chest and let the illusion go. Life around them went on as normal. Everyone was just as they'd been before—unharmed.

He wasn't broken anymore. Lindsay felt more than just successful, he felt secure. Finally, he was safely down in the depths of the world, not drifting exposed on the surface. "Wake me up when we're home."

"I will." Dane stroked Lindsay's hair as he fell asleep to the sound of Dane's big heart beating slow and steady—all was right with the world.

# Chapter Fourteen

LaGuardia was too bright and too loud, after the dim, muted cabin of the airplane. Lindsay had slept well, warm and safely tucked against Dane, but he was glad to be off the plane and out of the cramped confines of his seat. He arched and stretched as they walked out of the gate, easing his muscles into movement.

Dane kept a hand on him, looking around them warily. He hadn't seemed this nervous in the forest or on the streets of Cholula. His mood effectively shut down Lindsay's lazy contentment. If it hadn't been for the stress of wondering where Moore's people were—if they were here at all—Lindsay would have loved travelling with Dane.

"Luggage, then home," Dane murmured.

"All right." Lindsay tried to see what Dane saw, but he didn't know what he was looking for. "Let's go."

This was where they were going to be most vulnerable, Lindsay realized, between here and the safety of Cyrus's house. If they were followed, it could spell disaster for everyone. That thought almost frightened Lindsay more than the idea of being captured again.

At least if it was only him who got taken, the others would come for him. The thought startled Lindsay so badly that he almost tripped over his own feet. He caught up to Dane with a hop and a skip. They would come for him. He'd never had that feeling before, and he had no idea when it had crept in, but all the time he'd spent with Dane had given him some secret hope that it was true.

"It'll be okay," Dane said, watching over his shoulder to make sure Lindsay came back to his side.

"Do you want me to..." Lindsay looked around them, at the crowds, at all the movement and light around them. The air was full of voices rising to the ceiling, bouncing off the walls. There were so many of them. "I could try to hide us." He could help. He wanted to help, to be useful, like the rest of them.

"I don't want to lose track of you." Dane guided him around a kiosk and headed for the luggage carousel.

"I could exclude you. Like on the plane." A tall man, cell phone pressed to his ear, bumped Lindsay with his shoulder and knocked him back a pace. He stifled his noise of pain and took a few fast steps to catch up with Dane again. He hated airports.

"You think you can do that with this many people around?" Dane frowned. Lindsay could see him calculating the distance between them by the way his eyes flicked over Lindsay and the way he reached for Lindsay's hand.

Even if Lindsay had ever wanted to resent the gesture, he simply couldn't have—it felt too good and safe, on a nearly primal level, to slide his cold hand into Dane's warm one.

"I can try." He let Dane draw him in close. Yes, he was getting better at taking care of himself, but until they were with Cyrus and Vivian, neither he nor Dane could relax. Maybe not even then.

Dane's beautiful human face was stern, and he stopped walking to draw Lindsay into the relative shelter of an ATM kiosk. "Try," he suggested. "If it doesn't feel good, let it go."

"Okay."

Lindsay swallowed a stab of nervousness and straightened his shoulders. He had no idea how Dane managed to focus in places like this. After the peace of the forest and the mystical calm of Ezqel's house, Lindsay's human senses were overwhelmed. *Everyone else is overwhelmed too*, he told himself. *I can use that to my advantage. No one wants to notice us. No one cares.* Hiding from people who didn't care would be the easy part. He hoped it would work on the people who did care.

"Don't let go." Lindsay squeezed Dane's hand.

That got Lindsay a smile. He was used to the flash of fangs and a feral glint in Dane's eyes, but Dane was human again—or more than human—and this smile was beatific, like an angel or a saint, and the heat in Dane's eyes was pure gold. For a moment, Lindsay forgot about everything except for Dane's beauty and the realization that he was looking at his lover. *His lover.*

"We'll be home soon," Dane promised, ducking his head so that his words drifted warm against Lindsay's cheek. He pressed a kiss where his words had landed and a shiver ran down Lindsay's spine.

Lindsay slid his free hand up along Dane's neck, feeling the beat of Dane's pulse alive and strong against his fingers. *Home.* It sounded so good. Moore and her lackeys were a small shadow on the brightness that was his life right now. Home, magic, future... Months earlier, Lindsay'd had no hope of anything, and now he had it all.

"I'll try to get us there." He kissed Dane's silky golden skin where his fingers lay and tasted that familiar musk that was *home* already. "If you can find our luggage, you'll be my hero."

"I'm not already?" Dane pulled away, laughing. "I'm wounded."

"You'll heal, remember?" Lindsay said dryly, elbowing him. "Look for our luggage, so I can do my job."

"Get to it." Dane squeezed his hand and Lindsay took a slow breath.

There was a hollow in the center of his magic, like the eye of a storm, and Lindsay made sure that he and Dane were safe within it. He began to erase them from everyone's attention. In the confines of the luggage area, it was easy to do, but he couldn't make things quiet. The chatter around him increased, intensified, until he was wincing from the noise.

"Are you okay?"

Lindsay could barely hear Dane's voice over the clamor, but he nodded. He was aware of Dane gathering their few things, slinging bags over his shoulder, sliding his other hand into Lindsay's.

"Time to go. Seems like it's working."

They moved in a blank space in the world, people veering around them without looking, always at the same distance, like there was a wall around them. A wall of *nothing*. People's eyes slid off of them as though even the air around them was hard to look at.

*I can do this,* Lindsay said sternly, trying to calm the panic that started to rise in his chest. He felt claustrophobic. Had it been this noisy before he'd put his magic up?

*I think he's cheating on me.* What? Dane wasn't, wouldn't, they weren't even... *I wanted to go to Hawaii, but, no, she had to have Disneyland.* Hawaii, who wanted to go there? Lindsay had never even considered Disneyland... *I'm hungry, I'm hungry, I'm hungry!* A toddler's wail cut through Lindsay's focus.

*Oh, God.* Lindsay clung to Dane's hand so hard that his own knuckles cracked.

"Lindsay?" Dane's gentle rumble cut through the noise.

"I'm okay," Lindsay lied. There had to be a way to make it stop. *Why now?* It would have happened on the plane, if... Lindsay bit his lip, trying to breathe through his nose and not panic and keep the illusion up all at once. Someone was watching, looking for them. He could feel it like paranoia creeping up the back of his throat.

On the plane, there had been a soft whispering that he'd ignored because Dane's kisses felt so good. Maybe he'd been able to hold on because of that distraction, maybe there'd been fewer minds on his. It was so loud, Lindsay just wanted it to stop. *Please.*

They wouldn't be in the airport much longer. Lindsay's head was throbbing, but he made himself hang on to the illusion. The idea that they were being watched was getting stronger and stronger. If he was hearing the thoughts of everyone around them, there could really be someone there. If he dropped the illusion and they were found—or worse, followed—it would be his fault. He didn't want to be weak.

*I'm so tired of being afraid.* Dane was a tall, dark shadow at the margin of his awareness. Safety. Haven. Dane would protect him. Lindsay just had to hold it together.

Taniel had talked about shielding the mind. Lindsay hadn't thought it was necessary, he hadn't felt anything from Taniel or Dane, so he'd never thought to pursue the idea. It was too late for that. When he could, if he got through this, he'd work on it. But now, he had to survive.

The Institute had taught him things, Lindsay realized. He recognized the sensation of drawing into himself, detaching from his own body. There was something about working magic that was akin to clenching a muscle rather than sustaining a thought. His mind could hold the illusion even while his thoughts—his self—slipped away.

It still felt like hell, but Lindsay had survived hell before. He had survived Moore and her artifact. He could survive this. *I am stronger than you.* Remembering that gave him more strength against the bullet thoughts firing through the minds that were all linked to his in the moment. It let him keep walking.

Lindsay had no idea where they were. He was blind. Belatedly, he realized that the last thing he'd seen outside of the illusion was the sign as they'd left the baggage area. His eyes were working—how he knew, he couldn't tell—but he couldn't see, and he couldn't hear, either. His mind was full of so much vision, so much sound, everything anyone under his spell was experiencing, that he was deaf and blind...and dumb. If he opened his mouth, he had no idea if his own words would come out or someone else's.

And that was when he panicked. He tried to pull out of the illusion, tried to get his mind back. He'd been under an illusion of his own—that magic *worked.* That it was simple. That he'd been *defective* and that was why he couldn't control it, why he couldn't use it to save himself. But he'd been wrong. There was nothing magical about magic at all.

Lindsay tried to talk, to tell Dane he couldn't do this anymore. He fought to get into his own body, to be the one behind his eyes—*his* eyes and no one else's eyes. He couldn't draw attention to them, he couldn't give in to the urge to claw at his head and tear at his hair so he could feel it and know that this was his body, his own body. His jaw was clamped—he thought it was *his* jaw—on desperate whimpers.

Just when he felt a scream about to break out of his throat, everything was silent, even him. As though someone had dropped a bell jar over a candle, the world was utterly still and the fuel for Lindsay's panic was used up and gone. He was locked in stillness like an insect in amber, alone except for a sense of sympathy.

"It's hard, isn't it?" It was a woman's voice, one Lindsay had never heard before.

Dane was drawing him off to the side, so they were close to the wall, out of the immediate press of bodies, but everything was still moving around them, everything was chaotic. Someone's luggage fell off of a cart with a crash, and a mother with two suitcases and three children stopped right in front of them, forcing Dane to step away from Lindsay or run them over.

*Dane.* Lindsay reached for Dane, but the impulse never made it to his hand.

"Don't worry," the woman said. "It'll get easier once you learn. I'll be there to teach you this time."

"Lindsay..." Dane said his name, trying to reach for him, but that was all. Lindsay watched him wind down like a toy. His eyes were open, but all the light drained from his face. It was as though he'd simply left his body there and gone somewhere else.

"Let's all stay very calm." The voice in Lindsay's head was cool and precise. "Making a scene will just get people hurt."

Lindsay could feel his magic still working, but there was a power more controlled than his behind it now. He felt empty and limp, like a puppet. It was a sensation so familiar that he could hardly fight it.

"It's time to come home," the woman said. Not the woman. *The girl. Lourdes.*

Somewhere, Lindsay was screaming in terror and outrage, but it never went beyond that small place deep inside where he'd been locked the whole time he was at the Institute.

"Don't run." There was hot breath on Lindsay's hair and big hands on his shoulders. The voice was horribly familiar. *Jonas.* "Let's get you someplace safe."

Lindsay tried to struggle, but he couldn't fight himself. His body wasn't here anymore, and his mind was gone as well. He was a walking dead man.

"Dramatic, but accurate." There was laughter in Lourdes's thoughts. "Hush. If one of us slips while we're playing this game, it could kill us all."

Lindsay knew he was walking, being guided by Jonas's hands on his shoulders. Dane followed behind like a dog.

*Could kill us.* Lindsay was willing to make that sacrifice. He gathered his courage.

"All of us?" Lourdes's thoughts were a chiding tap on Lindsay's soul. "Even him?"

Lindsay had a flash of awareness that Lourdes had her mind on both of them. She felt impossibly powerful. Under the moment of horror and awe, he felt that she was having trouble holding on to Dane. The mind could make up hope from nothing.

"Why don't you both come this way?" There was a nearly invisible door in the wall that led off to a service hall, easily missed until now. A beautiful young woman in an airline uniform stood there, holding the door for the three of them. "Jonas, if you'd escort our friend to the car, I'll make sure Dane joins us. It is Dane, still, isn't it?" She gave Dane a bright smile as though he could see her, as though he'd answered. "I thought so." She held out her hand and he came to her, letting her take his hand.

Jonas steered Lindsay toward the door and his claws slid through Lindsay's clothes to dig into Lindsay's shoulders. "Feel free to try that game of yours on me again, little man," he murmured. "Any time you like." Trickles ran down Lindsay's arms under his sleeves.

Why couldn't Ezqel have let Jonas die?

Jonas laughed softly as he guided Lindsay through the long, white hall under the strings of fluorescent lights. "Too bad you can't fight, pretty. Worse that I have to keep you in one piece. I'd like to take you apart in front of our friend here." He rumbled, sounding so much like Dane. "He died too soon last time, would have missed the whole thing." His breath was sweet against Lindsay's cheek. "He did die last time. I remember it now. Can't wait to do it again."

"If you're good." Lourdes's voice was light, floating in the stale air of the hall. "If I have to kill him to keep him quiet, you don't get to. Can't you watch your paws? The smell of his little friend's blood is making him harder to handle. I'd rather kill Dane now, but I'm trying to be civil to you. Do you think Cyrus could grow a new dog if we sent him the head? I'd know that already if you'd let me cut yours off, Jonas."

Jonas laughed again. "Let's see what you have to give me before we talk about me giving you anything, girl."

*Please don't hurt Dane.* Lindsay had watched Dane die once already. He never wanted to see anything like that as long as he lived. He reached for his magic, heart racing with fear and anger when it still wasn't there for him to use. The place where it was, here and not here at once, was empty.

"Has to happen sometime, Lindsay," Lourdes said blithely. "He's done too much damage. We can't keep him. He is a lot prettier now, so I see why you'd be upset. Did he put on that pretty face just for you? Underneath, he's just a flea-bitten old thing. We'll get you a nicer dog. Nicer than Jonas, even. Look."

There were stairs that led down, and a pair of tall, solemn men, twins, stood waiting on the landing. "Hello, gentlemen," Lourdes said cheerfully. "Lindsay, meet Hesham and Mahesh. They'll be taking care of you. I know how much you like being cared for and I wouldn't take something away from you without replacing it with something better. I'm sure Dr. Moore will let you keep them." The two men bowed in unison, extending their hands to Lindsay.

They looked like corpses, fallow skin tight over dry bones; they smelled of cedar and sandalwood and roses and dust. Lindsay tried to back away from their reaching hands, even though it put him in Jonas's arms, against the feral's big chest. Suddenly, even Jonas seemed better than whatever these men could do to him. And Dr. Moore. Her name was laced through all his worst memories.

Jonas shoved him away. The twins caught Lindsay gently and righted him, each taking one of his arms. "I need my hands free," Jonas said roughly. "Come on, girl, enough socializing. Let's get the hell out of here."

Lourdes was sauntering down the stairs behind them, her arm looped through Dane's. Her mind slid away from Lindsay's as soon as the twins had hold of him, but Lindsay's magic was still locked out of reach. Now, he was terrified. His magic was *gone.*

"You think you have a grip on him, but it might not last." Jonas snarled as he spoke. "It doesn't last on me, not forever."

Lindsay struggled against the two men who held him, hoping that Jonas was right, that Dane would break free of Lourdes's hold on him. Whatever she was doing, Dane had to get free. Lindsay had to get free. He didn't want to go back to Dr. Moore, not again. Not ever.

"Come, sir." One of his two keepers spoke, and the man's accent was British. They were gentle with him, smoothing his clothes and hair as Dane would have done, always keeping an iron grip on him, and they guided him down the stairs. Under other circumstances, they would have been comforting, and that thought made Lindsay ill.

Together, they all went into the lower levels, through winding tunnels, and came out in a service bay where a van and a limousine stood waiting. The driver of the van, a broad, flat-faced man in coveralls, got out and swung the back open to reveal the cage inside.

"Say goodbye, Lindsay." Lourdes let go of Dane and he stood still. "He's going with Jonas and McKay, in the van. We have other things to do." Hesham and Mahesh turned Lindsay so that he could see Dane, each with a gentle hand on one of his arms, as though they were supporting him instead of holding him prisoner.

It was Dane's body, but was Dane really in there? Lindsay wouldn't say goodbye to him, either way. It felt wrong. He wished he could see into Dane's mind, to bring him back to himself.

He stepped forward, and they let him, their hands still on his arms so he couldn't run. When he was close enough to touch Dane, he leaned up and brushed a kiss over Dane's lips. *Wake up.* Lindsay kissed harder, desperation and fear building up inside him and seeping out from between his lips. His magic was gone, but he still had his body. Lindsay swallowed a scream and pushed his tongue into Dane's mouth, trying to elicit some response, anything.

Nothing.

Dane stood there, as still as a corpse. Lindsay's stomach twisted and he barely kept from retching on the asphalt.

Jonas snorted, and he grabbed a handful of Dane's hair and shoved him toward the van. "All that effort and no show." McKay, standing by the door, laughed and helped him throw Dane's unresisting form in the back.

The limo driver, a slight, gray woman, was holding the door. "Come along, Lindsay," Lourdes said. "We can't keep Dr. Moore waiting."

Lourdes patted Lindsay on the cheek as she breezed past. He flinched at her touch, but he couldn't get far enough to avoid the warm brush of her fingers. Dr. Moore could wait until hell froze over. He was going to find a way out of this, one way or another.

His new guards guided him toward the limousine, helped him in, and settled beside him on the seat facing the back.

Lourdes sat across from him, phone in hand. "Would you tell Dr. Moore that I've got what she wants?" she was saying to whomever was on the end of the line. She gave Lindsay a sweet smile once he was settled. "Yes. We're looking forward to seeing her too."

Lourdes's mind—it must have been hers—was still clenched around Lindsay's magic, keeping him from it without any sign of effort on her part. He had thought she was gone from his mind, but he had no other explanation for it. Unless...he glanced at the twins, and one of them, he thought it was Mahesh, smiled at him. Lindsay stomped on his panic at the idea that he had to deal with three mind mages at once, and sorted the information he could get.

*Guests.* So Dane was going to the same place Lindsay was. That made him feel a little better. With the way Lourdes held his magic in check, he couldn't imagine what he'd be able to do with that, but knowing that Dane's mindless husk wasn't being taken somewhere so that Jonas could kill it while Dane couldn't fight back was a relief. It would make it easier for Lindsay to find Dane when he got out. He pushed for his magic again. That he couldn't feel or hear Lourdes in his head was no reason to think the grip on him wasn't hers. All Lindsay could do was wait for a break in her attention.

Lourdes tucked the phone away in the purse that sat on the seat beside her and folded her hands in her lap. "We're so glad you're back," she said pleasantly. To his dismay, Lindsay had the distinct impression that she was sincere. That made things so much worse, that these people might care about him as though he were one of their own, as though he were a wayward little brother. "Everyone's just dying to see you again."

Dane knew exactly what was happening the moment the world slowed. He tried to say something, managed to get Lindsay's name out, but that was all. He even knew who was doing this to him. How had Cyrus missed this? How had *he*?

As he stood there, frozen, fighting to keep his awareness connected to his body, he could see Jonas stepping out of a service hallway. He could see the widening terror in Lindsay's eyes as Jonas laid hands on him. As he was falling away from himself, he saw Lourdes.

*Not for some days.* Ezqel's voice and Cyrus's sounded the same in the fading echo along the hallways of his mind.

She looked much as she had when he'd seen her last, though the childish roundness was gone from her face and her body. Now, she was slim and willowy, her fine red hair pulled back tightly in a twist at the nape of her neck that reminded him of Moore. Lourdes's pale, pale eyes were the last thing in his vision before he was gone.

Dane woke with a collar around his neck and his hands trapped behind his back in iron gauntlets. He was in a moving vehicle, his back pressed up against bars. He'd been here before. Maybe not this exact van, but one like it, more than once. He didn't have to open his eyes or do anything beyond inhale to know that Jonas was there with him.

"So, do you ever get tired of failing?"

Yes. Yes, he did. "Fuck you, Jonas." Dane got very tired of failing. In fact, he was exhausted from it. Failing all by himself was one thing, but this new twist of failing Lindsay was something else altogether.

"So, the elf fixed you did he?"

When Dane opened one eye, he saw Jonas sitting across from him, back to the bars on the other side of the van, trapped in here with him. "Looks that way."

"I'd forgotten what you looked like." Jonas sounded almost thoughtful. He stretched his legs out in front of him and crossed his arms over his chest. He was ugly, brutal-looking like a club or an axe, but he was still human on the outside. "Pity you got so pretty just in time to die."

"Who says I'm going to die?" Dane didn't have any intention of dying. He had a lot of fucking up to fix; he didn't have time to die. Lindsay hadn't even had a chance to live, not really, not whole, and Dane planned to make sure Lindsay got every chance he deserved.

"Me. They won't let me kill your scrawny little boyfriend, so I'll have to be satisfied with killing you."

Dane lunged forward, trying to get his feet under him, but his collar was chained to the bars and he was wrenched backward before he managed to get any momentum. The metal squealed in protest but didn't give, even when he tried again. Jonas sat there and laughed, watching him strangle himself as he fought to get free, blood trickling from where the collar cut into his neck, and his claws splintering on the inside of the gauntlets.

Finally, Jonas stopped laughing and moved enough to slam one foot into Dane's face as Dane surged forward again. Dane felt his nose crumple and his teeth crack. Blood poured down the back of his throat and his head smashed into the bars. It should have hurt worse than it did, but all Dane felt was a rush of ecstasy as his magic flowed through his flesh and began to knit it together again.

It took everything he had to keep from laughing, to make himself sag in his bonds and fall limp against the bars. Jonas was mocking him again, oblivious to Dane's deception. The smell of blood must have been thick enough in the van that it covered anything else. Or maybe Jonas never had grasped the idea of self-sacrifice.

Dane hung there, his breath barely rasping past the pressure of the collar on his neck, as Jonas got to his feet and, holding the bars overhead for support, kicked Dane over and over again, cracking bone and pulping flesh with glee. Dane lay there and let Jonas break him, soaking in the pain and waiting for his chance to get free.

*For every purpose, there is also a season*, Ezqel had said while he was being healed. *Your season can begin again. You think you have much left to do. I can see it in you, you know. You will fail, and fail, and still not end.* At the time, with his magic fading and runes burning into his skin, it had felt like a fresh curse.

Jonas wrenched Dane's head back and, for a moment, Dane was looking up at the man who had been his friend. For a moment, there was regret on Jonas's face. The regret was gone as soon as it had come, replaced by hate. Dane mustered up a smile as Jonas slit his throat. *...and still not end.*

Lindsay tried to watch out the window, to figure out where they were going. No tunnels yet, and no bridges, so they were still in Queens, or in Brooklyn. Traffic was thick, but even so, the street signs were too dark and went by too quickly for Lindsay to read. He wondered if that was Lourdes's doing, or if it was simply the way the car was moving.

There weren't any skyscrapers to help Lindsay guess where he was. Most of what he could see out the window was too dark to make out, though a trick of the streetlights made a massive cemetery just barely visible. The only damn thing he could see, and it had to be something that wouldn't do him any good, because he didn't recognize it.

"Are you sure that what you're seeing is real?" Lourdes had been reading something on a small device she'd pulled from her purse, but she stopped to look over at Lindsay.

"I'm sure that you're a bitch," Lindsay muttered. "Does Moore have you trained to sit up and beg too?"

"Spending time with that animal has taught you poor manners," Lourdes said primly. "I'm Dr. Moore's colleague, not her pet. You know, your education has been sorely neglected, Lindsay. You're remarkably lacking in deductive reasoning."

"Just offering you the benefit of the doubt. I'd respect you more if you were her pet. At least then you'd just be following orders." Lindsay slid his gaze back to the window, not wanting to miss the changes in his surroundings.

"You could be so powerful." Lourdes's expression shifted, softened. "I know you hate what they did to you, but now that you're free of it, you could negotiate, you know. You could be useful to them. To us. We're not puppets." She gestured at Hesham and Mahesh to either side of him. "Ask your friends here. We're not fools, either. We have purpose of our own."

"Why would I want to work for the people who tortured me?" Lindsay flicked his gaze back to Lourdes incredulously."For two years, they kept me strapped down and drugged up, poked and prodded me and experimented on me. Why would I want to be a part of that?"

"Better to be a part of it on your own terms than on theirs." Lourdes shrugged and smiled at him. "I should know. It's not so terrible, and they're not necessarily wrong. There's so much you don't know, Lindsay. So many things Cyrus and his pet and his woman didn't tell you about us, about our people. Did you ever stop to think about it, how little you know?"

*Yes.* Lindsay looked out the window again. He didn't care what Lourdes said, he didn't want to be a part of the organization that had tortured him like that, not on any terms.

One of the twins, Hesham, patted him on the knee. Lindsay flinched from the touch, pulling his legs tighter together. The touch was soothing, and he hated it.

"There are many benefits to being agreeable," Lourdes said. "Including never again having to be as afraid as you are right now." Lindsay glared at her and was met with a frightening wealth of understanding and sympathy. She folded her hands in her lap and looked out the window. With her pale, pale skin, and her pale gray-green eyes, she reminded him too much of the mirror.

Lindsay didn't answer Lourdes, didn't speak at all for the rest of the drive. It was just as well that only a few minutes later, the car went dark as they drove underground into some kind of tunnel beneath a building. The sign out front had said something about a battalion. Lindsay's stomach twisted with fear, and he felt around for any scrap of his magic, any thread he could use to unravel Lourdes's hold over him.

"It'll hurt less if you don't struggle." Lourdes smiled at him just before the car dipped into the dark and kept going along aslow curve. Lindsay realized that she meant it, that she cared. He would rather it have been an illusion, a trap. "Dr. Moore is going to be so pleased to see you," Lourdes said. "You don't need to be afraid. One way or another, everything will be sorted out soon."

# Chapter Fifteen

Lourdes, Hesham and Mahesh escorted Lindsay from the limousine and led him into the heart of the complex. They passed men in uniform who stepped aside respectfully, nodding to Lindsay and the other three as though he were a guest. There were colored lines painted on the walls and, after a while, it became obvious that they were following the green stripe. It led through one set of security doors, and another, and finally to a double set of doors marked with black and yellow warning bars.

"Home, sweet home," Lourdes said cheerfully. She stepped into a yellow box painted on the floor and a panel in the wall by the door slid open. A scanner read her palm and her retinas, and cameras at the ceiling whirred as they scanned the group. The doors opened up and Lourdes led the way deeper still.

The air here smelled of disinfectant and electricity. Lindsay was escorted to a hall that looked like it had been transplanted from a hospital, or from the facility he'd been held in before. That had been in DC, he reminded himself. This was New York. It wasn't the same, but he promised himself that the end result would be the same. He'd get out of this. He had to.

They passed door after door, all offset so that from the window of each, one could see nothing else but the opposite wall.

"You'll be safe in here." A swipe of a key card Lourdes pulled from her purse opened a door like all the rest, and she gestured for Lindsay to step in. He dug in his heels, but Hesham and Mahesh pushed him forward—gently, like a parent urging a child into class on the first day of school—and he crossed the threshold.

The first thing Lindsay recognized were the markings on the walls and floor and ceiling: one from the floor of Ezqel's study, and another from the white marble circle, one from the symbols Taniel had written in a book that Lindsay had seen from the corner of his eye, another from the mirror's frame.

"We don't want you to hurt yourself."

Lourdes's voice came from a distance, reaching where Lindsay was caught in his memories. A needle slid into his arm and, before he could panic, warmth and pain spread out from the prick of it in his skin. Lindsay could see, in his mind's eye, Moore's notes. He remembered watching, strapped upright in a cage, his mind recording his surroundings long after his consciousness was gone. Why his mind was tormenting him with that, he couldn't tell.

"It's for your own good."

Hesham and Mahesh were coaxing his faltering body into a straitjacket. Lindsay wanted to protest, to scream, but he couldn't move. He couldn't move and it wasn't just the drugs. *What did you do to me?*

"Just a little cocktail," Lourdes answered. The twins were guiding him down to the floor in a corner of the dim room, taking his shoes and socks and belt, everything he could use to hurt himself or someone else. Lourdes crouched so that she could see his eyes, and Lindsay realized that she thought he was talking to her. "The twins know what they're doing." She took his face in her hands so that he could see her in spite of how heavy his head was on his limp neck. "No one wants to hurt you, Lindsay," she said tenderly. "Sometimes, to save everyone else, one of us has to suffer. I promise we'll make it up to you when we're done."

Lindsay tried to spit at her, but the medication made him so uncoordinated, he only dribbled saliva down his chin.

"I know." Lourdes wiped his face clean with her sleeve, mopping his cheeks as well. It was only then that Lindsay realized he was crying. "It's going to be okay." She kissed him on the forehead before she rose. "It was hard for me, too. And look at me now. I'm fine."

She left, swiping her key card through the inner lock this time, and the ghostly figures of Hesham and Mahesh followed her out. Her mind slid away from Lindsay's at last, her presence and her locks drawn away, and he could feel his magic again. He could feel it, for all the good it did him. The medication and the cage of runes locked him down, locked him in. He let his head fall on his knees, and dreamed.

His dreams were strange, and in them Dane was dead, and he woke sobbing and high and he knew that Dane was dead. He knew it like he knew there were walls around him. The runes made him sick and dizzy. They floated down and loomed large in his vision, jostling with one another for his attention, as though they all knew each other and him. He had seen all of them before, he realized, in the memories that Ezqel had dredged up from his time with Moore.

"I know you." His voice was loud even though his mouth didn't move because of the drugs. His muscles spasmed against the straitjacket, but it was as though he wasn't there to experience it.

*On bypass.*

What had Ezqel done to him? Or had the mage done anything but show Lindsay where he had been? Now, Lindsay wished that he'd been less filled with loathing and self-pity and fear, that he'd had the detachment to watch his own torture. Now, he understood the detachment he'd hated in Cyrus and Ezqel, the detachment Dane lacked because of what he was.

Ezqel had seen Moore's research as much as Lindsay had, or more. He had seen, through Lindsay's memories, the way that Lindsay had escaped the collar and the cuffs. The runes fell over one another to line up in three rings. One for the throat, two for the wrists. And, now, they were on the walls.

The haze of drugs was wearing thin. He'd been given them the entire time at the Institute and now they didn't last. As they cleared, Lindsay remembered that he had escaped the runes once. He knew that they had broken him when he did it. And he knew that Ezqel, healing him, had known what they were. Maybe even that Lindsay would see them again.

No one was coming for him, though his body said that hours had passed. It was time for another injection, and yet it hadn't come. Lindsay reached for his magic, and through it, he reached for the runes. *Come on,* he said to them. *I remember you.* Slowly, his mind slid up and down the razor edges of them, tracing them over and over until he found the weak places into which he could sink his magic.

Moore understood that he had broken the artifacts—by sheer strength, it had seemed. Lindsay's magic was huge, yes, but it was not the size of it that had broken the collar and cuffs. It had been his will to survive and the strangeness of his mind that had found the way out. Moore had done it to herself, his parents had done it to themselves—it was their own fault that he was shaped as he was.

Lindsay wedged his will into the cracks in Moore's knowledge, the places where the world and magic had changed over the centuries and the runes were no longer strong enough to hold either in check. He pressed slowly and cautiously, bracing illusion up against reality to give him more strength, and when he felt the bindings crack, he stopped and waited.

Time passed. Hesham came and attended to Lindsay's body, and went. Mahesh came and filled him up with drugs, but not full enough. Lindsay let the little illusions of his body hide his awareness with closed eyes and slack limbs, hid his magic away in the runes around him. Finally, *finally,* Moore came, and Lindsay's fear, peering through the cracked runes, could feel her coming from far down a long hall.

The door opened and the twins came in first. Hesham—and Lindsay still had no idea how he knew which was which—picked him up and set him on a chair put in place by a white-clad tech. Another chair was set across from him for Moore. Mahesh pressed a hypodermic injection to the base of Lindsay's skull. The cold sting had hardly faded before Lindsay was awake, shockingly awake, with the hardness of the world all around him bruising his tender consciousness.

"Hello again, Lindsay." Moore sat, crossing her legs at the ankles and letting her empty hands lie folded in her lap on the tight stretch of her tweed skirt over her rounded thighs. Today, her chestnut hair was loose and fell around her shoulders in soft waves. It made her seem disarmingly gentle. Behind her glasses, her eyes were the color of tea, with dark flecks like leaves. "I'm glad you're back, and well."

Lindsay's tongue stuck to the roof of his mouth, but he managed to peel it away and speak. "I'm not."

"Not glad or not well?" Moore smiled at him and gestured for Hesham to bring forward a glass of cold water—Lindsay could smell it—with a straw in it. He drank, letting the ache of remembering Dane overwhelm him for the moment. "Mahesh, let's be civil. Undo that jacket, he looks like a psychotic."

"You'll get to see him again." Lourdes stepped in and stopped behind Moore. "Apologies," she said to Moore's stern expression. "I had something that needed my attention."

"He's dead," Lindsay said to her, speaking past Moore. He was done speaking to Moore. The flicker of surprise on Lourdes's face was gone almost as soon as it came. "And you know it."

"You have so little faith," Lourdes said quietly.

"I have so little reason," Lindsay shot back. But he knew, suddenly, that Dane was still alive; he fought it, so he wouldn't have any reason to hope. He let Mahesh peel the straitjacket from him and relaxed into his chair, gathering himself.

"We have work to do." Moore tried to bring their attention back to her. "We require cooperation, Lindsay. We need to discuss your circumstances. Your healing. Lourdes." She snapped her fingers at the other woman. "Give me his mind."

*Have it.*

Lourdes reached for him, wide open, to draw him in, and Lindsay lashed through the cracks in the room's binding, splitting the runes open and stabbing into her with all his might. He forced himself on her, pushing his magic through her, crushing her mind into the back of her awareness, moving through her and out of her to blanket everything with illusion.

*Nothing is wrong.*

The runes on the wall were bleeding fire and ichor, alarms were sounding everywhere, but Moore—half out of her seat at the first sign of trouble—sat again, eyes fixed on Lindsay. There were no shouts of alarm. Nothing was wrong.

"Now," Moore said pleasantly. "Let's talk."

"Go right ahead," Lindsay muttered. Lourdes clung to the back of Moore's chair, blood running from her eyes and from her bitten lip. He wondered if he'd broken her. Hesham and Mahesh stood silently. For a moment, Lindsay was afraid they were unaffected, but when he moved, neither looked his way.

Lindsay ached, but his body answered well enough when he tried to stand. He got out of the chair and grabbed Lourdes by the front of her shirt, pulling her into his place. She sat obediently, staring blankly into his chest, while he searched her for her security clearance and key cards. Already, his head was throbbing and his magic felt strained.

"Where's..." Lindsay started to ask her where Dane was, but realized that he no longer existed for her. He'd done that on purpose. Turning to Moore, he ordered, "*Ask her where Dane is.*"

"Where did you leave your friend?" Moore asked Lourdes, smiling sweetly. Lindsay didn't want to touch Moore, but he searched her, stealing from her everything he could find, from her key cards to the green pendant around her neck to her oddly ugly little stone earrings. *We call it a kuni*, Ezqel had said. *In some places, they are gateposts. Others are simply stones set in rings.* And earrings.

"Where he belonged," Lourdes replied. "Medical testing, Level Minus Nine."

"Thanks," Lindsay muttered. Reaching, he could feel the quiet minds of the guards outside the door. They stood at attention, oblivious to the rain from the sprinklers that had doused the smoldering runes. He prodded one of the guards' minds and, a moment later, the door swung open.

"There you go, Dr. Moore," the man said politely, giving Lindsay a smile. Lindsay noted the gun at his side. Guns. He hadn't dealt with those before.

"Thank you kindly. Lock up, will you?" Lindsay stood and watched the man do it. "Now, shoot the lock out, please."

"Bastard!"

The shout came from down the hall and Lindsay wheeled, almost losing his magic, to see Jonas bearing down on him like a freight train. He ran, not waiting to see whether the shot that echoed off the walls had found its mark. He could hear someone squealing and dying, could feel it through the tiny tendril that had connected him to that guard, and he ran faster, forcing his drug-heavy limbs to obey.

"Hurry, hurry, hurry," he chanted, shoving Moore's card into the elevator slot with shaking hands. The door slid open and Lindsay slipped in, shoving Moore's card into the inside slot—how many times had he seen her do it?—and hammering the override button. The door closed on Jonas's howl of rage, and Lindsay's reflexive terror weakened his illusion more. Jonas's claws shrieked against the elevator's reinforced doors as Lindsay escaped.

"A little longer." He leaned on the wall of the elevator for support and clutched at his head. The detachment that the drugs had given him was wearing off, and the minds all around him were pressing into his consciousness. *Just a little longer.* Fumbling, he found the button for Level Minus Nine and felt himself drop faster.

There was no way he could hold the illusion any longer, he could feel it coming apart at the edges. Something outside was trying to get in. Lindsay opened Moore's phone and it lit up, set to "intranet". *Oh, God or whatever, thank you.* Blood dripped on the screen and Lindsay realized that his nose was bleeding. He wiped it away and, hoping for simplicity, hit the keys, *-9#*.

"Medical testing, Ambrose speaking, how may I help you?" The man's voice was pleasant and, as soon as he spoke, Lindsay could feel his mind as well.

"This is Dr. Moore. I need you to release the restraints on the new feral you're holding." Please let it be enough to back up his illusion. "There's been a misunderstanding. I'll explain it when I get there."

"Of course, Doctor. I'll see to that immediately." The line went dead and Lindsay slid to the floor. All he had to do was keep his hold on Level Minus Nine. He let go of the shearing, collapsing periphery of his illusion to focus on the inhabitants of the level where Dane was being kept. Jonas would probably take the stairways down and be there already, unless he'd gone back to get Lourdes and Moore out.

Lindsay had no idea how to beat the man, but he was damn well not going to let Jonas live this time, not if he could help it. The elevator stopped and Lindsay struggled to his feet. He couldn't rest yet. Not yet.

The doors slid open on an empty hall lit up with red emergency lights. Lindsay had no idea where to go, but he remembered the green lines on the wall from his own imprisonment. Green. He put his hand to the stripe on the wall and ran.

Lindsay ran until his lungs burned, his bare feet stung, his fingers bled, and his head knew nothing but the sounds of other people's voices and other people's thoughts. Once in a while, he fought to peer out through his own eyes. One time, he gathered enough of himself to grab a white coat and pull it on. A handful of toweling from a handwash station mopped the blood from his face.

Blood. It was important and he couldn't remember why. At an intersection of hallways, under the flash of emergency lights, he lost track of everything. Green. Blood. He was somewhere in the clamor in his head, hammered by the ringing of claxons, turning around and around, trying to find the right direction, trying to hold the illusion together even as chaos crept into this level.

"What do you mean, escape?" Someone ran past him, shouting at someone else. "None of the alarms are going off!"

*I can't, I can't, I can't,* bubbled up inside Lindsay, hysteria rising, something in him screaming to try to get himself back. *I can't.* He couldn't stop the illusion, couldn't get out of it. His head was full of *everyone* and he couldn't get out. The voice screaming *I can't* was so loud that he finally understood that it was out loud, that it was him, and he was screaming. Men and women in white coats were hurrying past him in all directions, but not looking at him—all directions and he had no idea which direction was right.

"I see you."

The roar echoed down the corridor, startling Lindsay into silence. He couldn't see all the way to where it came from, but he knew Jonas's voice like he knew everything else he feared. Lindsay spun around, not knowing where he was going except that it was *away* from that voice, and ran. He ran straight into something, smashing into it like it was a wall, a wall that hadn't been there a moment ago when he had seen through his own eyes.

Before he could fall, the wall caught him, wrapped him up and swept him in. "Lindsay." Dark hair fell all around him and a kiss was pressed to his hammering temple. "Lindsay, let it go."

Lindsay's hands scrabbled for handfuls of cloth even as his mind scrabbled free of the illusion. The illusion shattered, making him cry out against Dane's chest, but then the only chaos was outside of him, outside of the tiny well of calm that was Dane's body sheltering him from the rush of frightened people.

"She said, she said..." It was caught in Lindsay's head and he sobbed it into Dane's shirt as he shook. *She said you were still alive.* He couldn't understand why she'd told him the truth, why she'd told him then.

"Doesn't matter now." Dane tilted Lindsay's head back, wiped Lindsay's face clean with his sleeve, eerily echoing

Lourdes's actions. How any bit of his ragged clothing was still unbloodied was beyond fathoming at the moment. "We have to go. You have key cards?"

"Yes, yes..." Lindsay couldn't stop shaking—he wasn't made for this, he wasn't built for fighting and running and being terrified—but he got the cards out and held one out to Dane.

"Good. You did good." Dane took it and shoved it into his pocket. "Now you have to run. Down this hall. Take the stairs up." Instead of pushing Lindsay away, he pulled Lindsay to him with a hand in Lindsay's hair. He kissed Lindsay fiercely, like he was pouring life and heat into Lindsay's blood like that, and it worked.

Lindsay threw his arms around Dane's neck and, in the midst of the chaos and the approaching sound of dozens of pounding boots, kissed Dane back just as hard. And just like that, it was all okay. His head was throbbing and his heart was pounding and he was terrified, but he was himself again, and they were both alive, and nothing else mattered.

"Disgusting." The sound of boots petered out into the sound of weapons being readied. "Touching, but disgusting," Jonas rumbled.

Dane's hand in Lindsay's hair kept him from turning to see what awaited them. Instead, he was looking up into Dane's beautiful golden face and its frame of bloody, matted hair. "Run," Dane said softly. "Run to Cyrus. And don't look back."

"If you kill the little one, we're all in the shit," Jonas said to his men. "The other one, on the other hand..."

"I promise," Lindsay whispered. He'd disobeyed Dane before, but he wouldn't now. He understood. Dane moved so that his body took up most of the hall and, when Dane straightened, his arms falling away, Lindsay did what he was told. He ran.

"You said what about me?" The words were hardly out of Dane's mouth when Lindsay heard the frantic rattle of guns firing, and Jonas snapping orders, and someone screamed. The red exit sign was so close and yet so far.

The door opened when he hit it—of course it would, in an emergency—and he burst into the stairwell. There were feet descending, multiple booted feet. Lindsay mustered up a tiny illusion and laid it over himself. It was a blonde woman, not a man, who threw herself out of the way of the soldiers.

"That way." Lindsay pointed downward. He didn't need to feign the tremor in his voice. "There's an animal..." The illusions were easier when he lied less, at least when he was tired.

"Keep going up, miss," one of the men said to him. "Level Zero and follow the escape lights."

"Thank you!" Lindsay took off, taking the stairs two at a time. The ground floor and the escape lights. But Dane had said to run to Cyrus.

Run all the way home? Lindsay had nine floors going up to think about it. He couldn't run all the way home. He kept his illusion up, finding himself in the company of others struggling upward.

Level Zero. Lindsay watched the man in front of him shove the door open and escape onto the main floor. The door was open long enough for a blast of cool, sweet air to touch Lindsay's face. *Run to Cyrus.* Cyrus wouldn't be on the ground.

Oh God. How far to the top? The safety strips on the stairs made his feet burn like they were being flayed. Lindsay ran past the Level Zero door and kept going. Cyrus wasn't on the main floor. Cyrus was in the air. The sky. The roof. Fighting his own mind, Lindsay tried to spread the illusion that he and Dane had gone out the door he'd just passed, together.

Lindsay had no idea what floor he was on, only that he had to keep going. He fell to his knees again and again, gasping for air, his lungs burning.

Then he heard footfalls behind him. Just one set. *Jonas.* Terror pushed Lindsay to his feet when he stumbled. He grabbed the rail and kept going.

"Didn't think I'd beat him?" Dane's voice was raw and wet, like his lungs were torn, but one big hand grabbed Lindsay's and pulled him upward.

"I just..." Lindsay hadn't dared to hope. Besides, better to think it Jonas and keep going than to think it Dane and get caught.

"I know. Smart." Dane kept moving, eating up the stairs like a machine, half-carrying Lindsay along with him.

Lindsay's senses weren't as good as Dane's by even half, but the smell of blood and gore on his protector was overwhelming. From the way Dane moved, Lindsay knew that too much of it was his own. But Dane didn't stop, and Lindsay knew why when the stairwell filled with shouts and the sound of boots again.

"I don't," he gasped. "I'm trying. I don't know why they know..."

Dane pointed at a camera in the corner of a landing when they reached it. "Feed's been transferred outside. Too far away for you to reach. Don't waste your strength."

One floor, and another, and then Dane threw Lindsay against the wall and fired down the stairwell, over the rail. Lindsay hadn't even known he had a gun in his other hand, but there it was, an automatic rifle he must have taken from a soldier. Lindsay, pressed close to him, focused and realized that the strap still over Dane's shoulder must have been another gun.

There was answering fire and something ricocheted off of the stairs going up. Dane threw up his arm almost before Lindsay heard the ping and Dane grunted as the thing bit into his flesh. Lindsay didn't have time to cringe with guilt before they were moving again, so he put the energy into running.

When they finally burst out onto the rooftop under a clear black sky shattered by spotlights and helicopters, there was a moment when Lindsay realized he'd never expected to make it this far. He could see for miles up here—the bright lights of the distant city, the black brow of a looming storm front rushing toward them. The air smelled like snow was on the way, sharp with anticipation.

"Run." Dane fired at a trio of soldiers, backing them up toward the shelter of the ventilation system. At least this time he came with Lindsay, using his body to shelter Lindsay from the wind and the bullets rattling off the rooftop around them. The bullets stopped. "They don't want to kill you."

The helicopters kept circling, like buzzards. "How..." *How are we going to get out of here?* Terror kept banging up against Lindsay's ribs, trying to climb up his throat.

"Trust me."

A pair of jets from the nearby air force base shrieked overhead. *Oh God.* Lindsay did trust Dane, but things seemed impossible, even if no one wanted him dead. They were almost at the edge of the roof and the wind was pushing them from behind even as it was shoving the storm toward them.

A helicopter dropped down and Lindsay could see the soldiers inside. One of them fired at the edge of the roof, drawing a dotted line, warning them not to cross.

"Hold on."

Lindsay had no idea what he was supposed to hold on to when Dane dropped the guns and swung Lindsay up onto his back. Lindsay had no choice but to grab handfuls of thick black hair, clinging like a burr as Dane took the last step. They were airborne, the wind lifting them up.

The wind couldn't hold them up forever, though. They dropped, and Lindsay screamed. "Dane!"

Lindsay could feel Dane shifting under him and then they were rising. Lindsay raised his head and his eyes widened. They should've been falling still, plummeting toward the ground, but they weren't. Far from it. They were *flying.*

The wind gathered up under them, vaulting them high into the air this time. Behind them, Lindsay felt as much as heard a great thud and when he glanced over his shoulder, he could see the fire flowering where a helicopter had crashed into the building. Clutching Dane's mane, he cast about to locate the other just in time to see the wind drive it down and down, until it burst into flames on contact with the ground.

*Cyrus. Run to Cyrus.*

"Come home," Cyrus murmured in his ears. The storm front yawned open and the wind pulled them into the howling and the snow.

In the last of the starlight, before the storm closed on them, Lindsay looked down to see huge wings spread out on either side of him. "Dane." He leaned forward, burying his face in a great, warm mane that smelled familiar and safe, and wrapped his arms around a thick, strong neck. The heat of the creature under him kept the worst of the cold away and he could feel muscles surging with each wing beat as Dane followed the wind home.

As the terror that had filled Lindsay was washed away in the wind and passing minutes, he was nagged by a quiet thought that had been waiting to be acknowledged. He had left everyone behind him alive. Even Moore. Even Lourdes. His time of brokenness was past, and he'd freed them on his own terms. Smiling, he pressed closer to the neck of the beast and closed his eyes against the wind.

Lindsay was half-asleep when the storm pulled away and dropped them into the sky above a house he recognized, even from the air. Dane spiraled down and down and down until his four paws touched the ground and—light as a feather—they landed. Still drained, but driven by anxiety and the need to make sure Dane was well, Lindsay all but tumbled from his back.

The doors to the third-floor balcony were open and, in the light that spilled out into the silent garden, Lindsay could see what had carried him. Urging his legs to hold him up, he let go of the mane and stepped back to look.

Dane shook his wild mane as though to settle it back, just as he did when he was human.

A lion. Lindsay could have believed that without a moment's pause, a beautiful golden lion, as gold as Dane with a mane as black as Dane's hair and just as beautiful. But the wings, black and gold and bronze and...Dane spread them, snorting like he was laughing, and Lindsay realized that he believed that too. He could even believe that Dane was so stubborn as to give up all that beauty and freedom to keep his pride.

"Dane." Lindsay threw his arms as far around Dane's thick neck as he could reach and buried his face in Dane's mane. Dane was huge next to Lindsay, and so soft and warm. "You're beautiful," he whispered, rubbing his cheek against Dane's softly furred face. Maybe "beautiful" wasn't how he was supposed to describe a creature like Dane, but Lindsay didn't have a better word for a lion, for whatever Dane was. A gryphon.

Dane spread his wings wide, and in the next moment, Lindsay was in his arms and he was bending to kiss Lindsay all over again. The familiar warmth of Dane's body—alive and whole—was a welcome sensation, after the night of illusion and fear.

Dane got his hands in Lindsay's hair and he kissed Lindsay with all the wantonness that he'd had the time Lindsay's magic had slipped and taken away his self-control. He was breathless, his body taut and trembling, but he seemed well, his flesh intact under his shredded clothes when Lindsay's hands skimmed over his body.

They were both alive and whole and safe again.

Dane pulled back to look at him in the light that spilled out of Cyrus's window above. "Did they hurt you?" He cupped Lindsay's face in his hands and tilted it up.

"No," Lindsay said, meeting Dane's eyes. "I'm all right. They drugged me again, but I'm all right. She didn't get me, not this time."

"I'm sorry." Dane kissed Lindsay's cheeks and his mouth before pulling away again. "I am so sorry. I keep failing you. You deserve better." He looked like he had when they'd first met, feral and ragged again, but his expression was so soft now.

Lindsay clenched his hands in Dane's ragged, filthy clothes, still shaking his head. "No. I deserve what I have. I'm yours, remember?" He'd never belonged to anyone before, never meant enough to anyone that his connection to them *mattered.* Belonging to Dane, being *Dane's,* felt like the best thing that had ever happened to him. "I deserve *you.*"

Dane was frozen for a moment, and then he swept Lindsay up off of his feet and kissed him. His soft growl was familiar and shamelessly possessive, sending another wave of relief through Lindsay. Dane wasn't going to give him up or give him away.

Above them, someone pulled the balcony doors shut and drew the curtains, leaving them alone in the dark. It was cold outside and clouds heavy with snow were moving on the hard wind. Dane settled Lindsay in his arms, sheltering him, kissing him all the while, and headed for the back stairs. He carried Lindsay in and up the narrow, winding staircase, down the hall past Cyrus's room and up another tiny, creaking set of stairs at the front of the house.

In the little garret room at the top, Dane set Lindsay on his feet and kissed him once more, tenderly. When Dane pulled away from the kiss, Lindsay looked around. The room was filled with books, a wardrobe, a desk and an old iron bed. There was no light in here, no warmth except for a glowing heater tucked in a corner. Snow was rattling against the windows and the roof, and the wind wailed around the corners.

It was so different from the room they'd given to Lindsay. Where Lindsay's room was furnished and ornate, with a large fireplace to keep it warm, Dane's was spartan. It was definitely Dane's, though. Lindsay's room could have been mistaken for anyone's—there were no personal items but his clothes. In Dane's room, the books and the furniture had obviously been gathered over years, each thing kept because it mattered. And here Lindsay was, with all the rest of the things Dane wanted to keep.

Dane peeled off his coat and shirt at once, the fabric tearing as he shrugged out of it and tossed it into the corner by the door. His bare skin was marred with twisting new scars, knots and ropes that were slow to fade. He shook back his hair—something about the shifting had left it clean—and reached for Lindsay again, as though he was unwilling to stop touching even for a moment.

Lindsay still had blood on his hands and clothes from when he'd touched Dane before they escaped, but he didn't care. The blood was Dane's, so it was as good as clean.

He stepped into the circle of Dane's arms and Dane ran his hands up and down Lindsay's back. He wasn't kissing yet, it felt like he was inspecting what was his. He growled and bit Lindsay under the ear with a hot, sucking kiss that was all sharp teeth. Lindsay shivered, his head dropping to the side to bare his neck for more.

Dane bit him again and this time, as he did, his claws cut through Lindsay's clothes. There was no method to it, just his hot mouth on Lindsay's throat, claiming it for his own, and his claws shredding fabric until the pieces fell away. As eager as he seemed to get Lindsay bare, his claws never left a mark on Lindsay's skin.

Lindsay wasn't even cold anymore, especially when Dane's fingers slipped between his thighs. "Please?"

"Anything." Dane was so incredibly good to him.

"Keep touching me?" That was all Lindsay wanted. He needed to be touched so he could have the reminder, again and again, of what it was to be Dane's.

"Come to bed."

The bed frame was old iron, but the mattress was soft when Lindsay crawled onto it, and the covers were filled with down, as were the pillows. The sheets were white cotton, cold with the winter chill. Lindsay curled up on them and then stretched out, feeling the smooth fabric slide against his skin. Dane shed the last of his ruined clothes and crept into bed next to Lindsay, pulling the blankets over them both.

Lindsay rolled over to face Dane, his cheek tucked against the crook of his bent arm. Dane didn't pull Lindsay into his arms, but lay there a moment instead, just looking. Even without being touched, Lindsay felt warm and content. Dane had brought Lindsay to his space, to his bed, because Lindsay was his too. Lindsay was still vibrating from the adrenaline and the drugs, and his head ached, but being in the haven of Dane's bed was enough to soothe him.

Dane traced Lindsay's features with a fingertip and put his finger under Lindsay's chin, tilting his face up for a kiss on the mouth. It was chaste and tender, like this was the first time.

Then he rolled Lindsay onto his back and kissed him down into the pillows. Dane's body was so warm against his own cool skin. Dane lifted his head and petted Lindsay's hair. He kissed Lindsay on the forehead, once, warm and gentle.

"Mine," he said seriously.

"Yours." Lindsay hadn't known enough to want it, but now that he had it, he didn't want to give it up.

The faint gray snow light from outside and the glow of the heater gave enough light that Lindsay could see the tenderness in Dane's expression. He reached up to cup Dane's cheek in his hand and brushed his thumb along Dane's jaw.

Dane lay back, coaxing Lindsay up to straddle his hips. Lindsay was still a bit sore, but by the time he was settled with his hands braced on Dane's chest, he was happy with the view. How had he managed to get so lucky? Wanting Dane, wanting *sex*, hit him all in a rush and Dane had to be able to smell it thick on the air.

"Tell me what you want." Dane smiled when he said it, showing Lindsay a flash of sharp white teeth.

"Don't you know?"

Dane laughed. "I like hearing it."

"I want you," Lindsay said. "I want whatever you'll give me, whatever you'll let me have. I want to give you what you want. And I want to make you come."

"You can have all those things." Dane's voice was rough. "What I want is you, any way I can have you. I want to hear you come, watch you come. I want to watch you be alive."

"I'm alive." Lindsay leaned in to kiss Dane on the mouth. "I'm alive. Thanks to you."

"That's what I want most." Dane cupped Lindsay's face in

his hands and kissed him hard and deep.

Lindsay wanted Dane *now*. He had no idea how he'd ever managed to be patient before. He licked at Dane's mouth and his jaw, working his way under to lick the tender skin of Dane's throat. He might have been on top, but he knew how to be submissive nonetheless. Dane's groan was proof enough that Lindsay had learned well.

"I want." He nipped to punctuate his demand and got a low rumble from Dane. "Fuck me."

"Anything," Dane said again. "You want that, go get the silver tin from the right-hand drawer in the desk."

In the drawer, on top of an old pistol and a cigarette case, Lindsay found the tin and turned to hold it out.

Dane was leaning on one elbow watching him, smiling, and Lindsay caught a glimpse of something in a mirror that stood in the far corner of the room. The person in the mirror wasn't thin and bent anymore, and not a boy, either. The person there was tall enough to be a man and lean but not thin. He seemed healthy, and there was enough light from the window on his face that Lindsay could see that he looked happy.

"That's what I want. Come to bed, little bunny."

Lindsay took one more look at himself, at the young man who seemed so surprisingly strong, and then turned away. Dane was waiting for him. Laughing, he ran across the room and jumped into bed, making the frame groan.

"Not so little anymore," Lindsay said, pushing Dane over on his back and crawling on top of him.

"No." Dane let himself be moved and fell into the pillows, still smiling. "Not so little anymore."

Lindsay dipped his fingers into the tin, finding something inside that felt like thick cream. It smelled of beeswax, but Lindsay didn't investigate further, setting the tin aside instead. He found Dane's hard cock, still ready for him, and stroked it, getting a delicious noise from Dane.

"I want you," Dane murmured.

It wasn't as though Lindsay couldn't tell, but Dane was

saying it because he knew how much Lindsay loved to hear it. "Did you...before you told me?" He stroked a while longer, reveling in touching Dane so intimately. If he hadn't been giddy with relief and success, he wouldn't have asked, but Dane had said such sweet things already that it made him bold. He wanted to know so much, to hear Dane say it.

"Yes." Dane's voice was rough with need and it made Lindsay shiver. "Even when you were angry at me. Before I should have."

Before...*oh.* God, it seemed a century ago that Lindsay had been angry at Dane, angry at him for something as trivial as fooling around with Kristan.

"Oh." Lindsay blinked a sudden welling of tears away and moved to kiss Dane as he slid his slick fingers into himself this time. "That's a long time."

"It'll just get longer." Dane's hands were all over him, touching him like Dane was claiming him.

Lindsay's hand was shaking as he guided Dane into him; his whole body was full of a flood of emotion. He whimpered and Dane stroked his hair, making soothing noises. "I'm okay," Lindsay managed to say. "I am, I am..."

God, he was more than okay, he was perfect. Alive and wanted and *real.*

Dane leaned up, effortlessly pulling himself to almost sitting, and kissed Lindsay on the mouth. "I'm proud of you."

Lindsay sucked in a breath, surprised by the praise. "Th-thank you," he managed, licking at Dane's mouth like the words might've left some residue he could taste there.

"You rescued me," Dane pointed out, wrapping his arms around Lindsay and kissing him back. "You didn't panic. You saved us. Saved me. Your magic worked." He brushed a kiss over Lindsay's lips. "You made me proud. I still am."

*Dane was proud of him.*

"Thank you. I'm glad I wasn't too late." Lindsay let Dane's pride and affection wash away the worry that he could've gotten there too late, that Dane could've died for good this time. He moved again, rocking his hips to let Dane's cock slide in and out of his body.

"Lindsay..." It was little more than a groan, and Dane shuddered under him. He was always so composed in bed, at least until now. Whatever Lindsay was doing—maybe just being himself—he was driving Dane crazy.

"You sound so good like that." Lindsay could *hear* how much Dane wanted him, and it was incredible.

Dane wasn't one to be passive, but he let Lindsay have him. Like this, Lindsay could see his face; it was overwhelming how much he could see, and how much it mattered to him.

Lindsay got lost in the way Dane responded to him, listening for every moan and growl, feeling for each arch of Dane's back into his touches. Making Dane feel good was its own reward, and Lindsay worked for it. "Tell me what you need?"

"You. Just you." Dane opened his eyes, focusing on Lindsay. "Just fuck me. I want to see you, want to hear you. You are so beautiful."

"You can have all of that." Lindsay's words trailed off into a moan as he wrapped one hand around his cock and stroked himself. Dane could have all of that, and more.

Precome slicked Lindsay's hand, easing the way as he stroked himself. His breath came faster with every pull, and he fucked himself on Dane's cock, rolling his hips to get it in deep. His hand moved faster, his body moved harder, until he was shouting Dane's name and coming all over his hand and Dane's chest.

Dane was growling softly under his breath, still moving. "Don't stop." It sounded as close to begging as Lindsay had ever heard him. His breath was broken by desperate hitches and he writhed until his back came up off the bed and his hands dug into Lindsay's hips, slamming him down and holding him tight. Then he was coming, and Lindsay soaked up the sound of his name in Dane's gasping, pleasure-drunk voice.

Eventually, Dane managed to muster up a tender smile

that was exactly what Lindsay wanted to see. He shifted to cradle Lindsay against him, snuggling down until they ended up nestled in the sheets, still entwined as close as humanly possibly. "Sleep."

Lindsay woke up already humming with contentment. He was cuddled up against Dane, warm and safe, and Dane was nuzzling in his hair. The sun was creeping between the broken clouds and through the window into Dane's little garret room. It was perfect. "Mmm. Morning?" Lindsay lifted his head, blinking at Dane with a soft smile.

"Morning," Dane said, laughing quietly. "We're still here." It was a victory, just that they were still here together. He ducked his head to nudge at Lindsay's cheek, hunting for a kiss.

Lindsay rubbed his cheek against Dane's and pulled back to brush his lips over Dane's. "It's a good morning, then." He kissed Dane again, soft and sweet.

They were still kissing when a knock came at the door. Dane's head jerked up, his body went tense, and a growl rattled in his chest.

Lindsay stifled his own nervousness and reached up to cup Dane's cheek in his hand. "We're at home," he reminded Dane. No one would hurt them here. He hoped.

Dane grumbled at that and got out of bed to pull on a pair of jeans that were folded on a chair by the bed. Lindsay hadn't seen it last night, but it was so *Dane* that the jeans were there with a pair of boots on the floor by the chair and a shirt folded over the back. There was an old, dark coat hanging on the back of the door. Of course. In case Dane wanted to go out the window instead of getting his coat in the front hall. Lindsay was filled with a wash of tender affection for his eccentric lover.

"Wait," Dane snapped, when the knock came again. The tone made Lindsay feel safer—there was no chance Dane was talking to him that way.

Dane offered Lindsay the shirt from the chair and Lindsay wriggled into it. He didn't have to undo anything to get it on, and it came to his thighs when he smoothed it down. His hands were lost in it, so he pushed the cuffs up. He tugged the blankets around himself again and sat up against the pillows, giving Dane a smile. He wasn't ashamed of being nearly naked, or of being marked with the reminders of their sex.

"All ready now," he said. Dane pressed a kiss to Lindsay's forehead and went to answer the door.

"I thought you might be hungry." It was Vivian's voice. "And I wanted to speak to you. Cyrus said you would be awake." Dane checked over his shoulder one more time before letting her into the room. "Good morning, dear," she said to Lindsay. She was carrying a tray laden with food, a newspaper propped up against the coffee carafe.

"What do you want?" Dane leaned against his desk, arms crossed over his chest, and watched her with more suspicion than Lindsay thought she deserved.

"Aside from bringing you breakfast," Vivian said as she put the tray on the chair by the bed, "I came to give you my apologies." When she straightened, she clasped her hands and gave Lindsay a bow. "I am sorry for failing you both."

Lindsay felt a shock of concern and then a rush of awkwardness. He wasn't used to anyone apologizing to him. "You didn't..." he began.

"She did," Dane said flatly. "What happened?" Lindsay hadn't seen him look so dire about anyone but Ezqel or Jonas.

"I miscalculated," Vivian said simply. She faced Dane's anger without flinching. "I thought Moore would be controlling the girl. She's more of a free agent than I ever expected Moore to allow. She must have found Jonas on her own, but I have no idea how she knew you would be in New York when you were."

"She had other people with her," Lindsay blurted out. The memory of the twin mages and their hands on him wouldn't fade any time soon. He remembered their names, but he couldn't bring himself to say the words out loud, like speaking would summon them up again.

"Who?" Dane's voice made Lindsay jump and clutch the

covers tighter. He hadn't been afraid of Dane since he'd woken up in this house, but he was now, just for a moment.

"Two men." The names wouldn't come out; Lindsay's tongue refused to work. He had to focus on Dane to keep talking. "She said I could have them, instead of you." His throat got tight at the memory and his vision blurred. "Because she was taking you away."

Dane crossed the room so quickly that he was already there when Lindsay blinked away his tears. He sat on the bed and let Lindsay burrow into his arms. "It's okay," Dane said gently, stroking his hair. "I'm here now. You did that."

The petting worked, it always had. Lindsay took a breath and tried to shake off the flood of misery that was trying to drown his memories. "They were twins," he managed to say, taking comfort in the fact that his voice didn't shake that much. "Tall and thin. Like polished wood."

"Dark skin and hair and eyes? Older than you?" Vivian asked. Lindsay could only nod. "I'll have to tell Cyrus they're here. That explains much."

"It does?" Lindsay pushed away from Dane enough to look at her. He didn't want to lose Dane's comforting presence, but he wasn't going to cower and cry when Vivian knew something he didn't.

"Null mages." Vivian's face was tight and pale. "And they have other tricks. But they are at their best—their worst—when they're together. I wonder what the girl did to draw them in."

"You know them?" It still felt that Lindsay needed a map to his own country.

"Of them." Vivian looked at Dane, then back at Lindsay. "We are not all so interesting that those among us with extraordinary powers don't go unnoticed by the rest. And she may not be able to keep them." She picked up the paper that was on the tray and unfolded it, offering it to him.

Dane let Lindsay go and Lindsay took the paper to read it. The front page documented a terrible accident at a National Guard base miles away. Another failure for Moore. "Is she in trouble?"

"In disgrace, I'd call it," Vivian said quietly. "Once more. I'll be leaving for Washington in a few hours. I may not be back for some time. I'm leaving Kristan here to help out, for now. She knows what I need her to do."

"Are you…?" Lindsay pulled his eyes away from the paper—he could hardly make sense of it all right now anyway—to look at her. *Are you in trouble?* As soon as he knew what he was thinking, he couldn't say it. "It wasn't all your fault. You can't know everything."

Vivian gave him a warm smile. "I can try. I should go prepare. I need to ensure that Moore and her people lose as much power as possible. The lobbyists are making my job harder than ever in DC. But I'm glad you're home safe." She came over and leaned in to kiss the top of Lindsay's head. Once, it would have made him cringe, but now it felt comforting. "Take care of each other, and Cyrus."

"Don't worry about us," Dane rumbled, concern on his face. It looked more like irritation, but Lindsay knew better.

"Well, I won't worry about *you*." Vivian gave him a stern look as she stepped away. "You shouldn't have bothered escaping. They'd've put you out on the curb in a day or two."

Dane laughed at her and shook his head. "They just don't appreciate me like you do."

"Me, yes. Cyrus, not so much," Vivian said dryly.

"Not my fault he can hear everything." Dane got up to walk her to the door and Lindsay resisted the urge to hide under the covers, cuddling up in the pillows instead.

"You make it impossible for him not to," Vivian chided. At the door she stood and tilted her chin up, obviously demanding a kiss, which Dane gave to her on her cheek. "Do try not to get yourself thrown out before I get home."

"I'll behave," Dane promised solemnly. "I'm a new man."

"You are." Vivian reached up and patted his cheek. "Welcome home, Dane." With that, she was gone. Dane closed the door on the sound of her heels on the stairs.

Lindsay looked at Dane carefully, but Dane seemed well enough. "What?" Dane asked, giving him a grin.

"You didn't tell me Cyrus could hear everything." Lindsay wanted to hide all over again. They hadn't been quiet last night. *Everyone* had probably heard them, now that he stopped to think about it. At least Vivian and Cyrus had.

"Cyrus is an old stick," Dane said loftily. He came back to the bed and bent to give Lindsay a long, hot kiss, one hand tight in Lindsay's hair. "Besides," he murmured, sitting beside Lindsay. "It's no one's business what I do with what's mine."

"You like everyone knowing I'm yours," Lindsay countered. He liked it too. He liked the idea that someone could hear his voice and know, could see the proof written out on his skin, that he belonged to Dane. Lindsay liked that he could look at himself in the mirror and know it. He also liked being able to show Dane with the sound of his voice how good Dane made him feel.

Dane purred and nuzzled Lindsay's cheek. "You might have a point." His hair was all over the place, the scars were faded to almost nothing under the silky fur on his chest, and his jeans were sliding down his hips and barely containing his cock. "You don't object."

"I like it too." The marks on Lindsay's skin, scars and bite marks alike, wouldn't fade nearly so quickly as Dane's had. He'd wash away the sweat and come, but he didn't think Dane's scent would be so easy to shed, either. Especially not if Dane kept putting it right back on.

Dane gave him that feral grin and kissed him hard and fast. He still didn't seem too interested in food when he asked, "Hungry?"

"Depends what you want to feed me."

"Better feed you something that'll do you good." Dane kissed him tenderly this time, and rolled off the bed. He stretched as he walked back to get their breakfast tray. "Cyrus may have decided I haven't completely ruined you, but he's not going to take me starving you."

"I'm not going to starve if I skip breakfast," Lindsay said, laughing.

"Fine, but I might." Dane set the tray on the end of the bed, and shucked his jeans, tossing them over the chair again. "Besides, you need your strength, little bunny." He slid into bed next to Lindsay.

Lindsay looked Dane up and down, and laughed again. "If you wanted me to focus on *food*, that was not the way to go about it." He sat up a bit more and looked at the tray.

There was meat there, a sliced steak on a plate, barely cooked. Vivian apparently knew Dane's preferences well. There was toast for Lindsay and cheese and fruit along with the coffee and a dish of fried potatoes. Maybe he was hungry.

Dane stroked Lindsay's back when he leaned forward to get a slice of toast. Lindsay smiled, wriggling into the touch as he sat back again and nibbled the edge of the toast.

Dane rumbled softly, letting Lindsay see how much Lindsay affected him. Lindsay was starting to understand what worked best, if he were of a mind to get something out of Dane. Dane leaned forward to tug the tray closer, until it bumped into one of his knees. "Think you can remember how that whole vacation thing works?"

Lindsay tilted his head. "I think there was sunshine involved. And sex."

"Very good." Dane picked up a fork and stabbed a slice of steak, popping the meat into his mouth. He looked thoughtful. "Won't be sunny here for a while yet."

Lindsay worked his way through the slice of toast, and reached out for the bowl of fruit. "It's not like I'm going to get a tan anyway," he pointed out. "I can improvise."

"I'm sure we can find something to do." Dane offered Lindsay a piece of steak and gave him a stern look.

When Lindsay saw Dane's expression, he sighed and obediently opened his mouth to take the bite.

Dane fed him, and leaned in to kiss him with a satisfied grunt. "You're going to need your strength for your vacation," he murmured.

"I'd better eat up, then." Lindsay stole another kiss, and then stole Dane's fork to get himself another bite of the steak.

Dane laughed and slid his arms around Lindsay, getting Lindsay in his lap once Lindsay ate a little more. "Good. I'd hate for anyone to say I'm not doing my job."

Lindsay snuggled into Dane's lap, getting comfortable, and tipped his head back so he could see Dane's face. "Oh, I think you're doing excellent work," he murmured, popping a bite of melon into his mouth.

"So you'll be keeping me, then?" Dane teased gently, holding Lindsay against him.

"I belong to you, not the other way around." Finally, Lindsay felt perfectly comfortable with who and what he was, and his place in the world. He rubbed his cheek against Dane's bare chest. He knew Dane wouldn't willingly give him up, not now.

Dane was quiet a moment, and he pressed a kiss to Lindsay's forehead. "Yes," he said. "You have it right. That's how it is." His arms tightened around Lindsay and he ducked his head so that his hair fell all around them and Lindsay was wrapped up in him, safe.

# About the Author

To learn more about Anah Crow and Dianne Fox, please visit www.anahcrow.com and www.foxwrites.com. Send an email to Anah Crow at anahcrow@gmail.com or to Dianne Fox at fox.dianne@gmail.com or subscribe to the Fox & Crow Newsletter to join in the fun! www.foxwrites.com/newsletter

*The only way to break free is to let go.*

# Lynx

## *© 2010 Joely Skye*

In order to protect his shifter kin, FBI agent Trey Walters hides his ability from his employers. For him, a vacation means a whole midwinter month in the Canadian wilderness, free to live in his wolf skin.

When he happens upon a rare lynx shifter, he's fascinated. And his protective instincts kick into overdrive. The young man needs to be shielded from werewolves and humans alike, whether he likes it or not.

Jonah can hardly wrap his head around the fact that other shifters exist, much less endure the presence of a stranger in his lonely sanctuary. Blaming himself for his brother's death, he lives in self-imposed isolation. Trust? Forget it. Yet Trey's patience penetrates Jonah's fear, and it doesn't take long for him to fall like a rock for the wolf.

Trey hadn't planned to embark on an intense, passionate affair, but he finds himself vowing to return after his next undercover mission is over. As months stretch into years, however, Jonah fears that Trey has broken faith with him—or is dead. There's only one way to find out. Leave the safety of his lair and venture into a dangerous, deadly world...

*Warning: violence, explicit sex.*

LaVergne, TN USA
23 March 2011
221260LV00004B/2/P